FOR MARIAN

FREEING DRUIDS

THE DARK ORDER
BOOK 2

WAYNE UDE

Sunbreak Press
Clinton, WA

Copyright 2021
For information about permission to reproduce selections from this book, write to Permissions, Sunbreak Press, PO Box 145, Clinton, WA 98236

ISBN:
ISBN: (epub)

Library of Congress Control Number: 2020944410

Published through Sunbreak Press (imprint of Blue & Ude Writers Services, PO Box 145, Clinton, WA 98236)

Cover Art: Jane Mortimore https://janiemortart.com/
Cover Design: Marian Blue
   Maps: Steve Swanson

Thanks to the members of the Reading Glass Writers group for their responses to my work, and especially to Janie, Scott, and MaryEllen, who've seen this series from chapter one. As always special appreciation to Marian, who continues to be my toughest and best editor.

Manufactured in the United States of America
This book is printed on environmentally responsible paper products not sourced from endangered old growth forests, forests of exceptional conservation value, or the Amazon Basin.

CONTENTS

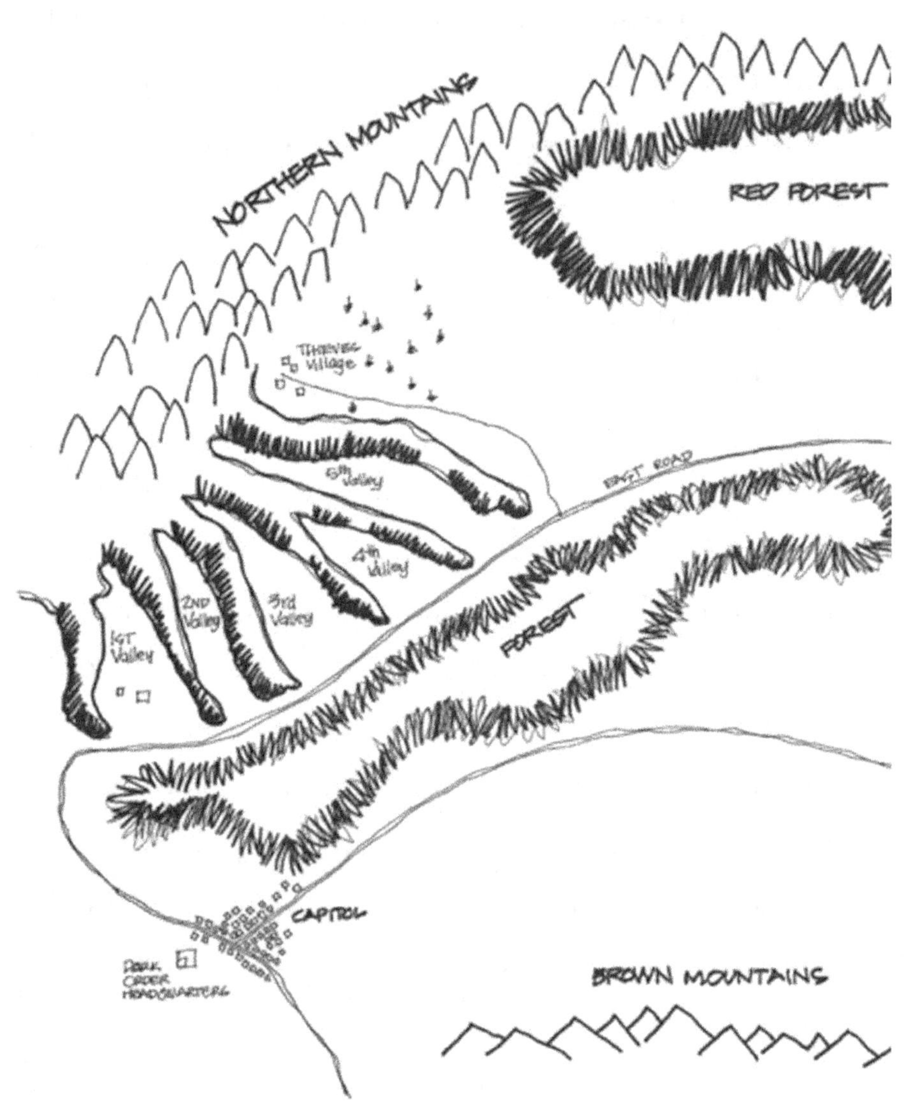

NORTHERN MOUNTAINS
RED FOREST
THIEVES Village
6th Valley
EAST ROAD
4th Valley
1st Valley
2nd Valley
3rd Valley
FOREST
CAPITOL
PARK ORDER HEADQUARTERS
BROWN MOUNTAINS

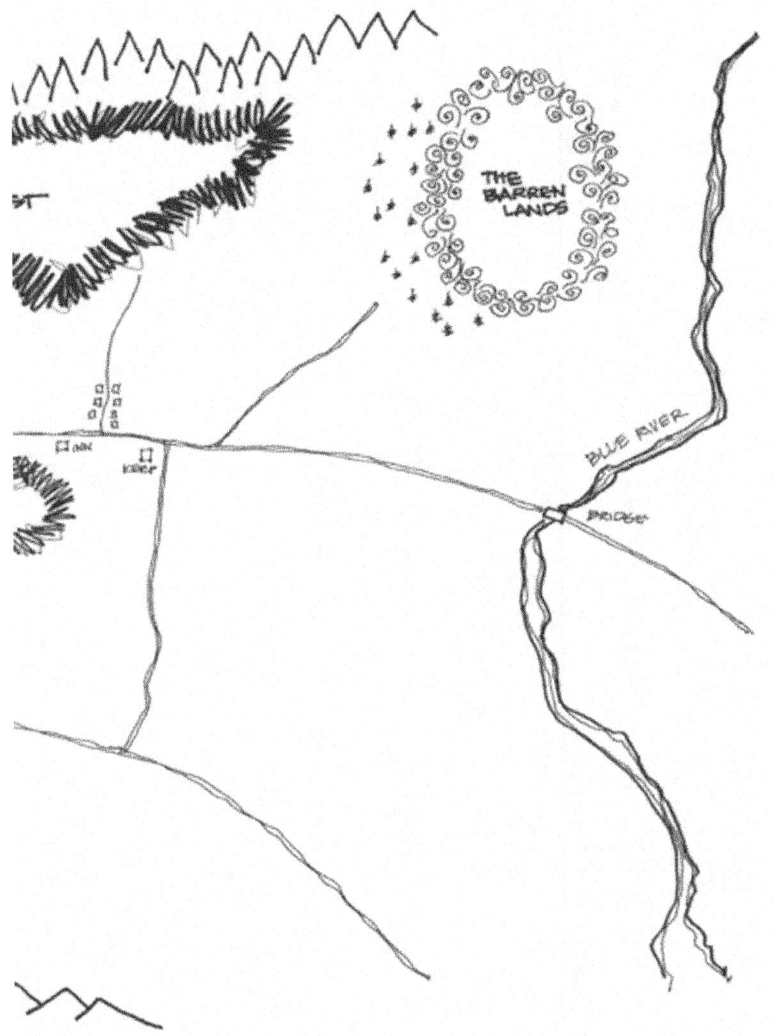
THE BARREN LANDS
BLUE RIVER
BRIDGE
INN

THE DARK ORDER:
BOOK ONE, FLIGHT

SUMMARY

The Dark Order is a fairly traditional fantasy series set in a quasi-medieval time. People travel by horseback or wagon, and magic is a stronger force than arrows or swords. The novel begins in the Five Valleys, a normally fertile area suffering from a five-year drought.

The land is dominated by the Order of Dark Wizards. Wizards draw their powers from the natural world: Green Wizards from lush valleys and forests, especially in the area north of the mountains; Brown Wizards from arid lands such as those to the south; Blue Wizards from the rivers, lakes, and even the deep blue of sky to the East. Most powerful are Dark Wizards, who draw power from the darkness of night as well as deep dark places within the earth.

The other Orders tend to use their powers to tend the earth, often to heal people and the land. The Dark Order seeks power for its own sake. This Order has begun to steal other orders' scrolls containing their spells and methods. For the past five years, the Dark Order has created and sustained the Fifth Valley's drought, using a scroll stolen from the Brown Order. The Dark Wizard Rath has been in charge of maintaining the drought in the normally fertile Fifth Valley.

Living in the Fifth Valley as the novel begins is Bird, an eight-year-old foundling. Unknown to her family, Bird has power far beyond her understanding. When she calls rain back to the Valley, breaking the Wizard-induced drought, Bird sets up an increasing conflict with the Dark Order.

It's only after Bird's older brother Aren returns from two years' service in Lord Ryd's Guard that anyone in the family begins to understand Bird's role in all that has happened. Aren convinces their parents that before the Dark Order discovers that she is the source of their problems, Bird must leave the valley in search of those who can help her understand and control her powers. He and Bird leave, travelling east.

In book one, they travel as far east as Lord Rand's lands, called the Holdings. In the meantime, the Order has discovered Bird's identity. Three wizards are sent after her, accompanied by a half-dozen guardsmen. The Order has also alerted a wizard living to the east. He is to instruct that area's Lord to seize any girl travelling with a lone former guardsman. The result is a disaster for the Order, for Lord Rand and his Keep (a small castle-like fortress), and for the people of the Holdings. When Rand orders brother Aren to be hung from the Keep's battlements, Bird reacts with fear and anger, screaming, "I hope you die! I hope you die, and your Keep falls in on you!" Without a lord and his fortress, the people of the Holdings are defenseless against thieves or the predations of neighboring lords. To Bird's shock, the people of Rand's Holdings fear her.

Leaving behind the rubble which was Rand's Keep, the pair realize that at least one Wizard will be coming toward them from the east in addition to those following from the west. They see no choice but to travel north toward the mountains. Just short of the mountains, they learn, lies the Red Forest, a place avoided by both Wizards and local farmers. There the pair hope to be safe for a time as they continue their search for those who might recognize Bird's nature and perhaps teach her to control her powers.

CHARACTERS IN BOOK ONE

Dark Wizards and associates

Rath, Second most powerful member of the Order of Dark Wizards. Lost right hand when trying to reinstate drought after Bird ended it. She inadvertently sent lightning through Rath's great crystal, destroying the wizard's right hand and his tower. Most powerful of group pursuing child-witch (Bird).

Soren, Chief Mage, Dark Order. With Rath, planned drought. Ordered pursuit of child-witch who ended drought. Monitors pursuit from Order's headquarters.

Haster, wizard, advisor to Soren. Functionary.

Lorit, powerful wizard, advisor to Soren. Nominal head of pursuit.

Oleg, Loremaster. Presides over Order's archives. Never demonstrates power, but believed to be most powerful member of Order.

Roke, junior wizard. Lives east of Rand's Keep. Relays order to seize Bird. Becomes part of pursuit.

Tarh, junior wizard, formerly apprentice to Rath. Part of pursuit.

The Dark One. Ancient being. Imprisoned beneath the Order's headquarters. Only Oleg visits, and only in search of ancient knowledge. Oleg's records say the Dark One taught the first wizards.

Snake. Chief Mage Soren's chief spy and assassin. Assigned by Soren to serve as scout for wizards sent after Bird and Aren.

Dog. Short, squat gnarled being. Ugliest person in any crowd. Called "Ryd's Dog" by mercenaries led by Lord Ryd in northern mountains. Became Ryd's finest scout and chief confidant. Came south when Ryd became Lord of Five Valleys. Ordered by wizard Rath to scout for pursuers of child-witch. Has own plans. Converted Snake to loyal follower by opening chasm beneath assassin. In private, Snake calls Dog "Master." When speaking to Wizards, makes the title an ironic "Maaaster Dog."

Other Valley folk

Lord Rand. Harsh ruler of lands to the east of the Valleys, known as Rand's Holdings. Elder brother of Ryd. When Rand became lord, he turned Ryd out, suggesting Ryd become mercenary in little wars up north.

Lord Ryd. Fifth year as Lord of the Five Valleys. Previously leader of mercenaries in small wars to the north. Drought began about time he arrived. At end of Book One, doesn't yet know of Rand's death.

Lir Bywater, father of Bird and Aren. Farmer. Found Bird in basket under oak tree in yard.

Reya Weaver, mother of Bird and Aren. Leader of Fifth Valley's council.

Rom Horseman & Alta Beekeeper, nearest neighbors to Lir and Reya. Rom raises horses and mules, Alta raises bees.

CHAPTER ONE

Aren and Bird rode slowly north through the village, hoping to attract as little attention as possible. As the landlord had suggested, the place seemed deserted.

With Aren's silence, Bird kept returning to what she'd done that morning. This was more than the death of a single dark wizard trying to enter her valley. She'd destroyed a whole way of life, left a village, no, a whole land defenseless against thieves. What of other lords who might raid? Aren said any of those things might happen. While Bird didn't understand how that might be, she believed her big brother.

Worst of all, perhaps others had died in the rubble, people who were innocent except that they served Lord Rand. She sobbed again, quietly.

As they passed through the town, Aren allowed Bird to weep without attempting comfort. She wept quietly, head down. He hoped a weeping child would not be identified with the small being whose anger brought down Rand's fortress and left him buried under the rubble.

Once past the town, Aren picked up the horses' pace to a fast walk they should be able to keep up for hours. He'd been leading; now he dropped back so the two rode side by side. Still he kept silent, occasionally putting out a hand to touch his sister's shoulder.

As the child's sobs lessened, he spoke. "Bird, that man was going to hang me and turn you over to wizards. You saved my life, and probably your own. His death is nothing to weep over. Think of how Reya and Lir would have taken news of our deaths."

That last hadn't been a good choice. Bird wept harder and added "I want to go home!" to her woe.

From time to time Aren looked back at the way they'd come. He didn't think the guard would organize a pursuit, and certainly villagers would not. But the guardsman had mentioned a wizard to the east who'd been sent for, and Bird had said she could sense wizards behind them on the East Road. While Aren suspected that Bird could deal with one or two wizards, he didn't want to test the idea. The mountains were further off here. He had no idea how soon Bird could call up thunder and lightning from this distance.

Though, now that he thought of it, she hadn't called up lightning to strike Rand and his keep. She'd simply—simply!—commanded him to die, and within minutes his keep became rubble. Apparently it took a keep only a little longer to, well, die than it did a person.

Rath's tower, he recalled, had taken a few hours to collapse and another day to turn to dust. Talk said that tower had been built in a night using powerful magic. Perhaps that was why its fall took longer even though it was smaller than Rand's keep. Still, even Rath's magic had not been able to stand against Bird. Perhaps she could order a wizard to die and he would. But suppose he took a day or two in the process, his strength only gradually failing.

Both he and Bird needed to know more about her powers, immense—and terrifying—as they seemed. Their only choice would be to keep moving while he kept watch on their back trail. Sooner or later the approaching wizards would send someone to look along this north road.

During his two years as a member of Lord Ryd's Guard, Aren had ample opportunities to watch Rath's apprentices as they practiced spells. He'd come to understand that most spells involved spoken formulas. Some also required herbs, potions, perhaps parts of animals. He suspected that as wizards grew in skill they no longer had to voice a spell.

Or at least lesser spells, ordinary spells. Lir and Reya maintained that they'd heard chanting from the two apprentices Rath sent into the Valley the night his tower fell. Perhaps some powerful spells required speech.

Lir and Reya insisted that Bird's only words that night had been a wish—a hope, she insisted—that lightning would chase the chanters from the valley. A few minutes later she hoped a bolt would shatter their crystal. She'd spoken no formula, certainly had not chanted.

Aren had been present the afternoon Bird hoped lightning would strike any wizard who set foot in the valley. No spell had been chanted. Surely such an---order?—to the lightning must have required a spell of great complexity if spoken by a dark wizard.

Whatever power Bird possessed, it didn't require spells or chanting. It seemed to come from her own will. But how could that be? And what might be its limits?

Suppose Bird became so homesick she wished she were dead, or had never been born. Or wished he were dead. Or wished them both back home. She didn't need to command lightning to kill Rand, or to destroy a lord's keep. She simply hoped. What else might she hope?

Surely somewhere were those who might recognize Bird for whatever she was, might understand her power and its limits. Surely there were limits.

In the meantime, they had to make their way north across Rand's holdings. The whole holding might quickly become lawless without the lord's strong hand. Aren wasn't worried about an encounter with a handful of brigands, given Bird's ability to charm horses. A troop of renegade guardsmen would be another matter.

Surely the pursuing wizards would be able to speak to one another through their crystals. No doubt they'd meet at the rubble which had been Rand's fortress.

Wizards, from what he'd seen of Rath and his apprentices, tended not to know much about roads and trails. Or landscape, for that matter. They'd have to rely on those who did. He'd better do the same as they moved further from the East Road. He'd watch for a farmhouse where he might ask directions, but not today. Today they needed to put miles behind them.

Aren realized that Bird had almost stopped sniffling. He reached out a hand and patted her shoulder again. This time she gave him a small, sad smile and spoke.

"Do—do you think that man really would have killed you?" Her lips trembled as she held back tears.

Aren nodded. "That kind of man doesn't take anything back. He'd have had me hanging in a few minutes. Then he'd have tried to turn you over to the wizards."

At that Bird's eyes darkened nearly to the slate of her angriest tantrums. "I wouldn't have gone. And I'd never let anyone take you away!"

She grew quiet then, her eyes clearing. "All those sad people. They were afraid of me." She turned in the saddle to face Aren directly. "Do people really depend on a lord so much? We almost never see the lord in our valley. You and Lir have swords and bows. Why are these people so afraid without a lord?"

Aren sighed. They were getting into deep waters now, but it was better than having Bird weeping or growing angry again at the thought of what might have happened. "Bird, not all places are like the Five Valleys. Most lords won't let their people have weapons or learn how to use them. Those lords hire professional guardsmen, mostly mercenaries who are paid to follow the lord's orders. Those might include protecting the people, or might not."

They rode in silence for a while. Then Bird voiced another question. "So if something happened to Lord Ryd, Lir and Reya wouldn't be afraid the way those people were?"

Aren chuckled at the thought of Lir or Reya being afraid at a Lord's passing. "No, little bird, they wouldn't. They might wonder a little, as they did when Ryd came. The custom of training our people as guardsmen and letting them keep weapons is too strongly ingrained for any new lord to change. At least not unless he brought a hundred of his own mercenaries with him, and even that might not be enough. "

"But what about all those people standing around the—the keep? Who's going to protect them, if their people have no weapons?"

"That I don't know." Aren considered the question. "That guardsman I spoke to seemed intelligent enough. He may be able to hold some of the Guard together, and that would give the people some protection. Their lord seemed to care little about his people. Look at these farms." He gestured toward the fields on either side of the road. "Every field we've passed since we came out of the hills has been over-worked, over-grazed. Remember those workmen we met on the road? They spoke of taxes so high that farmers planted every field each year and still lost their land to Rand for taxes."

Aren looked again at the lands to both sides of them. "I think Rand was a greedy man. Whoever takes his place can't be any worse. The council of lords will probably select someone to replace Rand, if a powerful neighbor doesn't take the land first."

Bird didn't care about the next lord. Her attention was on the fields as they rode by. "The land is tired. Lamar hasn't walked here in a long time."

Aren's eyebrows rose. Lamar, again. He'd always wondered how Bird was aware of Lamar's approach well before the man came in sight. He'd never heard Lamar make the faintest sound as he moved about Lir's farm, working for food and a bed in a hayloft. As nearly as Lir and Aren could tell, the man labored for the sheer pleasure of planting and shaping and weeding and harvesting. Not for the first time, Aren wondered about Lamar's warning that Bird need to leave. How had the man known that wizards would be after her? Aren shook his head, scolded himself: one unusual being was enough. He didn't need to start imagining things.

Bird's next words brought him sharply back to the present. "There's someone up ahead."

Aren began to draw his sword but paused with the weapon half out of its scabbard. If the one ahead were a wizard, a sword would be little use. He could see the figure some distance away. On foot: that suggested a wizard, though others also travelled by foot. Bird's face was puzzled, with none of the fury he'd seen when she'd called down lightning in the Valley or told Rand's keep to fall.

Bird whispered something too softly to hear. Aren leaned toward her, not taking his eyes from the figure, and asked what she'd said.

"I keep losing my sense of her. I think she doesn't know what she is."

Slowly they approached. Aren drew a sharp breath as he saw that the woman's robe was the grey of a novice whose power hadn't manifested. If that power didn't appear, the novice might walk in grey forever.

Bird spoke again. "She's different from dark wizards. They feel like an absence. She's a presence, but kind of flickering."

"Are you sure she's not some kind of dark wizard? Or under their control?" Aren was a little surprised at how quickly he'd come to believe his little sister could sense the presence of wizards. That she could determine a wizard's Order was something new. He could see the lone walker more clearly now.

"Should we call to her?" Bird's voice was curious, unafraid.

That was something: Bird neither afraid nor angry. If she could call down lightning on a dark wizard and destroy a Lord and his castle, surely she could deal with an apprentice wizard, flickering or not. He hoped. "No. We'll catch up soon enough. We'd better keep an eye out, just in case."

Concerned that he'd allowed his thoughts to distract him so Bird was first to see the walker, Aren began to search more carefully the fields around and the road behind them. Just in case, he loosened his sword in its scabbard. "Be watchful," he cautioned Bird. "If you see anything which might be magic, urge Pony to run past her. That may disrupt any spell and allow me time to forestall any further spell-casting with my sword. Let us hope it won't be necessary."

Bird nodded, slowing Pony so she rode slightly behind and away from Aren. He noted the tactic and nodded: a little distance might make casting a spell over both more difficult. Too difficult, he hoped, for a novice.

The woman stopped walking and turned to face them. She held her head high, her lips firmly closed. Aren watched those lips carefully for any sign of a murmured spell. If she were advanced enough to cast a spell by reciting the words in her mind, he'd get no warning. Given that her robe was a nondescript gray, he hoped she'd not be that advanced.

This gray-robed apprentice couldn't be far along—but on which path? A new, untried apprentice might still attempt to curry favor with the Order.

The woman let them come within ten feet before speaking. "Would you prefer I keep my distance, or come within reach of your sword? I won't approach the child or attempt to walk between the two of you." She gestured toward her robe. "As you can see, I was an apprentice, but not of these dark wizards." Her next words were addressed to Bird. "You need fear no treachery from me. My small power is as nothing compared to yours. That much but no more, even I can discern."

She waited a few moments. When neither Bird nor Aren spoke, she offered more. "My name," she said, "is Brenna. I do not ask your names." Again she paused for an answer. When none came, she went on. "If you would rather, I will step aside and remain here until you pass, though I am also eager to make my way quickly through these open fields. Dark wizards have no love for those to whom I was apprenticed."

Aren continued to eye her skeptically. She seemed harmless enough, but still… "Remain where you are."

The apprentice nodded, her hands still held where he could see them, her lips firmly closed when she wasn't speaking.

Aren continued. "You say dark wizards have no love for your order. What order is that? I know only of dark wizards in these lands. Why are you here, in the midst of the dark Order's territory?"

Her smile was rueful. "When the Order of Blue Wizards dismissed me from my apprenticeship, I thought only of leaving before I did any further damage. With nowhere else to go, I decided to return home. I thought to visit, at least, with my family, though they'll be disappointed in me. Clearly I had not thought enough about the Dark Order. As I came into their lands, my foolishness became clear."

"If you're from these lands, how is it the Order didn't take you?" Aren was skeptical; he couldn't imagine a wizard from another Order recruiting apprentices here.

She nodded. "It's a good question. My parents, as I said, are farmers north of here." She broke off. "But should we stand talking? I wish to reach the forest ahead before night. I would guess that you have some purpose other than a ride in the country on a fine day. I am capable of speaking while walking if you care to hold to my pace. Or I can remain here until you have gone on."

Aren stood in his stirrups, left hand shading his eyes as he looked back down the road they'd followed. She was right. They were wasting time. So far he'd seen no sign of treachery. Of course, if she were accomplished at treachery there would be no sign until she struck. With a sigh he gestured for the newcomer to walk to his right and slightly ahead, then motioned Bird to keep to his left. Even if this woman caught him off guard, Bird would have time to do something. He hoped.

They went in silence for a few moments, Aren holding Blaze to a slow walk for the woman's sake, before he reminded her. "You spoke about your parents being farmers." Behind him he sensed Bird stirring and Pony moving a little closer as Bird's homesickness increased with talk of farmers.

Brenna seemed to come back from some distance. "What? Oh, yes. My family farm here in the north of Rand's Holding. When I showed signs of power, my parents first tried to discourage me, keeping very quiet about what they'd noticed. Here nothing good is heard about the dark Order.

"My parents didn't want that life for me, though they'd seen few enough dark wizards. There are no women among them, though the Order does from time to time take a female child who's shown power. That also frightened my parents: what happened to those girls? When a dark wizard did come through, which wasn't often-- farms are few this far from the East Road--they would hide me. If time allowed, they'd send me deep into the Red Forest. Those woods have a bad name. Gossip says that members of the Order tend to avoid them."

She lapsed into silence again. Aren prompted her. "Sooner or later someone must have noticed your powers."

Brenna shrugged. "My parents feared that possibility. My mother came from further east, near the edge of Rand's holdings. She'd heard of another kind of wizard beyond the river. Among the people she came from, those wizards were rumored to practice healing, even to measure power by a wizard's ability to heal."

This caught Aren's attention. Perhaps those wizards further east would recognize the source of Bird's power. Had Lamar intended them to travel that far? Perhaps this failed wizard could tell them. Could he trust her words?

Brenna continued her story. "It was a long chance, but when I was thirteen and the signs of power too strong to hide any longer, they sent me east. I would travel as a lone girl with a story of dead parents and one relative somewhere beyond Rand's holdings."

"Sounds like us." Bird's murmur was just audible. Aren hoped it didn't carry to this failed apprentice.

If Brenna heard, she gave no notice. "Perhaps I was lucky, or what power I had protected me. As I encountered other travelers, few as those were along this northern edge, I prayed they wouldn't notice me. None found me worth bothering. When I neared the river which marks the end of Rand's holdings, I was met by a wizard. He wore a robe of blue so deep that I thought it black. Then his robe caught the sun and I breathed again."

"So you had used power without realizing it?" Aren asked.

"Yes," Brenna replied. "The wizard who greeted me said his crystal had picked up brief flashes coming toward the river, flashes which could only mean a potential wizard. He suggested that I had been protecting myself with power I could barely use. That was probably a good sign, he said. We rode his horse through the river. Rand's guards wouldn't have allowed us to use the only bridge."

"What are blue wizards like?" Bird moved up beside Aren, but didn't come any closer to the young woman.

The apprentice leaned forward, looking past Aren at Bird. "It is true, child, that they value healing, but they practice other powers as well. Some, they say, are to defend themselves against dark wizardry. My apprenticeship ended before I learned any of those. Basic healing and a few other spells were as much as I mastered." She fell silent.

"Do blue wizards also draw their power from the dark?" Aren asked.

The woman chuckled. "No, they draw their greatest power from lakes and rivers, even the sea."

"These—blue—wizards draw their power from water?" Aren was skeptical.

"From blue waters, but also from the blue sky, just as dark wizards draw their power from shadows and night."

Aren nodded, partly convinced. "What happened after you crossed the river?"

Brenna's gaze focused far away. It took her moment to reply. "This blue wizard's talk reassured me that what my mother had said was true. I went with him into that coastal region. I stayed in his household, studying what I could with his apprentices, until the next meeting of his Order of Blue Wizards.

"All seemed unlike what I had heard of the Dark Order. He presented me, told my story, and proposed that I be formally apprenticed. It was only at that meeting that I realized that Charl—the wizard who had befriended me—stood second in the Order. Much later I learned that there had been some doubt about the nature of my power. A proposal for apprenticeship presented by a lesser wizard might not have passed. As things turned out, those doubts were justified. In the meantime, I remained there on the coast, studying, until I was dismissed." She paused, her face sad.

Aren wondered why this one had been dismissed, but held back the question. They rode in silence for a time before Brenna spoke again.

"You will need to make a decision, you and the child. Not far ahead the road turns east to skirt the forest. The way is easy, though you'd be visible at a distance in this flat country.

"I will enter the Red Forest. I've known those woods since I was a child, and I'll be safe enough there. There are tales enough about dark wizards avoiding those woods that at least some of them must be true." For the first time since she'd joined them, Brenna smiled. "It may be that they're not aware of me, though I suspect that power of the kind this child holds will draw them. Even I can feel her strength."

That caused Aren to bring his horse to a standstill. "You said before that you can feel her power. Does that mean that dark wizards can trace her?" This was bad news, indeed, if wizards could sense Bird's presence, as she could that of wizards.

Brenna also stopped, turning to look up at the two of them as they sat on horseback. "I've learned, even in these few days of walking these lands, to keep myself aware of anyone holding power. It is a defense taught by the blue Order, who are only too aware of dark wizards' preference that no other Order should exist." She regarded Aren closely. "I was not looking for the child, but feared to come upon a dark wizard without warning. My small powers would not protect me. A wizard not scanning for signs of power might not sense the child. Indeed, they may not know of her; it was only by chance that I sensed her."

Aren found the apprentice's—or former apprentice's—words to be some comfort, but not much. Surely by now the Order would be searching for any use of power. What Bird had just done to Rand's keep must have been visible to any seeker. When two sets of wizards met at what was left, they'd quickly realize that he and Bird must have come north.

After a time, Aren said, "You have guessed correctly. I wish to keep my sister out of their hands. How might we best travel east but avoid the roads? " If this half-wizard spoke the truth and her own danger were something like Bird's, she might give what aid she could.

Brenna shrugged. "Best to continue north to the Red Forest. From there, you might slip away into the mountains, or travel east through the trees." Cautiously, she offered, "I know the forest as well as any. I could guide you to the eastern edge. There you would be near the river where the land becomes broken by streams and gullies. That might be your best chance. If nothing else, the Order might have to look for you to the north as well as along the forest edge. I doubt they would enter, but they might well be waiting when you leave."

Aren had to think for a while. Their best chance, or this apprentice wizard's best chance to betray them? She'd done nothing so far to hinder them. He'd seen no signs of spell-casting. She'd not brought out a crystal, so she'd probably not communicated with the Order.

He'd feel safer in a forest than in strange fields and roads. Forest ways he knew from wandering among the hills around the Fifth Valley. If nothing else, he and Bird would be harder to spot there. "We'll into this forest, though I would not endanger you by drawing the Order."

Brenna shrugged. "I doubt they'll notice my little power, with the child's to follow. I'll do nothing to attract their attention. If necessary, I could play hide-and-seek with a half-dozen guardsmen, or slip out to the northern mountains. That may be my lot in any case." She stopped walking and turned to face Aren. "I'm in greater danger if your sister remains in the forest. Guiding her to the far edge may keep the Order from noticing my presence at all. I have but to remain quiet as the two of you leave."

For a time Aren walked his horse in silence. Then he nodded. "We'll into the forest, then, and thank you for your assistance."

***

Oleg was not an early riser. He preferred to work late into the night, when his concentration was greatest. On this day, Haster awakened him with word that Soren wished the Loremaster to join him as soon as possible.

Haster hadn't seemed to quail at rousting the Order's Loremaster in mid-morning. Whatever news had come in must indeed be urgent. Grumbling less than he might have, Oleg poured a little water from the carafe into a basin, splashed his face, pulled a robe over his head and started up the stairs.

Oleg's tap on the door of the Chief Mage's observatory was answered by an abrupt "For darkness' sake, come in!"

Soren stepped aside from the great crystal, gesturing toward it. "Look."

Oleg hadn't needed prompting. He stepped forward, puzzled for a moment at what he saw. Was this Rath's tower? No, that had crumbled into dust some days earlier. This pile of stones and rubble must have been more than just a single tower. He looked an inquiry at Soren, indicating the crystal with a wave of his hand.

"Go ahead," Soren said. "Shift the view as you will."

Oleg nodded, willed the crystal to show a wider view. At first he saw only a greater pile. A still wider view showed a high road and across it, a field. A wider view yet, a town perhaps a half-mile to the west.

Oleg began to know what he was seeing; somewhere on the East Road, the remains of what probably had been a keep. Taking a closer view, he saw people standing a fearful distance from the rubble. Some were in servant's clothing, while a few were clearly guardsmen. Most stood stunned; a few wept.

He turned to Soren. "Whose?"

For a moment Soren didn't answer. "Rand's. Lord Rand's keep. Turned to rubble in moments."

Oleg widened the crystal's view again, this time focusing on the grounds around what had been the keep. The central building was gone, as were the outer walls. Beyond and behind the rubble still stood outbuildings: stables, storage sheds, granaries, housing for servants and guardsmen.

"This looks recent," Oleg noted .

Soren took the prompt. "Very. Very." He breathed deeply. "Early this morning, Roke reported that he'd received word that a guardsman and a girl child had been taken. An hour later we heard again from Roke, who'd arrived to find the scene we see now. The child, from all Roke could make of garbled accounts, ordered Rand to die and his keep to fall in upon him. There was barely time for the servants and guards to escape. The pair walked away."

Oleg chuckled without humor. "Surely no one there would have attempted to stop them." He thought a moment. "She told Rand to die, and he did? There were no signs of a spell being cast?"

"So two of the guards insisted. A third, their sergeant, was already so far gone in drink that he made no sense at all. They felt the building shift and they ran, the child and the male prisoner running with them. None stopped to check on whether Rand was actually dead. He certainly is now." For a moment they regarded the pile of rubble which had been the strong center of the keep, around it a smaller circle of rubble which had been the outer wall.

Oleg broke the silence. "Where did they go? Surely someone wasn't afraid to watch, at least."

"Roke asked that question of several. They started toward the village, but no one watched for long."

"Fearful, no doubt, of attracting the child's attention. With good reason," Oleg mused.

"What do we do now?" Haster asked. "Ordering lords to watch and apprehend these two clearly won't work." He stood just out of reach of the crystal, as though the witch-girl could reach through to seize him.

"Slowly, now; slowly," Oleg answered. "We know what we're looking for. Her power is stronger than we thought, or is growing. She can control rain and wind, lightning, horses, and stone." He considered the new evidence. "She can tell a man to die, with no need of lightning." He turned to face Soren. "Perhaps there is nothing in nature which she cannot command. For now, we'd better assume her power extends to trees, water, perhaps the earth itself." He became thoughtful. "This is an interesting problem."

Haster, a little recovered now, snorted. "Interesting!"

"Oh, yes," Oleg responded, despite Soren's look of outrage. "Very interesting. She can command one man to die; could she command a force, say, of fifty guardsmen to do the same? Perhaps, but perhaps not. Could she command arrows to drop from the air before they reached her? Perhaps. And what of the guardsman who accompanies her? Her supposed brother, Snake reported. No one seems to have said that he was extraordinary. So she needs a guide?" He fell silent, thinking, before continuing.

"Whatever she is, she's taken the form of a child. Does she have more than a child's understanding? Perhaps not, or she might have taken another form and gone out into the world on her own. Had she a full understanding of herself, she might have stayed in the Fifth Valley and defied us. Can she, I wonder, instruct a wizard to die?"

Haster shivered at that thought. Soren, again, looked outraged. Ironic, that, Oleg thought, given the half-dozen wizards Soren had directed Snake to kill.

Soren regained control of himself. "I've instructed Roke to remain in the area. He will take rooms at the Inn for Lorit and Rath. In the interim he may learn more."

Oleg shrugged. "I doubt he will learn much. Shocked servants will not easily speak to one of our Order." He considered the situation. "With any luck, Snake will arrive a day or two before the others. He should be able to loosen tongues."

For a time the three stood looking into the great crystal as first guardsmen and then servants drifted away from the rubble.

"Lorit should report sometime today. I've tried to raise his crystal, but he's no doubt placed it in his pack. I'll warn him." With orders to give, Soren seemed more nearly himself. "In the meantime, now that we know who to look for, Haster and I will spend some time scrying the East Road for our fugitives."

Oleg nodded. "And I will have more to report to the Dark One. Perhaps this news will shake some information from him. Certainly Selik's death by lightning seemed a surprise, though only briefly. He laughed and said we would not want to encounter the one who could control lightning. From what we've seen today, there was truth in that." He smiled at thought of a mystery to be researched. "I've put apprentices to searching the earliest scrolls. They're to bring me anything, no matter how fragmentary or unbelievable, which speaks of powerful beings, including Druids." Looking hard at the Chief Mage, the Lore-master spoke slowly: "Something is loose in the world. I doubt that it's new."

At Soren's gesture of dismissal, Oleg bowed and left the room. He wouldn't immediately seek out the Dark One; he'd want to think for a time first. Still, that visit would have to be made soon, before Soren called him again.

***

The wizards started early on the morning after Snake and Dog departed. Even though Rath was recovering, they made slow progress. A day later, when the group paused for their mid-morning break, Lorit prepared to report to Soren. He walked into the woods for privacy, but quickly returned.

"Rath, Tarh, come with me."

"What is it?" Rath looked up angrily from where he lay on his face while Tarh kneaded his back. "Can't you tell us here?"

"No," Lorit answered. "This is for our ears only."

Tarh assisted a complaining Rath to rise. They followed some forty feet into the woods before Lorit stopped, gestured them closer. He spoke softly but urgently.

"I've just heard from Soren. He sent Roke with word for Lord Rand to detain the two we spoke of. Apparently Rand did as told. By the time Roke arrived, he found a pile of rubble where the keep had stood, surrounded by a crowd of frightened villagers and farmers."

Lorit gathered himself. "The only coherent witness insisted that the child told Rand to die. Then she ordered the keep to fall in around him. There was barely time, this fellow maintained, for the living to get out before the whole place came down."

Rath choked on his attempt at a laugh. "I think we can forget any doubts about whether we follow the right quarry. I assume no one attempted to restrain them. Or are they waiting for us to catch up?"

Lorit leaned against a tree, his face ashen as the import of this story continued to sink in. "They were gone when Roke arrived. Soren has told him to learn all that he can, but take no action until we arrive." He looked hard at Rath. "How fast can you move? Snake will learn more than most, but we need to make haste."

Rath ignored the question. "Snake will learn what can be learned. There is no more need for haste than before. Perhaps less. We must consider how to deal with this witch-child. I shall someday destroy her, but would rather not be destroyed myself in the process."

Lorit stood, facing Rath. "Still, we should move as quickly as we can. I propose to force a faster pace on the guard, in whatever way we must. We know that men are capable of more than they believe, given the right incentive."

Rath shrugged. "As you will. If the guard carry me all night, I will survive it. In the darkness, spells will cause our guardsmen to keep going longer than they will in daylight."

***

By late afternoon, Oleg had reviewed every note he'd taken. He'd gone back to crumbling scrolls whose partially-readable text hinted at wild stories of beings with incredible powers, scrolls whose writers had clearly not believed such tales. He'd learned nothing of substance.

That left his final resource. He scolded his apprentices one last time, told them he was not to be disturbed. Closing his study door, he set a closing spell no apprentice and perhaps only Soren or Rath would be able to break. Then he unlocked the cabinet whose false back wall led to the darkest areas below the building, lit a lantern, and started down into that deep darkness.

As usual, the Dark One heard him coming. Oleg carefully shielded the lantern so what light it gave shone behind him. Even that dim glow usually set the Dark One complaining from the farthest wall of his rough cell. Today Oleg could see the shape standing just inside the bars. Apparently the thing had become interested in their recent conversations. Oleg was not entirely certain that was a good sign.

"So, master of lore, you must have more questions. These are more visits than I've had in many years."

Oleg grunted. There was no reason to let the fellow know that things appeared desperate, his knowledge perhaps essential. "I have found some odd bits and pieces in my researches, it is true. Old parchments with much damage. They talk of powerful beings who could control lightning, with power over animals and even stone. Such possibilities of course intrigue me."

The Dark One's laughter was harsh, as though it no longer quite remembered how to laugh and could only approximate the effect. "You do not fool me, wizard. Even these spell-haunted stones below your spell-riddled building can feel that something is happening. If you would ask questions, you must first tell me what transpires in the bright world. Otherwise, I'll remain silent and wait for these stones to hint at what takes place above. There is little you can do to compel. Had you been able to destroy me, you'd have done so long ago."

Oleg stood silent for a time, considering. What the Dark One said was true enough. Not even foxglove had been able to kill him, though it deadened his powers sufficiently to allow those early dark wizards to transport him to this deep cell. They'd taken the precaution of sealing the bars and the walls with powerful spells. Each month Oleg renewed those spells, just as he continued to feed this dark being a diet laced with foxglove and every other poisonous plant the Order could find. To frighten him or find a way to worsen his captivity would be, Oleg more than suspected, beyond their powers.

"Don't think too long, wizard. Finally, after all these years, you may have a tale which interests me. Speak, tell me your tale, or return to as much light as you can bear."

Oleg set the lantern down and leaned against a wall. "All right, Dark One. We will trade. I will tell you a tale, and you will tell me what it suggests."

A sigh came from the cell.

"A being unknown to us walks the earth. You've guessed that from my earlier questions. She commands wind and rain. Beyond that, she's set a permanent ward over a certain valley and called lightning to enforce it. None of our Order may enter that valley on pain of death, though our servants may."

"This much I'd guessed. Tell me something new." The Dark One pretended boredom.

"Now we learn that this same being can command horses, and we suspect other animals as well."

The Dark One said nothing.

"Further: today, this being was taken captive by a lord, to be held until we could arrive."

The Dark One's voice was incredulous. "You didn't tell this lord what he dealt with?"

"We tell lords only what they need to know."

"And he didn't need to know what sort of being he was told to capture? I can foretell the end to this tale, wizard."

"Perhaps. At any rate, this being ordered him to die and his keep to fall."

The Dark One chuckled again, sounding no more accustomed to the act than before. "I presume this being escaped." He paused. "You're being a little too careful, wizard. In our last conversation you let slip that this being is a girl child. I doubt that there's a second such walking your lands. Nor is she likely to have achieved adulthood or changed gender. You're faced with a girl child who can command lightning, rain, wind, animals, stone, and death. This is the second building she's caused to collapse, but the first may have been through lightning—am I not correct? This time, she simply commanded the stones. And she commanded a man to die. He obeyed." Again what passed for a chuckle. "Wouldn't your Chief Mage be delighted by that sort of power?"

The dark being said nothing more. Oleg waited a moment. "All right, I've told you a tale. Now it's your turn to tell me one."

"Your problem is quite clear, wizard. Does this being possess great power which she's just learning to use, or is her power growing? It's a fine distinction, but of little use to you, I think. Either way, her power is beyond anything your entire Order could bring to bear. Better sue for peace, I think. Stop pursuing her. If she returns to that valley, give it a wide berth. If her travels continue, allow her to travel to whatever destination she seeks, and stay away from that destination."

When he spoke again, his words came more slowly. "I've known only one being who could command air and fire, stone and water. Commanding death puzzles me. The one I recall could have, but would not. Had she, I'd not have been available to teach your ancestors the rudiments of power. Nor could they have learned enough to trap me in this cell."

He was silent for a moment as Oleg waited, barely breathing. This was more than he'd hoped to hear. How useful it might prove, he was uncertain.

The Dark One spoke again, thoughtfully, as though alone. "Yet he calls her a girl child. A child? How a child? Unless—but that's unlikely." He recalled Oleg's presence. "That's as much as I can decipher from what you've told. That you call her a child puzzles me. Perhaps if you return with more information I will be able to enlighten you further. Such enlightenment, I fear, will be the closest to real light within these walls until the day they crumble." Again he was silent. "I will say this much, master of such lore as your Order has managed: that she has twice commanded death should frighten your Chief Mage, as it does me."

Oleg waited for a time, in case the being would offer more; but the Dark One returned to the cell's far wall. As nearly as Oleg could tell, he had lain down upon the stone bed cut out of the wall. Oleg turned and walked away, toward the lighter world which awaited above.

***

Snake had travelled the East Road in the past, but never at this pace. He knew very well that the walk to Rand's Keep would take fully four days, and then only with an early start. He and Dog hadn't set out until late afternoon. Nonetheless, he found himself jog-trotting up to the Inn near Rand's keep in late afternoon of the third day. To his astonishment, he felt strong enough to continue at the same pace.

Dog halted at sight of the Inn. "Good," he said. "Drink. Eat. Order pay. Listen." He turned to Snake, who was busy marveling at how fresh he felt after their long jog. "Good?"

Snake nodded. "Ale, food, and a room full of gossip and tales. Lead on."

Dog shook his head. "Snake lead. His dog follow." He gestured for Snake to go ahead. After a moment's hesitation, the assassin did, adjusting his expression and posture to what would be appropriate for a servant of the Order with two powerful wizards following behind him.

The place seemed awfully busy for mid-day. Nearly every seat was taken, and the hum of conversation was constant. There must have been some great event in the village. Perhaps their quarry was nearby, or captured. Snake was not at all certain how Dog would react to such an event.

The assassin led the way to the bar, where the harried host busily filled mug after mug with ale or spiced wine as he shouted instructions to the barmaid and kitchen. When the man turned with a hearty, "What's your pleasure, gentlemen?" Snake held out a ring. On its stone of black obsidian was carved the Order's symbol: a dark hand holding a dark moon. "We'll want a table, ale, and rooms," he said with just the right amount of sternness.

The host's good humor vanished immediately. "One of the Order is already here, sir. He has taken six rooms—the entire second floor— in anticipation of your party's arrival. Are the others with you?" He shouted over his shoulder. "Pate! Show these--"

Snake cut him off. "The others follow. We can find our rooms later. Now about that table–?"

The host nodded. "Give me a moment." He came out from behind the bar, walked over to a small table by a wall and spoke to the two men sitting there. Snake, who could read lips well enough, read "wizards' men" on the host's. The two quickly picked up their mugs and sought a table on the room's far side. The host gestured for Snake and his follower to approach.

"Will this do, sir? I can provide another if you prefer."

Snake shook his head. "This will do fine." A glance at Dog's satisfied countenance assured him that was the case. "And now, if you will, two mugs of ale. If there's food in the house, something to eat."

"Right away, sir. We've been so busy we're left with a smaller menu than usual, but I can offer a fresh loaf, fine cheese from a local farm, slices from a roast. Will that do?"

Snake caught Dog's nod and said yes. The two had barely settled into their chairs before the ale arrived, followed shortly by the loaf, fresh though no longer warm, a large platter of steaming beef, and a round cheese.

Snake detained the servant. "You have quite a crowd here. What's the occasion?"

The servant stared. "You've not heard?"

Snake, stern now, shook his head.

"Why, Lord Rand's keep lies in rubble, the lord himself beneath! A child witch, they say, taken at the request of the Order, destroyed the keep and the lord himself. You've not heard?"

"We've been on the road from the west for several days." Snake did not need to pretend his shock. Dog's expression, he noted, did not change from mild interest.

"Ah, that's it, then," the servant responded. "This happened two mornings ago. Since then, we've been full up with townsfolk talking over the fall and others coming to gape at the ruins, then here to chatter and ask questions. Oh, it's been a great thing for business, it has, though no one has any idea what will happen now."

Snake raised his eyebrows, his surprise still genuine. "And this child-witch? What of her?"

"Ah, that's the question, isn't it? They say she and her guard walked away, that's what they say. I hope she's not hanging around somewhere!" The man clearly was prepared to talk on, but at a shout from the landlord he scampered off.

Snake watched him go, then turned to face Dog. "Master, what do we do now?"

Dog smiled. "Drink ale, eat meal, see wizard, look at ruins." He chuckled. "Someone angry, maybe."

That was all Snake was likely to get. He focused instead on listening to the locals' chatter, trying not to wonder just which side Dog, and so himself as well, was really on. He hoped it was the child's. He wouldn't like to find himself serving some third power which might pit itself against both the Order and whatever this girl-child might turn out to be. Snake had survived more than one struggle between powerful beings; surviving this time might not be so certain.

CHAPTER TWO

Chatter filled the Inn. Men wearing field servants' clothing told of hearing a rumble from the Keep. They turned to see guards and servants running from the front entrance. Others, in house servant's garb, told of stone dust drifting from the ceilings and walls. At the sight they ran blindly for the nearest door and into the bright day as the upper walls came down. That's not right, said one of the watchers. The upper walls didn't fall first; the whole keep came down at once.

Snake, playing the hardly-believing stranger, asked how many had died.

A half-dozen answered at once: only one, and he was dead before the Keep fell. "The Lord himself it was," an old house servant added. He looked around, saw none of Rand's guard, and went on. "Rand was a hard man, and none who served him will be sad to see him no more."

"Perhaps," said a portly fellow, a shopkeeper by the look of him, "but who will stand between us and thieves? Many such live in the woods to the east, and north along the mountains."

"And whose fault is that?" answered another who by his clothing was most likely a farmer. "Rand's taxes drove families off their lands. And what good did his taxes do him? What he didn't spend on losing wars he spent on guardsmen to enforce higher taxes. He built nothing!"

Over the murmuring which greeted this last, Snake asked, "So you think it was not the earth quaking which brought down Rand's keep? He must have angered some mighty wizard." He looked around carefully then, as though fearful of seeing such a wizard entering the room.

The old servant spoke again. He seemed a spokesman for the keep's staff. "From what the guards say, this was no ordinary wizard. Three were with Rand, and they claim the sorcerer was a child, a little girl, though some say it must have been he who claimed to be her brother."

Another voice put in, "Or the child was a powerful wizard in disguise."

Some nodded at that, but the old servant turned toward the voice and spoke scornfully. "And why would a sorcerer so powerful bother to disguise himself? Why not just curse the keep and its lord from outside? Why enter?"

A farmer replied, "It's said that the child ordered Rand to die, and he did. An enemy might well wish to watch." Other farmers sitting nearby nodded as though they'd also have liked to watch Rand die.

"And then have to run for his life, with guards and servants?" came a voice from the room's far side.

Snake voiced skepticism. "A child told him to die, and he did? And with his death the keep fell in? Was this Rand both sorcerer and lord, so his keep died with him?"

The white-haired servant shrugged. "I know only what the guard claimed to have been true. I was upstairs, supervising preparations. Rand had told us to expect important guests, so everything had to be in order."

"He ordered the kitchen to prepare for guests as well," said one dressed as a cook's helper. "We had just begun to clean vegetables. Some were about to go into the yard to select fat capons from the henyard when we felt the first tremor." He leaned forward, explaining for the strangers' benefit what the rest of his audience knew. "The kitchen was on the lowest level, a terrible place to be if the walls fell. We took little time leaving. Better the Lord's wrath if it turned out to be just a little shaking, than a sure death if not."

Snake looked around the room. As the new and amazed audience for these tales, he was the one person everyone in the room wished to convince. "So where are these guards? Has some son of the lord's gathered them to defend the holdings?"

Another villager spoke up. "Our Lord Rand was busy with wars to the south, trying to expand his holdings, when not meeting with other Lords to secure his position as head of their Council. He couldn't be bothered with a wife. Even if he had, any child of his would doubtless be too young to command. Rand was not yet forty."

"So where are his guards, then?" Snake repeated. With a dead lord, no heir, a keep destroyed, it would be essential to know what the guard were up to. They might rampage through the land, taking whatever they could as they abandoned this cursed place. Or a strong captain might hold them together and claim the lordship. That had happened more than once, Snake knew. Either way, he'd wish to avoid the guard, and he'd bet his new master would feel the same. A quick glance at Dog told him nothing. The broad man appeared only mildly interested in the story as it unfolded.

"I'll tell you about some of those who came to this inn early that morning to arrest the child and her brother," said Pate the waiter, who'd stopped to listen after delivering a tray of mugs to a nearby table. "I went to the Keep as soon as we heard—not believing until I saw for myself, you know. I saw six guards, still wearing Rand's livery, riding hard to the south. Two of them I recognized as being among those who'd taken the witch-child and her brother from the Inn."

A farmer who'd spoken earlier supplied the rest. "My land is not far from the Keep along the south road. I heard the rumble and was walking to see what had taken place when six guardsmen came galloping by. Their faces were white, and they kept looking over their shoulders as they whipped their horses. I'll wager they're well away by now."

The old servant nodded. "No doubt afraid the sorcerer would come after them next." He chuckled. Clearly there was little affection between Rand's guard and his other servants. Apparently the villagers and farmers shared that dislike: laughter spread around the room.

"But what of the others?" Snake insisted. By all accounts, Rand kept a guard of fifty, the largest garrison in the land. That many could present a problem if they took to marauding.

"Some gathered what they could carry and rode away. Others have remained, waiting to see what happens when more wizards gather," said another servant.

"Aye," said a kitchen servant, "but it's not their sergeant who rallies them. He was one of the three who took the pair into the keep. Now he stays in his quarters drinking the last of the wine he pilfered from Rand's cellar. It's a young guardsman who's called together the twenty or so who remain. He speaks of building a low wall from the rubble, to make some sort of defense."

"Probably hopes to move enough rubble to reach Rand's treasury. The gold must be somewhere under the pile," came a voice.

Dog's low rumble carried to each corner of the room. "What now for village and farms?"

All heads turned to the squat man. His question brought silence.

It was broken by the portly shopkeeper. "My question exactly. It's all very well, guardsmen talking of building a wall while others leave the country, but who's to protect my shop if those last twenty guardsmen leave? And who"—he turned to a table around which were gathered farmers—"who will protect your farms once word spreads that we're without a lord? What will prevent neighbor lords who lost land to Rand from taking back their losses and raiding into our lands and homes?"

Dog sat back, muttered in a voice which still somehow carried, "Not good for seek work. No sense stay." His wink alerted Snake, who rose to the hint in what he hoped was the intended manner.

"What of the child-witch and her companion?" Snake asked. "Where did they go—or have they remained? I would not encounter them! Perhaps they plan to rule in Rand's seat. Power which could take down Rand's keep would doubtless build anew as quickly. Perhaps you're to be sorcerer-ruled, my friends."

This brought a wave of protest. "The Order would never allow it!" "What if the child were a dark wizard in disguise?" "Wizards don't care to rule. They let lords manage things while they busy themselves with other mischief."

"They let lords believe they rule, you mean," said a servant. "A wizard visited the keep the afternoon before, and he didn't wait to be announced or invited in. After he left, Rand sent for the sergeant of the guard. Shortly afterwards several guardsmen rode out to watch the roads."

"Those sent in this direction didn't go far." This was the host's first contribution. He'd come to see what was taking Pate so long. He sent the man about his duties, but stayed for the conversation, smiling at the sight of his full room, with beer or wine on every table. "That half-dozen came here and sat in the window seat"—he pointed—"drinking ale and watching the road."

"Well, but where is this witch-child now, if witch-child she actually is?" Snake brought them back to what he thought Dog wanted him to ask.

Several answered at once: the two had walked back east, toward the Inn. Perhaps they'd kept going, or turned north, through the town. No one from the town had noticed them, not with the news of Rand's keep to draw them.

An argument began over whether the child-witch had continued east, gone north, or lingered in the area. Snake let it run on for a time before he broke in again. "What of the watch Rand's guard were keeping for those two the night before? Did the pair spend the night in Rand's dungeon before taking down his keep?"

Here the host spoke up. "The man and child spent the night upstairs." Heads turned to look. A few nodded. They'd heard this already, but it was a day for telling and re-telling stories.

The host was just as pleased to recount the Inn's part of the tale. No doubt it would keep the village coming in to hear and argue for years. "The pair seemed ordinary enough, an older brother and his child sister. Their tale seemed true: parents becoming ill while he was in service as a guardsman for some lord, the parents dying soon after he returned, the farm lost to taxes. He set out to find work as a guardsman, some place where the sister could also take service. The child seemed sad enough, though she perked up considerably when he ordered her a cup of chocolate."

The host spread his hands helplessly. "She seemed ordinary enough, and he a farmer's son, though it was clear he'd served in the Guards. In fact," he leaned forward, lowering his voice and speaking as though in confidence, "he offered for sale three swords with scabbards and belts, all of which he said he'd taken from thieves who'd beset them along the road. I purchased them for a fair price. The swords are hanging there." He pointed toward the wall behind the bar. This was something else which would bring the village to look and talk. He might wish to keep those swords hanging permanently.

Several scoffed at that 'fair price,' having had dealings with innkeepers.

Snake raised an eyebrow in Dog's direction, received a slight nod, and asked, "Did the fellow also offer three horses for sale?"

The innkeeper turned, surprised. "Why, yes. How did you know of that?" There was suspicion in his voice, and suddenly in the faces around him as well.

Snake decided that a version of the truth would serve him best, since the child and her brother had already been identified as sorceress and guard. "On the road some days back we came across three men who claimed to have been set upon by a witch child and her swordsman. The child, they said, bewitched their horses. Gentle beasts, they claimed, which had never given trouble before. Suddenly they found themselves on the ground, looking at a guardsman's drawn sword, their horses gathered around the witch-child. The swordsman took everything they had and sent them on their way." He glanced at Dog, saw a look of approval.

The innkeeper shrugged. "I must say that I did wonder at a single man, even a guardsman, taking swords and horses from three thieves. I thought perhaps the horses were all that was left of the farm, and the man simply wanted to sound fearsome. After all, it was no business of mine. Well," he said, "I guess it goes to show that one should not be too trusting." This brought another round of chuckles at the thought of an innkeeper being too trusting.

Snake, who'd dealt with more than one sharp innkeeper during his early career as a thief, joined the laughter. After the laughs died down, he asked the host, "Did not guardsmen take them that evening?"

The host shook his head. "No. Lord Rand preferred to take prisoners just before dawn and hang them by ten o'clock." There were solemn nods all around. "His men came early, and," he said, looking around at his audience, "the prisoners went with them quietly."

"You may be glad of that," came from a customer. "Suppose the child had commanded your inn to fall and the guards to die."

The host threw up his hands. "Don't say it! I could have lost everything, and no doubt few of my guests could have escaped!"

The evening had gotten late. After another good laugh at the innkeeper's expense, with here and there a muttered "at least we'd still have the protection of a lord," the crowd soon dispersed.

Dog and Snake dawdled over their ale. Dog had little to say other than "In morning, see wizard." No doubt, Snake guessed, the one who'd left orders for Rand to take the guardsman and child, then send word. He was not certain how Dog would react to that wizard.

***

Snake awoke as soon as the room grew light. At first he thought that Dog had arisen even earlier, then realized that the man's bed had not been slept in. That might have been worrisome had Snake been the actual leader of their expedition. Since he wasn't, he rose and went downstairs to see about breakfast.

The Inn was just coming to life. He could hear activity in the kitchen. A quick look around the common room showed no dark-robed wizard.

In Rath's absence Snake would have to report to him, but preferred Dog's company when he did.

Dog, Snake guessed, would not be indoors. He stepped out the front door and after a glance up and down the road headed toward the stable. Perhaps he could surprise Dog still abed in the loft. Snake adjusted his pace to walk even more softly than usual.

No such luck. Dog sat on a workbench, chatting with the ostler as the man dumped oats into the mangers. The stalls held a half-dozen horses. When Snake appeared in the open door, the squat man rose and walked out to join him in the early morning sunlight.

Dog inclined his head as would a proper follower. "Hope Master slept. Puzzle: ostler says horses gentle. Child leaves, horses bad-tempered. Ostler try make friends again."

Snake nodded. "The child's control over them, perhaps. A little more information for the wizard, though," he looked inquiringly at Dog, "nothing we hadn't told him before, I think."

Dog smiled. "Ostler maybe saw walkers turn north…"

Snake caught on. "We might take a look up the road leading through the village. Perhaps talk to the villagers in case someone saw them." He more than half suspected that Dog knew enough already to start out immediately on the fugitives' track. No doubt he was content to keep talking and questioning until Rath arrived.

The guardsman and child had most likely escaped north, up the village road. To the west they'd have encountered the wizard who was now asleep upstairs in the Inn, and to the east he and Dog would have met them. The mountains were a good ways off up that north road. Perhaps a young man from the Five Valleys would not realize just how far. Dog's tactics would allow the fugitives time enough to ride a good part of that distance, if that were the broad man's game. Snake wasn't about to ask questions.

They were under orders to gather information, not to go after the child themselves. Confronting the fugitives was a wizard's task, not his.

The ostler returned from feeding and watering the horses. He came to the stable's open doors to take a breath and bowed when he saw Snake. "Good morning, sir. May I assist you?"

"Well," Snake replied, "I understand the host may have horses and tack for sale. Might I look?" A nod from Dog confirmed the broad man's approval. So they'd continue to gather information which no doubt Dog already knew.

"Oh, yes, sir," the ostler replied. "They're right this way, in the three end stalls. They're a bit gaunt, but a few days of good feed will take care of that. There's nothing wrong with them that I can see. Feel free to look as carefully as you'd like, and call if you have any questions." He was as pleased not to accompany this fellow. The man might have money with which to buy, but the ostler wouldn't care to know just how he got it.

Snake nodded and waved the man away. He'd seen similar looks on too many faces to be irritated. If anything, the bit of uncertainty he'd seen in the ostler's eyes suited him just fine. A bit of fear was generally useful in his profession.

Leaning on the stall gates, he looked in at each horse in turn. They appeared about as he'd expected: underfed by thieves who were barely able to keep themselves and took their anger out on their horses. At least the animals would eat well here. They might even find better treatment from those who could afford to purchase rather than steal them.

Snake turned to face Dog, who'd come to look at the horses. "I suppose," Snake said, "there may be some breakfast ready indoors. No doubt the wizard upstairs will arise soon or later. I suppose we should await him and report before we look at what's left of Rand's keep. No doubt the servants and guardsmen there will have more information to include in our report to Rath."

Dog smiled. "Want give full report." He turned and led the way toward the Inn.

The host met them at the door. "Good morning, sirs. I hope your beds were comfortable? Breakfast is ready. We can offer eggs cooked as you'd like, a good cheese of course, fresh bread or griddle cakes. If you'd like a table, I'll have the cook's helper come right out."

He led them to a table by a window which looked out on the road. As he turned away he seemed to remember something and turned back again. "I—ah—believe there was another member of your party who arrived earlier yesterday. When he comes down, would you to like me to invite him to join you?"

Snake saw, out of the corner of his eye, Dog's quick nod. "Yes," the assassin replied, "please do so. "

"Would you care to have him awakened?" The host was clearly uncomfortable at the thought of waking a member of the Order, but nearly as concerned about offending Snake and his follower.

"No, I think not. He's perhaps tired by recent events. I understand that this particular member of the Order arrived at the ruins not long after the keep fell?"

"Within the hour, I believe, though it was some time later before he came to us and reserved rooms. He actually told me to put other guests out if necessary. A terrible thing to ask of an innkeeper, but of course one does not question the Order." The innkeeper stopped himself, afraid he'd said too much.

Snake reassured him. "A wise choice, landlord, a wise choice. Do ask him to join us when he appears, if you will. I think we'll wait here until he comes down, in any case."

With that the host bowed and was off. They could hear his voice in the kitchen for a time, then out at the counter, bustling around as though he had to awaken the building itself for the day.

Snake and Dog had finished their meals and were sitting back, sipping from mugs of mulled wine, when a dark-robed figure approached. Snake stood immediately, inclining his head respectfully. Dog seemed to take a moment to understand, then scrambled to his feet and stood with his head slightly lowered, his hands fidgeting nervously, a perfect abashed laborer.

Snake recognized the wizard: Roke, ordained perhaps a dozen years earlier. Roke recognized him as well.

"Soren must be worried if he sends you, Rath, and Lorit. Good. He should be." Without asking permission, he dropped into a chair, leaned his arms on the table. "Have you seen what's left of Rand's keep?"

The innkeeper appeared, hovering beside the wizard. Without looking up, Roke said, "I'll have something hot to drink. And to eat. Whatever is available."

At the wizard's gesture of dismissal, the landlord tiptoed away, returning immediately with a mug of mulled wine. His face, as he softly placed the mug on the table, was sour. Around them, the room had begun to empty when the wizard entered. These three were nearly the only guests remaining, and the Order might or might not pay the bill for their food and drink.

Roke looked like a man who hadn't slept in the two days since the keep fell, which didn't surprise Snake. His frank speech and informal demeanor did. The fall of Rand's keep must have shaken him deeply to cause him to forget the distance wizards kept between themselves and others.

He'd be more shaken to know that he shared this table with a being who might drop a keep into a sudden fissure in the earth.

Snake's own position in all this wasn't the most comfortable. He would speak and move with caution despite this show of frankness from the wizard.

The wizard's inquiry about whether they'd seen the ruins remained unanswered. Snake collected his thoughts. "No, Master, we've not. We arrived last evening, eager for a meal, and found ourselves surrounded by servants, farmers and villagers gossiping about the keep's fate and that of its master."

Roke stared into his wine. "How far behind would you guess Lorit is? I understand that Rath One-Hand is not yet fully recovered. He must slow them on a long walk."

"I expect they'll arrive the day after tomorrow, late," Snake responded, "unless perhaps they found a wagon soon after we left. Rath requires long rests at mid-morning, noon, and mid-afternoon. I doubt he can resume travel after the evening meal, despite being carried."

Roke grimaced. "Perhaps with the news, Master Rath will have to put up with the discomfort of forced marches. I would have his and Lorit's counsel." He regarded Snake for a moment. "And what of you two? Sent in advance, but for what reason? Is it a thing of which you can speak?"

Snake spread his hands. "Normally, perhaps not. But you know of what happened here, and of the persons involved."

Roke nodded. "Unbelievable though it is, a guardsman and a child. Though which possesses the power I'm not able to tell. Yet, why bring the child unless she bears power?"

Snake kept one eye on Dog during this exchange, watching for any slight head-shade of disapproval. "We have been on their trail for some time, Master. From what we've been able to learn, it appears that indeed the child has power. She has commanded horses, we believe, and before that, rain and lightning. This is not the first time she has killed."

Dog, Snake noted, did not appreciate that last, but his slight frown quickly vanished. The wizard, fortunately, continued to ignore the poorly-dressed laborer.

"Killed? How? And who?" This news clearly disturbed Roke.

"With lightning, Master," Snake replied. "A member of the Order may have attempted to pass a ward she'd set." That last was something uncertain in Snake's eyes, but he could see no other reason for the lightning to have struck just where it was said to have done.

Roke looked down at the plate a serving-man had silently slipped onto the table, seeming surprised to see eggs, a half loaf and a small block of cheese. For a time he ate, absently and in silence. Finally he looked again at Snake.

"And you say you haven't yet visited the rubble that was Rand's keep?"

Snake shook his head. "By the time we'd heard enough gossip to believe that the keep had fallen, it seemed wiser to wait."

Roke shrugged. "We have to wait for Rath and Lorit. In the meantime, visit the place. Should Rath and Lorit arrive tomorrow, they'll want a complete report."

Snake had already begun to rise when the wizard spoke again.

"Did you learn much from the gossip? Men cease to speak when I enter a room, so I've heard nothing."

"Not much of real value," Snake admitted as he sat back down. "The villagers and farmers worry about who will protect them. That's as close to grieving their lost lord as I've heard." It was safe, he knew, to disparage lords when talking to wizards, and wizards when talking to lords. Both groups knew the true authority lay with wizards.

As Snake expected, Roke smiled at the comment. "I also heard nothing of sorrow when I arrived at the ruin, perhaps an hour after the keep fell. Rand's people were too shocked, perhaps, to keep silent in my presence. The only point of calm was a young guardsman who seemed to have taken charge.

"He was calm enough to recognize me for what I am." Roke's tone was dry. "The man and child, he said, had walked away, back toward the inn and the village, but he'd been unable to watch them for long. Where or how far they'd gone he didn't know, though he doubted they'd have settled back into the inn." Roke paused for a long while, gazing unseeingly at a front window which looked onto the East Road. "What did gossip here at the inn say of how the keep came to collapse?"

Snake told him, dryly and without comment.

Again Roke remained silent, looking at nothing, before he spoke. "Close enough to what I heard that morning." He smiled unpleasantly at Snake. "You, however, have many ways of gathering information. What a pleasant face may not gain, a tickle with your blade might. I would know whether any of the guard or servants are hiding some knowledge of where the two might have gone." This time he made a gesture of dismissal. Snake and Dog rose and left Roke to his meal.

***

Aren had assumed that some variety of red trees gave the forest its name. He hadn't expected the trees to be oaks, nor had he expected red leaves long before fall. On the forest's edge he stopped, turned to Brenna, a question on his face.

The apprentice wizard laughed. "Lore says these are the only red oaks in the land. The very earth itself seems red, but that's an effect of light filtering through the leaves. As a child I took handfuls of forest dirt out into the clear sunlight. I found only good brown earth."

Bird sat her pony, mouth open and eyes wide, gazing at the trees, her fear and sadness forgotten. "You played in this forest when you were little? It's wonderful!"

Brenna smiled sadly. "Yes, it was a good place to be a child. And later a safe place when dark wizards came looking for children of power. They did not enter here. Here, perhaps dark wizards cannot draw on their power. Even during the moon's absence, darkness in this forest is not complete."

For a time the three gazed up at the trees. Brenna turned to Aren. "I'll lead you as best I may, but it's three years since I wandered these trails. Some will have changed. If I'm fortunate in my memory of the way, I may be able to offer you a better campsite than just a clear patch of ground."

Aren soon lost any sense of the direction Brenna took as she followed one path then another through the trees. He wasn't helped by the forest's perpetual early twilight; the huge oaks allowed only a little light to reach the forest floor. Brush was at most knee-high. In many places the ground was almost bare. Brenna might not have visited in some years, but change here would be slow.

Sometimes Bird and Pony were able to walk beside Aren and Blaze. Bird appeared to have forgotten her sadness as she gazed at reddish trunks and at red leaves far above. She spoke only once, to ask "Do you think everything is red but the earth?"

Brenna smiled. "I wondered about that, too, when I first entered these woods. I used to pick leaves from the lower branches and carry them into the sunlight. They remained red." She chuckled. "So I set a snare and caught small animals—a rabbit, a squirrel—and carried each into the sunlight before releasing them. They were also reddish in color. There are berries—red raspberries, red huckleberries, even what taste like blueberries. Can red blueberries still be called blueberries, I wonder?"

Bird laughed at that. "Or red blackberries."

Brenna joined in her laughter.

"Does the forest offer any food besides berries?" Aren asked. He didn't know how long it might take to travel through the trees. If they moved too slowly, he feared what might be waiting for them on its edges.

"Roots," Brenna answered. "There are wild potatoes near the forest edge—red potatoes, of course. Were we to stay, perhaps we'd show red ourselves." She turned to look again at Bird. "Would you enjoy being a little red girl?"

Bird shook her head. "I'm used to being just like I am now," she replied. "Except I'll get bigger sometime, like Reya." Her face saddened at the thought.

"Who would Reya be?" asked Brenna.

"She's our mother," broke in Aren, concerned that Bird would begin weeping. He shifted the conversation. "I can't tell how far we've come into these woods."

"Some miles, I think," Brenna replied. "We're far enough in to be safe. Men don't come here for wood, nor clear trees along the edge to enlarge their fields. It's not only dark wizards who avoid this place. I'm one of the few who ever came more than once. No one else ever stayed long."

"Why did you keep coming here, if no one else likes these woods?" asked Bird. Aren was glad to see her attention shifting from thoughts of home.

"I don't know, exactly. I've always felt--comfortable, I guess. Perhaps because dark wizards never come here. I learned early that I could do things other children couldn't. It became wisest to hide that. Here I could play, explore the little power I had. Sometimes I felt stronger in this place, but I think that was a child's imagination. Among these trees I didn't worry about being found out. I felt free."

"What sorts of things could you do?" Bird was very curious now. Perhaps this woman could tell something about her own power. Aren was paying quiet attention. Even a failed apprentice wizard must know more about power than did he or Bird.

"Oh, just small things.," Brenna said. "There are apple and other fruit trees along the forest edge, and I learned to call a ripe apple to me from a branch I couldn't reach. I seemed able to convince an occasional fawn or rabbit or squirrel to allow me to come near." She laughed at the memory. "That may have merely been because they grew used to seeing me in the forest."

Bird nodded. "I can do that, too."

"And more, I've no doubt," Brenna answered. "But here we are at last! I wasn't sure I could find this spot."

They'd reached the edge of a wide clearing surrounded by some of the largest oaks Aren had ever seen. They made a perfect circle which to his eye didn't appear natural. Why such a perfect circle, and why had oaks never taken over the clearing? He hesitated about entering, but Brenna and Bird had already walked into the center. With a shrug, Aren followed. If the place were dangerous, he would hope Bird could command safety. He doubted any danger would come from Brenna, who seemed honest enough. He doubted she would be likely to turn them over to an Order which would also take her captive. Assuming, he reminded himself, that her story was true. She still hadn't revealed why she had been dismissed from her wizard's training.

Brenna interrupted Aren's thoughts. "We can rest here for the night while you decide what to do next." She stretched and looked around as though arriving home rather than in a clearing in the woods.

Aren watched Brenna walk around the clearing. She stopped in front of one oak, larger around than the others. It was impossible to tell which might be tallest. Their trunks disappeared into a roof of red leaves far above.

"Oh, look! My hideaway!" Brenna gestured for them to join her, then apparently stepped into the tree.

Aren gestured for Bird to stay back. He approached the tree slowly, carefully, circling at a distance. As he circled to the place where he'd last seen Brenna, he saw that the tree wasn't entirely solid. Its walls were several feet thick, but the side he now faced was open for more than a man's height. Within was a hollow, and in its center stood a beaming Brenna. Aren removed his hand from his sword hilt, not that he'd expected a sword to be of much use against magic. He waved Bird forward. With an exclamation of delight, she dashed past him and into the tree.

"Oh, it's wonderful! You could live in a hollow tree, just like a bird or squirrel!" Bird walked around and around within the trunk.

"I suppose I could," Brenna laughed. "When dark wizards were rumored to be in the area, this was my hideaway. See," she said, pointing toward the far wall, "there's even a sort of bench that served me as a bed. It's not soft, but with a layer of blankets it served well enough. Go ahead, try it!"

Bird sat carefully on the bench, then swung her legs up and lay back. "It's wonderful," she giggled. "If only I had some nuts stored away!"

"Oh, you could have those as well," Brenna smiled. "There are nut trees along the forest edge." She turned to Aren, standing in the room's opening. "You're safe enough here. Those who follow you will take a day at least to reach these woods. They'll be reluctant to enter, though not so reluctant with dark wizards urging them on. Tonight you may rest and make plans."

Aren stood watching her, still reluctant to enter a living tree.

Brenna held her arms out, palms up. "There's no danger. The tree isn't enchanted. It won't imprison us. It's just being hospitable, as it always has been."

At that, Aren spoke: "Do you count it as conscious, then? Intending to offer you sanctuary?"

"Perhaps," she answered. "I always felt these trees were aware of my presence." She seemed to be listening for something Aren could not hear. "I may be only half a wizard, with just enough power to attract the Order's attention, but I can feel the trees' welcome."

She turned a rueful face to Aren. "While I could be wrong about that, I can be certain that I'm safer here than in the home where I grew up. Should the Order's servants invade this place, I can go further north. This forest stretches to the mountains. Even the Order's servants are unlike to pursue a small power such as mine that far. They would not go into the north and face green wizards, who would have no love for the Dark Order."

This was a bit much for Aren to absorb in one day: first they'd been captured and he, at least, sentenced to death; then Bird destroyed her captor's keep. Next he learned of blue wizards, drawing their power from blue sky and water. Now Brenna spoke of green wizards to the north. How many kinds of wizards were there? On the night Rath's tower crumbled, Lord Ryd had spoken of wizards other than those of the dark Order. At the time, Aren had paid little attention, but he was certain blue wizards had not been among those mentioned by the lord.

He voiced a question. "If there are blue wizards to the east and green wizards to the north, how many kinds of wizards are there?"

Surprise showed in Brenna's voice. "Well, you know of dark wizards and blue wizards. Green wizards tend to live in forests; their power comes from anything green and growing. The only other order I learned of were the brown wizards. They live in the dry lands to the south. They take their power from the brown earth itself and from plants which grow in the dry lands." She thought for a moment. "Those are all I know. We learned a little of each, but not much."

Bird had come to stand beside her. "Are they all as nasty as the dark wizards?"

A good question, Aren thought. If wizards studied and sought power, then perhaps all were dangerous. That didn't seem true of the blue, from what Brenna had said. Still, she was a failed apprentice, so there were doubtless depths to which she'd not been admitted.

Brenna considered Bird's question. "I think not. Advancement in the blue order, we were told, came through demonstrated power to heal. An adept heals not just people, but diseased streams and rivers, lakes, to some extent the ocean itself. We learned much less of the green and brown orders. What little I recall had to do with tending the land itself: mountain forests to the north, dry lands to the south. " She was silent for a time. "Only the Dark Order seeks power for its own sake, drawing on the darkness of night and the darkness within men."

The three fell silent at the thought of wielders of such power seeking them.

Aren ended the silence. Activity would give them something else to think about. "We could do with some food. The landlord gave orders for us to be provided with provisions for several days; let's see what's in these saddlebags." He turned toward Blaze and Pony. "There should be plenty for three."

"I'm glad to hear it," said Brenna. "I have food enough if I also pick berries and apples and nuts and find a few potatoes, but what I've brought may have to last some time."

Aren looked quizzically at her. "Do you build fires for cooking, or do you eat those potatoes raw?"

"Oh, I build fires for cooking. There are plenty of dead branches on the ground. There's a fire pit," she pointed to the center of the clearing. "I put it together years ago. I wouldn't want to use an axe in these woods, but," here she laughed, embarrassed, "the trees don't seem to mind a small fire made with dead branches."

Bird nodded. "They wouldn't, would they? Even trees die. They shed their branches almost like animals shed hair in the spring."

Brenna looked down at the child, surprised. Aren smiled. He was used to this sort of comment.

"Why, I suppose you're correct," Brenna said. "I hadn't thought of it that way. I always felt a little badly about gathering wood for fires." She paused, thinking. "Yes. Thank you."

It was Bird's turn to look surprised. "Why, you're welcome," she said.

Aren unsaddled the horses, removed their bridles, and put hobbles on their feet to keep them from wandering too far during the night. He brought their saddlebags to the clearing's center where several logs gave places to sit and began to unpack their meal.

Brenna went off into the forest for apples, returning a few minutes later with a half-dozen.

As they ate, Aren asked about the forest's size.

"It goes for miles and miles to the north, all the way to the foothills. If you chose to go that way, you could be in the mountains in a few days. Once there, you'd be out of reach for dark wizards, unless they chose to risk a confrontation in those green mountains. How strong green wizards might be, I'm not sure. The lessons I recall didn't speak of them in terms of power to use against others, but rather as a way to help the land. Still, they must be able to put up some sort of defense. When blue wizards spoke of conflict with other Orders—well, really with the dark Order—it was always about preventing them from crossing the river into the shorelands."

"Would green wizards be able to help us understand Bird's power? Have they that sort of knowledge?" Aren asked. "Going north might be safest. If those who pursue us must go around this forest, we could be well into the mountains before dark wizards entered them."

Brenna was silent while Aren and Bird watched her hopefully. When she spoke, it was slowly and uncertainly. "I would guess not, though I don't think any of the orders fully understands the power of any of the others. The blue wizards with whom I studied might understand more. Though I think, Bird," she said, looking at the child, "you might also terrify them. Still, it's worth a try. They might turn you away, but they would not harm you."

Aren smiled sadly. "They'd be wise not to, I'm afraid."

Aren's statement made Brenna pause before she spoke again. "Power can be frightening, child; I only hope you can control it." Brenna's voice was sad, her face concerned.

Bird became defensive. "I haven't bothered anyone who wasn't trying to stop the rain or wanting to hurt someone."

Brenna nodded. "Yes, but how carefully did you think before you acted? Did you become angry and then use your power?"

Aren became watchful. Brenna's questions were important, but he feared she'd ask more than Bird could deal with. If his little sister became upset, he would need to intervene.

Pale now, Bird swallowed before replying. "There—there wasn't time. Things were happening. I had to do something."

"That's the most dangerous of all," Brenna said. "I can at least tell you that much. Did you know what you could do before you did it, or were the results a surprise?"

Bird frowned. "When I sent lightning to chase dark wizards who were trying to stop the rain, I kind of knew. When I told the lightning to keep wizards out of our valley, I didn't really know it would strike one. Though I guess I wanted it to."

"What about the lord and his keep?" asked Brenna.

Bird looked at the ground. When she answered, her voice could barely be heard. "I was frightened. He was going to have them hang Aren. I just burst out that I hoped he'd die. He began to laugh and I said it again and said I hoped his keep would fall in on him. He stopped laughing."

Brenna remained silent for a long time, her face ashen. This was destruction beyond anything she'd heard of among her former teachers.

Faced with Brenna's shock, Bird looked pleadingly at Aren. "I couldn't let them hang you, Aren. I didn't know"—she turned back to

Brenna—"what the keep meant, or that it would cause so much trouble when the people's lord died."

Brenna tried to say something less serious. "I don't think lords would be happy to hear that."

Aren helped her. "I think all lords know that the Order is the real power," he noted. Then he leaned toward Brenna, his face serious. "You've mentioned a disaster which caused you to be dismissed from your apprenticeship. I would be more comfortable, to be honest, were I to know more, if you're willing. It's a worrying thing to leave hanging in the air. Bird has spoken honestly of her own mishaps."

Brenna hesitated. "I suppose you have a right to know." She saddened. "My disaster, as you call it, wasn't unexpected. I had struggled for some time.

"The day started well. Brother Turl had roused us early for a test which promised to be a bit of a lark," she said, shaking her head. "It would be less a test of power than of control. The task was straightforward: lift a single curved tile from the cookhouse roof, then gently replace it. The skill would lie in setting the tile down so softly that it did not crack. Any whose control slipped would have to shape a new tile, clamber onto the roof and make the replacement. Turl warned us that it would be no easy task to slide a new tile beneath two overlapping from above. More than one novice, we'd been told, had broken several in the process while the cook stood glowering in the cookyard.

"My fellows' first several attempts went well. On the fourth, a cracking sound could be heard as the novice tried to reinsert the tile into its proper place in the layers. Our laughter mixed with condolences. The next two succeeded. Then it was my turn."

Bird leaned forward, fascinated. Aren was only a little less so, his interest kept in bounds by the growing sorrow on the failed apprentice's face.

A moment passed before she continued. "I found myself wishing I had not waited until last to make my attempt. I wished that if I were to crack or worse yet break my tile, I'd done so when others would follow and take the focus away from my failure."

Again she paused to pull herself together. "It was a beautiful morning. The sun rose among scattered clouds in a flaming sunrise. Beyond it the sky was a deep, vibrant blue. I was certain that if I were careful enough, I could control my power.

"I selected a tile and concentrated on raising it slowly and carefully. It did not seem to move, so I increased my concentration just a little. It was hard to focus over the mutterings around me. Those were rude: novices were supposed to keep silent and allow the one being tested to concentrate. I saw a little waver in the tile, a hint of motion, so I increased my focus once again.

"There were shouts of 'No! Stop!' I struggled to ignore them, to maintain control rather than drop the tile." Brenna took a deep breath. "The entire roof now hovered a foot above its normal place. Turl was shouting, 'Hold it there until the cooks can escape!' Somehow I did.

"Then, as the final cook's helper dashed into the yard, I began to slowly lower the roof." She smiled crookedly. "I nearly succeeded, too. One corner settled first, placing too much weight on a single roof joist which cracked. I tried to lift that corner just a little, and the far edge came down, tiles breaking, joists cracking. I lost control completely and the entire roof fell, taking joists with it into the kitchen. Pots and pans which had hung from rafters joined the tumult. Nothing was left but the walls, and not all of those, either." Brenna sat with her eyes closed as she relived the memory.

"I stood weeping in the red sunrise. You know the result. I was dismissed from the school. Too many failures, my power inconsistent, either not present at all or out of control. I felt little choice but to return home. Only too late did I realize that it would have been wise to change out of this robe before I started." She fell silent.

Bird stood, walked softly to where Brenna sat and hugged her tightly. "I know what it's like when something turns out badly."

Brenna returned the hug, and for a moment the two held each other. Aren stood, unable to think of anything which might be appropriate to do or say. Finally he spoke. "I'm sorry. I shouldn't have asked you to tell that story. I thought—I don't know what I thought. Perhaps that it would tell us something more about the nature of your power. I can't help but worry, with dark wizards after us."

Brenna nodded. "I understand." Her voice was husky. "If I'd thought to change my clothing before I started out, I might have turned off the road and gone to my parents' house before you ever saw me. Or not have been concerned that you'd see me and take me for an apprentice to the dark Order."

"But you brought us here," Bird said. "And this forest feels—I don't know—friendly. And safe."

"Yes," Aren said, grateful that Bird had found the right thing to say. "You've given us a safe place for the night. We'll move on in the morning, before our pursuers arrive."

Brenna stood. "I will guide you. Once away from the forest edge, as we are now, the forest can be confusing. For now, let us get some rest."

CHAPTER THREE

As they left the inn, Snake asked Dog, "Where do we go now?"

Dog shrugged. "Wizard say look rubble. We look. Couple days, lead north. No rush." He smiled.

Snake joined in that smile. This business of wizard-fooling was a fine new game, the danger involved adding to the zest. He hadn't felt this pleased about an assignment in years. Surprisingly, he was carrying out the letter of the assignment, though he doubted Soren would agree. He wasn't going to think about Soren.

They walked slowly along the East Road. Ahead Snake could see a very large pile of rubble. A few people walked aimlessly about. Snake had more or less believed the reports, but now, seeing for himself, he was surprised at how completely the Keep had been destroyed. No wonder Rand's people were afraid.

As they approached, he could see that much of the rubble had sunk into what had probably been the dungeons. Rand's dungeons had rarely been used, he knew. The lord preferred a quick whipping or execution over maintaining dungeons. Rand wasn't a man to waste food on prisoners.

With Dog leading, Snake walked past the rubble which had been the low outer wall and towards the larger pile which had been Rand's keep. Here and there he could see a fragment of furniture or a bit of cloth, all that was left of Rand's wealth. Recalling some local's comment the night before about digging through the rubble for Rand's gold, Snake chuckled. If Rand's small wars had left much gold in his vault, Snake wished luck to any who came after it.

He looked east toward where he could just see a road coming up from the south. Behind him, just west of the Inn, another road came down from the north. Rand's keep had been placed half-way between. No doubt some ancestor believed he could charge a toll on both roads where they joined the East Road. With men enough, he certainly could.

Looking beyond the rubble, Snake could see that the Keep had been unusual among lord's fortresses. The only buildings nearby were those belonging to the keep: guards' and servants' quarters, stables, storage sheds, a blacksmith shop which appeared unused. That the town had grown up a good half-mile away suggested that the townspeople had come to prefer a little distance from their protector.

Dog gave the rubble a disinterested look, and went on to the outbuildings. After a few moments, Snake hurried to catch up.

They could see a mixed group of guardsmen and servants standing or sitting before what Snake guessed were the servants' quarters. Dog picked up his pace when he saw the group, Snake hurrying to keep up.

The small crowd circled around two men, one young and in a guardsman's uniform, the other the old servant who'd spoken up at the Inn the night before. They seemed to be disagreeing, though not quite arguing.

The older one was speaking as Snake and Dog approached. "...but who will pay us? Or pay accounts in the village, for that matter? Rand had bills everywhere. Shopkeepers traded them among themselves, knowing he'd pay sooner or later—"

"Mostly later!" came from someone in the circle of twenty or so.

The old man ignored the call. "No one will sell for anything but coins now. Rand's coin lies somewhere in the ruins of his dungeons!"

The younger man nodded. "True enough. But we still have gardens, chickens, milk cows, pigs. And what is in the granary for bread. Here we can at least feed ourselves, and we have roofs over our heads."

"Crowded roofs," came another voice from the crowd, this time from a guardsman, "now that keep servants have lost their rooms."

The young guardsman held up both palms in a near-shrug. "Ten guardsmen have already left, and more may go. Their rooms will be empty."

Another voice asked, "What of thieves? Who will protect us from thieves? What if shopkeepers come, claiming what little we have in payment for Rand's accounts? "

At this the guardsman unsheathed his sword and held it over his head. "This will protect you, as it always has. Six guards have agreed to stay for a time, at least until we learn what is to come. Others may join us. Six will suffice to turn away angry townsfolk and at least a dozen thieves. We'll hold watch over the garden and animals and granary as well as over your rooms. That's what guardsmen do." He looked around, saw nods. "It's not new duty. We will not stand alone for long. A wizard arrived yesterday. More must be on the way, if only to look into what happened here." He smiled as he sheathed his sword. "If you were a shopkeeper, no matter how large Rand's accounts, would you make any move to seize what's in our storeroom with wizards present?"

There were mutterings. They'd be safe enough from shopkeepers and thieves so long as no one knew what wizards might be planning.

"Wizards won't stay, will they?" a woman asked. "Won't they set out in pursuit of the witch-child? Surely she was no member of the Order. They couldn't have done this." She gestured at the pile of rubble.

"A good reason for them to delay pursuit, which would keep them here for a while," said the old servant. "I for one would as soon see them move on quickly. Nonetheless, their presence will at least allow time for a new lord to appear."

"How?" asked another. "Rand had neither wife nor child. Who would take his place, with not even two stones of his keep standing? A fine fortress that for a new lord!"

The old man smiled knowingly. "He was not without family, none the less. There was a brother, younger. He went for a mercenary in the North. Were word to reach him, he would claim the rule, if he's not won through to a northern lordship by now."

Another servant, nearly as old as the spokesman, was skeptical. "What is there to bring even a younger son here, with no keep, no gold where it can be gotten at, nothing but debts and a few wooden outbuildings? How would a penniless younger son rebuild?"

The young guardsman answered. "Power would attract a younger son with no lands of his own. Perhaps not power such as members of the Order possess, but power nonetheless. There is land here, if a new lord can hang on to Rand's holdings. There will be a harvest soon, and taxes to be paid." He turned to look at the rubble which had been Rand's keep. "Though I doubt Rand's tax records are of much use now."

That brought laughter. The young guardsman looked around, pleased to see there was still some spirit in these people. "Rand's tax gatherer will know what taxes are owed. Where is the man?"

A guardsman spoke. "He was among the first to flee."

More laughter. "Probably expected to be torn to pieces by the first group of farmers he met!" someone called.

The young man's shoulders slumped for a moment. "We'll have to figure out something. Farmers said Rand's taxes were too high, but they'll surely expect to pay something."

The old servant nodded. "All right. What you say makes sense, if you and the guard will stay and protect us."

Before the young guardsman could answer, another voice, badly slurred, broke in. "Whosh gon' protect us 'gainst the child-witch, hey?" Everyone turned to look at a man in a disheveled, stained guard's uniform, a sergeant's red stripe across his chest. He came stumbling toward them, waving a half-empty bottle of wine.

Dog, who'd been listening intently, turned to gaze at the newcomer, a look of delight on his face. Snake muttered, "What's this? Court jester?"

The sergeant stumbled into the group's center, shaking his bottle in the old servant's face. "You—you didn't see her!" He turned in a circle, gesturing with the bottle to include his entire audience. "None of you did. I—" he stumbled, caught himself—"I was there. I saw her eyes, black as midnight! I saw the way she stared at Rand! 'I hope you die,' she said, 'I hope you die and your castle falls in on you!'" He paused, turning slowly to look at each one in turn. "Rand started to laugh, but nothing came out! Nothing! He was already dead! Mortar and bits of stone started down and we all ran! Like rats!"

He scowled at the crowd of servants and guards. "What can you do against that? Dark wizards can't order a man to die. They have to in- in- inflict fear and let it kill him. They can't command a keep to fall!"

Once more he swung around in a circle, then staggered toward the guards' quarters, the crowd opening to let him pass. His voice came back to them, "No sensh leaving! She'll catch you if she wants you!"

Ten or so guards in the group loosened their swords in their scabbards, looking around as though the witch-child might be creeping up at that moment. The servants stood motionless.

Again the young guardsman spoke. "I was also there. Rand ordered us to take the man up to the battlements and hang him. You all know—" he turned, looking at each member of the circle—"what sort of man Rand was." Again there were nods all around. "Until then the man with her had kept the child calm. When Rand gave that command, she spoke his death and the death of his keep. Not before."

He paused. "In that moment before she spoke, I saw a frightened child. You know the rest. But—" here he again turned to look in turn at each member of the crowd, raising one finger for attention—"but when I reached safety outside the falling keep, the girl was right behind me, the man carrying her. She was crying! Crying, like a frightened child!"

He waited another moment while his words sank in. "I was afraid— who among us wasn't? I bowed to the man and asked his pardon. He said little, though he demanded my sword and belt." He smiled without humor. "You can imagine that I quickly handed him both. He buckled on the belt, then lifted the child again, trying to comfort her."

The guardsman spread his hands, palms up. "If she had wished to visit her wrath on anyone but Rand, would she not have done so then? Instead, her brother—for I'm certain they were brother and sister, though of what parentage I dare not dream—carried her away to the west even as the villagers rushed to find what had happened. I think we have nothing more to fear from those two."

There was silence for a time before the old servant spoke. "I will remain, and I ask every servant who is willing to remain to come with me to the storehouse. We must determine what foodstuffs we have. Cook," he turned to a round-faced, well-fed fellow who'd stood silent throughout all the talk, "Master Cook, can you manage meals with your kitchen and all its equipment somewhere under the rubble?"

The cook shrugged with just a touch of arrogance. "A good cook can make a tasty meal anywhere. Let us visit the stores. If we must, I'll see what kettles may be borrowed from the Inn."

The elderly servant turned to the young guardsman. "I doubt the sergeant will be of any use even after he's run out of Rand's wine. You must deal with the guard."

The guardsman raised his eyebrows, his hands coming up as well in a gesture of helplessness. "We will talk. Many are senior to me, though some of those may not stay. I will do what I can."

"So must we all," answered the old retainer as he turned to follow the cook and his fellow servants toward what Snake guessed must be the storeroom.

A dozen guardsmen gathered around the young man. One, scar-faced and well-muscled, perhaps fifteen years older, spoke. "Those of us who stay will do as Tavnor has said. Those who would prefer otherwise may leave." He looked around at his comrades, saw nods of agreement. "I will take the first watch over the animals. Who will stand with me, and who will take the first watch over the dwellings and storage areas? We should have two for each, and replacements at mid-watch."

One guardsman came to stand beside the scar-faced man. Two others stepped forward. The scarred man turned toward the younger but spoke to all. "For now, the four of us will secure the stables and storeroom. The rest of you go with Tavnor. He has shown the most sense of any. Are we agreed?" More nods.

He looked Tavnor in the eye. "It seems we have selected you as our sergeant. Lead us well." With that he and a second guard turned toward the stables. The other two moved toward the storeroom, talking and gesturing as they worked out their watch.

Snake watched all this with great interest. He'd never seen honest men organize themselves. His experience had been with thieves and later with lords and wizards who simply gave orders. Dog stood, smiling, at Snake's shoulder.

Tavnor took a deep breath and said, "Let us look at our quarters and see what remains. We'll hope there are still some horses left in the stables. I suppose"—here he looked at the eight guards who remained around him—"I suppose we'd better set a rotation of guards. First let's see how many remain and how many empty rooms we can offer the keep's servants." He and his retinue moved away.

"Interesting," Snake commented. "They seem willing to work without any assurance that there will be a new lord, or that he will reward them. Or even retain them."

Dog was puzzled. "Why not reward? Doing his work."

"So they are," Snake said. "Lords prefer their own servants to think little. These people may be sent away because they've shown initiative."

"Rand," Dog noted, "one such." He was silent. "Maybe new lord better."

They watched as guards and servants organized and set about their duties. Snake noted that several took horses from the stables and rode away. No doubt each felt that a good horse, saddle and bridle were more than they could hope to attain by staying. Snake noted that two guards attempted to take several horses, but the scar-faced man said a word. The pair settled for one horse each. Snake wished he'd been close enough to hear that conversation.

Dog and Snake pretended to be simply two more of the curious. Some could be seen walking around the rubble, while others looked closely at the stables and the storeroom with its broken lock, the key now somewhere below the rubble. The guardsmen keeping watch over storerooms and stables sent the too-curious on their way.

The cook and what remained of his kitchen staff spent much of the afternoon fixing up an outdoor kitchen which seemed not to have been used for some years. At times the cook conferred with the old retainer. From the way the old man took charge, Snake decided he must have been the house steward. At such times Snake would wander close enough to overhear. The cook wanted the village carpenter sent for to patch the roof over the stove, but the steward noted that the carpenter would wish to be paid. Another argument had to do with the cook's wish for a stone mason to build an outdoor bread oven. There were no coins with which to pay either the carpenter or the mason.

Snake shook his head. The weather was warm now, but before long they would need an indoor kitchen. To rebuild the keep, even on a smaller scale, would be the work of months if not years. Should work begin immediately and the workmen built in stages, he supposed they might finish a portion before winter. Such a quick start seemed unlikely.

At mid-afternoon, Dog suggested they return to the Inn. They might learn what, if anything, Roke had heard through his crystal during the day, if the wizard were still willing to share information with underlings. As they strolled toward the inn, for Dog seemed singularly unconcerned about speed, the broad man began to instruct Snake.

"Today say, wizards: no lord, lands maybe violent."

"Why would wizards care about such a thing as that?" asked Snake. In all his long years of service, he'd never noted any such concern on the part of Soren and his lieutenants

Dog nodded. "Wouldn't. Violent lands, search harder. Calm lands, search easier. Wizards give money, guards stay."

Snake nodded. All this made sense; a search in troubled lands would be more difficult. A thought struck him. "Would you not prefer that the wizards' search be slowed?

Dog shrugged. "No reason people suffer. Snake, Dog"—here he actually slapped Snake companionably on the shoulder, much to the assassin's surprise—"Snake, Dog slow well enough."

As they reached the inn, Dog said, "Now write note."

Snake stared. A note? That was not something he'd expected. Who would he write to? The assassin shook off his wonder. "Of course, master."

Pausing at the Inn's counter, Snake asked for paper, pen, ink, and sealing wax. Once in the room that, in theory, they shared, Snake sat down at the small table and arranged his writing materials, then looked expectantly at Dog. "I'm ready, Master."

"Short note. Write, 'Rand dead. Keep rubble. Bring men, gold.'"

Snake wrote quickly, waited a moment before asking, "Will that be all?"

"Enough. Give."

Snake handed over the note. Dog took up the ink-pot, smeared ink on three knuckles and the thumb of his right hand, then pressed the knuckles and thumb just below the line of writing to create what looked like the imprint of a dog's paw. He blew on the pawprint for a moment before returning the sheet to Snake. "Fold, seal."

Snake folded and sealed.

"Address Lord Ryd, Manor, First Valley."

Snake's eyebrows went up as he wrote the address in a careful hand. Of all the things he'd come to expect of this being, giving orders to a lord had not been among them. Rath had said this man was Ryd's dog, a sort of spy for the lord, a useful tool. Apparently the lord knew more about this being than had Rath. Snake began to wonder just who in that relationship was the dog and who the master.

Snake had thought of Ryd as a minor lord with no apparent ambition to expand his borders. Should Ryd arrive quickly with men and gold, he would become lord of the country's entire north, and thus the most powerful lord in the land. If, that is, his farmer-warriors would follow him away from their own valleys.

"Have money?" Dog demanded.

Snake nodded.

"Pay messenger, promise lord pay again. If need horse, buy. Go."

Snake left the room. Within minutes, a rider was on his way, encouraged both by Snake's coins and by the sight of his knife, backed by a promise to track the man down if the message weren't delivered.

***

Rath had claimed he could travel the rest of the day and all night. By midnight he regretted that boast. Lorit allowed only the briefest of pauses: at mid-afternoon to change Rath's bearers, near dusk for a quick and unsatisfying cold meal, and at midnight to change Rath's bearers again. At each break, Tarh helped Rath out of the sling, held him up while the wizard regained his balance. The two walked carefully along the road's edge, Rath complaining the entire time.

Lorit used each break to contact Soren, but found there was no more news. Rath held himself from groaning as Tarh helped him back into the sling. The guardsmen lifted it, then started off at the near-trot they'd maintained since word of Rand's keep came during their noon break a dozen hours before.

For Rath the rest of the trip became a blur. He was certain he did not sleep, but there were periods of which he was, mercifully, unaware. They paused in the dawn for a hasty breakfast, indistinguishable from their meal of the night before. Rath had no appetite but ate a little, hoping to have some strength left when they arrived. He did not want to appear a complete invalid. According to Soren, Roke reported an inn near what had been Rath's keep. He'd taken rooms on the second floor. Rath hoped to walk the stairs without assistance.

At mid-afternoon they reached the Inn. Tarh moved quickly to help Rath from the sling before the guardsmen who'd carried it on the last stage of the journey let it drop. They joined their fellows who already sat against the inn's front wall. Lorit allowed them a moment. They had made the journey as quickly as he'd hoped.

He felt tired enough himself after walking through the night and most of this day. But it would not do to let these guardsmen think a wizard was as subject to exhaustion as ordinary men. Lorit and Tarh's sustaining spells had been most effective during the dark of night. In daylight they'd been of some use, but not enough to keep Lorit from feeling the beginnings of exhaustion. That would grow as his most recent casting of the spell wore off.

Tarh, blast him, looked better than any of them. Well, that was one advantage of being a young wizard, Lorit supposed. Rath looked ancient as he tottered toward the inn, leaning heavily on his former apprentice. Lorit would settle the One-Hand in a comfortable bed and get some rest himself before seeking out Snake. There was no hurry. The assassin was far too experienced to wander off when wizards would expect a report. None of the wizard's party would be fit for much before morning.

Guardsmen could find whatever rooms awaited them in the inn. Lorit would send for them if he had further need.

Rath and Tarh entered just ahead of Lorit, who stepped past them to the counter where a man who looked like a landlord stood waiting. Three men in dark robes, followed by a half-dozen guardsmen, needed no introduction.

The landlord bent his head. "Greetings, masters. We have expected you. All our rooms are at your service. One of your number has taken one. Two of your servants are in another. The remaining four are vacant. I'll be pleased to show you the rooms. Their doors are unlocked, the keys on a table in each room."

Lorit nodded; there was no need for an answer. He gestured toward the stairs, and the landlord darted from behind the counter. Behind him came groans which Rath could not quite stifle. Lorit didn't need to look back to see Tarh assisting his former master. There was no way the man could climb stairs unaided after that trip. Indeed, it was a sign of Rath's will that he could walk at all, even with assistance.

The One-Hand had not, Lorit knew, been fully recovered from his injuries when they began this trip. The last day must have set him back. Rath would not admit to any weakness; he would insist on being present for Snake's report as soon as that villain appeared. Lorit would plan to have that session take place in Rath's room. But not before morning.

Lorit told the landlord to lead them to his largest room, then waved Rath and Tarh in. Rath would need the younger mage's assistance for at least the next few days. Lorit took the room next to Rath's. He wanted to know of any of Rath's comings and goings once the man had recovered. This mission was his to lead, and Rath might well attempt to wrest that leadership.

The guards took the two remaining rooms, which were designed to sleep as many as six men each. They saw no reason to cram themselves into one, given that the inn's entire upper floor was available. In any case, the landlord would be unable to convince any travelers to sleep on the same floor as four dark wizards.

In fact, and the guards chucked at the thought, they'd probably have the inn's tavern to themselves as well, once word spread that the inn was now headquarters to a bevy of wizards. That would mean better service and more drink for them, assuming the wizards didn't come up with errands. The manner in which Rath painfully mounted the stairs suggested that the party would not immediately.be travelling on

Once Rath was stretched out on one bed, where he almost immediately fell asleep or lost consciousness, Lorit instructed Tarh to rest as well. Lorit did not care what might be Rath's condition, so long as the man was quiet.

The landlord had pointed out which room was already occupied by a wizard and which was occupied by the two servants of the Order who'd arrived earlier. Lorit went to Roke's room, knocked twice, and entered.

The younger wizard stood up quickly from where he'd been sitting, looking out the window toward the keep. "Master!" he said. "I did not expect you until tomorrow."

Lorit gestured for him to sit. "We walked all night after we heard the news. Rath is resting. I will take your report now, in brief. Rath will wish to hear full details when he is able, which may not be until morning."

Roke told of the word he'd sent to Lord Rand. The next morning he'd received a message that two prisoners had been taken and were being held at Rand's keep. He had used his crystal to inform Soren, then set out immediately. It had taken him perhaps an hour to reach Rand's keep. There he'd found only a pile of rubble. He'd gotten little sense from what servants and guardsmen remained, and he was uncertain whether to believe even that little. Soren said that he was to leave the inquiry to Snake, and he had awaited the assassin's arrival.

Lorit listened without interrupting. He could feel his own exhaustion growing. He would rest now. Roke would awaken him in time for a late supper. The innkeeper would expect to bring a late meal to their rooms. The guardsmen could take care of themselves.

In the meantime, Roke could make certain that Snake and this Dog fellow would be available once Lorit and Rath had rested.

Roke inclined his head in acknowledgement. Lorit barely made it to his room before his legs began to tremble. In a few minutes he, too, was asleep.

***

Lord Ryd lounged in a chair placed against the Manor's west side. He was reasonably safe from interruptions here, his spot for sunning himself. It was also his preferred spot for talking with Talon or Dog. Conversations with Dog were choppy but interesting. This day he felt he had earned a bit of the early autumn sun: he'd worked out with his guardsmen that morning, taking part in weapons master Talon's drills as though himself a guardsman.

Then Talon had put the men to work in single combat with blunted swords, something Ryd always enjoyed. None of this group could offer him much challenge. He missed Aren from the Fifth Valley, whose two-year hitch as a guardsman had ended that summer. Aren gave him a workout whenever Ryd joined the training, though Talon complained that the other guardsmen tended to stop their work to watch the two. Still, it seemed to Ryd that there was some benefit in having their lord work out with them and even risk defeat in single combat with their fellow Valley farmer.

A servant came around the Manor's corner. Ryd groaned inwardly. Some minor problem, he supposed, which his major domo should take care of. Still, there was no sense in taking it out on the messenger.

"Yes, Joh?" Ryd sat up in his chair and faced the servant. He was followed at a short distance by another man. This was not one of his servants nor, he'd wager, one of the Valley farmers. None dressed that shabbily, nor became uneasy in the presence of a lord.

"My lord," Joh said, "this fellow brings a message for you, and says he's been promised payment for delivering it."

Ryd's eyebrows rose. This was unusual; who would be sending him a message by this sort of messenger? A fellow lord would have sent someone in livery, with no talk of being paid. He would give the fellow something anyway. A reputation for liberality never hurt on those few occasions when he left the Manor for meetings of the Council of Lords. When his fellows complained of the service they received from one another's servants. Ryd would keep silent and smile to himself. Giving a little something for service cost little and gained much.

Ryd had been silent too long. "Well, let's see the message, then." He reached into the small bag of coins he always carried for such moments and took out three silver pieces. The look on the messenger's face let Ryd know that the man had not expected this much. He'd probably been given a smaller amount to carry the message in the first place. This was another fellow who'd have good things to say about the Lord of the Five Valleys, and at a pitifully small cost.

"Where do you come from, lad?" Ryd asked.

"From Lord Rand's holdings, my lord," the fellow replied.

Ryd frowned. A message from his older brother was never welcome. Usually it meant Rand had some plot underway and wanted Ryd's support if the Council of Lords objected. There was little chance that

Ryd would offer such support; Rand ought to have known that by now. "Is it from Lord Rand, then?"

The man made an odd sound then, a sort of snort, Ryd thought. Not the reaction anyone living under Rand's rule would have at mention of the lord's name.

"No, my lord. Lord Rand won't be sending any more messages."

Ryd's eyebrows rose again. This seemed a day for surprises. "Well, let me see it. Wait a moment in case there's a reply. Joh, take this man to the kitchen and see that he's given something cooling to drink and something to eat."

Both men bowed, the messenger looking even more pleased than when he saw the coins. Ryd waved dismissal and turned his attention to the message. It was addressed to him, all right, and sealed. He broke the seal and spread the message, noting first the dog's paw signature at the bottom. A message from Dog. That was something new.

Dog. The lord knew that the name originated among his mercenaries as a scornful "Ryd's dog" before they realized how valuable the man could be. Ryd himself had never liked the name, even after it began to be spoken with respect. It had been some time before the man had shared his real name, and then only with a demand that Ryd never speak it where others could hear. Lamar. Ryd thought it was a good name, but honored Dog's wish that it not be spoken.

Ryd looked at the words in Dog's message for a moment before he could make sense of them: Rand dead, his keep fallen? And a command: bring men and gold.

Ryd thought for a moment. If Dog said 'bring men and gold,' then he would do so. The man had never misled him, starting with the day Dog walked out of the forest and into Ryd's camp in the north country. Thanks to Dog's advice, Captain Ryd's band of mercenaries had been the most successful of those fighting in the northern lord's petty border wars.

Prior to encountering the squat fellow with his odd pattern of speech, Ryd had conducted himself as did most mercenary captains. He fought the enemy where he found them, with no regard for damage to crops, barns, or even cottages. Further, he'd taken supplies from those same peasants as he had need.

The mercenary forces involved were too small for full-scale battles. Most were not likely to stand and fight if a skirmish began to go against them. It had been Dog who suggested that selecting skirmish sites with an eye toward doing as little damage as possible to the land and buildings would avoid alienating the locals. The man offered an even more startling idea: pay them for supplies, try to avoid damaging their property, and the whole region would become his spies.

Dog's suggestions had worked so well that occasionally a particularly vicious band of mercenaries would find themselves attacked from behind by a band of furious peasants. With axes, clubs, shovels and pitchforks, farm folk slaughtered those who accompanied any supply wagons. Then, with swords and spears taken from supply wagons, they'd come after the mercenaries themselves. Such attacks tended to result in quick surrenders: mercenary leaders knew they'd fare better as captives of another mercenary band than dealing with angry peasants. What such farmers might lack in fighting skill they'd make up with rage.

If Dog said no more than "bring men, gold," there was little likelihood that some rival lord had sacked Rand's keep, hung Rand and torn the place down. Tearing the keep down would have been no small task. Ryd remembered the keep's solid walls from his boyhood, before their father died.

Rand was dead, the keep at least badly damaged, and no enemy in the field. Bring gold and men: of course. Rand would have died owing every tradesman in the village and probably most of his servants as well. Only his guardsmen could count on being paid regularly, since they were his hold on his people. Few of those guardsmen would remain once Rand would no longer be paying.

Experienced guardsmen could find employ with another lord or even the Order. A band of as few as ten guardsmen could find employment as a unit with some lord's guard or as a company within a larger mercenary force. Servants had a harder time finding new positions and were usually more timid about making any sort of change. That would especially true for servants who'd served for any length of time with a lord such as Rand had been. If Ryd arrived soon enough and offered to pay back wages, any remaining staff and guardsmen would no doubt stay.

Ryd's smile was not exactly pleasant. Bring men, Dog had instructed. He'd put ten of his Valley guardsmen up against any thirty of Rand's guard. He knew precisely how skilled each of his men was with sword and bow. And exactly how willing to fight, if it came to that.

Most of all, he knew that going east after word that Rand was dead and his keep rubble would intrigue his Valley Guardsmen. All knew the tale of Lord Gerlach, Rand and Ryd's father, and his attempt years ago to conquer the Five Valleys. He'd brought a force of eighty men, an army by the standards of any Lord in these lands, expecting to lay siege to the Manor of the Five Valleys. The peasant population would cower in their valleys as his army passed.

At first it had gone well. Gerlach led his men without resistance along the East Road, past openings into three of the valleys. Somewhere between the opening of the third valley and that of the second, his small army came around a curve to encounter fresh-cut logs blocking their way. Arrows began to fly from behind the logs and from the woods on each side of the road. Twenty of his men were down before Gerlach could order a retreat.

He and his retreating men found their way blocked by more logs, freshly felled, and more archers. Soon half Gerlach's men were dead or wounded, and the remaining forty were primarily occupied with looking for a way out of the ambush into which he'd led them.

If they could even hear his commands, they weren't paying attention. A few attempted to charge into the forest and were quickly wounded. Most threw down their weapons and stood with their hands out to both sides, palms up. Lord Gerlach himself was bound and brought before Lord Fas of the Five Valleys. Fas had a reputation as a calm man, but Gerlach quailed at the anger in the man's face.

Ryd had heard this story from their father only once or twice, when the old lord was in his cups after a night of drinking. Only at such a time would the old man admit that he felt some fear of dying right then and there.

He hadn't. Lord Fas gave orders that his wounded were to be treated, his dead loaded into wagons, and the twenty still whole were to be held until the wounded were ready to travel. Their weapons would, of course, be forfeit. Lord Gerlach himself, Fas said with an unpleasant smile, would remain as his guest until a suitable ransom had been paid.

The ransom was large enough to leave Gerlach unable to increase the size of his guard from the twenty whole men who returned from this attempted invasion. Of the thirty wounded who returned to Gerlach's holdings, ten did not survive. The other twenty left the lord's service as soon as they were able, not waiting for his return after his ransom had been paid. In fact, most of the remaining twenty left within the next year. Trying to rebuild his coffers and then his guard, that first Lord Rand had raised taxes, which left him using his guard primarily to accompany his tax gatherers on their rounds.

Yes, Ryd thought, guardsmen who'd grown up in the Valley and heard of that fight from their grandfathers and fathers would be eager to see the ruin of the current Lord Rand's keep. That their own Lord Ryd was now mostly like Lord of both the Five Valleys and Rand's holdings would delight everyone in the Valleys, Ryd thought—not least of all Ryd himself.

"Talon! Joh! To me!"

Joh would have passed word to Talon of a message from Rand's holdings, knowing that if armed action were called for, 'Talon' would be first name Ryd would speak. The two came around the corner at once.

Ryd stood and faced them. "Rand is dead, and his holdings in turmoil. I'll take the ten most experienced guards. Talon, you're in charge of the guard in my absence, and Joh, you're in charge of the Manor. I'll want two saddlebags of gold and two of silver coins. Tell the cook to prepare rations for three days; we can ride the distance in two if we take two horses for each man, but if things are bad enough we may encounter bands of thieves along the way, and we'll want to take time to deal with them. Talon, you can wipe that smile off your face," Ryd finished, but then was unable to hold back his own smile. Rand had been a terrible brother and a worse lord; the land would be better off without him.

***

Dog and Snake had been relaxing in the inn's main room over mugs of ale when Rath stumbled through the inn's front door, aided by Tarh and followed by Lorit and the half-dozen guardsmen they'd seen only a few days before. Snake was surprised that they'd made the journey that quickly. Then, taking a second and closer look, he saw the exhaustion on the faces of the guardsmen and the wizards and realized they'd walked all night, forced on by spells which were now wearing off. The whole group would sleep for hours, perhaps until morning if Lorit left no orders to waken them. Within the hour Roke would be the only wizard on his feet.

Snake looked to Dog for guidance. Normally he would report to Lorit and Rath as soon as they reached their rooms, but neither would be in any shape to hear a report for some hours yet.

Dog smiled. "Sad-looking lot. No reports tonight. No company. Peaceful."

Dog was correct. Locals had already begun to gather for the evening's gossip, but at the sight of more dark wizards they finished their drinks and departed. When Roke came down the stairs, Snake and Dog were the only ones left.

"So here you are," he said, as though he'd been looking long instead of finding them where he expected. "You visited the ruins, then?"

"As you instructed, master," Snake replied.

"I'll wait to hear your report when the others do. They rest now after the strains of their journey, and probably will not wish to hear from you until morning. Still, remain in the inn. Take care," he said, glancing at their half-empty mugs, "do not drink so much that you're unable to report clearly. Lorit and Rath will be in no good mood when they wake." With that he returned to his room.

The landlord remained behind his counter while Roke remained. Now he entered the common room, looking mournfully around before walking over to the pair. "Ah, well," he said, "these strange events bring customers, and then they bring strange custom. Begging your pardons, gentlemen, for speaking so of your masters. Still, their presence does have a dampening effect on trade."

Snake chuckled. "We take no offense, landlord. Members of the Order do empty a room, even where the ale is fine. Is it of your own brewing?" He gestured toward a chair, with a quick glance at Dog, who smiled blandly. They would have some time before the wizards called them, and they might as well pass that time in the bar. Should Lorit recover more quickly than Snake believed likely, they would be available.

"Aye, the ale is my own brewing. I've brewed our ale since my father, may his soul rest in peace, began training me when I was just a lad. 'Learn to brew ale worth drinking,' he used to say, 'and you'll never lack for customers. If you're the brewmaster, you'll always know the quality of what you sell.'"

"High quality," Dog put in. "Don't drink own ale?"

The innkeeper laughed at that. "Oh, I'll take a mug from time to time, but not so often that it gets a hold on me. Since it doesn't appear we'll be busy tonight, or that your fellows will be coming downstairs soon, I will take a sip myself. If you don't mind me joining you."

"Not at all," Snake answered.

The landlord excused himself. He returned with a brimming mug, plus two more for the table. "Here you are, friends. I'd not have you dry and me able to wet my tongue." A moment later, a servant appeared with bread and cheese. "Here's a little something to take the edge off. Help yourselves, help yourselves."

Dog and Snake murmured their thanks, breaking the bread and digging into the cheese. After a healthy swig of ale, the innkeeper joined them. "Ah," he said, eventually, "it's a good cheese, this is. Comes from a farm not far north of the village. One of the few who's managed to keep his land even under Rand's taxes."

Snake had heard something of Rand's taxes earlier in the day. "Taxed heavily, did he?"

For a moment the innkeeper had the look of a man who'd said more than he'd meant; then he recalled that Rand could no longer object. "Aye, that he did. Too many of his little wars against his neighbors. Just like his father in that. Always wanting to expand their lands, were Lords Gerlach and Rand. when they weren't having to defend their lands against their southern neighbors.

"There was never any fighting here, but our farmers say they suffered almost as much from Rand's wars as did those against whom he fought. They had to pay the costs, you see. When they couldn't pay, Rand would take their land, put a servant in the farmhouse, and take the entire harvest. Harvests shrunk, and Rand seemed unable to understand why. Put a servant in charge who's never farmed and pay him a servant's wage, your crops will shrink. Still, even with smaller crops, taking all instead of just a part probably kept Rand from noticing that crops were shrinking. Or caring, so long as he could support his guard and live as he chose. It mattered little to him that fewer and poorer farmers spent little in the village or in my inn."

"The farmers who lost their land?" Snake inquired, though he knew quite well where they had gone, had known even before his visit with Dog to the thieves' village.

The innkeeper became evasive. "Well, that's hard to say. Surely some went into the woods and became thieves. Others hired out where they could. Most simply left, looking for work in other places. I doubt that many became thieves, though some will claim otherwise."

"What will happen now, do you think?" Snake asked. This, he knew, was apt to be uppermost in the innkeeper's mind, as it would for the villagers and farmers as well.

The innkeeper shook his head. "Ah, that's the question, isn't it. Some will talk of not needing a lord, but that will last only until danger threatens, whether from thieves or some southern lord seeking to claim Rand's holdings. Thanks to Rand, this is now a poor land. Most farms produce barely enough to pay their taxes, or produce crops only for him. A lord bent on conquest won't care, and there'll be no one to resist."

"Still," Snake pointed out, "a new lord's guard will drink ale and wine and wish food from time to time. And the village will remain."

"That it will," agreed the innkeeper. "But the village grows poorer each year. With farmers driven off their land, there's less business. Now, with Rand dead and no doubt owing everyone in the village, the townspeople will be poorer than ever. There'll be no getting to Rand's coin beneath what was his keep, though it would not surprise me were some to try."

The innkeeper was silent for a time; then he changed the subject. "But what of this witch-child who men say brought down Rand's keep? The first of your masters' Order arrived quickly after. So quickly, I'm told, that he must have been sent for earlier. If you should not speak of it, forgive my curiosity. I would not question or meddle in the Order's affairs."

Snake was a little uncertain just what his new master would have him say. He took a deep breath and made his best effort, keeping a wary eye on Dog. "We know little ourselves. We have tracked her for some miles at our masters' orders, not yet certain who or what she is. That, at least, she seems to have answered. Why the Order wishes her followed we know not, nor would wish to."

At a look from the innkeeper, Dog nodded agreement.

"Your wizards fear her power, I would guess," the innkeeper mused, "were I to guess concerning the Order's business. Which I do not," he said, leaning across the table and looking carefully at each in turn. "So," he continued, "you also know nothing of what she is or where she came from? Ah, it's safer that way, surely, for all of us—to know as little as possible about the Order's business!"

"Good advice," Dog agreed.

CHAPTER FOUR

Snake rarely tired of sitting in a tavern and listening to gossip. On this morning, there was little gossip to enjoy. Customers continued to arrive, but left after one drink as they learned that the inn had been occupied overnight by wizards.

Dog didn't speak for an hour at a time. He seemed to be communing with his soul, if his sort of being had a soul. Snake wasn't sure he wanted to learn just what his new master might be. He remembered too vividly the earth separating beneath him on their first meeting and had no wish to repeat the experience. Occasionally he wondered whether Dog and this witch-child were similar, but dismissed the idea. Dog opened the earth itself, while the child had control above the earth, or so it seemed.

Snake settled for watching the east road through the large front window, or watching the inn's staff as they went about their tasks. He'd analyzed each one's strengths and weaknesses, could have tricked any without difficulty. For a more immediate result, he would bribe or frighten each into doing anything he wanted done.

For the moment there was nothing Snake wanted done. Eventually the wizards would awake, still exhausted. Snake knew what that kind of spell-enhanced forced march did to men.

Given what Snake had seen of that young guardsman's following among what was left of Rand's guard, the remnants of Rand's guard would take care of any unrest among the people. The half-dozen of the Order's guards shouldn't be called upon to do much until the wizards set out travelling again. He thought of sharpening his dagger, but a touch of the edge with his thumb confirmed that wouldn't be necessary. There was nothing to do but wait.

Eventually it became time for the noon meal—roast beef, roasted potatoes, green beans, fresh bread, cheese, a fresh mug of ale. Snake had nursed a second mug through the morning. He didn't want to face wizards with a swimming head. Certainly not when he was pretending that he, not Dog, led the effort to track the child-witch and her brother.

After a time, Snake noticed servants carrying meals for four up to the second floor. The Wizards were awake. Guards would not have ordered meals sent to their rooms; the inn's main room would be far more attractive to them. Snake began to reach a hand to tap Dog and draw his attention to the parade up the stairs. The broad man had been watching all along.

"Soon," Dog said softly. "Wizards call. Tell what seen, heard." He paused for a moment. "Trail lead north. West, Roke meets; east, Rath meets." He smiled, not pleasantly. "Frighten, frustrate wizards."

Snake listened carefully. "There is nothing you would not have them know, Master?"

Dog shook his head. "Nothing. If lucky, won't catch girl. Maybe try take Rand's guard. Not good. Deserve better than wizards."

"If I may, Master?" Snake began, cautiously. At Dog's nod he continued, "I think they will leave those guardsmen in place. The Order assumes that only two of every six guardsmen will be loyal. The others serve for pay, or from fear of refusing. Members of the Order watch carefully every guardsman they employ to make certain that two loyal men accompany any travelling wizard. To take any from Rand's survivors would be too great a risk. Such men might desert even if they had to kill loyal guardsmen to get away. Even wizards realize that fear can guarantee only so much loyalty."

Dog sat back in his seat, regarding Snake with new interest. "Very good. Guardsmen stay, wait Ryd."

Snake needed a moment to recall Dog's note to Lord Ryd. "You are certain, Master, that the lord will come?"

Dog smiled. "Lord come. Lands, people, much to Ryd, nothing to wizards. Soon wizards go north. Best Rath, Ryd not meet. If meet later, in other hands."

From time to time Dog said something which suggested that he did not regard his own power nearly as highly as did Snake. Just who these other hands might belong to worried the assassin. Surely it was not this witch-child. Though her powers were demonstrably greater than the Order's, she fled from them. Her actions seemed random, responses only to danger, if one included drought as a danger. As the child of farmers, no doubt she agreed that drought was a great threat to that way of life. Snake had never worried much about farmers, though his new master had a fondness for them.

They sat in silence, sipping what remained of their ale. Eventually Roke appeared and gestured for them to follow. As they mounted the stairs, he cautioned: "Rath is in a foul mood. He suffered on their journey. Lorit is merely irritable. Still, you would be wise to answer fully. Cease speaking should you sense you are saying more than either needs. I would not see your mind blasted into chaos only to have one of my superiors regret it the following morning."

Snake nodded. Apparently Roke didn't know that Soren had long since provided him with an amulet to protect his mind against any but the strongest spells. Lorit was one of the few who would know of that amulet.

Snake heard Dog's very faint snort. He wondered what would happen should Lorit or Rath try to cast a spell on that being. It might be like trying to command a stone cliff. Which left Snake between a cliff and a whole order of wizards and enjoying every minute of it. At least most minutes. Perhaps not those to come this day.

Roke led them into a large bedroom situated near the top of the stair. Snake took in the room with one swift look. One bed, so probably Lorit's own room. That would make sense. Lorit was nominally the highest-ranking of the wizards present, though Rath, if fully recovered, might possess greater power. That is, if he had not been too badly damaged by his encounter with the child-witch when his tower fell.

All four wizards sat in over-stuffed chairs, no doubt ordered by Lorit so he'd not have to argue with Rath about putting the invalid in the room's only easy chair. Tarh sat close to his former master, his attention on Rath One-Hand more than on the meeting.

Rath One-Hand. The stump where his right hand had been was very much in evidence. That arm ended in a sort of leather cup which extended half-way up the forearm. How healed that stump might be, Snake couldn't guess. Wizards usually knew healing spells, though he'd never heard that those of the dark order were particularly potent.

It would not do to look too long at Rath or his stump. Just past Rath sat Lorit, with Roke off to his right so Lorit took up the center of their semi-circle, a small reminder that he was the leader of this little expedition. Their six guardsmen were not present. The less they knew, the better.

Snake stood, waiting. Wizards preferred to be the first to speak. Behind him he could hear Dog already fidgeting. If Rath chose to attempt to punish or silence the man, Snake would be careful to dive out of the way. Dog might or might not be able to cause a keep to fall, and perhaps he couldn't cause an entire inn to vanish into the earth, but Snake wasn't eager to find out. If it came to actual conflict, Dog would know what he was up against. Wizards would not.

Lorit regarded Snake for a few moments before he spoke. The wizard looked tired, a different sort of tired from Rath. The One-Hand appeared ill, a man who'd tried to do too much before fully recovering. Lorit's exhaustion was that of one who had replaced sleep with nights full of questions for which he could find no answers. Off to his right, Roke merely looked serious. Seeking answers would be a task for his superiors. Any thinking he might do would likely get him reprimanded.

"Assassin, what have you learned?" Lorit asked. "We will not visit what is left of the keep until tomorrow, but would hear what we'll find there." He seemed to notice Dog for the first time. "Do we need this minion of yours?"

Snake inclined his head just enough to substitute for a bow. He was, after all, not just any assassin, but the Chief Mage's own. "He is a fine tracker, master. You may wish confirmation of what we have learned." When Lorit said nothing, he continued. "You'll find little of the keep, master, other than a pile of rubble. Everything has fallen: outer wall, the keep itself, all. Rand himself, so say the servants and guardsmen who remain, lies somewhere beneath that pile."

Out of the corner of his eye Snake could see Rath's scowl deepen. The wizard spoke. "How long did the keep's fall take?"

"All say it was a matter of moments." Snake spread his hands in the manner of one who is doubtful of being believed. "The witch-child commanded Rand to die and his keep to fall in on him. The keep began to crumble even before Rand lay stretched on the room's floor. Others in the room—three guardsmen, the witch-child, and the man we believe to be her brother-- barely escaped before the entire place came crashing down."

Lorit turned to Rath. "As I recall, your tower took most of a night to fall and turn to dust." He faced Snake. "Have the stones in that rubble turned to dust?"

Snake shook his head. "No, Master. I've not touched them, but they appear unchanged. The mortar holding them turned to powder, say those who were in the keep."

Tarh spoke softly. "That was unlike the tower, which seemed to fall from the top down."

Lorit agreed. "And the tower's fall, you say, was the result of what appeared to be lightning striking your crystal several valleys away. Somehow it came through to Rath's great crystal atop his tower." He thought. "This destruction took place much more rapidly. Let us consider that."

They sat in silence before Rath spoke, reluctantly. "The child-witch did not make use of lightning. She gave an order to the stones and they obeyed."

"And to Rand himself, and his body obeyed," noted Roke.

"She has given orders to lightning and it has obeyed." Lorit looked around at his fellow wizards. "She has used lightning a second time. She put a ward over a valley and caused lightning to enforce it. A wizard died testing that ward."

"She has powers over animals as well, master," reminded Snake. He glanced over his shoulder at Dog, who appeared to have fallen asleep standing up. Eyes closed, the squat man gave a slight nod.

That news startled Roke. "Over animals as well as lightning and stone?"

Snake looked at Lorit, eyebrows raised. The wizard nodded permission. Snake turned to address Roke. "The child and her brother first travelled not on the road, but over wooded hills on the valley's east side. Maaaaster Dog"—he was careful to say the name with just the right amount of scorn, though the effort cost him no little inner trepidation—"tracked them over the hill to a forest road. On the way, he discovered that they were shadowed the entire time by wolves. From the tracks, they appeared very like an escort. This continued down to the forest road, where all four left. Master Dog doubts that took place by chance."

Lorit was skeptical. "This power does not sound as though it would threaten." His smile was slight. "Unless she should call a wolf pack." Even Rath smiled a little.

Tarh spoke for the first time. "So she commands lightning and rain, wild animals, and stone. What, I wonder, are the limits of her power?"

"That," Lorit said sourly, "is what we seek to learn."

Rath shot an angry glance at his former apprentice, then sat glowering. Roke and Tarh held silent, Tarh regretting that he'd spoken at all. This mission began to look more deadly each moment.

After a time Lorit spoke again. "And what of Rand's servants and his guardsmen? Have they all departed, now that no wages will be paid?"

"No, Master," Snake said. "Most of his guard left soon after the keep fell. A dozen or so remain, as do many servants. Both guards and servants appear to intend remaining until a new lord appears. Perhaps they hope to serve that master."

"A loyal group of servants, indeed," put in a sour Rath. "They know not who they might serve but are already loyal to that imaginary being."

"If I may make a suggestion, Masters," Snake said, his voice as uncertain as he could manage.

"What?" asked Lorit.

"If the land falls into chaos, your search may be affected. It might be worth a few coins to anchor the guard and servants for a while, at least."

Lorit nodded. "That does make sense. While we would not be affected, getting information could become more difficult. Tarh, you carry our funds. Give our scout what he feels will be sufficient."

Snake breathed more easily until Rath spoke.

"You, fellow," the One-Hand said, looking sharply at Dog, "do you have anything to add?"

Dog seemed to jerk awake. "Eh? No, no, master speaks straight as furrow in good ground. Furrow in good ground," he said a second time, as though pleased at the image.

Snake kept a straight face as Dog played the simple rustic.

"That is enough," Lorit said. "There is nothing more to do until after a night's rest. In the morning we will examine for ourselves the extent of the destruction." He focused again on Snake. "What have you to say about where the witch-child and this brother have gone?"

"North, we believe, masters. They seem to have taken the road which passes through the village. Had they gone west, you would have encountered them. Had they gone east, Roke would have seen them. They left the ruins and started back toward this inn. No one seems to have seen them after that."

Lorit stroked his chin. "North, then. Toward the mountains? Perhaps seeking allies in the green Order to the north?"

"Arrr," Dog broke in. "Red Forest close. Hard to find, in forest. No roads."

This surprised Snake. Dog must want these wizards to concentrate on that forest. Did that mean he knew the pair wouldn't be there, or would? It was hard to tell who the broad man herded most: these wizards, or the pair they followed. Snake wasn't about to ask. When or if Dog wanted him to know, the earth-shaker would tell him. Until then, Snake would focus on remaining on this strange being's good side.

All four wizards reacted to mention of the Red Forest. That was interesting. Snake had heard of the forest but never had occasion to visit. There were no lords or wizards that far north in this land, so little need for his skills whether as spy or assassin. This time, however, he appeared likely to get to know that forest more fully than he'd have thought necessary. Or desirable.

These wizards clearly did not care for the thought of pursuing their quarry into those woods. Perhaps their powers were weaker there. That the forest was ancient and it trees actually red were the limits of Snake's information about the place.

"Be ready to accompany us to the ruin in the morning." Lorit gave a wave of dismissal. Snake bowed, then turned to leave. He noted that Dog had not bowed before following him out.

Snake waited until they were down the stairs before speaking. "That was easy enough, I suppose. They didn't care for mention of the Red Forest." When Dog didn't respond, he asked, "How about one more mug of ale before we sleep?"

Dog smiled. "Best idea entire night. And wizards pay. If at all."

That much was true enough. The Order had a reputation for not paying its way as its members travelled. Most were good enough about paying when in the Capitol. There they needed at least a little good will from shopkeepers and their staffs, Snake supposed. Passing through the land, most didn't expect to return often enough to care.

Snake hoped that Dog would say something about their next steps. The fellow simply looked pleased, drank his ale, said goodnight, and left the inn for the stable loft. Snake was just as happy to make his way upstairs alone. Sleep came only intermittently, mixed with worries about where all these events would lead. Unusually, he wondered whether he would be among those who survived. That his new master would survive he took as given. He hoped Dog would somehow bring him through as well.

***

In Lorit's room, the wizards conferred for only a few minutes.

"I think," said Lorit, "it's up that village road to the north for us."

Rath wasn't so sure. "And what if they go east once they reach the forest, or even before then, going across the fields?"

"This fellow Dog apparently tracks as well as any. He can be put to checking any possible route across the fields. With two horses, they'd leave tracks."

The answer didn't precisely satisfy Rath, but he sat back in his chair and said no more.

"There is one other thing we might do, however," Lorit said. "Roke and Tarh, take three of our guardsmen and go east on the main road. Work your way north to the eastern end of the forest. If they go that way, you might arrive before them, or soon after. In the morning, we'll seek information about how far east the forest goes, and the best way to reach it from here."

Roke cleared his throat. "I've been up that way once or twice, tracking signs of power. There is a sort of trail which heads north at least part way. It leads to a few scattered farms, so it's little used but passable. There are no farmhouses or tilled fields near the forest, just pastures."

Lorit nodded. "In the morning, Snake and his minion can seek more about this road north. Snake won't have much trouble convincing even the most reluctant to speak. If there is any reluctance; no doubt the villagers would as soon see us go about our mission, so long as it takes us away from here." He stood. "Get some rest, all of you. We'll need to be walking tomorrow. Master Rath, with half our guardsmen going east with Roke, I'm afraid you'll have to walk with the rest of us."

Rath hadn't ceased to scowl the entire evening. It would have been difficult to tell whether his scowl deepened at Lorit's words. "I'll be ready. I've had enough of being carried in a sling like an infant." With that, he stumped out of the room.

Lorit turned to the two younger wizards. "Prepare yourselves for tomorrow's journey. Stay only long enough to see if anything new is learned at the ruin, though I doubt there's much to see that Snake has not already noticed. We can send messages through Soren once we're all on the road."

The two bowed and left. Lorit stood for a few minutes looking out the room's window. He found little comfort in the darkness. Sighing, he went to his pack and removed his crystal. It was time to contact Soren, He had little news, other than that they had a reasonable notion of where the pair had gone. They were only two or three days behind the two, so that was something.

***

Soren became steadily more irritable as two days passed with no word from Lorit. Surely they had been able to reach the ruins of Rand's keep by now. Lorit would not have allowed Rath's weakness to slow them once they'd learned of Rand's death.

The Chief Mage called Haster and Oleg to share his frustration. Neither said much.. Haster knew that silence was the safest choice. Expending all this energy in frustration didn't make much sense to Oleg. If you weren't getting information through your crystal, look for it elsewhere. Or sit back and think about the situation until you achieved greater understanding.

Soren's crystal had remained silent, only a slight glow in its depths revealing that it was active. Now the glow brightened and Lorit's face could be seen. "Chief Mage, we have reached the area where Rand's keep stood. We will not visit the site until tomorrow. We kept on for a day and night and arrived here in early afternoon, exhausted. Our party rested all last night and most of today. We have just met with your spy and his minion."

Leaning over the crystal, Soren asked, "And what have you learned? Have you caught up with this witch-child?"

Oleg suppressed a grimace. Had they come upon that one in their state of near exhaustion, it was unlikely either Lorit and Rath would have ever reported again. That Soren asked such a question was a sign of how distraught he'd become over the past few days. Oleg would rather have had Lorit, or even a fully-recovered Rath, as Chief Mage at such a time as this. He would not say so.

Lorit looked taken aback. "No, Chief Mage, we have not. Snake has learned that the child and her brother left the area quickly after their escape. It appears that they must have gone north. There is a road which leads through the village. Tomorrow we will make a brief visit to the ruin before following hem."

"Are you certain they've gone north?" This from Haster.

Lorit nodded. "We are certain of that. We know they did not take the south road back toward the Capitol. Had they gone east or west they'd have met our party or Roke."

Thank the Dark they didn't turn south, thought Oleg.

"Have you learned anything of their likely destination?" Soren asked.

"That remains unclear," Lorit replied. "The road north leads to the Red Forest. Once in the forest, I suspect they will continue east. If so, making their way through the trees will slow their progress. Snake and his Dog will track them within the forest, while Rath and I travel along the edge.

"Roke and Tarh will move to the forest's east boundary, where they should arrive before the fugitives. I hope to catch them between our parties."

Soren brooded. "The Red Forest. It has a bad name." He turned to Oleg. "Find out what you can about this forest. There may be a good reason for members of our Order to shun it, or you may discover only farmers' tales. I recall nothing but the name, and that our members do not go there." He turned to the crystal again. "Have you any greater knowledge of the place, or do your companions?"

Lorit shook his head. "None of us know any more than the name. Roke says there is no reason to go there, and he never has. Occasionally he has travelled among the area's few farmhouses, seeking those who've shown signs of power,."

"Is there no other news, then?" asked Soren.

"Nothing yet. We may learn more tomorrow."

Soren could think of no more questions. "Report tomorrow night. In the meantime, Oleg will see what he can learn about this Red Forest and any powers which may lurk there."

Lorit barely inclined his head in acknowledgement before Soren's great crystal went dark. The Chief Mage turned to his two assistants. "At least they're on the ground, though they've not learned much. What do you think of their plan?" This was addressed to Oleg.

The Loremaster raised his hands, palms upward. "It's as good as any. By following they can at least keep track of the pair. With any luck, they'll not be confronted by the child before we've learned something of use against her." He became thoughtful. "Roke has perhaps the more dangerous part, should he and Tarh find themselves between this being and someplace she wishes to get to. He could join Selik on our honor roll of those who've died to learn something of her powers."

Soren's gesture was dismissive. "There are other wizards as accomplished as Roke. A wiser man might have remained with Rand after delivering our message. At least he'd have seen these two. Should he die, we may learn something from his death."

Oleg suspected that had Roke remained with Rand, he would have already died. Such a death would not have brought any knowledge not gleaned from news of Rand's death and that of his keep. Instead of voicing that thought, he said, "I'll put the apprentices to work searching out what they can learn of the Red Forest. In the meantime, the Dark One may know something, if the forest is old enough."

✱✱✱

Oleg put his apprentices to work through the night. Look for anything about a Red Forest, he told them. This forest would be located along the north end of the land. They were not to be bound by that geography; any references to a red forest, no matter where or what the reference, were to be brought to his senior apprentices for their review. He would be busy for a time with his own researches. When those were done, he would look at what they'd found. They'd better have found something.

With those words of encouragement, Oleg left them, carefully closing and sealing his office door behind him. Then it was into his closet to light the dark lantern and open the hidden door leading to the dungeon.

"So you have more news for me, Loremaster." As always, the title was said with just a touch of irony, the Dark One's reminder that even Oleg's lore was small compared to what lay within his mind.

"Of a sort, Dark One," Oleg replied. "What do you know of a forest to the north which men call the Red Forest?"

There was a slight grunt from within the cell, the sound a man might make if stifling his surprise. That was something, Oleg thought. Perhaps this forest had more meaning than he'd expected. "So," he said, "you know of such a forest, I take it."

"Does it still exist, then? To the north, near the mountains?" The voice was almost eager.

"It exists," Oleg replied, keeping his voice disinterested. "What of it? There are many forests."

"Ah, but you do not ask about many forests. In all the times your kind have visited me, none have asked about forests, much less a red forest. Tell me, Loremaster, what do you know of this forest?"

"Little but the name, which tells us nothing."

At this the being gave what might have been a slight laugh, though unlike any laugh Oleg had ever heard. "You didn't look at that forest through your mighty crystals to see if you could tell from where its name was derived? Now that was careless, Loremaster. Still," he went on, thoughtfully, "you can do that soon enough, and there's little to be gained by sending you away until you've looked.

"Only oaks grow there, oaks with reddish bark and red leaves. The forest's red tint can be seen in the distance. It grows stronger the closer you approach. All else that grows within that forest is red as well: reddish-brown deer, squirrels, even rabbits. Farmers living nearby do not harvest wood from those trees, or did not in my time. I doubt they've become bolder in all the long years." He fell silent. "Why do you ask about this forest, Loremaster?"

Oleg often wished he could pretend idle curiosity when speaking with the Dark One, but he knew the futility of such a pretense. Idle curiosity would never bring him into these depths. "The witch-child appears headed there. We suspect she will continue east through the woods."

For a while there was silence from within the cell. "It were best for your order that such be her purpose. The Red Forest is no source of strength for your sort, wizard. It is an ancient place, powerful enough--and bright enough--that none of your order could call on darkness when within. In that place, even your Chief Mage, or you who pretend only to study power, would feel that the power of darkness had never existed."

"You tell me this, more than you've ever offered—why?" Oleg was inclined to believe none of what he had just heard.

There came another of those sounds that Oleg suspected were bits of laughter, long unpracticed. "Perhaps because talk of that forest almost brings a bit of light to this place. Listen well, Loremaster: if she is not yet aware of her power, or if it has been growing within her, time spent within that forest may well bring her to fuller awareness. Certainly she will be strengthened, if strengthening she need." He fell silent. Oleg, accustomed to the creature's moods, waited.

"Long ago, a Druid weakened by whatever cause would come to that forest to regain strength. From what you have said, she needs little such strengthening. She commands lightning, she commands stone and mortar, she commands death. Have you news of else she commands?"

Oleg was glad the Dark One could not see him clearly. That the child might be strengthened and that this forest might be alien to the Order's powers was far more than he'd hoped to learn. The learning was not all that satisfactory.

"What is it you think is to come, Dark One?" Oleg was not certain he wished to hear, but this day the Dark One seemed willing, almost eager, to talk.

"Loremaster, even you must be able to foretell that. I see two paths, but doubt your Chief Mage will see more than one. He could order this child left alone. That would buy time to consider what sort of being she is, and most of all, what she is apt to do with her power. So far, she seems to have acted only when attacked. A wise man would cease attacking while he still has the choice."

Again he fell silent. "Your Chief Mage would not like such advice, and it might be dangerous to offer, even for you. He will choose the more dangerous course. That is what a Chief Mage in your order will always do. And what is that course? To find a way to destroy or at least neutralize the child?

"If your Chief Mage wishes to join the darkness, your present course will lead him there. It will not be the darkness he seeks, that of the full power of the Dark, but the dark of oblivion. Can you not see that even such power as this child has shown is far beyond any you can summon?"

Oleg was becoming more and more uneasy. This was unlike the Dark One. He gave only a little at a time, and now he was volunteering more than Oleg had requested. "Why do you warn against the course that Soren is likely to continue? You bear no love for us."

"I do not. But I would not have your order destroyed if in the process your building above me turns to rubble, and my cell is buried beneath. Should she destroy all of you but leave this building untouched, over time the spells which hold me here will weaken. Then I will make my way into the night air, though I may be unable after these long years to bear the daylight. Should your Chief Mage come to his senses, nonetheless she will eventually become aware of my presence and seek me. I both long for and fear that day."

With that, the Dark One fell silent, and none of Oleg's questions would rouse him.

***

By morning Aren had made his decision: for good or ill, they would continue east through the forest. That way might lead into greater danger: as they reached the far end, he strongly suspected they would encounter at least one wizard and his accompanying guard. Only by going north into the mountains could they hope to completely avoid members of the Dark Order. Yet he clung to a hope that they might find someone to the east who could tell Bird what sort of being she might be, could teach her the extent and uses of her power. Why he felt that help could be found to the east, he wasn't certain. He doubted the feeling came only because Brenna had suggested that the order of blue wizards might be helpful.

Aren took time to prepare a breakfast of crushed oats boiled over a small fire he built from dead branches. Afterwards he packed up his and Bird's bedrolls as Bird cleaned up their bowls and the pan in a nearby stream.

"You plan to travel on, then," Brenna said.

Aren nodded. "We can do little good by staying here and waiting for wizards to catch up. It will not take them long to figure out which way we must have gone."

"They aren't close yet," said Bird, without looking up from packing the clean dishes. "I think they must be still on the road, or at the inn." After a moment she added, "I liked the inn. I wish we could have stayed longer."

Brenna's eyebrows went up. Aren caught her expression and said, "Yes, she can tell when wizards are nearby. It's handy."

"It certainly is. Can you tell that they're dark wizards, little bird?"

"Oh, yes," Bird answered, "just as I could tell you weren't. I'm not sure yet what sort of wizard you are, but you're not dark."

For a moment Brenna pondered this. It was more than her masters could discern. They identified her as a person of power, but not the kind of power. They'd assumed she could become a blue wizard. And now this child, who could spot a dark wizard at some distance, could say only what she wasn't. "Well, I'm glad I'm not, though I wish you could tell what I am. It would be good to know something definite about myself. I'm tired of living with failure." After looking down for a moment, she added, "But that's not your fault, child. You have more serious problems than figuring out my nature."

Aren had finished loading their few belongings onto the horses. "We had better be on our way, little bird. I have no idea how far we must travel to reach the end of these woods."

Brenna cleared her throat. "I'd be glad to guide you. The woods are open with little underbrush between these huge old trees, but it's easy to become turned around. I haven't any plans that guiding you would delay."

Aren looked questioningly at Bird, who clapped her hands. "Oh, yes! That would give me time to think about what sort of wizard you might be! You could tell us more about the people across the river, too." She gave her decisive nod. "I've never been this far from home before. Everything's new."

"Well," Aren said, smiling, "since Bird is certain you're not a dark wizard, we'll gladly take you on as our guide. The pay is meager—sharing our meals, such as they are. We'll be glad of the company."

Brenna had readied her bedroll while Aren prepared breakfast. She had only to tie it on her backpack and she was ready.

They spent a long day travelling through the forest. Aren hoped to reach the eastern end before one of the wizards could arrive there, but he didn't want to exhaust their guide. They moved more slowly than he would have liked, with more pauses.

Still, traveling at this pace would save the horses. If they did have to outrun pursuers, their horses should be fresh enough, though he wasn't sure Pony could outrun a guardsman on a full-sized horse. Fortunately, a wizard would have to move on foot, and his guards were unlikely to be allowed to ride while he walked. Even Pony should be able to outrun guardsmen.

Aren hoped they could avoid their pursuers. He wasn't eager to learn whether Bird could command the death of a wizard as easily as she could that of a lord. There'd been too much death already, and he feared Bird might come to find death too easy to command.

He watched as she rode through the woods, still wide-eyed at the size of the trees and at the occasional cardinals. "Look at how red that one is! Why isn't the other one that red, too? Is it young?"

Brenna laughed. "No, that's a female. The brighter one is the male. He has to be bright red to attract a mate."

"Hmpf," Bird replied. "I don't see why the lady bird shouldn't be just as bright and pretty. You're prettier than Aren, though I think he's stronger and bigger."

That got both adults laughing. "I'm just as glad not to be pretty," Aren noted, "so Brenna can take those honors."

"Well, anyway, I think they're both pretty. She's just quieter about it, that's all," said Bird, decidedly. Aren was glad to see her childish certainty returning. Maybe it wasn't so childish. She'd been certain about several things which happened precisely as she hoped.

They camped before it began to get dark. Brenna said they had another full day of travel, which would bring them close to the forest edge. Then they might see if any waited for them.

Aren agreed but wished to know how far they would be from the river at that point.

By horseback, Brenna guessed, perhaps two days. She had not walked straight toward the river for fear of drawing attention to herself, so she'd taken the better part of four days. There was a road a ways south of the forest which meandered toward the river but didn't reach it, and she'd followed that.

So, Aren thought, another two days of traveling to reach the forest edge, and then two to reach the river, where they might cross over and at least be beyond the reach of the dark Order. If, that is, they didn't find a wizard waiting for them at the forest's edge. Still, the forest was large. A wizard might well wait at the wrong spot, though a wizard of any ability should be able to find either Brenna or Bird by their powers. They'd have to chance it. Going back wouldn't do them much good; there were no teachers back home.

***

The visit to the ruins of Rand's keep told the wizards little, other than ending any thoughts they might have had about the destruction being less massive than they'd heard. Even Rath was impressed. They didn't pause to have Snake seek information in the village about the Red Forest. Roke had told them all they felt they needed to know on that subject. So they travelled north, moving more rapidly than Snake would have expected. He wondered if Dog's presence was having the same effect on these wizards as it had seemed to have on him earlier.

Dog kept looking at the ground, frowning and shaking his head. After a time, he gestured to Snake to lean close. "Walker ahead. Not sure who. Didn't expect."

Snake began paying closer attention to the tracks. Though the walker often kept to the side of the road while the horses tended to move in the center, occasionally the walker's tracks would be blurred or obliterated by those of the pony.

Some time later, Dog held up a hand. Snake signaled that the wizards and their guards should hold up. Dog spoke softly so only Snake could hear. "Riders catch walker. Pause, talk." His frown deepened. "Who walker?"

Dog's reasoning was clear: the horses stood for a while, their hoofprints imposed over one another while the walker's remained off to one side. For the first time, something worried Dog, and that threatened Snake's one bit of certainty in this wizard-baiting.

Snake turned to the watching wizards. "The pair caught up to a walker. They talked for a while."

"Can you tell anything about this third person?" Lorit asked.

"No," Snake said. "The footprints reveal little."

Dog moved to the edge of the road and walked slowly forward, examining tracks. Snake joined him. Dog continued to mutter. The only words Snake heard clearly were "why walker?" After fifty paces, they turned back.

Snake reported. "Tracks suggest the three went on together. The brother kept his horse between the child's pony and the walker. This probably wasn't anyone they knew well enough to trust, or perhaps knew but didn't trust."

Off to one side, he saw Dog's brief nod of approval. The tracker's face continued to show puzzlement over this new traveler.

As they drew closer to the Red Forest, Snake began to feel uneasy. The trees were very unusual for oaks, with reddish bark and red leaves. While he wouldn't have said the place glowed, it did seem to create more light than it absorbed from the late sun.

Lorit decreed a halt when they were still a good hundred yards from the forest edge. While the guards set up camp, Snake and Dog continued into the forest. The trail left by the horses was clear. Dog again set his fast travelling pace.

The trail led to a clearing where signs indicated that their quarry had spent the night. Snake more than half suspected that in this forest Dog's tracking skill owed something to the ground itself informing him of anything his eyes could not spot on their own. He wasn't about to bring up that idea.

That their quarry had moved on was clear, but Dog did not return immediately to the wizard's camp. Instead, he walked over to a huge tree, living and healthy despite an opening which let them see that the tree was hollow for perhaps a dozen feet up. Dog walked into the tree, Snake following a little behind, nervous about entering one of these red oaks. Suppose it closed behind them, as in an old tale?

Dog looked at the walls, the ceiling, the bench-like protrusion which offered space enough for one person to lie full-length, or to sit with back to the wall. "Interesting," he muttered. "Shelter offered. Woman returns. Welcome." He stopped frowning. "Good."

This was a bit much for Snake. Of course Dog could tell that the third who'd joined the brother and sister was a woman. Snake had also noticed that tracks were deeper than the child's and shallower than the man's. But Dog could tell that the forest welcomed the woman? Was the forest in some way conscious?

Snake had dealt with wizards for a good many years . He'd seen strange things, but those had been done by men using powers studied and honed for centuries. The possibility that a forest could will something was something entirely new. That one of its oldest and tallest trees might offer a shelter was more than Snake wished to consider.

Snake had already learned a great deal in the last few days, much of it unwillingly. This piece of knowledge struck him nearly as forcibly as had the moment when Dog put his hands together, then spread them and a crevice opened beneath Snake's feet. There were powers and minds in this world which Snake had never guessed at. How many forests he'd walked through had actually been aware of his passing? He wondered what might have happened had a forest not wanted his presence. What if this one decided he was a trespasser?

Dog left the shelter, walked once around the clearing. He sat on one of the logs laid out around a fire-pit which clearly had recently been used. Snake sat as well, glad to get off shaky legs.

After a time, Dog spoke as though to himself. "Well enough. Walker return. Why left? Safest here." He was silent, thinking. "Guides through forest, good. Says stay in forest? Will not serve." He looked up then, seemed to recall Snake's presence.

"So. Herd northerly. Wizards poor herd dogs." He shrugged. "We go back. Say, quarry east. Say, go forest edge."

"Then"—here Snake's new master leaned forward , speaking with greater emphasis—"say we go ahead, meet others, lie in wait." He said, almost to himself, "Gather wizards forest edge. Push child further north. Leave woods. What walker do?"

Snake inclined his head in obedience. "I understand, Master. We wish to hurry these wizards along, and to go out ahead of them to find the younger wizards. I will be convincing."

Dog chuckled again. He was enjoying this immensely, Snake thought. "That certain."

***

Since Tarh had only recently completed his apprenticeship, Roke claimed the role of senior wizard. He drove Tarh, their three guardsmen and himself hard. They travelled until well after dark, eating their meals as they walked. He allowed a halt only when he knew they must rest before going further. Their trail consisted of two ruts in the grass. It rambled, its only purpose to connect several small farmhouses with the East Road. Cutting across fields would have slowed them more, Roke believed, than did the road's windings.

By the second day they could see the Red Forest ahead. From then on, Roke drove his men across fields, unconcerned about any damage the five of them might do to crops. If any farmers noticed their passage, two dark robes would be visible from a great enough distance to keep them away.

That night they slept only a few hours from the forest. Roke could not feel completely comfortable, even at this distance. He'd felt unease when in the past he'd walked this northern edge, seeking after potential wizards, even though he'd not come nearer than the closest farmhouse.

They'd left the last house behind not long after mid-day. No wonder farmers built some distance off, though they farmed land closer to the forest than they were willing to live. That evening Roke's party came to the end of the crops and camped in untilled grasslands.

The two wizards spared little breath for speech. Neither expected to encounter the witch-child in the open fields, but only a fool would have failed to watch for her.

Roke slept badly, which allowed him to wake his guards at the first hint of daylight. He ordered them to go on ahead. Should the guardsman and the child be spotted, the beginnings of a plan had begun to develop in his mind.

When Lorit spoke of Selik's death by lightning, he'd also mentioned that he'd been able to send a guardsman as a scout into the valley. The guardsman had returned unscathed. That was typical of Lorit: send a guardsman, and if he returned unharmed, send a wizard and see what happened. Roke was glad he'd not been along on that mission.

Suppose this child were mortal, or some inhuman being of power wearing a human body. It might be possible for other humans to harm or even kill her—say, with arrows fired from some distance before she became aware of danger. His three trained guardsmen each carried bow and quiver as well as sword. If arrows could harm her, then so should a sword. If nothing else, perhaps his guardsmen could slay her protector, leaving the child alone and confused.

That should slow her journey to whatever her destination might be, though Roke suspected she sought support from the blue wizards across the river. She must be kept from forming such an alliance.

His instructions were to find her if he could, inform Lorit and Rath, then wait for them. If instead of waiting he could achieve more than they had been able, he might well rise within the Order. The credit would have to be shared with Tarh, unfortunately. He would see what his guardsmen might be able to do against her protector and perhaps against her as well. Tarh might object to the effort, but he'd have to accept orders from his superior in the order, no matter by how little that superior's status differed from his own.

CHAPTER FIVE

Ryd and his ten men kept a steady pace but did not gallop. Each led a second horse, and at each brief break they changed animals. Ryd wished to arrive with horses and men fresh enough to cope with whatever awaited them. That wish did not keep him from riding until well after dark before making a warrior's camp. After a cold meal, they slept in bedrolls under the stars. Each took one hour on guard, though Ryd doubted there would be danger until they were nearer the ruins of Rand's keep. If Dog said there were ruins, he was certain they would find ruins.

And Rand dead, however that might have happened. When word reached the southern lords whose lands Rand had constantly raided, surely one or more would send a force to claim the Holdings. Ryd would be ready.

At first light Ryd and his men were in the saddle again, eating a cold breakfast as they rode. The look of the land dismayed Ryd. These had been decent farmlands despite their father's taxes; now they looked poor, over-cropped. It would be some years before the land came back.

He would lower Rand's taxes; perhaps he'd collect no taxes at all until the land recovered. He could live with that. He'd managed well the income from the Five Valleys. Even with low taxes, rich farm land let him live as comfortably as he cared to while still maintaining a reserve which grew every year. During the recent drought years he'd lowered taxes even more. The response from his people more than made that worth doing. Possibly he could persuade some of the Valley's farmers to come east for a time to guide these farmers in restoring their lands.

Ryd found himself remembering the land well. He'd roamed throughout his father's holdings whenever the old man wasn't ordering him to train with Talon and the guard. The old lord's plan was clear: "You will serve as the captain of your brother's guard when he succeeds to lordship. It will be an honorable role for a younger son. and you'll be a more loyal vassal than would any other."

That role Ryd had expected to fulfil throughout his life, right up until the moment when Rand, their father dead and buried, sent him away. "Go north," Rand suggested. "Become a mercenary. It will be a good use of your skills. Do not return. I need no rival beloved by the people." That he might be beloved, or even liked, came as a surprise to Ryd. After all, he was his father's son, raised to regard the people as a lord's property.

In a rare moment of generosity, Rand announced that any guardsman who wished might join their former captain in his new life as a mercenary in the north. He even allowed Ryd a small bag of gold.

The new lord was dismayed when Ryd was accompanied by Talon, their father's swordmaster, and twenty guardsmen. The twenty best, Rand grumbled; but they were mounted and riding away before he could rescind his offer. Those twenty became the core of Ryd's band of mercenaries. Soon his band reached fifty, making it not only the largest but the most effective in those small northern border wars.

While it was still light Ryd ordered a halt, giving his men a welcome break in their hurried ride. They would rise early, he informed them, and arrive at whatever was left of Rand's keep well before mid-morning. What they would find there he did not know. Perhaps what was left of Rand's guard would be claiming ownership of the lands, or rampaging for what they could steal before leaving. He wanted his men to be ready for anything. There might, he warned, still be wizards about, in which case they would need caution.

Ryd's men were up and ready to move out before the sun had fully risen. They passed the village and the inn well before mid-morning. Though Dog's note had said the keep was destroyed, Ryd still wasn't prepared to see only a pile of rubble where his childhood home once stood. Behind him, his guard spoke in whispers as they neared the site.

The outbuildings still stood, and Ryd could see some activity there. He led his men in that direction, cautioning them to be wary. Rand's guard had reached fifty men again some time after Ryd had ridden north, and Rand had maintained that number. While it was likely that some would have departed after his death and the end of their salaries, there was no telling how many or what sort remained.

As Ryd and his men rode around the rubble and toward the outbuildings, a servant walking across the area stopped, stared, and dashed toward the guards' quarters. A moment later, a half-dozen guardsmen appeared. Oddly, their leader appeared to be the youngest of the group.

"Welcome," he said. "May I inquire who you are, and what you seek here?"

Ryd stepped down from his horse and walked forward. "Greetings," he said. "I am Ryd, Lord of the Five Valleys and younger son of Lord Gerlach. I am here to claim my late brother's lands."

Tavnor recognized a lord's bearing and dress. Whether this was Rand's brother he was not certain, but the man was definitely a lord. That he had brought with him only ten guardsmen suggested this was no attempt at conquest. Still, he had no way of knowing whether this lord's claim was true.

"My Lord!" came a voice from behind. Tavnor turned to see the old house steward approaching at what was as near a trot as the man could still manage. "Lord Ryd! It is Vernel, your brother's steward! Oh, my Lord! This is better luck than I dared hope!"

Ryd broke into a smile and stepped forward, lifting the old man from his attempted bow and embracing him. "Vernel, old friend! I had not hoped to see you again, though I wish it were in better times."

"Meaning no disrespect to your brother, my Lord, but if you indeed claim the lordship, surely better times must follow." The steward bowed deeply as he spoke, then turned to Tavnor and his retinue of guardsmen. "This is indeed Lord Ryd, younger son of Lord Gerlach and younger brother of the late Lord Rand. Lordship over our lands is his by birth. And if I may say it, he will be a far better lord than was his late brother." He turned apologetically to Ryd. "Meaning no disrespect, my Lord."

"None taken," Ryd laughed. "Your greeting delights me nearly as much as does your presence. Will you continue as house steward, once we have a house again?"

Tavnor broke in before Vernel could do more than nod vigorously. "My Lord, forgive my questions. I was only—"

Ryd reached out a hand. "My friend, you were doing your duty. I have only praise for such a man." He looked at the guardsmen who'd followed Tavnor from their quarters. "I take it that your fellow guards feel much as I do. Is that correct?" This was directed at Tavnor's fellow guardsmen.

Without hesitation all nodded. A rough voice spoke up and a scar-faced guardsman stepped forward. "Aye, Captain. Tavnor has taken charge and organized us. If I may make so bold, we would have him for our sergeant, the old one having been drunk ever since the keep fell."

It took Ryd a moment to speak. "Scar! You here? This is indeed luck!" With a laugh, he stepped past Tavnor and gripped the scar-faced man by both shoulders. "Greetings, greetings! Well met!"

Scar's attempted scowl couldn't hide a wide smile. "Didn't know if you'd recognize me, Captain. It will be good to serve with you again." He gripped Ryd's shoulders for a moment before dropping his hands. "But what about our sergeant? He's the best thinker among us."

"I take it you don't want the position, then?" Ryd asked, smiling.

"Nar," Scar said. "Tavnor saw what needed to be done almost as soon as the keep stopped falling, and he got people to do it. I'd have taken longer. He's the one, Captain."

"I concur," Ryd replied. "Sergeant Tavnor, please continue in your duties. Know of my gratitude for your efforts to date. And now" he said, turning to Vernel, "I suspect there are things to be ordered, and others to be paid for, including my late brother's debts. I've brought coin enough. Let us sit down, you and Sergeant Tavnor and I, and see what is to be done."

He turned to the ten guardsmen who'd accompanied him. "Get yourselves settled in whatever housing is available, or set up tents if necessary. Then join these loyal guardsmen and share their duties. I'm sure they can use the relief." With that, he followed Vernel into the serv-ant's quarters, Tavnor following close behind.

Within half a turn of an hourglass, they'd sent for the cook. Within a full turn, Ryd dispatched Vernel and the cook on a shopping and bill-paying visit to the village. They were escorted by Tavnor and three other guardsmen, one driving a wagon, along with two young manservants to fetch and carry. Tavnor carried a small bag of gold coins and another of silver, with instructions for Vernel to pay all legitimate debts. Both Vernel and the cook smiled at that "legitimate"; their new lord was no fool.

Whatever doubts the villagers might harbor about their new lord would, Ryd knew, be settled by prompt payment of Rand's bills. Fair-ness and promptness in bill-paying would always win over a merchant.

As they should, though Ryd had not thought much about that before he'd run across Dog during those northern days as a mercenary.

That led him to wonder where Dog was. There were decisions to be made, and Dog had been his best counsellor for years, something the squat man preferred to keep secret. Perhaps the fellow was back at the inn. If that were the case, no doubt Rath and his retinue of dark wizards would be somewhere around as well. It would be easier to begin to set things right if the wizards would move on. If they were in pursuit of whoever had destroyed Rand's keep, they might take their time starting out. Even a wizard should think hard about following someone who could do this.

Ryd hadn't taken time to let the enormity of what had happened to Rand and his keep strike home. Now that he'd given orders that would begin the recovery, he was free to walk around the rubble.

He wouldn't miss the keep. What he'd enjoyed of his boyhood had mostly taken place beyond those stone walls, whether in the yard training with Talon and the guardsmen or wandering Gerlach's lands. The farmers had treated him with suspicion at first, but after a time came to realize that he was neither as arrogant as his older brother nor a spy for his father.

Later they watched him a little more carefully if their young daughters were attractive. Even that did not seem to bother them terribly; young men would behave like young men. If watched carefully enough, no harm would come of it. They didn't dream about their daughters becoming lady to Gerlach's younger son, though one or two of the daughters may have.

So Ryd came to know these lands far better than did his older brother. It had been some fifteen years since he'd left for good, as he thought then. He suspected he'd still know the land better than would Rand.

Now Rand lay buried beneath what had been his keep, and there would be little mourning. Standing next to the rubble, Rand said a soft, "Good-bye, brother." He couldn't help feeling even that might be more than Rand deserved.

There would be planning to do. These people would need more than wooden servants' quarters and an outdoor kitchen with winter only a few months away. He wasn't interested in building another keep. Something like the Manor of the Five Valleys would make much better sense, but he wasn't sure how far along that might be before the cold arrived.

It did not occur to Ryd that he might not claim the double lordship of these holdings and the Five Valleys. Now he realized that they would give him lordship of the entire northern edge of the country, from the cliffs on the far west to the river which bounded the lands of the blue Order.

He chuckled at that thought. His father had attempted to wrest the lordship of the Five Valleys from its rightful lord and had his own power broken as a result. Rand had spent his short life taking minor bits of land from lords to the south, then trying to hold those lands. Once things were settled here, assuming he didn't have to repulse a raid from the south, Ryd would meet with those southern lords. Surely they could come to an agreement to settle borders once and for all. He could recall well enough what the lines had been all those years before. He was inclined to settle for those.

Once he'd instituted the same system for recruiting and training guardsmen that worked so well in the Five Valleys, he'd have a defensive force many times the size of anything even the entire group of southern lords could raise. At that point, they'd probably spend their time raiding one another.

Ryd was still standing by the rubble, absently-mindedly gazing while he considered his new situation, when he heard the wagon returning.

Servants and guardsmen quickly began unloading. The cook supervised placement of pots and pans and other tools in the makeshift kitchen while Vernel oversaw movement of foodstuffs into the storehouse. Some servants carried what appeared to be clothing and bedding into the servants' and guardsmen's quarters. Well, of course, Ryd thought. Those who'd had quarters in the keep would have lost everything. He smiled; Vernel had done well.

Tavnor came back from carrying a load to the quarters. He saw Ryd watching. "My lord," he said, "I have what remains in the bags you entrusted to me." He went to the wagon, reached under the seat, and lifted out two bags which seemed heavier than Ryd would have expected. Vernel must have bargained extremely well.

Ryd held up a restraining hand. "Take them to the steward. He will no doubt need to make other purchases in the days to come, and he should not have to ask each time."

Tavnor, startled, said a quick "Yes, my lord." Evidently Rand had had learned no more of trust than Ryd remembered from their childhood. Surely a house steward must be worthy of trust.

Ryd waited until Tavnor had taken the bags of coins to Vernel, who looked to Ryd inquiringly. He accepted them only after seeing Ryd's nod of approval. The old man bowed deeply. There, Ryd thought, that was a servant whose loyalty would now be even stronger than it had been.

He waited until Tavnor came back for another load from the wagon before calling the young guardsman over. "I will also want to hear from you what is needed for your guard, so give it some thought. We'll no doubt have workmen in shortly, and I will welcome your suggestions as we plan buildings. These"—he gestured toward the servants' and guardsmen's quarters—"do not look to have been improved in the years since I was a boy. They were old even then. If we're going to build, we might as well make a job of it." He almost smiled at the look on Tavnor's face; clearly the man was not used to much consideration from his former master. "You might start a conversation with your guards and with Vernel about more suitable arrangements. We can talk about these things later. Let's meet today's needs."

At that, Tavnor bowed deeply and turned toward the wagon, only to see that it had been emptied. A guardsman was driving it toward another outbuilding which held a carriage as well as another wagon. Ryd watched with interest as the man guided the horse along the front of the building, turning away at just the right moment to place the wagon before an empty space. A servant—probably the hostler—came forward and unharnessed the horse, then led it to the stables while another gathered up harness and followed. Two guardsmen came to join the man who'd driven the wagon. The three of them backed the wagon into the shelter, leaving it positioned for quick harnessing when next needed.

Ryd smiled, stepped forward and called, "Well done!" to the three. They beamed as though given a great honor. They'd soon enough become accustomed to praise. That would make accepting instruction or even blame that much easier, so long as they felt all three were warranted.

Behind him Ryd heard the sound of pounding. When he turned, he saw Vernel overseeing the setting-up of a large canopy. At his look of inquiry, the steward explained. "I thought we would need a shelter large enough to allow meals on inclement days. Between meals, it might serve as a temporary meeting space and great hall for your use, my Lord."

Ryd nodded. "A wise thought, indeed. What of tables? Rand's would be under the rubble, of course."

"I had thought of that, my lord. There is a good carpenter in the village. He could make us, say, fifteen or so with benches, and a suitable seat for your use as well."

"We may dispense with a suitable seat, but tables and benches make sense. He may want funds with which to pay for wood. Will he accept half now and the other half as he delivers, do you think?"

Vernel chuckled. "Oh yes, my lord. He's used to being paid some time after he makes a delivery—meaning no disrespect." Vernel looked worried.

Laughing, Ryd answered, "Do not concern yourself. I knew my brother well. If he couldn't avoid paying for something, he would pay as late as possible. Still, it would not be good to speak too freely of his ways. I would rather our people look forward than back."

"I will take care, my lord, to keep their minds focused and their tongues under control. They've already begun to praise you, if I may say so. Most will need only the occasional reminder to speak little of those who are no longer with us."

Ryd bowed at that. Vernel signaled Tavnor to join him. Then Tavnor went to the stables and came back with two saddle horses. The two mounted and rode off toward town. A cough from behind caught his attention and Ryd turned to see Scar.

"Well, Captain, would you like to see your quarters? It's the best we can do, the keep bein' out of service, so to speak. Still, it's better than some places we slept in the old days."

Both smiled at the memory. Then Ryd answered with false formality which brought another smile to Scar's face, "Indeed, that will be most satisfactory."

Scar turned and Ryd followed him to the guardsmen's quarters. They entered the room closest to the road. As Ryd looked around, he was certain this had been the sergeant's quarters. It was larger than the usual guardsman's room, with a table and chair as well as a decent-looking bed.

Nodding, Ryd turned to Scar. "Thanks for remaining. This Tavnor seems a good choice, but I think your support will be important. There is much to do, and we may yet have to deal with raids. What think you of the other guardsmen who've remained?"

"They're the best of the lot. If I'd had my pick of all fifty, it would have been these ten. That looks like a good bunch you brought with you. With them added, we've already enough to handle anything that might come up from the south. And as for thieves, they have only to see a well-disciplined troop and they'll give us a chase before we take them,." He caught himself then. "But maybe a lord doesn't care for as much opinion as did a captain."

"No fear," Ryd smiled. "I have no quarrel with honest opinion. For that matter, I'd rather be called captain than lord, if I could have my way. I share your value for those who came with me, and my value for those already here is just as high. Our people will be well protected, here and on the farms and in the village as well."

Scar smiled broadly now. "Them's good words to hear, Captain."

Ryd made a gesture of dismissal, and Scar gave him another of those head-bobs which served as his version of a salute and walked out, whistling.

***

Oleg's apprentices brought him more references to the Red Forest than he had expected. There were tales of dark wizards finding their powers useless in that place and fragmentary mentions of beings with powers unaffected by the forest. None of this was good news.

He waited until evening to report, hoping better news from Lorit might improve Soren's mood. The only truly good news Oleg could imagine wouldn't please the Chief Mage: that they'd lost track of the child. Perhaps Lorit would be intelligent enough to realize that losing her trail would be his safest course. Alas, he'd find that difficult with a revenge-hungry Rath at his side.

What if they did catch her? If wizards could not harm her, might she still be vulnerable to arrows fired by guardsmen? Oleg hated to ask the dark being such a question; it reeked of desperation. The Dark One would need little additional reason to think their situation was desperate.

Oleg entered the observatory to find Soren pacing up and down. Haster stood very quietly near the wall furthest from the great crystal. At Oleg's entrance, Soren stopped pacing: "Well?" he demanded.

Oleg shrugged. "The Dark One offers us nothing useful, though he said more this time than is usual for him. This witch-child clearly interests him. The little my apprentices have found about this forest does not contradict his words."

"What does he say of this child?" Haster asked, impatient.

"Much and yet little. He says that her power is great. We knew that. When told of the keep's destruction and the death of Rand, this second death clearly surprised him. He speculated that she might destroy this building, or instead destroy only our Order. His greatest hope seems to be that once we are gone, our wards over his cell will fail. He hopes to live long enough to return to the surface."

Soren was red-faced with rage. "He said that? He spoke of our destruction?"

Again Oleg shrugged. "Would it not take our destruction for him to escape? He will have thought of little else in all these years. Should our wards fail, he will have vengeance." When Soren made no response, the Loremaster continued. "It was by luck that he fell under our control. Our predecessors' attempt to poison him at least succeeded in blocking his powers. Fortunately, they left us the list of poisons which keep him powerless." Oleg leaned forward, his voice emphatic. "He has no reason, Chief Mage, to play the courtier and speak only what we would wish to hear. That makes him no pleasure to speak with. It also makes some of what he tells me useful."

"So," Soren was deadly calm now, "he has suggested no weakness, nothing we might use against her?"

"Only one: that she may not yet have grown into her full powers."

Haster erupted: "Not yet have grown into her full powers? What powers does he think she has not yet shown?"

"That he does not say. He did speak of this Red Forest." Oleg spoke slowly. "The ancient Druids visited it to restore their strength. Those woods were a place of power strong enough to negate that of any dark wizard who might enter." He paused, let what he'd said sink in. "Chief Mage, if that is true, should we not warn Lorit and those with him to stay out of that forest?"

Soren bowed his head in thought. "There is merit in what you say, Loremaster. Yet it seems to me that if this child and her brother do not understand her power, now is the time to attack. If her powers grow greater while she's in the forest, it would be worth even the sacrifice of another of our Order to drive her forth. Once she is in the open we may yet learn how to cope with this witch-child. We have not yet seen whether arrows or blades can harm her.

"No." Soren straightened. "We will not speak of this to Lorit. And when—if—we do, it may be to tell him to send Roke or Tarh into the forest to flush her out." He paused, rubbing his chin. "Yes. We will hold this for a time. When we do speak, it will be to Lorit alone. I do not fully trust Rath. Tarh was his best apprentice only recently. Rath might wish to spare him a walk in that forest."

Oleg rather doubted that. Rath's heart was darker even than Soren's. Until this recent set-back, he had also been perhaps more powerful. Oleg had been careful not to alienate the wizard, just in case the One-Hand decided to replace Soren. Though he suspected he could stand up to either Soren or Rath should that become necessary, Oleg hoped it would not. Destroying a Chief Mage meant becoming the successor. The duties of that position did not interest him.

"What news this night from Lorit?" Oleg asked, more to change the subject than for any other purpose.

"Little," Soren answered. "He has sent Roke and Tarh to search along the eastern edge of the forest while he and Rath follow the trail north. He divided their guardsmen between the two groups. Roke is to inform us should he come across the child. We will pass word to Lorit."

"He keeps Rath with him, then," Oleg noted. "An interesting choice."

"I also wondered about that," Haster said. "But Rath is still recovering, and in his weakness may let his wish for revenge overcome his judgment."

"Rath and Tarh," Soren noted, "have had the most direct experience of the witch-child's wrath, though Lorit has seen enough of the child's power to take no chances. Roke is the least certain of the four. He may not listen to Tarh should they encounter the child." He considered that possibility. "Still, Tarh has survived one encounter with the witch and should be cautious enough to survive another. If so, he can tell us how Roke fares. Eventually we may learn enough to counter her power, even if we cannot break it."

***

By the second day, travel through the woods had become less interesting to Bird, though she didn't display the restlessness to which Aren had grown accustomed. She seemed thoughtful, even a little distant. When they paused for a brief noon meal, Aren asked her what she'd been thinking about all morning. Brenna leaned forward a little, listening.

"Well," Bird took a bite of her bread, then added a bite of cheese, while she considered. "I'm not sure. It seems--I don't know--as though I'm more myself here."

Aren recognized another of Reya's phrases: 'I'm not myself today,' or more often, 'I feel more myself than I did yesterday, thank goodness.' "What do you mean, little bird?"

"I guess—well-- I feel better about having these—these things I can do." She looked down at the ground for a while before going on. "As though I could do something besides just smash and kill. But I don't know what." She looked over at Aren. "I wish I could figure that part out."

Aren nodded. "I also wish it, little bird."

Brenna spoke up then. "I feel something similar, Bird. Maybe I always felt it in this forest, but didn't know what I was feeling. My powers, weak and unreliable as they've always been, feel stronger here. I almost believe I could control them." She hesitated. "I don't really want to try. I've failed too many times already."

Bird listened attentively as Brenna spoke. She turned to Aren. "Remember when I said she wasn't a dark wizard, but I couldn't tell what sort she was? And that maybe she didn't know what she was either?" She faced Brenna. "I can almost tell. Maybe in another day I will."

Brenna smiled, though only slightly. "I'd be grateful for that. Still, it may be that I'm no more than a half-wizard, best suited to work in an apothecary's shop and mix potions for my betters. I'm tempted to return across the river to see if my old master might help me find that sort of work. If it would be acceptable, Aren, I'd travel at least as far as the river with you. It might be that my little power added to Bird's would be useful, though it might also make us easier to find. If we move separately, they might not find either, or might find only one."

That ended the conversation. As they travelled through the forest, Bird and even Brenna had almost forgotten who followed. Now the reality of their situation returned, full force.

"Well," Aren said, breaking the silence. "We'll have tonight and tomorrow to consider. Let's see what, if anything, lies in wait for us at the forest edge. I have no objection, Brenna, should you decide to accompany us as far as the river and beyond. From what you've said of the Blue Order, they would not hunt us as do these dark wizards. Perhaps you might introduce us."

Brenna smiled at that. "They might not trust my introduction, given how I left them. My master would greet me cordially, at least, so long as I wasn't asking to be reinstated. He would do the same for you as well,

I'm certain. I will consider more fully whether returning across the river is my best course. Surely it is a wise step for you, Bird, and your brother. There you'll at least be safe from the dark Order."

***

As he and Dog approached, Snake saw that Lorit had not ordered a full camp. A dying fire suggested that a meal had been eaten, and both Rath and the guardsmen lay stretched on bedrolls. There were no tents.

Apparently Lorit been eager for their report. He'd taken the first watch, difficult as Snake found that to believe. Even if the wizard were unable to rest, he'd normally have required one of the guards to serve as watch.

"Well?" Lorit called when they were still some twenty feet away.

"Maaaster Dog found their trail easily enough. We tracked them to a clearing where they spent the night. From signs, they left early this morning, headed east."

Lorit nodded. "Trying to reach the lands of the blue Order, no doubt. Roke and Tarh should interfere with that. I wish I could get a message to them; neither my crystal nor Rath's will work this close to the forest."

"If I may be so bold, Master?" Snake asked, seeing the opportunity to forward Dog's plan.

"What is it, man?" Lorit replied.

"Master Dog and I could go ahead with a message. We can follow the trail until we're certain the pair intend no change of direction, then leave the forest. Surely we can move rapidly enough in open country to reach your brother wizards before they can."

Lorit sighed. "That will have to do. Tell them to do whatever they can to impede the witch-child's movement."

Snake bowed. "We will depart, Master, and report to you as we may." He turned to Dog, who'd been apparently dozing nearby, and shouted, "You, fellow! Up! We have more to do this night!"

Dog came grumbling to his feet, shooting a grin in Snake's direction once Lorit turned away. They started again into the forest.

Dog set an even faster pace than on their first visit to the woods. As before Snake found that he could keep up a far faster pace in the squat man's company than he'd have been capable of otherwise.

Soon Dog led the way back out of the forest. Glancing back in the growing dark, Snake saw that they were out of sight of the wizards. He wondered if Lorit had yet been able to jolt his group into more movement. Rath might insist on a longer rest, though dark wizards were apt to gain strength and travel faster in the night.

The two trotted on without speaking. Early the next morning they came within sight of the forest's eastern end. Dog slowed, looking about carefully. "Now find young wizards."

***

By the time he and Tarh and their followers came within sight of the Red Forest, Roke had formed a plan. The witch-child might destroy a wizard or a lord, or a tower or keep, but she ignored guardsmen. Surely a wise wizard would send his guards into the forest. Even if the child could not be harmed by arrow or sword, that would not be true of her guardian. If she truly were some re-born being of power which had chosen a child's body, she might also have a child's mind. Left alone, she might not know what course to pursue.

Roke didn't bother confiding his plan to Tarh. The younger wizard might have objected. Roke wanted to try his cunning against this witch-being as soon as possible.

It was nearing evening, a poor time to send guardsmen into a strange forest. Nonetheless, he gave them their orders. Should they not return, he and Tarh would at least know the witch-child was nearby.

Roke took his crystal from his pack and attempted to contact Soren and report. The crystal didn't brighten; instead, it took on a reddish glow and showed nothing. Tarh tried his crystal, with much the same result. This Red Forest, then, did have some sort of power which interfered with that of crystals, or with the power of those who attempted their use. The two looked at one another, worry in their eyes. Neither spoke of their fears as they settled down to wait for the guardsmen who had gone into the forest.

***

Soren was furious. He'd had no report from Lorit or Rath, nor from Roke or Tarh. When he tried to contact them, his great crystal showed only an unsettling red glow. He'd scanned the area where they should be, well to the north of the East Road. Close to the road, he could see the countryside as usual, but his view became less clear the further north he scanned. Finally the landscape disappeared into that same red glow.

Oleg, sitting back in one of Soren's padded chairs while he watched the Chief Mage' anger grow, offered an observation: "It seems that what the Dark One said about that forest being a place of power was true. Something neutralizes your crystal, and I would expect it will do the same to the lesser crystals carried by our travelers. It will be," he said, rising to his feet, "interesting to see whether the forest has some effect on the witch-child. Had we bothered to learn more of that forest, we might have seen that she would be drawn to it. The question now becomes, is this her final goal or merely a pause in her journey? The old scrolls say nothing of any beings there who might teach this child. That at least is something. Her power may grow stronger, but at least she will learn no more about its uses."

"That's little enough solace," grumbled Haster, who'd been carefully keeping out of Soren's way and, as much as possible, out of his field of vision.

"But for us to be left blind!" Soren said. "For all we know, they've met the witch-child."

"You could send someone north after them, with orders to relay news," Haster suggested.

"It would take days, if indeed a seeker could find them. Who knows which way they'll go around or through that place?" Soren was in no mood for one of Haster's suggestions.

Oleg smiled unpleasantly. "I doubt they'll go through the forest. Once they realize that their crystals are powerless nearby, one of them will explore whether distance will allow a crystal to function. I'd expect that from Lorit or perhaps Tarh, if the presence of the forest hasn't affected their thinking. We know little, after all, about the forest's power other than that it exists, as we have proof in your crystal's red glow." He frowned. "We could have been investigating that forest, plumbing its depths, all these years."

"This isn't a learning experience for your apprentices, Loremaster," Soren said, his face sour. "Let us weep over lost opportunities another time."

Oleg inclined his head in acknowledgement, looking down until he'd managed to cease scowling. Soren was a power-hungry fool; a man of intelligence would have realized that knowledge led to power. No wonder Rath, himself a serious student of the old scrolls and of power of every sort, was rumored to have ambitions to replace Soren. Rath might not be ambitious at all, merely aware that Soren was becoming an impediment to the Order's survival.

"No," Soren said, "we will wait a day or even two. If by then they do not contact us, we may have to send someone. I'd as soon this remain unknown as long as possible, though the fall of Rand's keep makes that unlikely. No doubt rumor will reach the rest of our bothers soon enough. Some are already made uneasy by tales of Rath's injury and the breaking of his drought. Would I had never approved that scheme," he grumbled.

Would you had never conceived it and assigned it to Rath, Oleg thought. Rath will not like being made scapegoat if this turns out as badly as is likely, should he or Soren survive. The dark being in the dungeon believed the witch-child might turn this place into rubble. Where might a member of the Order seek refuge, should the witch-child turn her attention and her path toward the Order's headquarters?

***

They'd swung slightly south as Brenna led her companions along. "It's not far to the eastern edge now, or at least the edge nearest the river. The forest bends north and east before long, but if we're to make the river, we'll want to leave it soon."

Before Aren could respond, Bird spoke up. "There are dark wizards ahead. Two of them. Ahead and a little south. I don't think they're in the forest."

Aren pulled Blaze to a halt. "How far off are they, little bird? Can you tell?"

Brenna had turned to face Bird, her face ashen.

"They're pretty close," Bird said. "I could feel them coming yesterday, but I hoped they'd go on by, or turn away from the forest. It doesn't like them much."

Brenna's eyebrows raised at that. The forest didn't like these dark wizards? As a child, she'd sometimes pretended that the forest was alive in ways others forests weren't, but that had been a child's game, a child's imagining. Or, she thought now, maybe not; maybe her child's mind had perceived something her adult mind could not. Bird, though a child, had real powers, and some child-like things she'd said had turned out to be true. Perhaps she could commune with the forest in some way beyond Brenna's understanding.

"Didn't you know?" Bird asked her, as though she'd heard Brenna's thoughts, a smile replacing the seriousness with which she'd made her announcement about the nearness of members of the Order. "The forest likes you. It made that shelter for you."

Aren tried to ignore this latest revelation and keep focused on nearby wizards. "You said these wizards are close. Are they coming toward us?"

Bird closed her eyes, concentrating. "No. They're staying put. The ones behind us are coming this way, but they're pretty far off. I don't think they can catch up very soon." She concentrated again for a moment; then her eyes turned slate-gray. "One of them is that fellow from the tower who tried to stop our rain. I thought he learned his lesson!" Again she sounded for a moment just like Reya, using one of Reya's favorite lines whenever anyone repeated an action which had previously turned out badly.

Aren and Brenna exchanged glances before Aren spoke. "If there are wizards before and behind us, perhaps we should move north and east a little before trying to leave the forest. I doubt they can find us in here, even with their crystals. But they could send their guards to look. It would be good to move away from the forest's edge. We might as well make it as difficult for them as we can."

Brenna agreed and began leading them further into the forest. After a time, she spoke again, hesitantly. "With dark wizards this close, you may not be able to reach the river and the lands of the blue Order. If we continue north east, this forest comes close to the Barren Lands. There you could evade any searchers, from what little I know."

Aren looked searchingly at the apprentice. "What are these Barren Lands? Our home is in the west. Rand's holdings are further than most valley farmers have travelled. For us, these are unknown lands—forests of red oaks, coastlands with blue wizards, and now barrens?"

Brenna was surprised. "Not heard of the Barren Lands? Well, perhaps not. They lie north and east of Rand's holdings. No one claims them, though Rand probably would have insisted they were his."

For a while she rode in silence, thinking. Finally she spoke as though musing to herself. "The Barren Lands. No one knows much. They're a land of fogs and mists and yet not fertile. Blue wizards have attempted to explore them, but with little success; returning, they report being lost for days in the fogs before finding their way back out. Little grows there, they say. My master claimed that the dark Order had also tried to explore those lands, but with no more success, though dark wizards are rumored to see in the dark better than others. Still, he suggested, not even dark wizards can see through fog."

Bird asked, "Does no one live there?"

Brenna shrugged. "Stories claim there are shadowy figures in gray robes who avoid travelers or perhaps lead them astray. My master said he'd spoken with one very old wizard who had attempted to explore the Barrens. He'd gotten lost in the fog, but claimed he'd been guided out by one of the shadowy figures. He'd not seen the fellow clearly, though he could hear someone ahead of him in the mist. Since he was hopelessly lost he followed, hoping at least for food and a place to sleep. Eventually the mists thinned and he could see clear patches ahead. Soon he was out.

"When he looked back he thought he saw a figure turning away into the wasteland. Then the fog thickened again, rolling toward him, and, he told my master, he hastened away. My master asked how far into the barrens the old one had gotten and whether he had any sense of the size of the place. The old man chuckled, saying he might have been walking in circles in the same small piece of land the whole time." Brenna smiled. "He was never tempted to return."

"It doesn't sound very promising," Aren noted. "But if we're cut off by our pursuers, we may have no choice."

"Well, advice from a failed apprentice may not be the most useful, but if the stories are true, you'd be safe from wizards of any sort. If anyone does live there, they must have chosen exile long ago. Perhaps found it a place of refuge from the various border wars or even the dark Order itself. If they entered the place long enough ago, they may have preserved memories of Druids and other powerful beings.

"But," she finished, "you must make your own plans. What I do not know I cannot be forced to tell, should it develop that the Order is less wary of this forest than they have seemed. They may have never had a reason to enter this woods; now you have provided one, they may brave the place."

This disturbed Aren. "We would not have entered the place had we thought we would bring the Order down upon you. I would have taken our chances by riding east and past the forest rather than endanger our guide."

Bird spoke up. "It's bad enough they're chasing us! We don't want them after anyone else. And they would try to hurt you, too, just for helping us. Oh, I don't like dark wizards! I wish—" she broke off at the look on Aren's face. "I didn't say 'hope,' just 'wish.' Wishes don't make anything happen, you know."

"I know, little bird," Aren replied. "But a heartfelt wish from you might carry more weight than you think. It's better not to take any chances."

Brenna interrupted. "Should the Order come into the forest after me, I can retreat to the north and go into the mountains. It could make sense to do so in any case. Perhaps I would do better as an apprentice green wizard. They might know more about controlling an unruly power than do blue wizards, who are a civilized lot for the most part. Green wizards are said to live in caves and huts in the forest." She smiled. "I have options, should life in this forest become untenable."

"Well," Bird said, "I hope dark wizards stay out of this forest, so there!" She looked defiantly at Aren's frowning face. "That didn't threaten anyone, now, did it? I didn't call down lightning, or anything."

Aren shook his head wearily. "Bird, we don't know how that hope might be enforced. But it's been said, and I have no idea whether you can take something back once you've said it. I'd rather you not make any trials. But do be careful. If dark wizards can track power, as Brenna's blue master tracked her by her use of power, your hoping may lead them to us."

Bird's head drooped, her shoulders slumped. "I'm sorry," she whispered. "I didn't mean to do anything bad."

"And you didn't," Brenna responded. "It was a very generous hope, and I thank you."

At that, Bird looked a little less despondent, though Aren still scowled.

After a time, Aren asked Brenna, "Know you any offensive or defensive spells, should their guards find us? I can fight off two or perhaps three, I believe, but more than that number would present a problem."

Brenna hung her head. "I'm afraid not. I might be able to cause one to slow or be distracted long enough for you to strike, but that's about all."

"It could well be enough. Consider what spells you have and be prepared. Bird," he said, turning to the child, "ride on my left side; if they come at us, it will probably be from the right, from the forest's edge."

****

Roke's two guardsmen went grumbling into the woods. This business of going where wizards wished not to enter did not sound promising. Their instructions were clear: seek out the guardsman and the witch-child. Test whether the child could be hurt by arrows or sword. In any case, injure or kill the guardsman. Neither chore sounded promising. If this child could order a lord to die and his keep to fall in on him, she might destroy them with a look.

They moved carefully through the sparse brush, watching for any movement. Their only chance would be to see her before she saw them.

If they were unlucky enough to come upon the pair, one would fire at the child and the other at the guardsman. Perhaps both arrows would strike and they could return with the good news.

They would need to survive in order to report. Their knowledge would do the wizards little good were they both lying dead somewhere in a forest their masters refused to enter. If they were to wait long enough to see their arrows' effects, they might as well fire a second time before running. Unless the first arrows had no effect, in which case they'd better just run. Their quarry might take a moment to realize from where the arrows had been fired. That might make all the difference.

So they had a plan of sorts. They moved silently as they could manage through the forest. They'd come further than they'd planned before the older stopped, held up a hand, listened. There it was again. Something large was walking toward them. Though their masters could not ride horses, they knew the fugitives did. These sounded like horses. Walking, not running, toward them. The shot would be easier if the pair walked their horses. A little girl would be especially difficult to hit on a galloping horse. A guardsman would be none too easy, either.

CHAPTER SIX

Aren watched carefully as they rode. Though trees in this forest were large and far apart with little brush between them, they weren't spaced for far-seeing. Each was thick enough to block a good portion of the view. He kept Bird to his left, away from where trouble might come. Brenna walked a little ahead, hoping to offer some hindrance to anything coming from that direction. This wasn't her quarrel, and she knew what her master would have said about coming between members of the dark Order and their quarry. Nonetheless, she'd grown fond of this child.

The Order's guards were skilled at ambushes. They found spots behind two oaks more than wide enough to keep them from sight. Near each grew a patch of brush large enough for a kneeling man to wait behind, his bow ready, an arrow nocked. They hoped they were close enough to where the riders would pass. They'd had to guess from what they'd heard approaching through the forest.

A woman on foot came through the trees, which nearly caused them to curse at having found the wrong travelers. She was followed by the guardsman, clearly on alert. The child was barely visible behind him. Something had warned them. Perhaps the witch-child had sensed their presence. Both fired as soon as both guardsman and child were fully visible. Each nocked a second arrow as they watched for the effect of their first shots.

Aren cursed as an arrow went deeply into his side; he knew immediately that he was badly hurt. Bird was luckier, though she would not consider it luck. The arrow meant for her struck Pony instead, driving deeply into his neck. The small horse stumbled, then fell. Bird was barely able to throw herself just beyond his falling body.

Brenna turned, shocked and furious. She saw the two assailants raising their bows for another shot and reacted without thinking. As she'd done on her final day as an apprentice when she raised the entire cookhouse roof, she reached out, willing the two men to rise as she lifted and pushed.

To her amazement, the two men were thrown upwards and away, flying a good thirty feet in the air until they slammed against oaks. Brenna didn't watch to see whether they survived. She turned her attention first to Bird. The child appeared unhurt. She had crawled over to the dying Pony and sat weeping, her arms around the little animal's neck. Aren had fallen from his horse and lay bleeding, both hands clutching the arrow.

Brenna knew a little healing, but nothing about dealing with wounds of this sort. "What can I do?" she asked.

"Not much," Aren grunted. "We need bandages before you pull this arrow out." He grunted with pain. "There's not much time."

At the groan, Bird realized that her brother was hurt. She cried out, "Help him! Fix him!"

Brenna spread her hands helplessly. "Child, it would take a Druid skilled in healing to mend this wound. I have not the skill."

"Then a Druid had better come!" Bird shouted.

The air shimmered. A moment later a tall white-robed figure stood before her, looking around in confusion. "What?" she said, "Where?" She saw Bird. "Mother! Why have you called me?"

"I'm not your mother!" Bird shouted. "My brother is hurt! Help him!"

The Druid turned, saw Aren on the verge of losing consciousness. Quickly she stepped over to the fallen man, knelt, and grasped the arrow. Singing, she gently pulled the shaft until the arrow was out. Still singing, she placed both hands over the still-bleeding wound. She looked up at Bird. "Mother, you might call on the wound to heal."

Bird, a little shocked still at what she had already called, nodded. "I hope the wound heals quickly," she said. "I hope it stops bleeding."

The Druid looked a little surprised at her choice of words, but nodded.

Brenna took a small knife from her belt and begun slicing bandages from her robe. She handed those to the white-robed woman. The Druid took the bandages and wrapped the wound. "That should do," she said. "With the Mother's word that the wound heal, he should be safe."

Bird had time now for weeping as she reached for her brother. She knelt and touched his forehead. "Oh, Aren," she said between sobs, "I'm so sorry I caused all this trouble. I'm so sorry."

Aren tried a smile. "It's not your fault, little bird. It's those wizards who're causing all the trouble." He tried to rise, but the tall figure in white held him down.

"You'd best not move for a while. You've lost a lot of blood."

"What about those archers?" Aren asked. "They'll attack again!"

Brenna, still shaking from the power which had surged through her, replied. "I don't think they'll be back. Somehow I found the power to throw them." She laughed without humor. "They'll be badly broken, I think."

"Still," said the white figure, "we should check. If they attacked once, they'll no doubt try again. Where were they?"

"They came from that direction," Brenna said, pointing south.

The figure in white nodded, then turned to Bird and Aren. "Mother, would you stay with him? We'll not be gone long. Summon us if anything happens."

Bird was about to tell her again that she certainly wasn't anyone's mother, but at that moment Aren heaved a deep sigh. Her attention turned to him.

Brenna and the Druid walked cautiously toward where the guardsmen had been. They came across arrows scattered where they'd fallen from quivers, among them two bows. Further on they found the broken body of one guardsmen, and a trail where the other had dragged himself away. There was blood here and there on branches he'd grasped to pull himself to his feet for a few steps before falling again. They followed long enough to be certain he wasn't coming back.

Brenna had begun to think again, and most of her thoughts were questions. "Where did you come from? We'd have lost Aren without you."

"I was floating as part of the breeze and drifted this way. I dimly remembered red oaks from long ago, so I gladly became part of the forest, living within one tree or another. The trees healing power radiates, though they seem almost asleep. In another day your friend may be walking. He won't run for a time."

"You—you were floating on the breeze and then became part of the forest? What are you? No wizard could become part of the forest."

"I wasn't floating on the breeze. I was part of it. I've been part of many things since the Mother sent us back into the earth." The tall woman paused for a moment, remembering, a look of longing on her face. "The Mother had need of a healer and called, so I came." She looked around at the woods. "It is strange to wear this form again after so long. Limited, and yet I see the world in some ways more fully." She was quiet. "And you? I had not seen a red wizard. But no doubt time has passed since I last walked this land."

Brenna was trying to make sense of her words. What mother? And how 'back into the earth?' It took her a moment to reply. "I'm not sure there is such a thing as a red wizard. I was a failed apprentice with the blue Order. After I was dismissed, I didn't know where else to go, but often as a child I spent time here."

"Ah, the blue Order. I recall their beginnings. They were healers then. Are they still healers now, or have they fallen away?"

She recalled the beginnings of the blue Order? What sort of being was this? Brenna hesitated. "They're still healers, though they study other kinds of power as well. What sort of being are you? Were you really around at the blue Order's beginning?"

The tall one smiled. "I was a Druid, when I walked this land with other Druids and the Mother. Apparently I am a Druid again, or still. Healing was my interest—finding a sick tree, leaning into it, finding the source of its troubles, sending health from root to tip. Or coming upon a limping animal, calming it, sending my thought into its bad leg, and guiding its healing. I watched the early efforts of those blue-robed wizards and approved. The Mother said we were not to guide them and so I only observed." She looked at Brenna. "My name, to the extent we used names, was Hobard. I suppose that will do now as well."

"Who is this mother you speak of? How did she call you?"

It was Hobard's turn to wonder. "Who is she? I know not why she has taken the form of a child. To a Druid, her form does not matter; we would know her in any form. Surely you heard her call. She would not have needed to speak, so perhaps you did not."

They returned to the scene of the attack. Bird was singing softly, a lullaby, and Aren appeared to be sleeping. Hobard walked to Bird's side, knelt, felt Aren's forehead and listened for a moment to his breathing. "Ah," she said, "he's sleeping comfortably, and with less fever than I might have expected. But then," here she smiled at Bird, "he's had the best care possible, has he not?"

"Oh," Bird said, "I thank you so much for coming. I didn't know if anyone would really come, but I was hoping so hard. And there you were."

Hobard laughed happily. "You called, and I came. Had another been nearby, that one would have come just as quickly. It has been long since any of us met with you. To be in your presence again cheers my heart, my lady."

"Now you're not making any sense. I'm not a lady, I'm just a little girl. And I'm certainly not anyone's mother, either. My name is Bird, and this is my big brother."

Hobard was silent. "Then that is how it will be, lady Bird. I am Hobard. As always, I am your loyal helper."

"Well, that's good, then," Bird replied, "because I think we'll need your help. There are dark wizards after us. Two to the south, two more coming up from behind. Those men must have been with them."

Hobard's face clouded. "The dark Order still exists, then, and still behaves unwisely."

"They certainly do, and I don't like them at all. They won't leave us alone."

For a time Hobard was silent, thinking, before she spoke again. "Your brother may be able to ride by morning. If necessary I can carry him, or can craft a litter. This is a place of power, and our friend here," she gestured toward Brenna standing a little ways off, "is connected to it. She may use that power to protect."

Bird looked at Brenna and nodded. "Now I know what kind of wizard you are! I didn't know that kind existed. When you fought those men, your robe blazed red." She paused for a moment, looking Brenna up and down. Placing hands on hips, she said, in her best Reya fashion, "Well, that's settled. You're a red wizard." After another moment she asked, "Are there many red wizards?"

Brenna stifled nervous laughter. "So far as I know, one—if that's what I've become."

Hobard reminded them, "If a number of dark wizards are gathering, it would be wise to move on before they arrive. Unless they've grown in power far beyond what any would have guessed, they could do little against any of us, but they may bring more warriors." She stood.

"This has been a hard day for all three of you, but you are not safe here. We will move further into the forest. Then you may rest. I will watch, and the forest shall watch also. We will know if any approach."

Bird turned toward the horses, only then recalling that Pony had been struck by an arrow. With a cry, she dashed to the little horse, knelt and tried to raise the pony's head. She looked up at Hobard and asked in a small voice, "Can you do anything for him?"

Slowly Hobard came near, shaking her head. "I am afraid not, my lady. The poor beast passed on while we tended to your brother. There is nothing we can do."

Hobard waited a while as Bird wept, then reminded her again that they needed to move on. The girl rose, and with one look back at Pony, followed as Hobard gently lifted Aren. Brenna led them further into the woods.

***

Roke and Tarh grew more worried as the night came on and their scouts did not return from the forest. Perhaps, Roke thought, it would have been wiser to have the two report back before taking any action. At least he would know the witch-child's location. If both had been destroyed, he'd have some explaining to do when Lorit and Rath arrived. Nott that any explanation would do him much good.

Finally they heard a rough movement in the woods. Both walked forward cautiously. Dark wizards could see more in the night than could most, but they did not wish to be surprised. Their prey might have destroyed the guardsmen, then tracked them back to this camp.

The noise turned out to be one guardsmen, bruised and battered, bloody from a score of cuts and bruises. He dragged one leg behind him as he crawled, pulling himself from bush to bush.

The guard who'd remained in camp passed the wizards, half running to assist his comrade. He supported the battered man back to camp, laid him down by the small fire, brought him a sack of wine. The wizards followed, waited until the man had taken one long drink before beginning their questioning.

The guardsman held back nothing, though his tale was often interrupted by groans. Yes, they'd found the pair, but a third person, a woman, was with them. She must have been the walker they met on the road. The woman had worn an apprentice's robe. As ordered, they had fired arrows. His had struck the guardsman, who'd fallen from his horse. The other's arrow struck the pony on which the child rode. It had fallen.

They'd just nocked their second arrows when the apprentice waved her hands and they were thrown into the air. He didn't know how far away they'd landed. Raf had not moved; his neck was broken. No, he hadn't tried to bring Raf as well. It had been all he could do to drag himself back. In the morning they could bring his body out if the wizards wished. Raf could rot there in the woods for all he cared; he had no wish to enter that place again.

No, he hadn't seen how badly the guardsman was hurt. He didn't know whether the child was injured when her horse fell. But this was odd: he was certain that as the strange woman gestured, her robe suddenly glowed red, a deeper red than that of the forest light. He was sure he'd seen that, and also sure she'd worn an apprentice's robe when he first saw her.

Roke told the remaining guardsman to make the fellow as comfortable as he could. The two wizards walked off a ways to consider. This was news of value. If the guardsman were wounded, surely the child would travel more slowly, if she travelled at all. Perhaps they would wait while he recovered. The presence of this woman, apparently another witch, was a problem. Her robe glowed red? If there were a red Order, it had been kept secret. In this forest a red wizard would be a formidable foe.

In the morning they could send their remaining guardsman into the trees to see what he could learn. If this battered fellow were up to it, he could guide. This time, no attacks until they'd come back and reported.

"And now," Tarh said, "I think it is time I take my crystal and walk away from this forest until my crystal clears. We must report this to Soren, who may be able to contact Lorit with the news. If not, he and Rath will catch up to us sooner or later."

Roke agreed, though he'd have liked to be the one to report. On the other hand,, if Soren chose to be upset at this word, it might be better to let Tarh take the brunt. As leader of this part of their group, he should stay in camp and supervise.

So it was Tarh who walked into the night, stopping every quarter mile to take his crystal out and attempt to contact Soren. Finally, a half-dozen miles from the forest, the crystal responded to his will with its usual glow. He was able to call out to Soren's great crystal.

***

For the second day in a row, Soren's crystal glowed red whenever he tried to contact either pair of wizards. "Surely by now they'll have thought to send someone away from the cursed forest to report!" He started to aim a kick at the wooden frame which held the crystal, thought better of it and kicked his desk instead. Though the hour was only mid-afternoon, he'd grown too impatient to wait any longer to send for Oleg to share his and Haster's discomfort. Sometimes the Loremaster offered sage advice. Unlike Haster, he wouldn't shy away from pointing out hazards. While that was irritating, it was also useful.

"Perhaps" Oleg noted, "one of our brothers is only now walking away from the forest. They will not know, after all, just how far they must go. There may have been little to report, which could be a good sign. After all, they are not likely have entered the forest themselves. They'll have sent their guards or Snake and his minion . It may be some time before their servants return."

"If they return," said a sour Haster. "If they encounter this witch-child in a killing mood, they may die right there. Or return under compulsion to kill our members."

"That would not be easy," Oleg said. "Even Roke and Tarh are skilled enough to freeze guardsmen where they stand. I think we must be patient. No doubt Lorit and Rath must travel along the forest's edge as they pursue the pair. It will take the younger wizards a little longer, no doubt, to realize that they must report no matter how difficult reporting has become."

"Enough!" roared Soren. "If we must wait, let us at least do so in silence!"

It was another hour before the great crystal began to glow its usual white. All three moved quickly to look into the globe's depths. They saw Tarh, seeming to look up at them as he gazed into his own travelling crystal.

"Chief Mage," he called, "our guardsmen have encountered the pair and wounded the man. They fired an arrow at the child, but struck her horse instead. We know that the horse fell, but not whether the child was injured. They are near the forest's eastern edge."

"Well," Soren said, "that is something. This is the first damage we've done to either. You are to be congratulated, I think. But why did your guardsmen not fire a second time, and why are they unable to tell whether the child was injured?"

"Only one of them returned, Chief Mage, and he was badly injured. He spoke of a red-robed wizard, a woman, who gestured and sent both guardsmen flying through the air. His companion was killed in the fall. The survivor spent some hours making his way back to our camp."

"A red-robed woman with power?" Soren was incredulous. "What Order could draw upon red auras? And how would it find enough such auras? Your man must have mistaken a brown-robed wizard under those red leaves."

Oleg was thoughtful. "Unless that red-robed individual drew upon the forest itself."

Soren stared at him, as did Haster.

"The Dark One has said, Chief Mage, that this forest has long been a place of power. Should a wizard whose spirit is attuned to that power enter the forest, such a one would no doubt discover herself to be wearing a red robe." He almost smiled, but caught himself. "This is most interesting news. Perhaps there has long been some being residing in that forest who is able to use the forest's power."

Tarh had been straining to hear but picked up only an occasional word spoken away from Soren's crystal. Now Soren turned back toward the globe. "Have you seen anything of Lorit or Rath?"

"No, Chief Mage. The forest edge is not an easy passage."

"How far from the forest are you?" asked Oleg, curious as to how far the young wizard had to walk before his crystal would work again.

"Perhaps five miles, Loremaster. I tried my crystal frequently, but this is the first it has worked."

"Five miles," said Oleg, thoughtfully. "The forest must be a center of power indeed if a crystal will not work within five miles."

"Enough of this," Soren growled. "Have you aught else to report?"

"No, Chief Mage. In the morning we will send our remaining guardsman into the forest to see what he can learn. Perhaps Lorit will join us tomorrow and can next report for both groups."

"Good," Soren said. "That will do. I expect to hear from you again tomorrow night, or earlier should you learn anything of moment."

Tarh barely had time to incline his head before Soren's crystal broke the connection.

"Well?" the Chief Mage demanded of his lieutenants.

Haster was tentative. "Wounding of the brother is promising, Chief Mage. I doubt the damage our guardsmen experienced was indeed caused by some red wizard. The witch-child would have reacted with great anger, we know. I suspect that she and not the red-robed woman was responsible for whatever was done. Snake and his dog can no doubt go over the ground and tell us more."

"It is interesting that the child did not instantly destroy the two guardsmen," Oleg mused. "Since she did not, she may have been injured. It would not be like her to simply toss away men who had harmed her brother and her horse."

"Do you suppose this will turn her more completely against us?" asked Haster.

"How much more could she do?" Soren snorted. "She's destroyed Rath's tower, thrown lightning to kill Selik, destroyed a keep and its owner. She's had no fondness for us from the first we heard of her."

"She also ended Rath's drought," put in Oleg. "So far as we know, that was her first act. All this has come in reaction; she has not appeared to follow any plan. Suppose," he held up a cautioning hand, "suppose she should cease to flee and instead turns to challenge, even to attack us here in our sanctuary. It is a disquieting thought. She may have acquired a powerful ally in this red woman, if indeed she and not the child reacted to our guardsmen's arrows."

Soren and Haster turned pale faces to the Loremaster. "We must find a way to stop her first," Soren said. "Speak again to the one in the dungeon."

***

By the time Tarh returned to camp, Snake and Dog had arrived. Roke sent the pair into the forest with orders to find out what they could and report. Following the returning guard's trail was easy, even for Snake. For Dog it was plain as could be. The man had clearly taken some time returning. The seriousness of his injuries was obvious from both the blood and the track he'd left, crawling and dragging one leg.

Still, Dog did not rush. When he came upon the dead guardsman, he paused, shaking his head. Then he brought his hands together and moved them slowly apart.

Snake hurriedly stepped back as the earth opened. When the opening had reached the size and shape of a grave, Dog dropped his hands. He motioned for Snake to take the dead man's legs while he lifted the man's upper body. They gently let the man down into the grave. Dog stood looking down at the body before he raised his hands again. He brought them slowly together, closing the grave. Shaking his head in disapproval, he said, "Wizards leave body. Not good for forest."

Snake had to agree that the wizards would have left the body to rot. Dog hadn't seemed concerned about that, but about any damage it might do to the woods. That was puzzling. Snake assumed that sooner or later the body would have provided food for trees and brush, with some stench in the meantime. Apparently Dog liked a cleaner forest. Perhaps he felt that a servant of the Order had no place being allowed to slowly become part of the forest. At least if Snake died in the strange being's service, he could count on not being left where he fell. That was something, he supposed.

A little further on Dog pointed upward. Snake looked and saw a scrap of cloth caught on a high branch, then other scraps on other branches.

"Threw high," Dog commented. "Not child."

Further on Dog motioned for Snake to keep behind him. He began to move very deliberately as they reached the spot where, he indicated, the guardsmen had knelt and fired their arrows. From there they continued slowly forward until Dog stopped beside the body of a small horse. He knelt, stroked the pony's nose, and spoke so softly Snake could make out no words. When Dog stood again, his fists were clenched. Snake wasn't certain, but he thought the earth trembled just a little.

There was blood on the earth, though not so much as should have been caused by an arrow which would bring a rider to the ground, Snake thought. Perhaps the wound had not been so severe as the injured guardsman had reported. Clearly there been two horses, two riders, one walker. Even Snake could discern the child's small tracks from those of the woman. He could also see that somehow, a fourth set was present.

The brother—the wounded man—had not regained his feet. From the number of tracks and the way they'd been walked over, the group had remained for some time. Finally the brother had been lifted, Snake thought, by the one who'd joined them, and carried. The new being must have been quite tall, judging by the length of the stride.

Dog stood scratching his head as he examined that new set of tracks. He began talking to himself in that strange way which didn't acknowledge Snake's presence. "Aren hurt. Bird not." He knelt, rubbed the dirt under the woman's footprints. "Power here. Draws on forest." With a look of pleased surprise, he nodded. "Something new in world."

Dog rose and walked to where the new tracks first appeared. To Snake, he seemed almost to test the air. "She called—how know? Saved life. Power grows." He looked at Snake, seemed to take a moment to recognize the man. "Close to where must go. Now, herd carefully. Wizards too close. Tried attack without magic. May try others."

Snake had listened to all this in some confusion, trying to parse which "he" and which "she" were referred to. That the two they followed had been joined by a third person on foot, he had known for some time. He hadn't believed the tale told by that half-delirious guardsman about a woman in red whose gesture threw them into a tree. Only when he and Dog tracked the two guardsmen was Snake convinced that they'd been thrown some distance, enough to kill one and badly damage the other. On the other hand, he had believed that the guards had wounded the brother and also the child's horse. Guardsmen wouldn't mistake that sort of thing; it was the core of their business, after all.

Some fourth being joining the three, seeming to appear out of thin air? The tracks were undeniable; someone had joined them, tall by the size and depth of the tracks and strong enough to carry the brother. His injury must be serious. The new being's strides were longer even than the brother's.

So the situation had changed, and not in ways which would benefit the Order. The brother had been injured badly enough to be carried, but they'd been joined by a woman witch or wizard with some real power, and by another being of whose nature Snake had no idea. Both newcomers seemed to surprise Dog. That displeased Snake; he was much happier thinking that his new master could not be surprised, even if this surprise seemed to please the squat man. If Snake were going to change sides permanently, he wanted his new side to be the clear winner in whatever was to come. Fortunately, the Order didn't yet realize that he'd changed sides, so his new choice, unavoidable as it had been when Dog opened the earth beneath him, might not be irrevocable.

"Well," Dog said, calling Snake back from his thoughts, "Time start back. One thing first. Pony loved. Bury deep. No disturb." He paused for a moment. "Gather large stones. Small cairn. Pony deserve."

There were not many large stones lying on the surface in this old forest. Snake had to dig and force half-buried stones to where he could lift them, then carry them back to the site where the little party had been surprised. The little horse was safely underground when he returned, the earth smooth again. Dog had sought out a few stones as well. They each made one more trip before Dog declared enough. The squat man built a small cairn quickly and efficiently, then walked once around, testing to make sure it was solid.

One he was satisfied, Dog led the way out of the woods, instructing Snake as they walked. "Say, buried body. Tell what else found. Not fourth person. Say brother barely able walk, leaned on horse. Child's horse died.

"Say tracked while. Convince. Be good servant."

Snake did not much care for that last remark. It had been long since anyone had said to his face that wizards regarded him, as they did all who weren't members of their order, as a servants. Still, he knew it was true. At least now he served a man who was neither servant nor member of the Order, and that was something.

As they neared the camp, Dog spoke again, at greater length than usual. "Say quarry deep woods. Wizards move on, leave wounded. Send Dog, Snake, track fugitives. Convince."

That gave Snake little time to think through his story, to say nothing of figuring a way to give advice to young wizards. Older wizards were more willing to take suggestions, so long as those were framed in such a manner as to acknowledge the wizards' greater wisdom. Perhaps that would work as well with these two.

As his new master had predicted, Roke and Tarh were uncertain whether to be angry that Snake and Dog had not caught up with their quarry, or pleased that they had returned to report. Neither had credited the surviving guard's report of the presence of a woman in a red robe who was possibly some new kind of wizard. Now Snake confirmed that there had been a third person, probably a woman by the size of her feet, length of her stride, and depth of her footprints. If that much was true, perhaps the rest of the guard's tale was as well.

Snake noted that the two guardsmen had been thrown some distance, high enough that shreds of clothing remained caught high in the trees. He didn't mention the fourth person. That the child's horse had been killed struck the wizards as good news. That and the brother's wound might slow their progress.

Snake allowed them to think over his report for a time, stepping back a little as they discussed what it might mean. The pair speculated: perhaps their quarry had found some kind of wizard who might be leading them to a stronghold of some sort. Regardless, for the first time the dark Order had inflicted damage, however slight. Soren would want to know all this immediately.

That was when Snake very cautiously offered up Dog's instructions as his own hesitant suggestions. He began by apologizing for not including in his initial report that Lorit and Rath were following, probably a day and a half behind. He did not smile when both Roke and Tarh were visibly startled to recall their superiors.

After a moment, Snake suggested that their quarry had moved north and east, deeper into the forest. After a moment to let that thought sink in, he wondered if they'd wish to move their camp further along the forest edge as it curved northeast. He asked only, he was quick to say, because he and Dog would need to know where to report back later the next day, if they were to reenter the forest and track the fugitives.

He'd spoken carefully enough, Snake noted with some relief. He hoped that any violent punishment for his words might have induced Dog to drop the pair into a chasm, though he wasn't sure that was part of the broad man's plan.

The pair waved him away and sat down to talk. Eventually, Tarh took up his pack and walked away to the south, no doubt to report to Soren. Roke watched him go, then turned to his remaining healthy guardsman, who was attending to his damaged companion. "Make him comfortable, with food and water for a day or two. The rest of our party will arrive within a few days. He can report that we've moved on now that the pair we follow have done so. Can you manage that, fellow?"

The wounded man nodded, managed a low "Yes, master. I will tell them."

Roke turned his attention again to the healthy guardsman. "After you've made him comfortable, prepare to pack up the camp. In the morning we will move further along the forest's edge while these two," he gestured at Snake and Dog, "follow the track through the trees." He glanced at Snake, who inclined his head, then again at the wounded guardsman. "You, fellow, will report this as well."

With that, Roke moved to the tent shared by the two wizards. Snake turned to Dog, who nodded. They rolled out their bedrolls in the forest shade and lay down.

"Well done," Dog noted. "Wizards chase north and east. Will serve. Soon," here he rose up on one broad elbow to look closely at Snake, "have choice: continue, or return former life. Think; choice maybe sudden." With that, Dog's new master lay down again and soon began snoring lightly.

This was a new complication. Snake would have a choice whether to continue with Dog or rejoin the wizards as a loyal servant, as he hoped the wizards continued to believe? Neither struck him as terribly safe. On the one hand, he more and more doubted the Order's ability to cope with either his new master or the witch-child . On the other, he knew little of what Master Dog intended, and was still uncertain whether Dog were the child's friend or foe. Snake did not relish the thought of being caught in a cross-fire between one who could drop, he suspected, an entire keep into a chasm and one who could command the keep to collapse. Yet, if the two were friendly, or at least not hostile to one another, serving them would surely be safer than serving an Order of wizards without sense enough to leave them alone.

***

Soren was surprised and pleased to receive a second report from Tarh. That the brother had indeed been wounded badly enough to be carried was good news indeed. That they'd not been able to test whether an arrow would wound the child, however, dampened his pleasure. Still, they'd killed her horse. Now, with one wounded, they'd have one horse for the three. The experiment had been, all in all, a success. They'd lost only one guardsman, with another damaged but living. Much better than sacrificing junior wizards.

The woman who'd joined worried him. Snake and his minion hadn't been able to discern whether she had in fact been the one who'd tossed two guardsmen some forty or fifty feet in the air, though that didn't sound like the witch-child. She tended to call down lightning or order men to die. Perhaps the red woman was yet another witch, drawing power from the forest itself.

"That power is considerable and old," reminded Oleg.

"Yes, yes," replied Soren. He was silent as he searched for some hopeful thought. "Snake and his follower are present and will go again into the forest in the morning to follow the trail of these three. Snake will find them. Given the opportunity, he could well end our troubles with one thrust of his knife."

Haster snorted. "Not unless he could be certain that the knife would do the job. Snake wouldn't put himself in jeopardy, not even for the Order. He's wilier than the average guardsman." At the look on Soren's face, he wished he'd remained silent.

Fortunately, Oleg agreed. "Not until Snake had seen an arrow strike the child and do damage would he attempt to get close. He is clever with a thrown knife, so he could try that, if he were certain of throwing and immediately fading back into the woods. His henchman could watch from some safe spot, I suppose."

Haster had another suggestion, which he hoped might at least lessen Soren's impatience. "When Lorit catches up, no doubt he will also report. If he and Rath have been walking between the forest edge and farmers' fields, no wonder he's not moved far enough from the trees to use his crystal. Who knows what sort of rough lands those pastures might be? Surely they would not be croplands that close to the forest."

"All this will make for an interesting conversation with the dark being in the dungeon," Oleg said. "I will leave now, with your permission, Chief Mage, and see whether he'll reveal more, intentionally or otherwise. He grows more interested in this tale each time I visit."

Frowning, Soren gave a wave of dismissal as he moved to his desk, already deep in thought.

✳✳✳

Oleg had begun to find his visits to the Dark One less burdensome. On most visits he heard some new bit of information, at the least. The misshapen being had become more interesting as it became more interested. That the thing had a mind, Oleg had long known; but that it had personal experiences, ideas, even longings and perhaps fears, that was something Oleg had never considered. Nor, as nearly he could tell from the accounts of his predecessors, had any earlier Loremaster. Their only concern had been to glean the Dark One's considerable knowledge of power and its uses.

Oleg ignored his apprentices, not bothering with his usual brief explanation that he had work to do and needed silence. He closed his office door, cast a spell to assure his privacy and went straight to the closet which led to the dungeon.

As usual, the prisoner heard him coming. "Ah, Loremaster, your steps are quicker today. Something has happened. Well, don't spoil a good story by hemming and hawing. Are more of your Order dead? Or has another keep fallen? Come, come, man, speak!"

"Better news than that," Oleg said. "A guardsman's arrow has wounded the brother, and another's killed the horse on which the witch-child rode."

At this, the Dark One's voice became somber. "That will anger her, surely, as much for the death of the horse as for the damage to the brother. And what of the guardsmen? How did they die?"

"Only one died." Oleg paused. Let this dark being wonder for a moment. "A third seems to have joined them, a woman wearing a red robe. She threw the guardsmen some distance up and away. One did not survive the fall. The other returned, hurt but able to speak. He lies recovering."

"Ah. So the child did not respond to the attack this time. The wounded man must mean much to her, then, if she would turn her attention to him rather than to the attackers." Again he was silent. "As you would see it, your servants have done well, Loremaster. This is the first damage your Order has inflicted. Alas, your archers were not able to fire a second volley to test whether their arrows would strike this child. Still, you have achieved something. Or think you have—but what?"

"Of course," he said after another pause, "you may have simply turned this child from fugitive to attacker. Up to now, she has seemed intent on moving away from your followers. You might have allowed her to go and hoped she would not return. Now I think your course is set: who would forget the wounding of a brother, the loss of a beloved horse?"

"Why beloved?" asked Oleg. "It may have been just a mount, a way to get somewhere."

There came that rusty sound which might have been laughter. "If this is the being I suspect it to be, she will not have regarded the horse as a convenience, but a live being to be cherished. No, Loremaster, you have given her two more reasons to hate the Order. You began by trying to stop the rain, then attempted entry where she would not have you enter, followed by threatening to hang her brother—"

Oleg broke in. "That was not done by our order."

Again the rusty laughter. "Perhaps not, but her capture and the nature of the person who detained her were at your order and choice. She will not be fooled into thinking it was only his doing." Another pause. "Now you've actually harmed those who are dear to her. Only if you are very lucky will she not turn on you."

"What if she seeks some refuge?" asked Oleg.

"Perhaps she does, but I can think of none she would need," came the reply. The next words were spoken softly as though he'd forgotten for the moment that Oleg stood on the other side of his bars. "Unless… but would she know to go there? If she has chosen to return as a human child, she may not. And yet her path seems purposeful…" the voice trailed off.

Oleg had listened carefully. "Where might she be going? We did not know of the Red Forest as a place of power. Is there another such she might reach from that forest? Come now; you've said this much, why be shy?"

Again the rusty laugh. "No, Loremaster. You must return in a few days and tell me more. I would not miss the next step in this tale of yours. Perhaps this red being knows more than do your wizards. Shall I give advice? Very well. Your Chief Mage would be wise to order his pursuers to return at once. I suspect his one forlorn idea will be to attack again, quickly and without concerning yourselves with the loss of a whole mob of dark wizards in the effort." Again that maddening silence. "That is enough, Loremaster. Take what you've learned to your Chief Mage, and much good may it do him."

That was all the being would say, despite Oleg's best efforts to get him to speak again.

✳✳✳

For hours Hobard led them further into the forest, always moving north and east. She seemed unbothered by Aren's weight. Surprisingly, Aren seemed to sleep peacefully despite being carried like a sleeping child, one of Hobard's arms under his shoulders and the other under his knees. From time to time the Druid would stop and, without putting Aren down, ask Brenna to check the bandage for fresh bleeding. Brenna reported each time that there was no sign of blood.

Bird rode Aren's horse, sobbing from time to time and alternating that with anger: "Why did they hurt Aren? Pony hadn't done anything to them. I should go back and fix all of them, once and for all." Then she would weep again.

At those times Brenna would walk beside the child, comforting her, suggesting that they most needed to reach a place where the dark Order could not follow. Such a refuge must be somewhere ahead of them, since they knew there was no safety behind. Returning to where they'd been would only put Aren in greater danger, not to mention Bird herself and perhaps Hobard.

"And you, too," whispered Bird, a little hoarse from crying. "We brought them into your lovely forest where you might have learned how to be a red wizard. Now you have to run away, too."

"Once you are safe, I will return," said Brenna. "There is much for me to learn here. I doubt the Order will concern itself with me once you are beyond their reach. They may believe that I would not come back, should we reach sanctuary somewhere ahead, though I doubt that will be with the blue Order. Hobard seems to be taking us further north than their lands, though it's difficult to judge. I've not spent much time in this part of the woods. The shelter where we stayed our first night provided home enough."

She walked in silence for a time. "Indeed, we seem to have come further east than I knew the forest extended. It must be that the forest curves north here. That will at least give us cover for a while longer."

With that, Brenna moved forward to ask whether Hobard had a destination in mind. No, the Druid said, she simply wanted to put as much distance as possible between them and their pursuers. She suspected those would not return this night, but she preferred to ensure that they'd have to walk a long way in the dark should they attempt immediate pursuit. She had not seen them, she reminded Brenna. What sort of men were those who dared such an attack?

Brenna said they were ordinary enough guardsmen, from what she could see.

Hobard nodded. "Guardsmen," she said meditatively. "Yes, there were guardsmen, working for others who had declared themselves lords. The first wizards as well." She frowned at that thought. "Some used their power well, tending the land in places we had not reached. Others brought to the dry south crops which could live there. Yes, some deserved the faith some of us had given them. Sadly, others cared only for power: over the land, over the people. And so we were sent back into the earth itself so we could do no further harm."

Brenna was puzzled. "Who sent you? Who could send you where you didn't want to go?"

"As for who," Hobard replied, "another will have to answer that. It did not feel like a banishment. I have moved through the earth itself, into the roots and the trunks and leaves of trees, I have drifted on the breeze from place to place, I have been part of the highest mountains and the deepest lakes—oh, it has been a wonderful existence! From time to time I would encounter something which I knew was another of my kind. We would share for a moment the awareness of one another's joy." Her face turned sad.

"And now you are here," Brenna said, "because this child said a Druid should come."

"Is that how she called?" asked Hobard. "I wondered how I came to be chosen. I was no doubt the nearest when she spoke. That," she said, "is a relief. I feared I had transgressed in some manner and was being recalled. It is good to know that I came at need, yet the need saddens."

Brenna had to think about this. "What—what is she? Surely she is not the one who sent you and your kind into the earth?" Brenna could not believe the question even as she asked.

"Ah, that is something more which another must resolve for you. Here we are at a suitable place to spend the night. As it is about to get dark, let us stop here and get an early start in the morning."

Bird rode quietly through the forest, keeping her tears to herself, some for poor Pony but most for Aren. Once they stopped and Aren had been lain gently on his bedroll, she went to him and remained, sitting quietly, weeping only occasionally. Brenna had gone searching in the woods for plants which might help in his healing, as had Hobard. When they returned they made poultices and healing drinks, then removed Aren's bandages and examined his wound. Brenna had learned some healing as an apprentice, but Hobard clearly knew much more. When the Druid said the wound was already healing nicely, Brenna accepted her word. The wound looked well enough, but Brenna would not have felt able to declare it already healing.

Hobard spread their poultices on the wound, singing softly as she worked. Then she lifted Aren's head and got him to drink a little. He came to half-consciousness. After rebandaging the wound—strips this time from clothing in Aren's and Bird's packs—Hobard lay Aren again on his bedroll. "He will sleep until morning. Until then, there is nothing better we can do for him, my lady, than your best will for his recovery."

Bird thanked them both. With Aren seeming to have fallen asleep again, she spoke softly: "I hope you heal quickly." She was thankful that Aren wasn't awake to hear her voicing a hope. When she glanced up, Bird saw a look of satisfaction on Hobard's face. She hoped that meant she had not done something wrong yet again after promising Aren that she wouldn't use her powers.

Bird remained beside Aren, bending her head in concentration as she willed him to recover. She paused only when Brenna brought bread, cheese, and water and insisted she eat and drink. Afterwards she focused again on Aren, speaking softly: "Oh, Aren, I'm sorry. I'm sorry. If I'd left those wizards alone and let them stop the rain, you wouldn't be hurt. I'm sorry I can do things. Please get well; please get well; please get well; I hope you get well; I hope you get well" and so through the night.

CHAPTER SEVEN

Dog and Snake rose early, before the sun. Dog led the way into the woods, walking as briskly as though it were full day while Snake made his way as best he could. The forest was just light when they reached the place where the attack had taken place. Dog moved away from the dried blood already being absorbed by the soil. He sat, taking cold meat and bread from his pack, along with a small wineskin.

"Sit, eat. No hurry. Catch soon enough. No need wizards know. Plenty time."

Snake sat, accepted a pull from the flask, then a piece of meat, one of bread and took a bite from each. He asked, tentatively, "If we're in no rush, Master, why leave so early?"

Dog chuckled. "Before wizards change minds. Lorit and Rath not far behind. Paah! More herding. Watch wizards carefully. Not stop friends now."

Snake thought for a while before asking another question. "Master, could you not lead them yourself, if you know their destination?" To his surprise, Dog gave a long answer, though it left Snake as puzzled as before.

"Fair question. Maybe, must reach on own. Wears child's form. Some purpose. One place sure allies. Why appeared valley?" Dog shook his head. "Too much. Wait almost over. Now," he said, his tone changing as he came to his feet, "confuse Snake enough. Trail." With that, he led the way into the woods, following the track of a horse and two walkers, one weighed down by Aren's wounded body.

Before mid-morning they'd come upon their quarry's camp of the night before. Dog left Snake standing just outside the site while he moved slowly and carefully about, speaking loudly enough for Snake to hear. "Left early. Good. Need distance on wizards. Wizards walk forest edge. Travelers move straight line." A few feet further, he stopped, knelt down, his head hanging.

This time he spoke softly, more to himself. "Sat brother all night. Would not have had happen. Sorrow for brother." He knelt there a while longer, looking to Snake almost like a man kneeling in prayer, not that Snake had much experience with prayer.

The squat man rose and resumed his study of the campsite. "Red woman with. Maybe keep on, maybe turn back forest edge. Other remains. Soon, learn much."

With that he stood, gestured to Snake to join him. As they followed the tracks further into the woods, Dog noted, "New one walk lighter. Horse tracks deeper. Perhaps brother able ride, share horse. Red woman walks. Signs better." He turned to Snake. "Follow afternoon, quick back to camp. See what chaos wizards bring."

***

"The Dark One says," Oleg noted, "that we should recall our wizards and allow the witch-child to travel without hindrance." Soren's reaction, he expected, would be interesting, perhaps volcanic. Oleg would enjoy watching.

For a moment, Soren looked as confused as did Haster. "Why— why does he say that? What has he told you?" The Chief Mage looked frightened; up to now he'd been frustrated, angry, determined, but not quite frightened. The witch-child had done nothing new to raise fear in the man. Perhaps he'd had enough time to consider what her power must be. There was no telling what she might do as she grew older. If she grew older; after all, for the first time the Order had struck a blow.

Oleg shook himself out of his thoughts. "My apologies, Chief Mage. I was thinking over what he said. What I have just told you was clear enough, but there was something else, something he said almost to himself. I think he did not intend me to hear." Oleg gathered his thoughts. "The news has startled him. I would guess it's the first new thing he'd heard in centuries." Oleg raised his hands placatingly before Soren could become too impatient. "I asked him where she might be going. He claimed to know of no place she might seek. Then he seemed to think of a destination. He argued with himself about whether she would know it. He grew silent and refused to speak again until I return with more information."

Oleg leaned forward, speaking slowly for emphasis.

"There may be some place, some goal toward which she moves or is drawn. If she does not know the full extent of her powers, nonetheless she may be drawn to some place or some being. I wish I knew more. This is the first hint the Dark One has given us of a possible destination."

"But where could it be?" asked Haster. "The blue Order does not have the kind of power she displays. Beyond their land is only the sea. Might she be drawn to some place across the water?"

"I doubt that," said Oleg. "The men of that coast sail widely, and they've reported no islands, let along larger bodies of land, within reach of their vessels." At Soren's questioning glance, he explained. "I gather information of all sorts, Chief Mage, including reports from sailors. They'll speak freely for a few coins and many drinks. Maps of the coast are readily for sale in shops in those lands. From time to time a traveler returns with information and a willingness to sell. Other times some of Snake's old comrades venture beyond our lands. They've learned that if they return with anything of interest, here is a market."

"Then their goal must be somewhere to the north," Soren said. "What is beyond the river which bounds the blue lands?"

Oleg considered. "Little, I believe. The mountains and the river angle north, and the lands between the river and the mountains are of little interest. Neither are the lands this side of the river. I believe men call them the Barren Lands. They're believed to be a place of mists and fogs, where men and even wizards wander lost if they venture in at all."

"A place where men and even wizards wander lost…"mused Haster. "Might such a place serve as a refuge? Even in the Red Forest, guardsmen could find her; but if they would wander lost in these barrens—"

"The barrens might prove a better refuge. Yes," said Soren. "So there's another task for you, Oleg: find out all you can about those lands. A map, if you have one. At the least we can learn their location. There may be accounts of visits to those lands, though it sounds as though they won't have been fruitful. Still, some knowledge is better than none."

Impatient, Soren shook his head. "When next I'm able to converse with our wizards, I'll warn them to move to cut off any escape from that cursed forest into some land to the northeast. Perhaps by then, since they report rarely these days, you'll have more to tell, Loremaster."

"They must have some goal in mind," put in Haster. "Surely they've not gone east simply to travel."

"They might travel to escape the wizards we've sent to investigate," put in Oleg, dryly. It was, after all, as the Dark One had suggested, the Order's actions which had triggered all this. Though, in fairness to Rath, he'd spent five peaceful years establishing his drought with no signs of opposition before his plan—and his tower—collapsed. Five years, thought Oleg, fit perfectly with the time it would take a child to become aware of the drought.

If only Soren had had the foresight to wait until they knew more of this being before sending a party after her. But then, there had been Rath's right hand and his tower, and Selik's death by lightning. This witch-child had not been entirely benevolent. Still, Selik was no great loss. And Rath's hand, well, Oleg could live with that. Greater caution in dealing with whatever power had arisen might have left the witch-child in place, seemingly a farmer's daughter who could be quietly observed until they knew more.

Or until she grew into her full powers and full understanding. And who could predict what she might become?

***

Lorit and Rath walked all day after they sent Snake and his follower ahead, though they walked at Rath's pace and that meant slowly. Rath would no longer hear of riding in the sling. He'd been carried by four on the way to Rand's keep, but they'd sent half their force with Roke. Now the One-Hand would have to be hauled by two, with the third rotating in. It was probably faster to let Rath walk while his temper rose.

Rath did walk faster than Lorit expected. Fury at the witch-child who'd taken his right hand, his tower, his carefully-tended drought energized him as they closed in. Whether it also unbalanced him, Lorit was unable to say. He was not willing to engage Rath in any conversation which might reveal the state of the wizard's mind. There was no telling in what manner a powerful and unbalanced wizard might lash out.

If Rath were too furious and in too much pain to be rational at this moment, a few day's rest might still restore him. Lorit doubted they would have that rest even should Roke and Tarh succeed in flanking their quarry and forcing them to remain in the forest. At that time, Soren might order the four to see what their combined powers could do against this child.

That Lorit had been unable to contact Soren was a worry. Neither had Rath. Lorit guessed that Rath's fury at that failure added to his energy. Being without information was never something Lorit cared for. He should have been able to keep in close contact with Soren and thus with Oleg through their crystals. The odd power of this red forest was something entirely new. Lorit did not care for the way it hampered him; never before had he been unable to work a crystal. He had not believed that to be possible. Nor did he wish to enter that forest.

He was not afraid of the power of the other Orders of wizards, for he understood the natures of the green, brown, and blue Orders. He knew that none had studied pure power for its own sake as had the dark Order. Power of which he knew nothing worried him, and now he was facing two sorts, neither of which he understood in the least: that of the witch-child and that of the forest.

Should Soren order him into the forest, well, Soren was not present. Unlike the witch-child, the Chief Mage could not send lightning through a crystal. If anyone were to go into the forest, let it be Rath. The One-Hand was just angry enough to venture any place which might bring him near enough to strike out at the child. What Rath might bring to bear which might touch that being, Lorit could not guess.

At evening, Rath began to pick up his pace. As the night grew darker he picked it up again. All day he had walked abreast of Lorit, who had been careful not to draw ahead of the injured man. Now Lorit chose to remain a half-pace behind, letting Rath find his own speed. Behind them, the three guardsmen were glad of what was a more leisurely walk than they were used to. They'd guessed there would be no camping that night, and the slower pace would make travelling all night easier.

Morning found the group moving at the same pace. Rath was eager to reach the younger wizards' camp and learn what they had seen. By now, he knew, Snake and Ryd's Dog would have reported to Roke. Finally there might be information to use against the child.

His stub throbbed. This day and night he had badly overtaxed himself, but this was no time to consider anything but finding the demon-child. She must be stopped before she could cause more damage. He felt his power growing within him as he continued to recover despite his current near-exhaustion. His standing in the order had no doubt fallen; destroying this child would show that he was still one who could challenge and replace Soren whenever he wished—if he wished.

At mid-morning they came upon the young wizards' camp and were surprised to find no one but a single badly-injured guardsman. From him they learned of the attack on the travelers and of his comrade's death. Master Tarh, he told them, had walked some miles away from the forest and contacted the Chief Mage, who had instructed the two wizards to attempt to again get ahead of their quarry. The forest, he also told them, was said to curve north and east. Snake and his man had been sent into the woods to track the child. With her were her injured brother and the red woman.

The news was not as pleasing to Rath as it might have been, though it was good to hear that a blow had been struck. But they would have to travel further to reach the rest of their party. There would no doubt be more to learn by the time they caught up to Roke and Tarh.

Lorit made a quick decision. Rath was tired; even a short rest would help him. And he needed to contact Soren. He would follow the younger wizards' example and move away from the forest until his crystal became free of the baleful red glow. Then he would contact Soren, see if there were more news. Instead of returning directly back to this camp he would cut across country to rejoin the party further along. Rath and two of the guardsmen were to rest for an hour, then be on their way again.

One guard was to stay with the injured man until he was able to travel. Judging by the man's appearance, Lorit judged that might be some time. He suggested the two make their way to the inn near Rand's fallen keep, and from there back to the Order's headquarters. Given his preference, he'd have left the injured man alone with provisions enough to last until he could travel, and perhaps enough extra to supply him all the way back to the inn; but the Order had learned the limits beyond which guardsmen would begin to doubt that wizards cared whether they lived or died.

One guardsman more or less would make little difference. With the two they would still bring and the one remaining with Roke, they could strike the quarry at least twice more even should they lose guards on each attempt, or once more with greater force. With Snake as scout, they would not need guardsmen to survive and report.

Rath found word of the successful attack gave him renewed strength, but he knew that a rest would do him even more good. He grumbled a little about lost time as he gestured to the nearest guardsman to lay out a bedroll and to set a canopy. He was not willing to move so close to the forest as to lie in its shade, no matter how bright the sun. They could leave the canopy for the wounded man. That would save time when they started out again.

Lorit had walked through the night without resulting to a strengthening spell. Those, he knew, would work only so many times. He suspected he'd need them later on this quest. Now he cast such a spell to speed his way to a spot far enough from this forest where his crystal could work. Even so it was a full hour before the crystal cleared.

The news Soren added to what they'd learned from the wounded man troubled Lorit. The being in the dungeon had let slip something which led Oleg to believe that the travelers might seek a place called the Barren Lands. Accordingly, Soren had instructed Roke and Tarh to move quickly and get ahead of their quarry.

Soren commanded that when they caught up to the fugitives, Lorit send Tarh or Roke to contact him immediately. By then, Snake should provide information which might help plan their next attack.

Soren did not tell Lorit that the Dark One had suggested they partly withdraw and allow the fugitives to escape. Nor did Lorit reveal that the same thought had crossed his mind when he'd seen the wreckage of Rand's keep, and again when he discovered that his crystal would not work anywhere near the forest. The thought was not one he would share with Soren at the best of times, which this was not.

With that, Soren signed off. Lorit set out across the fields at an angle which he hoped would bring him into the cleared area close to where Rath and his two guardsmen would be. A quick finding spell would tell him if a being of power had walked there recently. If not, he would move rapidly after the young wizards. Rath could catch up as he might. It would be good to free of the One-Hand for a time.

***

Aren didn't recover consciousness until morning. By then, Bird had fallen asleep next to him. Hobard, who didn't sleep, had spread the child's bedroll over her. Aren looked around, starting at sight of Hobard, sitting against a tree on the other side of the little clearing. After a few moments, he signaled to Brenna to come closer from where she looked into the various packs to see what might be available for breakfast. He gestured toward Hobard and asked, very softly, "Where did she come from? What is she?"

His question hadn't been soft enough to avoid waking Bird. Groggily she worked her way out of sleep. "You were hurt, and I was afraid you'd die. Brenna said only a healing Druid could save you. Then one came and that was Hobard. Once they bandaged you, Hobard carried you and I rode Blaze."

Aren reached out and touched Bird's face. "You look tired, little bird. Didn't you sleep?"

Bird was indignant. "I did not! I sat beside you all the night, hoping you would get better. I didn't mean to fall asleep. And now you are better." She paused a moment, and then in her best Reya voice said, "You'd better not frighten me like that again, young man!" before bursting into tears. She threw her arms around Aren, but drew back when he winced.

"Hug me on my left side, little Bird," he admonished, and she did so.

Hobard approached slowly, allowing Aren time to come fully awake and grasp their situation. "You seem much improved, Bird's brother. I am glad to see it. Brenna and I will need to examine your wound before we travel on. I fear you and the Lady are not safe here."

With a resigned sigh, Aren lay back down while Brenna removed his bandage. Hobard placed a hand on the place where the arrow had entered, closing her eyes in concentration. When she removed her hand and opened her eyes, she was smiling. She turned to confer with Brenna. "I feel no fever heat from within the wound. It heals wonderfully, though that should be no surprise, given the Lady's vigil. Is there much blood on the bandage?"

Brenna had been carefully examining the bandage the entire time. "I find none. Not a trace, even." She shook her head in wonder. "How is this possible?"

"Many parts to this healing," Hobard said. "Healing power of forest, earth, Druid, sister's love. Now we add Brightsong." She began a soft, wordless song, gesturing for Bird to join in. The child began, tentatively at first. Hobard, eyes closed, smiled broadly as she sang.

The Druid brought the song to a close, opening her eyes as she did so to find Bird looking at her with a puzzled frown on her face. "You remember," Hobard said.

"But I've never heard that song before," Bird said. "How could I remember?"

With a slight shrug, Hobard replied, "There may be much for you to remember, Lady. I am pleased to help even a little."

Brenna suggested that they should eat something and get on their way, but Aren insisted that he could eat on the road. He was sure the others could as well. With Hobard's assistance, he stood, swaying for only a moment once he was on his feet. Looking about, he asked where Pony was.

That brought tears from Bird and an explanation from Brenna. Aren knelt and held his sister until the tears passed. When he stood again, he acknowledged that he was not up to walking, but could surely sit his horse. "And," he continued, "as I become stronger, the three of you can also take turns riding."

Hobard smiled at that. She would not need to burden the horse. She had been used to walking in the time before she went back into the earth, and she would enjoy the sensation.

"Before you what?" Aren began, but Brenna reminded him that later would be a better time for explanations. Just now they were followed by those who'd already attacked once. "No doubt they will try again."

"It would help," Hobard mused, "if we knew just where these wizards are."

For the first time since Aren had been wounded, Bird brightened. "I can tell you! Let's see…there are two that way." She pointed to the south. "Two more are coming behind them, but further off. The two further off make bigger holes in the day. Do you think that means they're more powerful?"

"Of course you can sense them," Hobard said. "I should have known." She laughed, then sobered and answered Bird's question. "Yes, they probably are more powerful." She added a slight bow. "Thank you, my lady. If you will, let us know from time to time just where these wizards are. I suspect they will try to hurry around the edge of this forest and set another trap. We must, I think, continue as we are and attempt to outdistance them."

"I didn't like dark wizards before," Bird said, "and I like them even less now. I hope"—she broke off at the look on Aren's face. "Yes, I promised. But if they send more men with bows…" she let her voice trail off, her eyes a little darker.

"I know, little bird. Let's see if we can outwalk them first," Aren answered, while Brenna looked on, puzzled. Hobard nodded as though remembering something she'd heard long ago.

They continued northeast, and as the forest began to thin around them their route shifted to become ever more northward. Eventually they could see that the forest to the north also thinned as though nearing its edge. At least there were no wizards to the north, Bird reported.

But those behind were coming faster now. The second pair had split up with one moving away from the forest while the other came straight along the forest edge. Now they were closing on the first two, and those two had turned along the forest's edge and were coming nearer.

They had travelled more slowly than they might have for fear of opening Aren's wound again. Now, at his urging, they increased their pace. Soon Bird reported that the wizards were no longer gaining, but weren't losing any ground, either. Ahead they could see the forest's end.

"I will run ahead," Hobard volunteered, "and see what lies beyond this forest. It may be that we must turn north and escape into the mountains, or turn again into the deepest part of the forest and then into the mountains where they lie closer." She set off, running fast through the woods, brush and small trees seeming to bend to make a clear path.

"Is she actually a Druid, come to life again?" asked Aren.

"It seems so," said Brenna. "She certainly knows more healing than do I. It was her actions which drew the arrow and then, separately, the arrowhead from your side. She did it by singing what must have been incantations. I think she did not touch the arrow, and when it appeared without the arrowhead, she sang the arrowhead to her. None of the blue order could have done such a thing."

"Well, of course she's a Druid," said Bird. "I called a Druid, and there was a kind of flutter and then there she was. Confused, too, for a moment," she giggled. "Then she got right down to work." She turned to smile at Aren. "I was afraid, but she helped you, and Brenna did, too."

"I did little," Brenna protested. "I helped with the bandaging, and when we made camp I helped find healing herbs; but Hobard knew best what to do with them." She paused. "Hobard does not seem to know of the Barren Lands. If they are what was told among blue wizards, they are a place where fogs always lie. You could perhaps lose our pursuers there. I doubt their guardsmen will fare any better in the Barren Lands than do wizards."

They rode on for a while, more slowly now. There was no sense in making too much distance should they have to turn and retreat further into the forest. "Hobard's coming," Bird announced.

She approached at a run, scarcely breathing hard as she reported. "The forest ends soon. There's an open plain, a few miles wide, before trees begin again. It's a mixed forest, no oak. Beyond the forest I sense another sort of place. I could not tell much, but it seems to be covered by bright mists which, I should almost say, have been called together. Perhaps it is a place of power as well, one which might resist the dark Order. Though it is covered by mists, there is a brightness about it, as the red light in this forest seems brighter than one would expect. I have never visited, either in former times or more recently. There is no better refuge in sight."

"What of the wizards who follow?" asked Aren. "If they come near enough before we reach the trees, they will see us. I can ride swiftly for a time, and Bird can ride with me. I see that our Druid friend can move as quickly as does Blaze; but can we outrun their spells?"

Brenna spoke up then, slowly and reluctantly. "I believe what power I have is drawn from this forest. When you break cover, I will stay behind and wait for the wizards and their guardsmen. I will call on all my strength and, so much as I am able, the forest's power. I should be able to delay them for a time. If not, I can at least confuse them.."

Aren turned to face her. "And when they determine where and what you are and four dark wizards combine against you? What then?"

Brenna laughed. "Why, it will be time to fade back into these trees. These wizards will not choose to seek me here, and I doubt they'll take time to send guardsmen when they have you to follow instead."

"It is a brave plan," Hobard acknowledged, "and our need is great. The forest is angry and growing angrier. I can feel tension all about us. I think it does not like its tenant being driven. But we should talk as we move." She lifted Bird unto Blaze's back.

Aren checked to be sure Bird was settled before asking, "The forest is angry? You can tell that?" He nudged the horse into motion.

"It's very angry," Bird affirmed. "And getting angrier. It doesn't like what's happening. I don't think it's angry at us."

Now it was Hobard' turn to be surprised. "My lady, no forest will be angry at you. But yes, that you must run from wizards is another reason for the forest's anger." She paused, turning to Brenna. "When first you suggested remaining behind, I thought it a brave effort which would doom you. As I feel the forest's will gathering about you, I think you may well survive. I hope so, at any rate." With that she bowed to the red woman.

"And now," said Aren, "we have come to the end of this forest and must move as rapidly as we can across this plain. Let us not run until our pursuers come in sight. Bird, will you warn us as they wizards come nearer?"

Bird nodded. "I can do that." She turned to Brenna. "I will miss you. Thank you."

"As will I," said Aren.

"I wish you goodspeed. May we meet again," Brenna replied as they moved out of the trees.

"Farewell, woman of the red forest," called Hobard as she trotted onto the plain. Brenna smiled at the title, thinking that it was one she hoped she would live to hear again.

***

Oleg's apprentices were becoming used to being driven harder than even they had ever experienced. To be told to work through the night if necessary did not surprise them—nor please them. But they knew better than to grumble where the lore-master might hear. They'd become accustomed to working among the oldest scrolls, and the best among them had begun to sense where the most useful information might be found. There was little method in the oldest storage areas, but there was some. Those who'd looked through those nooks most often had begun to realize where word might be found about this Barren Land, this place none of their order had entered within living memory.

There was not much, but by morning at least they'd found a few scrolls. Oleg looked at the meager group and grumbled that they should keep looking, though he was a little surprised they'd found this many. He retired to his office to laboriously decipher what he could.

The scrolls did not encourage him. As soon as he'd finished, he left the office and slowly walked up the stairs to Soren's watchtower. Haster was there, as he'd expected, and to his surprise Soren as well, despite the early hour.

"I do not sleep much these days," Soren said as the Loremaster entered. "At daybreak I looked into the crystal for any place of refuge to the east and north. I will show you what I found." He moved to the crystal, which glowed dimly as it sat idle. Oleg joined him. Haster came forward as well, though he'd seen the view earlier.

Soren sighed. "Here you see the land between Rand's keep, or what is left of it, and the Blue River. Now as we look further north, we see the river begin to curve away from Rand's holdings. Note the slight red glow of the damned forest to the north and west. Our view moves north and east, away from that glow, but see how it follows. The forest must take a similar curve, as though it wished to follow the river's lead. Watch the area north and east."

Oleg did as Soren suggested. He could see a sparse forest come into view. That would fit with a place called the Barren Lands; no doubt little grew there. He began to see a blur, a distortion in the view. Finally, as Soren willed the crystal's vision further north and east, the entire globe seemed filled with a pale fog.

Oleg stepped away. "You see," Soren grumbled. "Another place where power may keep us from seeing or acting. Perhaps it would be worth a lesser wizard to know for certain."

Oleg sat in one of Soren's soft chairs. "My apprentices have found some ancient fragments concerning this Barren Land." He gave Haster and Soren a moment to seat themselves, Soren behind his desk.

"And?" said an impatient Soren.

"The name 'Barren Lands' is old. It appears in one of the earliest fragments my students found. Our predecessors did attempt to explore the area, from what I can glean from a number of partial accounts, but with little luck. One scroll, older than that which first mentioned the name, speaks of a time when the mists came. It suggests a link to the disappearance of beings such as the Dark One. It speaks of the disappearance of beings who had taught our forefathers the rudiments of magic. Shining Ones, this account calls them.

"That line about 'Shining Ones' stuck in my mind, and took me to the ancient scrolls concerning our dark prisoner. I wondered if he had ever been described as shining, but found nothing specific to suggest such an epithet. Apparently he was a creature of midnight when first he wandered here."

Soren grumbled, "I care nothing about the history of your prisoner, Loremaster. What of these Barren Lands and the mists which infest them?"

"Of course, Chief Mage. There were attempts to penetrate those mists. Experienced wizards accompanied by guardsmen entered more than once. Some did not return, while others stumbled out weeks or even months later, Each told a tale of being blinded by the mist only a few feet into those woods, unable to find their way out even if they turned about immediately and retraced what they thought were their steps. Parties lost touch with one another, some immediately—those were the early attempts—and others more gradually.

"None who returned told much, but here is what little they could say: the place appears dry, despite the mists. They could see brown, dry grass. but only by bending nearly to the ground. Wizards went in at several times, and the grass was brown and dry all year round. They could see trees only from a few inches away. What trees there were appeared stunted, again as though the land were in a perpetual drought."

Mention of a perpetual drought brought a brief frown to Soren's face, to which Oleg responded with a blank gaze and an inner smile. Let the fool be reminded of his own folly.

"It seems indeed to be a barren place, Chief Mage. And yet the combination of mists and fogs—both words are used in the scrolls— and dry ground suggests something more than natural in those mists. That is supported by an experience which is repeated in several sources: while our predecessors found it easy enough to enter the place, they were unable to perform the simplest spells once there. Unlike the Fifth Valley, the Barren Lands did not seem to wish them ill; the land simply refused to welcome them.

Oleg smiled mirthlessly. "Perhaps, Chief Mage, the witch-child will have the same experience. If we're fortunate, she might enter and never return. Darkness knows we could use some good fortune, though I would not undervalue wounding of the brother."

Soren sat thinking for some time before he spoke. "You may have said more than you intended, Loremaster. If they enter those lands, we could do worse than keep vigil on them. There are more than enough of our order to sustain such indefinitely. Guardsmen can be bought in whatever numbers we need to set a cordon about the place, espe- cially if it borders on the sea. What do your ancient scrolls say of its boundaries?"

Both he and Haster leaned forward eagerly as Oleg responded.

"The scrolls speak of entering those lands from the east as well as from the north, Chief Mage. There are ancient maps, though not so old as the scrolls of which I speak, which show a vague area labelled simply "barrens." It does not reach so far as the northern mountains nor south to the Blue River. It is much smaller than the red forest. It would seem that we could wait out these fugitives should they reach these barrens."

"Perhaps," Haster ventured, "it were best they do reach those lands."

"Perhaps," Soren responded, grudgingly. "A surer course is to destroy at least the brother and if possible the witch-child before they disappear into those mists, and that red witch with them. We will allow the chase to continue. We have little chance of stopping it unless the chase moves far enough from that accursed forest for us to sustain contact. However," he said, moving to the crystal, "we can at least observe the area between the forest and the mists. If they attempt to cross there, we should be able to see."

The crystal activated, and they found themselves looking into a plain leading northeast into a sparse forest. When Soren widened the view, they saw an impenetrable reddish glow on one side and a white mist on the other. They settled themselves to wait.

***

Thankful that he had kept himself from using strengthening spells during the night, Lorit resorted to one to speed himself on his way back toward the Red Forest. He did not retrace his path from where he'd left Rath, but rather angled to reach the forest further on, as he'd planned. Walking over pasture land was unexpectedly difficult, he'd found on his way to contract Soren. The land had not been plowed in many years—never, in fact, he suspected, since it lay so close to the forest. Even at his increased speed, he stumbled often and sometimes had to slow down over a particularly awkward portion.

When he moved onto the margin around the forest, Lorit cast a quick finding spell and saw that two lesser beings of power had passed that way. Rath had not yet made it this far.

It didn't matter much. Soren had ordered that he be contacted if at all possible before their next attack. If they could make no contact with the Chief Mage, Lorit would have to direct the attack. Rath's presence would probably be a complication, given the One-Hand's state of rage. Lorit had hoped that would diminish as they travelled and Rath recovered, but instead he'd sensed growing anger in the wounded man. A coldly rational Rath would be valuable; an irrational Rath, especially if his full power or anything near it had returned, could be a danger to them all.

The forest edge began its shift to the north and east as Lorit's second strengthening spell gave out. With a groan he resorted to another. Some said it was possible to risk a fourth strengthening spell, but Lorit did not wish to take that risk. He could see movement ahead and hoped it would be Roke or Tarh, or both.

***

By afternoon, Dog and Snake were close enough to their quarry to listen in on their conversations, though remaining hidden became more difficult as the forest thinned and the party approached the edge. When they'd heard the plan for the fugitives to dash for the forest opposite and the mists beyond while the red wizard remained behind to slow their pursuers, Dog gestured for Snake to accompany him as they withdrew.

"Good plan," Dog said when they were out of earshot. "Go forest edge, seek wizards. Report. Dog follow child,."

Snake inclined his head in acknowledgement, then ventured a question: "What will you do, master?"

Dog rubbed his hands together. "Red woman delay wizards. Maybe not survive." He paused, frowning. "Don't like. Dog can do"—here he grinned—"some things. Wizards attack red woman, Dog act."

Snake shivered, recalling his first meeting with this odd being, felt again the shock of having the ground split beneath him. Once he'd delivered his report he'd head back into the forest again, even if he had to slip away. He did not wish to be among the wizards' party when his new master began weaving distractions. He turned to go, then paused. "Master, you said that soon I would be free to choose whether to continue with you. Is that time nearby?"

Dog had already started toward the place where they'd broken off their eavesdropping. He paused, faced the assassin. "Time near. Chase almost over."

Snake took a deep breath. "But the conflict with the Order is not?"

Dog chuckled. "Not yet."

"In that case, master, I would be your man among them, as I have been."

"Why?" Dog asked

Now it was Snake's turn to grin. "Master, I can assess strength as well as any man, not to mention over-reaching. I know not who these beings we follow might be, but I would rather serve you than Soren." He paused for a moment. "I am no fount of goodness, you know well.

But I have done less harm these past days than at any time in service of many years.

"Very well," the gnarled man said. "Child reach Barren Lands, play game little longer. Time right, leave wizards together. Will do?"

Snake knelt in acquiescence, something he'd not done even in Soren's presence. Before he could voice his thanks, Dog scolded: "Go! Events moving!" and turned into the woods. In a moment he was out of sight.

Snake stood, shook himself once, and moved quickly toward the forest's edge.

***

Lorit had nearly reached Roke and Tarh when beyond them a horse carrying two riders broke from the woods, accompanied by a tall woman in a shining robe who remained between the riders and the wizards. The guardsman accompanying the two younger wizards broke into a run, angling to intercept or at least come within easy bowshot of the horse. The wizards themselves stopped, appeared to cast spells but to no effect.

Lorit groaned. They were too far off. While their spells might affect the horses and the wounded brother, he doubted they would have any effect on the child. Or the tall woman in white. Lorit did not wish to think what she might be. Where was the red witch-woman?

That question seemed to receive an answer. The running guardsman suddenly flew into the air, rising a good thirty feet and coming down fifty or more from where he'd started. He did not move after landing.

With that, Roke and Tarh turned their attention to the woods. Lorit, running now with the last of his spell-induced strength, saw a red-robed figure standing just within the trees. She raised her hands and gestured toward the young wizards as though pushing them away.

Roke had just time to counter her spell but was still staggered, while Tarh reeled some yards, ending on his knees. With that, Lorit sent his most powerful fear spell at the woman, a spell which should have para-lyzed her in terror

She was not paralyzed, he could see, but certainly slowed. That allowed Roke, guessing what Lorit had done, to add his power. Now the woman reeled, still with no fear showing on her face. As she steadied herself, the ground beneath the wizards shook.

Standing well within the forest where he could see and not be seen, Dog had placed his hands together, then clapped once, sharply. After a moment, seeing the dark wizards still on their feet, he clapped again, then once more.

Only Rath, still some distance behind though with the plain in sight, kept his feet.

Dog watched for a moment while the wizards regained their footing. Then he placed his hands together, pointing away from his body and opened just his fingertips.

A gap in the earth appeared between Roke and Tarh.

Dog wiggled his fingers, and the gap extended, seeming to slither through the earth. He made a series of gestures then, moving his paired hands this way and that, sometimes in small circles, others in odd angles, wiggling his fingers the entire time.

Roke and Tarh found themselves unable to keep their feet in the midst of what seemed to be a weaving of the earth itself. Occasionally one or the other would rise to his knees only to be forced to roll away from a chasm which seemed to chase him.

Lorit, seeing no other foe, summoned all his power and again attacked the woman in red. Rath, nearer now, added his power, and Brenna crumpled to the ground.

At that, Dog made a noise low in this throat and turned his attention to the two senior wizards. Before he could act, he was thrown on his face by a force which came from behind and around him. When he struggled to his feet, he saw an empty plain where Lorit had been.

Dog shook himself, feeling aches everywhere, then turned to face into the forest. "Might warn!" he shouted, receiving no answer but a rustling of leaves which seemed angry. At that he shrugged. "Well," he muttered, "Lorit maybe decent compost. Red woman?"

He walked through the brush until he came to where Brenna lay, eyes closed. Dog knelt beside her and engulfed her head in his hands. "Now," he said softly, "time to return. Return," he said softly, almost a chant, "return to forest, return to shared spirit," while around him leaves rustled in rhythm with his words.

Dog knelt there long enough for Snake to find him. The assassin stood off a ways, watching for any signs of the two younger wizards or their guardsmen, his throwing knife ready in one hand, stiletto in the other. After a time, Brenna moaned and raised her hands as if to protect herself, her eyes opening as she attempted to rise.

Dog gently held her by a shoulder. "Must rest. Wizard gone. Forest needs time restore strength."

Brenna tried twice to speak before she could manage it. "Who—who are you?"

"What, better question," replied Dog. "Not today. Friends near Barren Lands. Forest remembers power. Use sooner next time. Now rest." He lifted her, one strong arm under her shoulders and the other under her knees, and stood. He noticed Snake for the first time, the assassin's eyes darting this way and that as he watched for enemies.

"What news?"

Snake sheathed both weapons as he approached. "I had nearly reached the forest edge, Master, when some power barely brushed me. Fortunately, it only knocked me down. When I looked up again, Lorit had vanished. One guardsman is down, the other seems dazed. Both young wizards are very quiet. Even Rath seems shaken. It seemed time to rejoin you without reporting to the wizards."

Dog smiled. "Good choice. We take lady into forest."

***

Hobard led the way across the open land between the Red Forest and the sparse forest just ahead, running while Aren, struggling to keep upright with Bird behind him, rode beside her. She glanced back once, then slowed their pace. "We can go more slowly. The wizards have other worries. The woods are near. Once in them we will be more difficult to find than here in the open. The red one has bought us time. Let us not waste it."

***

Soren stared at what his great crystal showed him. He had watched, with Haster and Oleg, as Roke, Tarh, and a single guardsman moved into view. Then a horse seemingly ridden only by the witch-child's brother and accompanied by a running woman appeared from the red haze and started across the plain. Cursing again the crystal's failure to show the child, he could only hope the witch-child was with them, He'd watched approvingly as Roke signaled to the guardsman to cut them off, only to see some force toss the man as though he was a feather. Quickly he'd shifted his crystal's view to the aural plane in time to see lines of force, red to his dismay, which led back into the red mist. With nothing more to learn there, he'd shifted back to temporal view in time to see Roke and Tarh stagger and fall as the earth beneath them shook.

Then came the most amazing thing: chasms opened as though at whim, making patterns unlike anything natural as though some powerful being were playing with the earth itself. Chasms extended in half-circles, then came back across themselves and circled around one or both wizards only to dart away again, if chasms in the earth could dart.

Soren had instinctively adjusted the crystal to view all this from a greater distance. Now Oleg said, "Look at what Lorit does," pointing.

Soren looked, saw Lorit seem to send a spell into the red mist.

"He must be attacking the red witch," Oleg said.

"And now Rath joins him," Haster noted.

In the globe's center the chasms had stopped playing. "This should settle her," Soren gloated, just before a red wave burst out of the mist and swept across their field of vision. When it had passed, Lorit was nowhere in sight. Some distance behind him Rath lay, apparently unconscious or dead. When Soren willed the crystal to show a wider picture, there was still no sign of Lorit. The two younger wizards, apparently further from whatever had taken Lorit, struggled to their feet, looking around in apparent confusion.

"The fugitives have escaped into the forest," noted Oleg. "No doubt from there into the Barren Lands. The red woman has provided a fine distraction."

Soren widened the field of vision even further. Oleg was correct; the fugitives were nowhere to be seen. "Can we be certain the witch-child was with them?"

Oleg did not share that concern. "I think we can assume that the brother would not leave his sister behind."

Haster nearly fell into the nearest chair, where he sat with his head in his hands. "What are we to do in the face of such power? And now there is another being residing in a forest which, you tell us"—raising his head to regard Oleg—"has long been known as a place of power. We know of no red Order, yet a woman appears wearing a red robe, residing in a red forest and seeming to draw upon its power, while we can't even be certain the witch-child went into the Barren Lands! Chief Mage, what are we to do?"

Until Haster's outburst Soren had appeared equally shaken; now he regained control. "We must wait for Roke to contact us. We could not see the red forest by crystal, but he and Rath can see it with their naked eyes, and their guardsmen have been able to enter. They should also be able to see the child. We know that the guardsmen they sent to attack her could see her."

"At some risk," Oleg noted. "Even wizards will find it difficult to persuade them to enter the forest again after this." He gestured at the crystal's view of the plain.

Soren was impatient. "True enough, Loremaster. Still, they will have seen what we could not."

"Could the earth-shaking have come from the witch-child? It seems more her sort of power than that of the red wizard." Haster was beginning to think again, Oleg noted, to the extent he could.

"I doubt it," Oleg responded. This was indeed an interesting puzzle. "It seemed the gaps in the earth began from the direction of the forest and moved from there, at least in the beginning. After a time, they appeared here and there with no particular pattern. Unless the child is very wily—and continues to be wily while escaping on a running horse—she would probably have directed those gaps from where she was at the time, rather than starting them from further away and guiding them back toward her location." He paused, thinking. "No, she has been more direct than that. Likely she would have destroyed all four wizards immediately. This was some being confident enough to play."

"You're correct, I think," Soren said. "This was a different power, one which felt no need to kill or even harm. The witch-girl strikes out of anger and even fear. The red wizard strikes to protect. This power, this earth-shaker, is as determined as are the other two but does not seem afraid or even angry. Playful, I would say, yes."

"But what play!" noted Oleg. This would be something of great interest to report to the Dark One. Still, he would rather hold that interview until they'd heard something from Roke, and from Rath if he survived this second confrontation. It seemed there would be no more reports from Lorit, which would leave a damaged Rath and two young wizards to deal with three beings of differing powers, each more powerful than Rath at his strongest.

No doubt some time would pass before any coherent reports would be forthcoming from those remaining on the ground. "Chief Mage,"

Oleg said, "with your permission, I will return to the archives and set my apprentices to searching for scrolls concerning beings with powers to shake and re-shape the earth itself. If you would send for me when Roke or Rath is able to report, I would much like to hear what they have seen this day."

Soren nodded and made a gesture of dismissal. Oleg departed.

***

Brenna had again lost consciousness as Dog carried her into the forest. Finally he paused before the hollowed-out living tree where she and Bird had spent their first night in the forest. He carried Brenna into the hollowed space and laid her gently on the bench which served as both bed and couch. Snake watched from the opening which served as a doorway.

Dog placed both hands against the inner wall of the tree and seemed to concentrate for a time, then turned and walked past Snake into the open air. Brenna had not regained consciousness as he carried her, and she did not do so now.

Snake was full of questions, but settled for one. "Will she live, Master?" He did not greatly care, but was curious about this woman who apparently was a new and powerful sort of wizard.

Dog smiled as he turned and looked back at the tree. The entrance had vanished, the tree's trunk now apparently solid. "Forest's center. Great power. Healing place." He shook himself, then moved off quickly. "Come! Rejoin wizards. Say knocked out. See what wizards plan."

Snake followed without any more questions. It was clear, as it had been for some time, that Master Dog was not on the side of the dark Order; but just whose side, if any, he was actually on, Snake was still uncertain. On the side of this new red wizard, perhaps, though that might have been simple convenience. Probably on the side of the child and her brother, though in that case, why not simply join and guide them?

That question continued to puzzle Snake, who was accustomed to taking the most direct approach within his world of spying, assassinations, and service. If someone were to be killed, then the quickest way was usually best, so long as there would be no link to Soren or himself. The same was true with spying: learn what he'd been sent to learn and return to the Order's headquarters as quickly as possible.

That was clearly not his new master's method. Master Dog could have ended the chase at any time by dropping the four wizards and their guardsmen into the depths and closing the earth over them, but had not. It was as though Dog, for all his powers, acted under some constraint which required him to let the child find her own way to a place of safety. To Snake's surprise, something about that pleased him, just a little, and he wasn't sure he liked the feeling. There were more powers popping up in this changing world than he would have preferred.

CHAPTER EIGHT

Some hours passed before Oleg was summoned again to Soren's observatory. Nor had they been productive hours. His apprentices had searched for mention of any being able to shake the earth but found nothing. Oleg himself had led the search in the very oldest scrolls but with no better luck.

Soren and Haster were bent over the great crystal when Oleg tapped once on the door and entered. Soren acknowledged him with a nod, Haster sparing him only a glance.

A battered-looking Rath gazed out at them from the crystal's depths. "…there are more forces at work here than we had realized, Soren. The child escaped into the green forest to the northeast while others delayed us. Lorit is gone, swept away by some force emanating from the forest. Roke and Tarh were knocked off their feet when the ground shook, as was I."

"Did this force which struck Lorit seem to come from the red wizard-woman?" asked Oleg. "We could not see; a red ward blinded us to the forest and for some distance beyond. When Soren shifted briefly to the aural plane, we could see red lines of power, something we've not seen before."

"I think whatever took Lorit did not come from the woman," Rath said. "Roke and Tarh were closer than I when they were knocked to the ground, though not hurt badly. They believe the red woman was not the source. Lorit struck her down and she did not move again. The second strike came only after Lorit's attack. It seemed to come from deep within the forest.

"That was not all," Rath continued. "You must have seen the way the ground shook, and then chasms opened as though directed."

Soren was silent for a moment after hearing of Lorit's disappearance. "So Roke and Tarh survived. What of your guardsmen?"

"Three remain. One died in the forest, and his companion was too badly damaged to continue with us. Lorit left another to assist the damaged guard, though I doubt that will make a difference. He will no doubt make his way back or die somewhere along the way. No matter; he will be of no more use to us."

"The witch-child was with them? My crystal could not show her." Soren was little concerned with guardsmen.

"She rode behind the guardsman as they made their way into the forest beyond," Rath said. "There is yet another new member of their party, according to Roke: a tall figure dressed in a white robe ran alongside their remaining horse, seemingly effortlessly."

This brought Oleg to lean over the crystal as though he wished to reach into it and take Rath by the shoulders. "What sort of white robe? Was it dull, perhaps dirty?"

Soren and Haster looked in surprise at the Loremaster. Neither had ever seen him appear excited.

Rath also seemed puzzled. "Not dull or dirty; almost gleaming, Tarh maintains. Almost too bright to look at."

"And tall," Oleg repeated. "Taller than a normal man, then?"

"Tarh says the top of the woman's head was level with that of the horse. Taller than normal, even allowing for the turmoil of the moment."

This was interesting news indeed. Oleg had read much in ancient scrolls only parts of which were still readable, some in languages so archaic as to be almost incomprehensible. References to Druids often mentioned their gleaming robes, those references becoming more disparaging as the dark wizards writing those accounts became more powerful. Height was not directly mentioned, but some drawings showed wizards looking up at taller beings. Occasionally an account of a meeting with a Druid might mention looking up at the being's face.

The Dark One would find this news of great interest, Oleg would wager. There was much to tell him: the witch-child appeared headed for the Barrens; she seemed to have found a Druid—found or called one; the red forest appeared to use power to protect the red woman-wizard; and some Power seemed able to play with the ground itself.

For all the interest the Dark One would no doubt manifest, Oleg found little reason for joy. As Rath said, there were more powers at work than the Order had expected. And each seemed greater than the previous. Though, he reminded himself, one appeared to be a child; what she might become when grown might be the greatest of all. He did not think they were working together just yet so much as working against the Dark Order, which seemed to unite them. Perhaps given time they would war with each other. Could the Order survive until such time?

Oleg realized that Soren had been speaking. To have missed Soren's first words was unusual for Oleg, who was careful to pay attention to the Chief Mage. "…when will you be able to continue in pursuit? If they are indeed headed for some sort of sanctuary in these Barrens, we may be able to set a watch along those lands. But we must know where they are."

Rath bent his head; when he looked up again, exhaustion showed clearly in his face. "It will be some time, Chief Mage. I used several strengthening spells in order to arrive when I did. It will be morning before I recover from that effort. Roke and Tarh are not much better off; they were badly battered. We will follow tomorrow, but I fear we will follow slowly."

Haster spoke up. "Chief Mage, perhaps we should send help to Rath and the others. All three are damaged now, and they've lost a third of their guard."

Soren frowned, then nodded. "Yes. We will think on this, and see who will be most useful." He focused again on the crystal. "Rath, prepare to follow in the morning. Snake should be able to track them, and that fellow with him is reputed to have some skill in the matter."

"If Snake and Ryd's Dog have survived," Rath answered. "They were in the Red Forest, sent there to track the fugitives. Roke expected them to report about the time the fugitives broke cover. Perhaps both perished in Lorit's attack on the woman, or in the forest's attack on Lorit. If they live, they may join us tonight. We will camp near here. Neither the guardsmen nor my fellow wizards wish to camp where the ground was torn, even though it is smooth now. I will keep my crystal nearby in case you wish to speak again, or something happens which I should report immediately."

Oleg's eyebrows rose; it was difficult to believe that Rath had said these words. The man had always been independent, arrogant, Now he spoke of reporting as though it were something he'd always done willingly. As much as anything else which had been reported that day, Rath's chastened attitude spoke of the magnitude of the powers he'd observed.

***

Hobard slowed to a walk once they were well into the woods. "It does not look as though anyone will follow us tonight. Let us save our energy in the event they pursue again."

The suggestion pleased Aren. He didn't believe his wound had begun to bleed again, but it surely would were they to continue at a fast pace. Blaze had a gentle gait when walking, though even that was uncomfortable.

"Do you know what lies ahead?" he asked.

The tall woman shrugged. "A place which may provide safety, if Brenna was correct. Behind us are wizards with reason to be angry, though I wonder why they pursue." She looked from Aren to Bird and back again. "I appeared only after they'd attacked you, so they would not seem to be pursuing me. I am surprised," she looked at Bird, "that you allow these attacks, my lady."

Bird sniffled. "I promised Aren I wouldn't do anything, even to dark wizards. A wizard and a lord are dead because I lost my temper twice. I don't like doing things like that."

Hobard was shocked into silence. As Blaze walked past her, she shook herself and hurried to catch up, then moved a little ahead to where she could look over her shoulder at Bird's slumped shoulders and unsmiling face. The child's eyes glistened with unshed tears.

"I think I understand, my lady," the Druid said. "I have come into a different sort of world than I left. There is much to learn. For now, let us walk as far as we're able before we camp."

***

In the morning Hobard set out a cold breakfast before rousing Aren and Bird. Both had slept well while she'd kept watch, occasionally murmuring words for the two which would foster sleep and healing. Bird jumped up, nearly her old self, smiling at the morning, bright even among the trees. Even Aren moved more easily than he had the night before.

Bird stood still, her face puzzled, seeming not to listen so much as recall. Aren watched her for a few minutes before asking, "What is it, little bird? Are wizards nearby?" Automatically he loosened his sword in his sheath, though he doubted he would make much of a showing in a swordfight.

Hobard also stood listening. "I do not think—" she began before Bird interrupted.

"It's not wizards. But the place up ahead—that way, I think." She pointed a little more east than they'd been going. "The place up ahead feels different, though I'm not sure just why." She not-listened again. "What's ahead isn't quite like the Red Forest, but it's more like that than where we are now. And I think--" She concentrated again, "I think," she looked up into Hobard's face, "there are people there who are a little like you." At the look of joy on the Druid's face she held up a cautioning hand, much as Reya would have done. "They're a little like you. If dark wizards are like a hole in the day when I sense them, you're a brightness. These people are somewhere in between. It's as though they're faded."

"Do you sense any danger?" asked Aren.

Bird shook her head. "I think they're too sad to be dangerous. Sad and yet hopeful, maybe."

"Are they near?" asked Hobard.

"I'm not sure." Bird not-listened again for a moment. "We might meet them today. They've been where they are for a long time, even longer than the people in the Five Valleys, I think."

"Well," said Hobard, "let us eat and be on our way. The sooner we start out, the sooner we'll see what's ahead. Those wizards may not be in shape for travel just yet, though I have no doubt they'll be coming after us. They seem slow to learn."

✳✳✳

Snake was also thinking that wizards were slow to learn. The pair came limping--very convincingly--into the wizard's camp at dusk. Snake told a story of having been struck down by a force surging through the forest. They came to their senses very late in the day, he added, then made their way back toward where they'd left the wizards. Dog had ripped their clothing and thrown dirt over both to make their appearances agree with their story.

When Rath questioned them about the nature of this force, Snake claimed to be unable to tell from which direction it had come. He admitted having seen Brenna send her power into the plain against the two younger wizards and again against Lorit. Then the older wizard's strike had burst into the forest edge, bending brush and trees alike as it struck down the red woman.

Snake did not tell Rath that after Brenna was attacked, the forest had seemed to shake with what Snake would have called rage had he been speaking of a person. Power rolled through the forest and away. After that, things became quiet again. Except that Lorit was gone.

The assassin maintained firmly that he and Master Dog had lain unconscious until late in the day, long after the battle was over. When they awoke they could hear no shouting and feel no bursts of power rocking the forest. For which, he added, he was grateful. Once was enough.

"You must have been on the edge of Lorit's strike, then," Rath noted. "Had you been closer, you'd not yet be awake, if you were to waken at all. Did you see anything of the red woman when you awoke?"

No, Snake asserted, they'd seen nothing of her. Perhaps she had been entirely destroyed.

Rath snorted at that. "Lorit was strong, but not that strong. Her body may lie there in the woods. We will leave it. For now, rest. We move into the far woods in the morning, and will have need of your dog's tracking skills."

Snake bowed and rejoined Dog, who'd been warming himself by a fire built by one of the guards. He sat just within hearing of Snake's report, sipping a little heated wine. With a wink, he finished his wine and curled up to sleep on the ground not far from the fire. Snake stretched out nearby.

***

Again Oleg made his way into the darkness below the Order's headquarters, and again the Dark One heard him coming. The rusty voice came out of the gloom. "Already more news, wizard? And more fears, no doubt. Well, let us hear it. Your world grows more interesting."

Oleg held his answer until he was standing in his usual spot before the door, just out of arm's reach, the dark lantern at his feet. "Yes, there is news, Dark One. It is time for better answers, lest I decide that yours are not worth the journey into this deep hole."

"A nice threat, that. After centuries in this dark, a little longer seems bearable. Sooner or later all walls fall. Eventually all bars rust." The voice paused. "Enough of this fencing. What setback have your wizards met with now?"

Oleg hesitated for a moment but decided to speak frankly. "Severe. A senior in the Order has been wiped from the earth. The child, her brother, and another have escaped the Red Forest and crossed into a lesser forest to the north and east. Before his death, Lorit cast a spell which struck down the red woman; then a far more powerful blast came, seemingly from the forest itself. Afterwards, Lorit was nowhere to be seen." He paused, thinking of the power of that blast.

A low, rusty chuckle came from the darkest corner of the cell. "Then the forest has remembered its strength. Even as it dozed, I'd wager no nearby farmer ventured to cut firewood or lumber from those oaks." There came the sound of the Dark One shifting on his stone seat. "The woman is at least a wizard; have no doubt of that. Attacking such a one on the edge of the Red Forest is something no sane being would have done. Your Order blunders into the awakening of one power, now into the awakening of another. How many do you think you can stand against? You've long avoided that forest, I'm certain. Now you may not even approach. One of your number was killed when he tried to enter a certain valley. How long, I wonder, before you cannot leave this building?" He chuckled, genuinely amused, Oleg thought.

"There is more," Oleg said. "We suspect that yet another power joined the conflict. Rath reported that the earth around the two younger wizards seemed to go mad. Trenches opened and ran here and there around them. The ground shook them off their feet."

"Now that is interesting," came the reply. "The--shall we say, child--you pursue might have done that had she thought of it. But such control—and the way it was used-- has the mark of yet another. Your wizards may be correct about that." His voice came more freely now. "Tell me, Loremaster, can any of your order command earth and stone? Hey? The child commands stone and mortar to fall, and now she seems to have an ally who commands the ground itself. You continue to pursue her?"

Silence grew before the Dark One spoke again. "Ah, I see there is more yet to tell. Out with it, Loremaster. How can I prescribe for your Order's trauma before I know all the symptoms? And yet even the most skillful healer cannot stave off death."

Oleg's voice was nearly a growl. "Another has joined them. This one is tall, robed in gleaming white, and travels on foot as rapidly as does a horse, even in flight."

"What?" The Dark One rose and came forward to stand with hands gripping the bars. "Tall, you say? White-robed? Moves swiftly and easily over the earth itself?"

"Taller than most men," Oleg replied. "A Druid, we suspect."

"You suspect rightly," came the answer. Then, more softly as though to himself, "She has called a Druid. She moves, whether deliberately or otherwise, toward the Barren Lands."

For the first time in Oleg's many conversations with the prisoner, there was something more than amusement, scorn, or hatred in the voice coming from that vague shape. The Dark One seemed shaken.

The voice spoke again. "Loremaster, this is where your Order's study, your learning, your search for greater and greater power has brought you. You have awakened those who will destroy you." Again a pause. "If you call off your wizards now, you may survive. I doubt your Chief Mage has wisdom enough to do such a thing. For myself, I hope you do not retreat and do not survive. I may never leave this dark hole, but it will be a comfort to know that those who imprisoned me are wiped from the earth."

That was all the Dark One would say. Oleg could tell from the sounds that he retreated to his stone bed and lay down. Deeply disturbed, the Loremaster took up the dark lantern and left the prisoner to brood alone. Oleg would do his brooding in his office.

He had much on which to ponder. The Dark One had named "Barren Lands," but would say no more. Surely that was the ancient name for the mist-filled area north of the Blue River and east of the Red Forest. Wizards had entered those lands in the past, though only to become disoriented and lost almost immediately. Within ten feet of entering the fogs or mists, said several accounts. Perhaps yet another ward protected them from intruders. Would such a ward protect against a force of fifty or so guardsmen, keeping so close to one another as to nearly touch?

Oleg shook his head, snorting in disgust. How had a Loremaster of the dark Order been reduced to considering a campaign using a small army of guardsmen in an area where wizardry might be of no use? If the barrens' fogs and mists were part of an ancient ward, strong enough to have continued through the years, he knew of no wizardry which might be useful against it.

The land was indeed, as the Dark One had chuckled, becoming smaller. For a moment Oleg felt almost claustrophobic, in need of a breath of fresh air somewhere outside the Order's building. He'd not felt such a need since his apprentice days. Quelling the feeling, he went into the archives to gather his best apprentices. He would send them searching for more about the Barren Lands, or any word of a land of mists and fogs between the Blue River and the mountains.

***

Dog woke at the first suggestion of morning light. By the time Snake rose from his bedroll, the squat man had a cold breakfast laid out on a small cloth. As the pair ate, the three remaining guardsmen also rose, made their own meager breakfast, then set about striking the tent in which they'd slept. As the three surviving wizards appeared from the tent they'd shared, a guardsman quickly set out their breakfast plus three cups and a flask of wine, then stepped well away from the three.

Rath, again assisted by Tarh, showed the greatest effects of the previous day. He walked slowly, occasionally unable to suppress a wince, groaning as he lowered himself to sit on a log the guards had provided. Roke was obviously stiff and sore, as was Tarh. Both moved gingerly around the camp for a time before joining Rath at breakfast. None spoke, the two younger wizards preferring to allow Rath to speak first so they could gauge his mood and moderate their own speech accordingly.

Rath ate in silence, with an occasional sip from the wine Tarh had poured. Finally he spoke. "Bring Snake."

Snake and Dog were not so far off that a call wouldn't have sufficed. Tarh walked quickly to where the two trackers had been relaxing, their meal long since finished and their bedrolls packed. Snake was already on his feet, moving toward where the wizards breakfasted, saving any need for words.

Snake gave his slight bow of the head and shoulders. "I trust you slept well, Masters."

Roke snorted at that, drawing a quick glare from Rath.

"You and your dog will go into the forest ahead and track our quarry." Rath's voice had regained some of its usual commanding tone. "Where the trail becomes dim or confused, leave some sign our guardsmen will recognize. If you come across anything of moment, either return to inform us or, if you think your minion can manage to convey a message, send him." For a moment he waited for any response. Snake merely nodded. "What sort of sign will you leave?"

Snake almost replied that he'd use his knife to scar trees where a sign would be needed, but he suspected Dog might not appreciate that. Instead he replied, "We'll arrange either a string of rocks or a series of branches in the trail to point the way."

Rath nodded. "Tell the guardsmen." He waved Snake away.

Again Snake's very slight head inclination. He took a step backwards, turned and walked toward the guards. They'd just finished packing up the wizards' tent and supplies. The oldest stepped forward. "We heard. You'll leave a sign in the trail, stones or branches."

Snake nodded, then joined Dog. Guardsmen, he knew, wished as little contact as possible with him. For that matter, he didn't particularly relish their company, either. In his days as a thief, guardsmen were to be avoided. Since becoming Soren's spy and assassin, he'd found them no more congenial than when they sought to catch and punish him. The one difference in their new relationship, of course, was their obvious discomfort and sometimes fear in his presence. He'd always enjoyed that difference.

Dog had already shouldered his small backpack . He held out Snake's own. As Snake took the pack, Dog turned and led the way into the thin green forest.

***

Though they'd moved at a gentle pace until mid-day, Aren was beginning to consider asking Hobard to stop for the night. His wound had been throbbing for some time, and he wasn't certain how much longer he could stay on Blaze. He saw the first thin tendrils of mist ahead just as Hobard announced that they would soon be free from concerns about pursuit. That gave Aren strength enough to continue, though he still hoped it would not be for long.

Soon they moved through a fog so thick that Aren could no longer see Bird as she walked alongside Blaze. Hobard's white robe vanished completely in the fogs and mists which swirled gently with their passage. Only occasionally did a swirl cause a momentary thinning which allowed Aren to catch a glimpse of Bird. Finally, reluctant as he was to ask for help, Aren called out, "Hobard, I cannot see you or Bird. I fear losing you."

Hobard appeared out of the mist. "I am sorry. I forgot that you might not see through the mist. It is impenetrable to your eyes?"

"It is," Aren admitted. "You can see clearly, then?"

Hobard nodded. "To my eyes, it is a very thin mist, more like gentle rain on a dark day than the thick fog which must appear to you."

"Well, Aren," Bird said, "that's not very good if you can't see clearly. I hope these fogs let you see right now!"

With that, Aren found he could see Hobard and Bird through what now appeared to be a light mist. Glancing back over their trail, he noted that the fog seemed to thin wherever he directed his gaze. On the edges of his vision it seemed as impenetrable as ever.

"Is that better?" Bird asked.

"Much," Aren answered. "You can see through this as well as Hobard can?"

"I don't know how clearly she sees, but I don't see any fog," Bird answered. "I can tell it's there, though. It's as though the fog wants me to know it's in place and doing its job. It's all very strange. I know what its job is: to set a boundary, keep out anyone except those I wish to have enter."

She paused, looked to Aren in appeal. "How can that be, Aren? I've never been out of the Valley. How could I have set limits on who can enter here?"

"That I understand no better than do you, little bird. If this fog serves to hold back the wizards and their guardsmen, I am glad of it. Perhaps here, with Hobard's help and that of the beings you sense within this place, we can learn more. If the fog is to keep out anyone that you would not want to enter, then those who live here may also have your permission, odd as that may sound. They may be able to tell you more."

"Well, I certainly hope so! The fog seems to welcome us. I don't sense much else, other than its focus on its job. It has been here a long time, and no one has entered who shouldn't. When I thought of dark wizards, the fog seemed for just a moment to become a wall; then I saw wizards wandering in circles until they finally wandered into the open again. Aren, I think we may be safe here. The fog will do its job well, as it always has!"

At that, the light mist Aren saw and the thicker fog on the edges of his vision seemed to dance.

Hobard stood silent, eyes wide. She opened her mouth to speak but closed it without saying anything. In another moment she suggested they move further from the forest's edge. Perhaps they could seek shelter with those other beings Bird sensed somewhere ahead.

***

The trail was easy for Snake to follow and certainly even easier for Dog. Though the child's light weight and small feet left little sign, a horse and a long-striding Druid left a clear trail through the small growth on the forest floor. Clearly they were making no effort to hide their tracks. Eager to reach a destination, Snake thought, no doubt the barrens he'd seen on maps but never had reason to seek out. How those might be safer than the Red Forest they'd just left, he wasn't sure. At any rate, the clear trail made it unnecessary to leave any markers for Rath's party to follow.

Once again Dog set a pace faster than Snake could normally have maintained. He'd become used to that and almost didn't notice, though at mid-afternoon the thought occurred that the wizards' party couldn't possibly catch up to them. Snake's master showed no signs of slowing or turning back to rejoin Rath's party.

Shortly thereafter, Snake began to catch glimpses through the trees of what looked like mist or fog up ahead. Dog slowed and finally stopped a dozen feet from what seemed a wall of fog. The trail continued into that wall.

Dog smiled. "Safe now." He turned to Snake, who stood bewildered.

"This fog will protect them?" Snake asked. "Won't wizards go in after them?"

"Wizards blunder in circles." Dog chuckled. "Easy walk back, take time. Make early camp, wait wizards." He tuned back along the way they'd come. "Stay while, listen to wizards' foolishness. Child where maybe intended."

Dog strolled, taking his time, cocking his head occasionally to listen to a bit of birdsong, pausing to watch a deer move through the brush or a squirrel scolding its way up a tree. Occasionally their route would pass near a large rock thrust up through the ground. Snake's master might stray from the path to stroke it as one would a pet. For the first time since they'd met, Snake sensed no urgency in this squat being. In its place, Dog seemed in and of the world around them. Whatever urgency, whatever crisis had impelled him seemed settled.

***

Blaze walked slowly now, Hobard insisting that there was no need for speed. The wizards would see no more clearly than had Aren. And no, she said, noticing Aren's raised eyebrows, wizards would have no power over the mists. Those mists were far more ancient than any magic a gaggle of dark-robed wizards might command.

Aren was grateful for the gentle pace, and even more for Blaze's apparent awareness that his rider was injured. Occasionally he dozed in the saddle, knowing himself to be a good horseman even when dozing. That, too, had been part of Lord Ryd's training. The lord would lead a half-dozen of his new guardsmen on long rides up the First Valley and along the foothills to find game trails and occasionally thieves' trails.

Ryd intended to keep his men in the saddle so long they'd learn to sleep while riding. Aren chuckled at the memory; of course each man dozed and fell from his horse more than once. Ryd would halt and lead the entire troop in a sort of riddle song: "Who fell off his horse?" "Aren fell off his horse!" "Why did Aren fall off his horse?" "Because Aren was asleep!" "Should Aren fall off his horse when he sleeps?" "No, no! Aren should keep his seat!" By that time, the sleeper would be awake, mounted and looking forward to the next poor fool who fell. By the time Ryd brought his men back to the Manor, all were eager for a good night's sleep in a bed, and all could doze while riding without fear of falling off.

Safe for at least a while, Hobard had time to look carefully at the world around her. The land appeared not so much barren as dry. Trees and undergrowth were more compact than in the green forests she remembered from further west and in the mountains to the north. She assumed those forests and mountains still existed; surely she'd have sensed that kind of absence. Long ago she had spent most of her time in those forests, studying trees and brush and grasses, listening to them, learning of the powers each might hold to help or harm. The Red Forest had been most interesting, fully awake and vibrant with its power for growth, health, healing. She'd lingered long in those woods.

Later, at the Mother's command, she and most of her kind passed into the earth and the lakes and the trees. How long she'd existed in that form Hobard neither knew nor cared. She'd no longer listened from outside plants; instead she moved from one to another, becoming part of each and staying, a welcome guest, for a time before moving on. The knowledge was like air to a Healing Druid, as she'd been back when she'd last had a body. Sometimes she'd come across a diseased tree or even a farmer's suffering crop, and with what she'd learned during those travels and something contributed from her own strength, she'd again be a healer. Always she returned to the Red Forest as it slept through time. Eventually, to the extent "eventually" meant anything in that existence, Hobard sensed a greater need for her skills and sensed also that the world was changing, though she had no idea why. Called back into her body, she did not much like the world she'd found, with what appeared to be its constant threats.

She'd existed without a body for a long time. Long enough, it seemed, for the one who'd called her to have forgotten herself, though Power still enfolded her like a cloak. No, like a swirl of colors, a blessing. Hobard could see, though either her caller in her new form couldn't or didn't notice, how alert plants became as Bird approached: the slight lift of their leaves, a just discernible lifting of branches, straightening of stems or trunks. As a healer, Hobard had always been most attuned to the life of plants. Now she could also feel the earth's welcome as this child approached, feel more than hear a quickening in the deep, slow song of stone far beneath a celebrating earth.

As they moved further into the mist Bird found herself feeling safe for the first time since she'd awakened to find men with swords threatening Aren. Only his quick word of warning had kept her silent then. Now she wondered if it would not have been better to have stopped the men who'd taken them, avoided reaching that terrible Keep. What had followed she didn't want to think about. Much better to look around at this strange dry land, dry in a way which felt natural, appropriate, so very different from the drought years in the Valley. Here the land seemed at peace with this aridity. Plants here, Bird knew without understanding how she knew, were adapted to little rain. They'd have done less well in the Valley.

Somewhere ahead, closer now, were those faded beings she'd sensed earlier. They weren't quite comfortable, that was certain, but Bird didn't think they were dangerous. Reya would have said they were sorry for something they'd done, perhaps even that they were trying to make up for it. Hobard said they would be safe here. Bird hoped Hobard was right. She didn't want to kill any more wizards or their helpers, but would if they threatened Aren again. And what of Brenna, who'd stayed behind to slow wizards? Bird hoped the Forest had kept Brenna safe.

They could see buildings ahead, a small village. As they rode slowly toward the place, Aren took the lead. Still very weak, he wouldn't be much in a swordfight if those who lived in these dry lands proved unfriendly. He'd have to count on his guardsman's bearing to intimidate. At least the fog had vanished as they moved further into this dry land.

The village wasn't promising. Though the small wooden huts appeared well kept, with solid roofs and tight doors and windows, nothing resembled an inn or house large enough to afford a night's hospitality. Aren had hoped for a night's rest in a bed, or even on a level floor with no stones digging into his back or side.

Near the center of the dozen or so huts stood about that many men. Aren halted Blaze a good ten feet away, inclined his head in a slight bow. "Greetings. Is there a place nearby where three tired travelers might rest and perhaps take a meal?" Glancing over his shoulder, he saw that Hobard had stepped off to his left, Bird standing between them and slightly behind. Hobard, he noted, looked puzzled.

Aren didn't spare more than that one glance, not with obviously uneasy strangers to deal with. These tall men looked confused. Each one's gaze kept shifting, from Aren to Bird to Hobard. Aren was unable to tell whether Bird or Hobard seemed most to worry them. Bird had said that these beings were maybe a little like Hobard, but if that were true, Hobard seemed puzzled by any resemblance.

They were tall, like Hobard. But where her robe was a white which Aren thought had gleamed while she murmured her healing chant over his wound, theirs were a kind of gray. Yet that gray was unlike the color Brenna's apprentice's robe had been. These robes seemed stained rather than deliberately colored.

Hobard kept her head turned slightly so Bird remained in her field of vision. As though these beings were somehow kin, Hobard could feel their uncertainty as their eyes darted from one to another of the small party. Bird had said that these people were sad but perhaps hopeful, and faded.

Faded. Hobard would think about that later. That these dozen beings were confused, even a little frightened, concerned her more. Fear could dominate actions, she knew from healing injured animals and people in the time before she'd gone back into the earth. If whatever hope they felt seemed fading, that could increase their fear. Should they attempt to harm Bird, she must stop them. As Hobard gathered her strength, her robe began again to gleam.

Aren caught the brightness from the corner of his eye but spared only a quick glance. These strangers still had not answered his question about whether travelers might find a meal and perhaps a bed. Perhaps asking again would convince these worried men that they were only tired and hungry travelers.

"May three travelers find a place to rest and perhaps take a meal? We mean no harm."

One villager stepped out from the group. The others huddled silently.

"My apologies. We see few visitors, and none of your sort for many years." His eyes flickered, darting from Aren to Bird to Hobard. He froze, staring at the Druid.

Aren risked a quick look at Hobard, saw that her robe had begun to shine. Immediately he shifted his focus back to the group of tall men with robes of that odd shade of gray. He allowed his cloak to fall away from his left shoulder and placed his left hand on his sword-hilt. If Hobard sensed trouble, Aren would be ready, despite his wound and weakness, to do what he could to protect Bird and buy time for Hobard to do whatever she might.

The tall fellow took a step back, raising his empty hands. The men clustered behind him did the same, stepping away from one another so each could be clearly seen.

Hobard watched the men, her robe gleaming, but didn't move. Bird looked at the Druid, then turned toward Aren, her face puzzled.

Aren broke the silence. "If it helps any, we're no one of us afraid of a little work. Surely there must be some elder whose wood needs chopping or water needs hauling. Both my sister and I can wash a dish or clean a floor, while she"—he nodded toward Hobard, never taking his eyes from the tall fellow and the villagers—"can mix a potion or set a broken arm."

The tall fellow answered now, but his voice shook just a little. He didn't take his gaze from Hobard. "Why, there is such an elder." He turned toward his friends for a moment, holding his hands before him, palms down in a calming gesture before again facing Aren. "Magda's wood always needs split, and as for her floors--!" The men behind him smiled at this, but the smiles were strained.

"That will do for us," Aren said. "Where can I find this Magda?"

The man half turned, his face showing relief which didn't quite hide the apprehension beneath. He pointed along the road which continued through the small village. Not far off, atop a small hill, stood a solitary hut which even at this distance looked to be in worse repair than those in the village proper. "That's it," the tall man said. "That's Magda's cottage. Tell her Inek sends his best."

Aren gestured for Bird and Hobard to proceed first, holding his ground until they were several feet ahead. He followed, left hand still resting casually on his sword hilt, walking Blaze as slowly as possible, his ears straining for any sound from behind. He heard little, mostly the kind of shuffling which usually meant a group standing but not attacking. After thirty feet, he glanced back.

As he'd thought, the dozen or so not followed. They were lined up across the road, watching the travelers move away. Aren saw in the villagers' faces open disappointment and more: dashed hope, and resignation which nearly drew him back to ask the reason.

Ahead was a building where they might hope for shelter and perhaps food. Bird and Hobard moved more rapidly than did Aren as he took up the rear, with several pauses to look behind. Bird already knocked at the door as Aren rode up.

A low half-groan, half-growl came from within. Bird knocked once more. This time brought a voice which might have been that of a woman or a very ancient parrot. "Who's there? Go away! What do you want? Stop that knocking!"

Aren dismounted and reached Bird's side. He took her hand in his left. The voice didn't sound dangerous, but who knew what someone irritated at visitors might do.

Aren knocked, louder and more firmly than had Bird. This time the voice sounded closer. "What's this, then? One knocks at the bottom of the door and the other at the top? Or is it Inek, playing his tricks again, hey?" There was a pause in which Aren could almost hear thinking from within the hut. "Is that you, then, Inek, with a bit of wine and a favor to ask?" The voice was softer now, muttering to itself. "No, not Inek. A dwarf and an ogre, perhaps? Well, that's better than Inek, at any rate. So you're—"

The door opened. In the doorway stood an old woman, bent but still tall enough that Aren had to look up to see her eyes under a wild white thatch of hair. She was older than he'd imagined a woman could be. She looked past Aren and down, to where Bird stood beside and slightly behind her brother.

For a long moment the old woman didn't move or speak, her eyes and mouth widening into "O's" of astonishment and, Aren thought, something very like joy. Finally she breathed in and then out in a great gust of wine-soaked breath, began to reach toward Bird with both hands, and fainted.

Hobard caught the old woman as she collapsed and carried her back into the hut. For the moment, she chose to lay the woman on the floor.

Aren called to Bird to shut the door behind them, and immediately wished he hadn't. The hut was dim and dank, with no candle and no fire on the hearth. He saw a small window on the wall opposite the door, but it took him a while to maneuver his way around a series of small tables piled with bottles, vials, and plants. Finally he was able to open a small shutter and let in light and, more importantly, air. He breathed deeply for a moment before turning back to the shambles of a room.

He wouldn't even try to guess how long it had been since the floor had been swept, what he could see of it between bags of what might be seeds and shocks of dried plants. Nothing above the floor had been dusted, either, and sunlight streaming through the west-facing window showed a near-curtain of dust stirring as they moved about.

The old woman lay on her back in only clear spot large enough to hold her. Bird stood a little further off by the open door. In what little floor space was left Hobard knelt and listened to the old woman's heart, touched her finger for a moment to the flutter of pulse in the withered neck, lifted an eyelid to look at the eyeball, leaned forward again to listen to breathing, ran hands over head and neck to check for injuries.

Finally Hobard stood, shrugging and raising her palms. "She seems fine. From the wine-smell, I'd guess she's passed out. Or perhaps she mistook us for someone whose appearance would be a shock. If she doesn't wake for a while, I can try a stimulant." She looked around at the bundles of dried plants. "There's got to be something in here which will wake her."

"In the meantime," Bird piped up, "There must be a broom somewhere. Reya would have something to say to us if we went to bed tonight in all this dust and clutter!" She had adopted her "little Reya" stance, hands on her hips, a decisive nod after each sentence. "Hobard," she continued, "can you look around and find places to put her plants so we don't stumble over them every time we move? "

One wall was covered with shelves full of baskets and bags of seeds on the upper levels, with large bins lower down. Here and there were strings of dried herbs. Hobard had already recognized enough of what she could see on the old woman's shelves to understand that the woman must be a very skilled healer, one worthy of her respect. Hobard would handle these herbs with respect. The number of seeds puzzled her; what could one person do with so many?

A healer could not be left to lie on the floor. "Lady," Hobard said, "there must be a bed somewhere. I will carry Magda to it, then begin sorting and shelving, with your permission."

Bird blushed. "Oh, I should have thought. I'm sorry. Put her to bed while I get started." She turned to her brother. "Aren, you need to rest and recover. Let Hobard and me do this. In fact," she said to the tall Druid as Hobard returned from putting Magda to bed, "I think you'd better check Aren's wound once you've settled Magda. I'll get started on the rest of this."

Hiding a smile but also fighting a surge of homesickness, Aren nodded.

"Let us go outside into the light, where the air is cleaner," Hobard suggested. Aren followed her out the door. He left it open for more light and especially air.

A table and benches stood in front of the small house. Aren sat and removed his jerkin. Hobard untied the flat knot she'd used to tie off the bandage, then slowly unwrapped and set it aside. She looked surprised when she saw the wound. Before speaking she carefully examined the bandage.

"The wound seems to be sealed," she said. "I expected to find some fresh bleeding, or at least signs that it bled recently, but I see nothing." She looked Aren in the eye. "You're lucky. That ride should have broken the scab which has been forming." She placed both hands across the wound and closed her eyes, concentrating. "I feel no heat coming from the wound. There may be no infection."

The Druid was quiet again as she kept her hands covering the wound. "I feel nothing which should hinder a quick recovery." She took her hands away. "I will find something appropriate for a bandage. Stay quiet and let the wound breathe a little. Contact with air will help the healing." She entered the cottage and returned shortly with a fresh cloth.

"I found this in a drawer which seemed to have kept the dust out. It should do."

As she re-bandaged his middle and tied off the bandage, Aren said, "You appeared concerned about those villagers."

Hobard worked in silence for a few moments. "They seem familiar, yet I'm not certain how that might be. I recall none like them from earlier times. Their robes are odd, the color almost not a color at all, as though the wearers do not quite exist. Yet they're here. I could feel the hope with which they regarded the lady, their puzzlement about your presence as though they'd not encountered humans in many years. When their eyes fell on me, I could feel their fear and then their disappointment as they looked again at the lady. It was as though they expected us, yet we were not what they expected." She finished Aren's bandage and stepped back. "That should do. You're in much better shape than I dared hope."

She was silent while Aren thanked her. "I sense no anger, nor that they are a danger. Yet they seem strange, alien to me even as I sense their responses more than I do yours, or did Brenna's." She shook her head, frowning slightly. "I do not know. We must wait and see what we learn. They seem guarded, yet even their guarding is clear to me. I don't understand."

Aren listened, hearing little reassuring even in Hobard's suggestion that these beings were no danger. In any case, he would continue to remain alert until he was certain that Bird would be safe, if such a time ever came. "I will be on my guard," he said. "We need no surprises."

Hobard smiled. "And I will help the lady clean this cottage," she said, leaving him to bask in the late afternoon sun.

***

Though the broom, dustpan, and mop all had to be taken outside and cleaned before they were of much use, two hours later the cottage's main room had been swept and dusted, with spider webs knocked from the ceiling.

Relying on such order as she found on the shelves and her own instincts about what would surely belong in the empty spaces, Hobard sorted and stored the herbs and plants littering the room. They'd opened all the windows as well as the door. A slight breeze moved through the room, but it would be a while before stale air was replaced by fresh.

Something about the old woman seemed familiar, but Hobard wasn't certain why. That could wait. For now, those villagers were uppermost in her thoughts. They, too, had seemed almost familiar. For all that Inek's rudeness, something else lurked just below his surface—something sad, almost hopeful but without hope, not that that made much sense.

She joined Bird in the yard. Aren had been dozing as he sat leaning against the front wall. He awoke as they joined him.

"I don't think Magda's been very happy," Bird said, bringing Hobard's thoughts back to the old woman.

"Or very sober," a reclining Aren added. He was just as pleased that Bird had ordered him to rest, as much as he hated to leave all the work to others. He wasn't yet himself, though he was feeling far better than he'd any right to expect, thanks no doubt to this Healing Druid. "What do you think, Hobard? Would drink and the surprise of seeing strangers at her door have been enough to make her pass out?" He looked at the open door, remembering Magda's greeting. "She didn't sound very pleasant before, and I don't expect she'll be any nicer when she wakes."

Hobard chuckled. "If she stays out long enough to sober up, the headache will keep her from wanting to hear her own voice raised. A good shout from any of us might bring her to her knees."

"Then let's not shout unless she shouts first," Bird said, grinning. "If she shouts, I'll raise my hand like this, and when I drop it, we'll all yell 'Don't shout!'" She giggled as she gave her sharp nod. "Good. That's settled, then. Now let's find her bucket and get this room mopped! Aren, you stay quiet. I know about mopping, and Hobard can carry water as I need it."

The sun was setting before the room was finally cleaned to Bird's satisfaction. Before they'd begun, she'd had Hobard carry the room's two small rugs outside for beating while the floor dried. Aren, she was pleased to note, had fallen asleep as he leaned against the cabin's wall.

Hobard agreed that sleep was the best thing for him. They took the rugs out behind the hut where they'd found a bit of clothesline. There they gave the things a good beating, leaving them hanging to air overnight. The sky showed no sign of rain. From the looks of the land, rain was rare enough.

Bird suggested that on the following day they could do a good washing. They'd better wash Magda, too, she said, wrinkling her nose. Aren woke from his nap, neck only a little stiff, just in time to hear that about doing a washing. He smiled at the words. This was the first time he'd seen Bird seem to completely forget her troubles since they'd left the Fifth Valley. Watching her channel Reya had always amused him, in part because Bird did it so well. He rose, stretched before he remembered his wound and was surprised it didn't pull at the movement.

Hobard saw Aren's look of surprise and the hand he placed over the place where the arrow had entered. "Does your wound pain you?" she asked.

Aren shook his head. "It feels better than I'd expected. I thought it would pull when I stretched, but it didn't."

"I hope it's all healed!" Bird said then. "I should have blasted those men—"

Aren interrupted. "Brenna dealt with the men who attacked us, little bird. Those two won't be after us again."

Mention of Brenna distracted the girl, as Aren had hoped, but also saddened her. "I hope she's all right."

Aren nodded; he too hoped the red woman had come through unscathed, but he feared for her. She'd slowed their pursuers, giving the trio just time to reach the sparse woods. In her place, Aren would have done the same, though his skills were only those of a guardsman. "She showed great courage," he said. He could think of nothing else worth saying. To distract Bird, he turned to Hobard. "I'm grateful for your help. I've never seen a healer with your skill."

Hobard shook her head. "This is not of my doing. I can begin a healing, but then it has to proceed naturally. Still, mine are not the greatest powers." She looked at Bird.

Bird stood uncertain whether it was too soon to laugh with delight at the news. "Well," she finally said, uncertainly, "I did hope you'd heal quickly. But I didn't know if I could do that. I've hoped for little good things before, but my big hopes haven't been so much for something good."

At this Hobard looked about to question her, but Aren quickly raised a cautioning hand and the Druid kept silent.

Aren reached out, drew Bird into his arms for a strong hug. "I think you helped Hobard's healing to work faster, little bird. And I thank you."

Bird was crying now, partly with relief, partly at the memory of all that had brought them to these barrens with their strange people, Aren wounded and Brenna—who knew what? And now they'd spent the afternoon cleaning the home of a woman who'd fainted at the sight of her, and what did that mean, anyway?

CHAPTER NINE

The old woman still slept. Aren and Bird decided not to wake her, though they'd have liked to ask whether there was any food in the house. They'd found none, and only a little dried meat and fruit remained in Aren's pack.

Hobard offered to walk to the village to see if she could beg some vegetables, perhaps a few eggs and some bread.

"Beg?" Aren asked. "There's no need to beg. See what these coins will purchase." He handed her three pieces of silver. "This should purchase several days' food." He raised a warning finger. " Don't let them take advantage of you."

Hobard nodded, unruffled by the advice. Trading coins for food was not within her experience. Druids had lived on fruits and vegetables, sometimes baking bread with flour made from various wild grains or creating wines from wild berries. Later, as humans came into the world, wandering Druids were welcomed to farmers' tables. Even when there was no need for a Druid's skills, one's presence was regarded as a blessing on the farmstead. Hobard never understood why.

She was eager to observe the people they'd met earlier. They had not seemed old in the way humans grew old, yet she could tell that they had been in the world much longer than any group of humans could possibly have lived. She'd sensed something else: they'd been full of hope as Bird's little party approached their village. They had expected something to happen, and it had not.

As she neared the small grouping of huts, Hobard realized that the inhabitants were still standing or sitting where they'd been when Bird's little group asked about lodging. She felt their hope, mixed with acknowledged error and responsibility. At some past time they had been found wanting. Hobard also realized that she should feel some familiarity about these beings.

Hobard's pace slowed. She looked carefully at these beings who were too long-lived to be humans. Except for their height they looked as human as did Hobard herself.

The man who'd directed them to Magda's house stood a half-step in front of the others. Hobard addressed him.

"Is food available? We are able to pay."

A great sigh went through the group. For a moment Hobard thought the man she faced might weep.

The fellow looked down, shoulders slumped. Then he straightened. "Yes, of course. We have food." He turned his head and spoke to the men behind him. "Bring it!" Again he faced Hobard. "We have fruit and vegetables, and we have milk, cheese and honey. Bread, and eggs if she wishes." He paused, watching Hobard closely, before venturing his next speech. "Magda will have wine enough, I warrant, but we have wine as well."

The entire group watched Hobard. She felt a growing sense of familiarity about these beings, something she should remember from before the ages she'd spent within the earth's green life.

The men Inek sent for food returned and knelt before Hobard. Clearly these beings were growers and potters of some skill. One carried a tray with bowls of apples, pears, melon and berries, another two large jugs of milk. He lifted one stopper to show a layer of cream. A third carried a small jug of thick dark honey and a small wheel of cheese. Two others carried bowls, one of brown eggs, the other of butter, and yet another three warm loaves. All looked anxious to Hobard, clearly seeking approval.

Hobard smiled broadly. "This is wonderful. She will be most pleased." She reached into her pouch. "We are able to pay," she said, drawing out her little group of coins.

Instantly the villagers' hopeful looks faded. Instead she saw tears not just in their eyes, but streaming down their faces.

The leader needed a moment before he could speak, and even then his voice was choked. "Do you think we would take money from Her?" Hobard could hear the depth of sorrow in the emphasis Inek placed on "Her." The word carried everything Hobard herself felt: all the feelings she carried for the Mother, all that she knew of who Bird must be and what she meant. Hobard's certainty was not affected by Bird's refusal to be called Mother.

Hobard stood silent, trying to absorb all that the man's single sentence had implied. Silence stretched until the man spoke again.

"Do you not recognize us? Have we fallen so far that these long years of work and repentance have meant nothing?" Inek gestured toward the crowd which now knelt, heads down. "We came to this sparse land as She ordered, and we have remained. With long years of effort, we learned to grow trees and bushes which will bear fruit and berries in this dry place. Slowly we enriched the soil to support those and the vegetables in our gardens. After years of listening to the earth and grasses we were able to grow fodder for our milk cows and feed for a few chickens. We set aside all our pride and ambition, our foolish seeking for ever more power. We sought instead to serve the earth itself, to serve Her."

He stepped forward, reached out to take Hobard by both shoulders, almost shaking the Druid. "Hobard"—Hobard started at the use of her name, which she knew no one had mentioned—"Hobard, elder sister, do you not recognize us? We were the ones She named Dark Druids. It was our error which caused the Mother to withdraw the rest of her Druids from the earth." He'd ceased to weep, but Hobard could recognize sorrow carved deeply into the lines of his face.

Inek recovered himself. He removed his hands from Hobard's shoulders. "I am sorry. I have no right to touch you, or even to speak in your presence." He gestured toward the kneeling men, who hadn't moved even to wipe their tears. "Tell Her the food and all we have is at Her service, now and always." He took a deep breath. "And, if you will, ask if we may show what we have done here. We seek no more than that. Tell her we offer what we have done, which is all we have and all we have become."

Hobard stared open-mouthed for another moment before she found her voice. "You are Kasen?"

This generated a violent headshake. "No! No—I was Kasen, but no more. As Kasen I thought I was wise. My name for these long years has been and will be Inek, which in one human language means "small." He knelt, looking up at Hobard. "I am Inek, and I will serve Her if she will allow, though I dare not speak Her name."

From behind him came, in unison, a near-chant: "So will we all."

Hobard looked at then one by one. Their eyes begged for a forgiveness she had not power to bestow. Beneath that supplication lay a resoluteness and, she felt, a faithfulness which would serve even if never acknowledged.

For several moments Hobard stared into Inek's face, then nodded. "I will tell her." She turned to the six who had managed to kneel even while balancing containers of food as, she realized, they would hold them before an altar. "Will you follow me to Magda's hut?"

All nodded as they rose. Hobard could see joy in their faces. As she turned to say farewell, she saw joy rising in Inek's sad face as well. "I will bring your gifts to Her, and tell her where they came and with what good will the offering is made. Most assuredly I will tell her of your wish to show her what you have made of this land." She paused. "What she will say, I cannot tell."

Inek bowed his head. Hobard turned and led the small procession to Magda's house, noting that as they neared the building, the carriers became increasingly uneasy. At the house she had each place his offering on Magda's outdoor table. She thanked them and, to their obvious relief, sent them back to the village. The villagers were or had been Dark Druids, and only one had been more proud than Kasen, now Inek. Hobard wasn't about to allow them into the hut with a child who didn't seem to know herself or her power.

She opened the door and began carrying food to one of Magda's small tables. Aren leaped to help, clearly feeling better. Bird came scampering. "What did you bring! Oh! Apples! And Pears! Raspberries and huckleberries!" She popped a huckleberry into her mouth and giggled with delight. "They're sweet!" She peered into the bowl. "And big, too. Reya would like to see the plant these came from. And these great big raspberries, too!" She took one. "Oh, yes—Reya will want to hear about these!"

Bird scrambled onto the bench alongside the table, knelt so she could lean over and look into the milk jug. "There's cream on top! And honey! Oh, and eggs, and butter, and bread still warm! It's a feast! I hope everything is as good as these berries!" She jumped down and skipped to a cupboard against the wall. "Hobard, will you check on Magda while I set the table?" She opened a cupboard and peered in. "Oh, my!" She turned to her brother, shaking her head. "Aren, will you get me a bucket of water? We're going to have to wash dust off these platters and mugs!"

Soon enough they were settled and eating, Bird offering each dish her highest praise: Reya would approve. About half-way through the meal, after Bird had mentioned again how much Reya would want to see the bushes which produced such large, sweet, juicy berries, Hobard ventured to pass on the rest of Inek's message.

"Inek, their leader, who says his name used to be Kasen--" she paused, watching Bird for any reaction to the name but saw none. "Inek and his people would like to show you their gardens and fields."

Bird's face glowed. "Oh, I'd like that! Then I can tell Reya about the berries, and maybe her bushes can become like theirs!" She beamed at Aren. "Wouldn't it be nice to bring something good back from all this fuss and travelling?" She bit into a pear, giggling as juice trickled down her chin. "And these pears, too!" she mumbled through a mouthful, then chewed and swallowed, holding a palm up toward Aren. "I know. Don't talk with your mouth full. I forget sometimes." She grinned at her big brother, then turned to Hobard. "Could you tell them I'd love to see their gardens—oh, and their fields and pastures, too!"

She glanced around the room and sobered. "We'd better finish mucking out this place and get Magda back on her feet again. That may take a couple of days. Would you be willing to go back down and tell them after we finish supper?" She took a drink of milk, then another. "Be sure to tell them how much we enjoyed everything. I haven't eaten this well since we left home, Aren!" For a moment her face saddened. "Yes, Reya would approve," she said softly.

Supper over, Bird sent Aren to the cookstove in the shelter next to the hut to heat water. She intended to wash all the dishes in the house.

Hobard walked down to the village. She found, as before, the villagers gathered where she'd left them. She wondered if they'd moved at all. This time Inek's false bravado was entirely gone. He seemed almost afraid to look Hobard in the face.

Hobard smiled at the group, her own uneasiness almost gone. "I bring to you Her thanks for a wonderful meal. She could not praise it highly enough. She accepts with delight your offer to show your gardens and orchards, and hopes to see your fields and pastures as well."

For a moment she thought Inek and his followers would weep again, this time with joy.

Some moments passed before Inek could speak again. "When we became aware of Her approach, we hoped. When She did not know us we despaired. What She wishes, we will do, as we have done."

Hobard hesitated, not sure how much she should say. Still, these were, or had been, fellow Druids. They already had questions, and soon would soon have more. It might be best to tell them what they surely would notice before long. "Why She has chosen to return in this form I would not attempt to guess. Dark wizards pursue her, and She does not seem to fully know Herself. Aren, the one who accompanies her, says he and the Lady hope to find those who can teach her the nature and uses of her power. She insists that Aren is her brother." She paused, made a wide gesture to include them all. "Here She has found those who can recognize her, as I do. But instruct her? I have not dared it."

Inek shivered slightly. "Nor should I. We had sensed an approaching presence. As She came near, we saw Her as we always did, at the center of a swirling rainbow of what those wizards call auras, as you must also see her, Hobard. And yet as She came nearer, we saw a child and wondered. Yet Her power, Her very nature, is clear to us, as you say it is not to Her."

A question came from one of the men gathered now in a half-circle around Inek. "But what of these dark wizards who pursue her? We bear the guilt for those."

Inek turned. "I agree, Oso. The Mother warned against teaching men more than they could understand, and we transgressed. Still, I doubt that even in these long years they will have learned enough to harm us. Yet, as She is in the form of a human child, it may be they can harm the shell She has chosen. Who could predict the result?" He paused, thinking. "If She will allow us, we may yet stand between Her and those who would do harm. We taught these dark wizards. It may well be that we must end them, difficult as we would find that after these years tending this land." He turned back to Hobard. "For a Dark Druid to offer to teach the Mother--!" The murmurs behind him expressed similar disbelief.

"She must have a reason for returning in this form," Hobard suggested. "Those who come into the world in Her present form seem to grow into themselves. Perhaps She wished that experience for Herself."

"Whatever Her wish," Inek said, "we will honor it. While we wait to learn what She most needs—if we do—we will continue to do as She asks. At the least, we can assure her safety. Wizards will not penetrate the mists, nor will their servants. Nonetheless, we will be on guard. Anything She asks of us, including any information, we will answer honestly, even when it concerns our errors."

Hobard nodded. "As will I." She looked carefully at each man. "I must return. She wishes to spend tomorrow resting, but will soon visit your orchards and fields." She didn't think it useful to tell a gathering of Druids that Bird wished to spend a day house-cleaning, or that Hobard herself would join in. Instead, she found herself saying words she had not expected. "It is good to speak again with Druids. That is a fellow-ship I missed, though occasionally I sensed a presence nearby with which there seemed some sharing."

Inek bent his head. "We thank you. It is good of you."

Hobard ducked her head in acknowledgement as she turned away.

* * *

To Snake's surprise, his new master not only camped after travelling only a half-day, but took his time breaking camp the following morning. The squat being built a small fire, heated porridge and two cups of wine, then lingered over the meal. "Rest today. Let wizards catch up." He chuckled. "Rath eager challenge mists, wander lost, lose temper. Bit of fun for Mist."

Snake wasn't sure just what Master Dog might mean by any of that. Nonetheless, he was willing to walk less and let the wizards come to them. Snake more than half believed that even if they'd come through thick brush and ground too hard to leave traces, his master could have instructed the ground to mark their passing.

For a moment Snake wondered if he wasn't becoming as gullible as his farmer ancestors who believed all sorts of unlikely possibilities. Yet he'd seen much which his parents would not have imagined, might not believe were he ever to see them again and tell this story. Not that they'd be eager to see him, or he them.

The wizards sent one of their remaining guardsmen ahead. The fellow came crashing along, something Snake would have doubted possible in a forest this thin and open. A certain kind of guardsman seemed to need to impress others with his brawn by making a racket. Perhaps this fellow needed to impress himself as well, or drive off any animals which he might otherwise encounter.

The guardsman came upon Snake and Dog as they had just ended their mid-day meal. Snake didn't bother to offer the man food or drink.

The offer would have been refused in any case. Guardsmen didn't share food with assassins who were no doubt also spies for the Order. Spies would report any careless word, or make one up for reporting later. Snake might offer poisoned food simply for the practice.

"Well, this is nice. Resting comfortably, are we?" the man said before realizing that was not the best way to greet Soren's pet assassin. "How much further? And what lies ahead?"

Snake smiled just unpleasantly enough to keep the man nervous. "To the fog, a couple of turns of the hourglass. How far back are the wizards?"

The guardsman snorted. "At least that many turns. Rath moves slowly, and the other two limp. They'll take half the afternoon to reach this place. I carry their tent and bedrolls"—he gestured at the large pack strapped to his back—"so that I can have the camp ready when they arrive. At least it's gear for only three wizards, now that we've lost one."

Snake was a little surprised at the man's frankness. He must have been tired indeed to speak so freely. Still, this pursuit would not have increased the guardsman's respect for Rath, and certainly not for Lorit.

"Well," Snake said "you might as well keep on. You'll find the fog easily enough. There's a clearing nearby which would make a good campsite. We'll report that you've gone ahead." He kept one eye on Dog and was pleased to see a slight nod. He was getting better at guessing what his master intended him to say.

The man nodded and set off down the path. Dog watched him out of sight, smiling, then lay down and closed his eyes. Snake chose to stay awake. He would not like to have Rath find him asleep while the wizard struggled on.

As the guardsman had suggested, it was a good two turns of a glass before the wizards and their two remaining guardsmen arrived. All three wizards leaned heavily on staffs, groaning a little as they walked. The appearance of Snake and his follower was occasion enough for the wizards to seek logs and sit down, complaining still more in the process. The guardsmen went off a little before letting down their packs and stretching out on the ground.

"Well," Rath grumbled, "how much further is it?"

Snake stood in an attitude of respect, Dog sitting against a tree just near enough to listen. "Another two or three turns of the glass, perhaps more, to the edge of the fogs. We met your advance guard. He's gone on to make camp. We should be able to get there well before dark."

Rath nodded. "What of this fog about which we've heard so much?"

"It's too thick to find one's way easily." Snake decided on a lie, knowing Rath wouldn't accept at face value his estimate of the fog's density. "I sent Master Dog in. He quickly became confused. It was some time before he was able to follow my calls and find his way back." Out of the corner of an eye he caught Dog looking very much like a man who'd nearly been lost for good in the fogs.

"This is similar to what we'd heard," Roke observed.

Rath did not seem pleased by the interjection. "We'll see whether wizards find this fog such an obstacle. We won't get there by sitting." With that he set his staff firmly on the ground and used it to pull himself upright, with several nearly-suppressed groans.

Snake wondered whether even a rested wizard in possession of his full powers could find his way through mists which Dog claimed had fooled wizards for generations. These three seemed much less than fully powerful at the moment. Still, he stood, as did Dog and the guardsmen.

Rath ordered the guardsmen to go on ahead. They could help set up camp and have a meal ready when the wizards arrived. The men didn't wait for a second invitation to get away from wizards for even a little while.

All three wizards took a few moments to gather themselves before they resumed walking. Dog walked ahead, as befitted a mere tracker, while Snake stayed with the wizards. At first he thought Rath might want to question him as they travelled, but the wizard had no breath for speaking as he made his slow way through the woods. It occurred to the assassin that it might be a mercy as well as a pleasure to put all three out of their misery. Alas, if Dog wished these three put down, no doubt he would open the earth beneath them.

Late in the day they reached the camp, just in sight of the mists. The guardsmen stood alertly, no doubt warned by Dog's arrival. Dog himself sat against a tree on the camp's far side, not bothering to stand as Snake and his three charges came up.

Roke and Tarh made as if to sit, but Rath stumped onward to the mist's edge. The younger wizards slowly followed.

The three stood with tendrils of fog touching their feet and ankles as though inviting them in. Rath announced, "I will chance this mist." He turned to Tarh. "I will call from time to time; do you answer me. A clear-sight spell should suffice to make short work of this mist. Roke, add your strength as well to my spell. Tarh, focus on listening for my call. If you cease to hear me, call every ten heartbeats."

With that he stepped into the mist. Those watching, Dog with a slight smile on his face, could see Rath dimly for only a short distance as he walked away. His calls came regularly, and Tarh's answered. The mist did not thin, though Roke began to strain with the effort of keeping up their shared clear-sight spell.

In the fog, Rath found he couldn't see his own knees. He paused, turned and begin walking to his left, all the while continuing to call at regular but shorter intervals. He was unable to hear Tarh. He began a slow circle to his right which should have brought him back nearly to where he'd begun. His own calls came quickly now. He was first irritated, then concerned, then approaching what in anyone but a dark wizard would have been called panic.

Outside the fog, Roke abandoned his spell and asked, "What can we do? We hear him, but he doesn't hear us. If we send someone after him, that one may wander off as well."

Snake glanced over his shoulder at his master. Dog was smiling broadly, obviously enjoying himself. Snake spread his hands in a questioning gesture. Dog shrugged, then joined the wizards. Nearby, the guardsmen had forgotten for the moment their uneasiness and came closer to watch and listen.

"Saw once," Dog grumbled. "Held hands, stretched into fog. One stayed back."

"Did it work?" Tarh asked.

Dog thought for a moment. "More men, would have," he answered. "Maybe wizard circle closer."

Snake didn't much like the idea of being part of a human chain going into that fog. If a guardsman or wizard lost his nerve and let go, they'd all wander as did Rath. He hoped his new master could navigate this mist or fog or whatever it was. He also hoped the odd being would anticipate use enough for his servant to bring him out.

The two wizards didn't like the idea either. Rath seemed to circle a little closer, his calls now louder and sounding desperate. Tarh sighed and said, "I'll go first. Snake, you stay in the clear. Come, Roke; you and I will have a better chance of dealing with this fog than will guardsmen." With that he seized the other wizard's hand and stepped into the mist. "Don't dawdle; Rath is closer, and we may not get another chance."

Roke stepped toward the mist, then halted, reaching for a guardsman's hand. The guardsmen held back until Snake tapped the hilt of his knife. One stepped forward, then the other two. The chain lengthened. Snake looked inquiringly at his master, who gestured for him to take the last guardsman's hand. Softly Dog said, "No worry. Fog not problem."

Snake took a deep breath and followed the guardsman. The minute he stepped into the fog, he lost sight of the man just in front. Nor could he see beyond the elbow of the arm whose hand the guardsman clung to. If he ever let go of the fellow, the entire line would be lost. He looked back over his shoulder and couldn't see Master Dog either, but felt the other's strong hand enveloping his own. They walked forward a dozen or so more steps before Snake felt the line stop. Since they'd stepped into the swirling fog, he'd not heard Rath's calls.

Dog's grip on his hand began to pull him gently back toward what he hoped would be the clearing. Snake in turn gently tugged on the hand of the guardsman. In a few minutes Snake stepped into the clear air, then guided the guardsman as well. Shortly the other guardsmen and the three wizards also stepped out of the fog. All six quickly sat down before, Snake suspected, they fell down. Rath appeared exhausted.

Back there in the fog Snake had had a moment of fear that perhaps Dog had had enough of his services and would leave him wandering. He was a little ashamed of the thought. Snake hadn't seen any signs yet that the broad man was unreliable. Certainly he had seemed determined to assist this child-wizard and her brother in their travels to the Barren Lands, though the two hadn't seemed to know that was their goal.

After a time Rath seemed to rouse himself, a little less pale than he'd been when he first emerged. All three wizards were rattled, that was certain. Snake had seen wizards unnerved, but only at the moment they realized that Soren's assassin was upon them. He found it interesting now to watch equally shaken wizards recover. Clearly Rath had not expected to be completely helpless once he entered the fog. Tarh and Roke had no doubt felt more trepidation, going where a master wizard appeared lost.

"What we have heard of this cursed fog or mist or whatever it calls itself is true, then," Rath muttered, just loud enough for his fellow wizards and Snake's keen ears. "I felt stripped of my powers. Yet they seem to have returned readily enough." With that, he looked at the guardsmen and smiled with satisfaction when each, though facing away from him at that moment, froze. He was still able to send at will a paralyzing fear of the dark. In reflex, Snake touched the amulet against dark wizardry which hung around his neck. More than once it had allowed him to walk through a dark wizard's power of fear and end that power with his knife.

"I felt it, too," said Tarh, and Roke nodded. "I could not see as far as the end of my arm, and I had no sense of direction. Had we lost one another's hands, we might never have gotten out."

"And yet," Roke noted, "before we entered the fog we could hear you, though it seemed you could not hear us."

"Not at all," Rath said. "Once I'd taken a step in, I could hear nothing. When I looked back, I couldn't see the fog's edge. I knew you would keep calling, and I kept calling as well, hoping you could hear me, at least."

"As we did," said Roke. "But it did us no good. Had not Master Dog suggested making ourselves a chain, we might never have been able to reach you."

All three sat silent for a time. No one offered up thanks to Master Dog, Snake noted. A glance at his new master showed an apparently impassive face which, to Snake at least, did not hide enjoyment of the situation. Again Snake realized that, though he couldn't exactly be said to have chosen, he was on the stronger side in an uneven contest.

On the camp's far side, the guardsmen had used blankets supported by strong branches set in the ground to create three comfortable seats. Once the wizards were settled, the guards moved to replenish the small fire and reheat wine, then set about cooking supper.

After a time, Rath called for his pack and took from it his crystal. He didn't bother sending the guardsmen away. If later there was need for secrecy, it would be easy enough to silence three guardsmen.

* * *

Soren had been expecting all day to hear that his wizards had reached the barrens. Haster had put up with his Chief Mage's irascibility and impatience the entire time. Oleg, who had fairly reliable maps and could read them, had a sense of when Rath would report. The Loremaster had been in the tower's observation room only a short time when Soren's crystal brightened. Rath's face appeared. The wizard did not look well at all.

"Well," Soren demanded, "have you reached these Barrens? Are they what we've heard?"

Rath sighed, which wasn't at all like the man. "We have reached them, Chief Mage. Those we follow seem to have entered them a day or so ago. Their trail ends here."

"What do you mean, ends?" asked Haster.

"I mean that fogs or mists don't allow us to track further," Rath snapped. "From outside the mist, we cannot see the ground; from inside, we cannot see as far as the hands at the ends of our arms."

"You have been inside the fog, then," said Oleg. "And you returned easily?"

Rath's laugh contained no pleasure. "Easily? No. I wandered lost. Those outside the fog could hear my calls, but I could not hear theirs. A clear-sight spell did not work, even with two concentrating. Had I been alone, who knows how long I might have floundered. Those who'd remained outside the fog formed a sort of chain, holding hands in a line which just reached me."

Oleg had another question. "Is this a power like that of the Red Forest, then?"

"Always the seeker of lore, Oleg." Rath shook his head. "This is different. The Red Forest's attack was stronger than any power I've felt. I was far from the center, which seemed focused on Lorit, or I might also have perished. This fog blinds everyone—wizards, guardsmen, assassins. None could have found our way back out without help. The fog didn't seem to care whether we were able to escape. It simply wished us to go no further into the land."

Oleg nodded. "That fits with accounts left by members of the Order of Blue Wizards. They report one difference: some being living within the fog led or pushed them in the correct direction. None was able to get a clear view of their rescuer."

"No one came to my rescue but those who came with me," Rath sneered. "Though perhaps I did not stay as long as have others. I'm not eager to try that experiment." He fell silent. "I doubt we could form a human chain long enough to explore the place. Even if we did, we would see nothing clearly. This fog felt as though it covers more than the borders. I sensed depth, duration. Oleg, how old are your reports of blue wizards trying the fog?"

"Not so ancient as those which tell of meetings with Druids, but old enough. At least a few hundred years, judging from the ages of their scrolls." Oleg had a thought which disturbed him even more than most thoughts these days. "Would you say this is the handiwork of the being who created the ward over the Fifth Valley? It sounds similar."

Even through the crystal it was clear that the same concern had disturbed Rath. "I prefer not to consider that. If this fog were created by the same being which set a ward over the Fifth Valley, then either we pursue the wrong power or it reappears from time to time. This fog was not set to kill; it merely prevented us from entering further. I suppose a lone entrant could wander lost until he starved to death, but there was nothing immediately fatal about the fog itself." Again he was silent for a time. Those in Soren's observatory waited; clearly Rath had more to tell but was reluctant.

Finally the wizard spoke. "There is one thing more. While in the fog, Roke, Tarh, and I all three felt not just as though a spell would not work, but as though we had no powers of any sort. Upon stepping out, those powers returned. I do not think wizards entering the fog, even if we can find our way around, would be any more powerful than mere men."

This brought a long silence from the three in the observatory. Soren finally rejoined the conversation. "Are you sure the child-witch and her companions did enter the fog?"

"Unless they flew," Rath answered. "Their tracks go to the edge without pausing."

Soren nodded. "Then let us try to keep them there. Oleg," he turned to the Loremaster, "can you produce a decent map of the boundaries of this place?"

Oleg nodded. "I have several. They disagree in small points, but wizards on the ground can correct any errors. If the fog persists up to the land's border, that will serve as clear demarcation."

"Then we will send other wizards and guardsmen to surround the place. Rath, stay where you are for the time being. Keep Roke and Tarh with you.. It will take a few days to make enough maps and to select members of the Order." Soren did not have to say that Rath would be in charge. All four wizards knew that Rath would accept no other possibility. Even in his weakened state, none of the Order but Soren would challenge him, given that Oleg challenged no one.

"Is there anything else you would tell us?" put in Haster, wishing to have some part, however small, in the conversation.

Rath shook his head, muttered a hoarse "no." With that, both crystals went dark.

"And now," said Soren, turning to Oleg, "put your apprentices to work making copies of your best map. Bring me the first. We will need to establish the number of wizards needed for this watch. See what the thing in the dungeon has to say, if anything."

Oleg nodded and left, not bothering to tell the Chief Mage that his apprentices were already at work. Once the barrens appeared to have become the witch-child's destination, Oleg had selected what appeared to be his best and most consistent maps of those lands and their immediate surroundings. These were chiefly maps of the borders and the areas around. A blank space marked the Barren Lands themselves..

For a moment Oleg considered whether Soren still hoped to find a way to reach into the fogs and attack the child, or wished merely to contain her in those fogs. Perhaps the Chief Mage's goal was to know if she left those dry lands, so he could once more order attacks. Of those choices, Oleg would have selected observation from a place close enough to see any party leaving those lands and distant enough to allow observers to get out of the way. Nothing of what he had heard led him to wish for any further confrontations with a being who either was allied with land and forest or could command them as she did weather, wolves, and stone.

By the time Oleg reached the archives, he could see that his five most careful apprentices were well into making copies of each of the five maps he'd selected. Nine copies of each, he judged, would be enough, with the originals remaining in his office and one set remaining with Soren. He doubted Soren would send as many as ten wizards. That would be half the Order. It would be good to allow for some survivors should the child-witch become seriously angry and vengeful.

His apprentices' work examined and approved, Oleg retreated to his office and made his way to the dungeon. The thing in the dungeon, Soren had said. The Chief Mage never seen the Dark One, never spoken to it. Had he done so, he'd have been a little more careful in his naming.

"So, Loremaster, you bring news from the world of light. What mischief have you wizards been up to now?"

Oleg ignored that question. "The three have entered the barrens." That should get the prisoner's attention.

It didn't have as much effect as Oleg hoped. "We expected that, Loremaster. You wouldn't bother with all those stairs to tell me only what we'd already guessed."

"There is little more at present. The mists and fogs which cloak those lands persist. Our wizards were unable to walk more than a few feet before becoming lost and having to be rescued."

"And how did that rescue work? Sending in a rescuer would not." Disdain dripped from the Dark One's voice.

"The listeners formed a sort of chain, holding hands tightly, one staying just outside. They were able to reach the one within the fog, though just barely."

The Dark One appeared to speak more to himself than to Oleg, a habit which the lore-master believed to be growing. Their news was affecting the being more than it wished to admit. "So they are safe now. And if Kasen and the others are still there—but where else would they be? And I thought them to be the fools!"

Oleg's question came quickly, hoping the Dark One would answer without thinking while he was in this mood. "Who are Kasen and the others?" He kept silent, hoping the being would reveal more than it usually intended.

"Wiser beings than I, clearly," the Dark One answered. "And now She has come to them, bringing with her a bright Druid."

After a time, Oleg tried again. "But who or what is this Kasen? And these others?"

The Dark One's answer was sharp, sharper than Oleg had heard since the breaking of the drought and destruction of Rath's tower. "Leave me, wizard. I have much to think about. I will say this much: if your Order would survive, do not attempt to enter the fog again, or interfere with any who appear from within. What this girl-child intends I cannot tell, nor whether she knows what she intends. You have angered her, and now you have attacked her directly. Long have you ruled these lands, and badly. I and my kind are partly to blame for that; we serve our punishment. Yours has not yet begun." With that, he withdrew to the stone which served as bed and said no more.

Oleg returned into the comparative brightness of his office where he sat thinking. The Dark One had said little more than previously, but with a new undertone, as though he'd been uncertain whether to hope for or fear something which he clearly expected, and now it had begun. But what? That this witch-child had reached the barrens, where she would be safe from wizards, guardsmen, or any other foes? But what in that should trouble the Order's prisoner, after all these years?

The Dark One spoke of punishment, for himself but also for others. For what? Revealing lore which led to the development of the Orders of wizardry? At times it was difficult to remember that this Dark One of the Order's dungeons may have been a Druid among Druids. There was little in the archives about that. Perhaps it would be worthwhile to search back through records of the Dark One's imprisonment, something which had never interested Oleg. He had believed he knew all which was needed: that the Dark One had long been the dungeon's sole prisoner. To keep his powers suppressed he must be fed foxglove leaves and wine laced with foxglove. Occasionally he would give information. Now Oleg was curious, and his curiosity was always to be satisfied.

In the meantime, he would pass on this latest, and most limited, information, and bring Soren a copy of his best map of the area around the Barren Lands.

* * *

When he re-entered Soren's observatory on the tower's top floor, Oleg was a little surprised to see that night had fallen. There were no windows in his records hall, much less in his office. He had no need for daylight. After his conversation with the Dark One, he must have thought much longer than he'd intended.

Soren never bothered with greetings. "What did the thing in the dungeon say this time?" He spared barely a glance for the roll of parchment Oleg lay on a table.

"Not a great deal, Chief Mage. He spoke of safety for those we seek. He seems to think that the witch-child will have found allies of some sort in the barrens. For the first time, he spoke a name: Kasen and the others, he said, must still be in that place. But who and what they might be, he kept to himself. I suspect they may be Druids, though why Druids would have withdrawn to such a place and remained there is beyond me. He spoke of punishment, for himself and others, which continues." Oleg paused for a moment, wondering whether to go on. "He also offered advice."

Soren and Haster both frowned at this. "What sort of advice might that one offer?" Haster asked.

"Similar to what he has said before: leave the child and her followers alone, withdraw, watch from a distance. The Dark One has no great opinion of our powers. He seems to forget that we've kept him prisoner for some time, despite what our records say of his strength." Oleg waited for Soren's wrath to erupt.

To his surprise, it did not. Instead, Soren appeared thoughtful. "This is nothing new. Yet the powers arrayed against us seem to have increased—powers we did not expect and do not understand. A forest which seems to awaken and wipes a wizard of Lorit's strength from existence? Another Power which can play with the earth itself, opening and closing chasms at will? Fog existing for centuries which confuses even Rath, a wizard stronger than Lorit?"

"Don't forget the ward over the Fifth Valley, Chief Mage, which we still have not managed to penetrate, though our lesser servants may. And the destruction of Rath's tower and Lord Rand's keep," Haster pointed out. Oleg was not surprised that Haster had kept count of their failures. His would have been the strongest voice for letting the witch-child go where she wished, had he dared to say words with which Soren might disagree.

Soren took a deep breath, squared his shoulders. "We will take one part of that dark advice: our watchers will select places at some distance from the fog, from which they can see and from which they may retreat at need. Should the child remain in that fog-ridden place, sentinels may be all we'll need."

"Should she remain there," Oleg repeated. "I have brought a copy of what appears to be my most accurate map. Apprentices are making additional copies of it and four others which vary slightly but appear to be accurate enough for our purposes. Once our sentinels are in place, they can send out guardsmen to bring back more accurate information."

Soren seemed not to be listening. His head bent, he appeared to be thinking deeply. Finally he spoke. "You said the Dark One spoke of punishment, his and that of this Kasen and others. His we know, though we've thought it only our protection against him. What of these others? If they were Druids, as he more than hints, what Power could enforce a punishment for them? If a group of Druids have occupied those lands all these long years, remaining there while a fog acts as a ward to keep others out, has the place also been a prison? We believe this witch-child created the ward over the Fifth Valley. What Power would have created a long-lived ward over the Barren Lands, one existing long before this witch-child was born?"

Oleg had thought long and hard about just this. "Or reborn, Chief Mage. Perhaps awakened. If the Red Forest could awake to its power, could not some other long-quiet being? Perhaps Rath's drought in the Valley roused whatever this child might be. Suppose"—he paused to gather himself—"suppose this child is a rebirth of the one who banished Druids to these Barren Lands, with power which Druids would obey through all the long years. Even now, after all our years of study and growth, the entire Order could not command the Dark One were he free, let alone several Druids." All three fell silent. "We had thought our knowledge and the power it gives us to be supreme and growing. Now we find ourselves facing powers which brush us aside, whose nature we do not understand. It is no easy place to be. The number and strength of those powers appears to be growing."

"Yet this witch-child appears human," Soren replied. "It may yet be that we will find a way to deal with her, or it. In the meantime, I agree: we must watch and wait," He changed the focus. "Let us look at that map. Haster, clear that table, then bring the roll of the Order's member-ship. If this is but a copy of your best map, we may mark upon it where our members should be placed on watch."

204 * FREEING DRUIDS

CHAPTER TEN

Rath had sent the guards a short distance away while he used his crystal to speak with Soren. Now he recalled his will and the crystal darkened. Tarh and Roke had remained nearby, listening. After a few moments Rath waved them over.

"So," he said, "since we cannot enter the Barren Lands, we will fall back. Roke, you and one guardsman will camp far enough from the woods to watch some distance along the edge. When additional wizards and guards arrive, I will send men enough to search northward. Doubtless we'll need another watchpost there. Tarh, you'll accompany me. I may need you as a messenger to our brothers as we extend our watch on these lands.

"We should have time. Our quarry has just entered this mist and should not immediately emerge again. Perhaps in the interim Oleg will devise some way to combine the powers of several wizards in a way which may overcome this witch-child. Surely what would kill any of us will prove to kill her—sword or arrow, or Snake."

Snake, sitting against a tree nearby, didn't care much for this idea. He looked to his new master. Dog gave him a shrug and what on anyone else's face Snake would have called a smirk. He supposed that was reassuring. If his dagger couldn't penetrate Dog's chest, who knew whether it could harm the child? Left to his own devices, Snake would have responded to an order to assassinate this witch-child with a servile nod. When opportunity allowed, he'd have chosen a swift knife-strike into Rath's heart. He suspected the wizard had one.

Dog rose as Rath called to the guardsmen to break camp. Snake joined him.

"You two," Rath said, "will accompany me. There will doubtless be need of your special talents, assassin. I would not have your minion left to wander freely, perhaps to babble of our plans and locations."

Snake bowed his head slightly in acquiescence. "He will not babble, Master. I will make certain of that. Should we need again to track these others, he will prove valuable." If his new master decided to leave, Snake doubted Rath could do anything about it.

Evening saw Roke and his lone guard camped between the sparse forest around the Barren Lands and the easternmost edge of the Red Forest. At least, Roke thought, they were not camped where Lorit had vanished. He was closer to the Red Forest than he'd have liked, but did have a clear view of the sparse forest's edge to north and south. It appeared that the forest's northern edge shifted away to the east just slightly. To the south the edge seemed to keep the same line for some distance. According to Rath, before long the younger wizard would have enough guards to send two further north and two further south, keeping at least one with him at all times. Not that he thought guardsmen would be much protection if the witch-child should appear.

Rath chose his own campsite carefully. The site sat on a rise, a good distance from the thin forest surrounding the Barren Lands. It offered a clear view in each direction, though Rath chose to avoid looking toward the Red Forest looming to the northeast. Tarh could keep watch on those cursed woods. Rath felt no particular grief at the loss of Lorit, but the man's power and experience would have been useful. He needed no reminder that the witch-child was not the only reawakened power in the land.

His guardsmen set about making camp, first placing two low camp stools for the wizards, then setting a tent for each before erecting their own some distance away. One scooped a hollow for a campfire for the wizards and gathered rocks with which to line it. His fellow built another, far enough off to avoid listening to wizards' talk.

Snake and Dog made their own camp, a small campfire and a single small tent for Snake. Wizards would lay out their own bedrolls; neither would want anyone else in their tents. Finally, the guardsmen set to work gathering firewood.

Snake and Dog gathered wood for their own cook fire.

While the others set up camp, Rath sat thinking. He was determined that Tarh would be his aide, regardless of the rank of any other wizards who would join them. As a recent apprentice, the man was used to taking instructions. Now that Lorit was dead, only Tarh, Owen and Rath himself had experienced a direct attack by the witch-child. Whatever power had exploded from the Red Forest, it had not come from her. When that blast erased Lorit, she had been fleeing to the woods around the Barren Lands, accompanied by a wounded guardsman and a tall figure in gleaming white. What that could be was a puzzle. Oleg suggested a Druid, but there had been no Druids in longer than the mind could comprehend.

Too many forces were involved, Rath knew. The witch-child was only one, though her power had proven far greater than he'd anticipated. If, as Oleg kept suggesting, she was only now beginning to learn the extent and nature of her strength, it might be that confronting her was not the wisest approach.

Yet he yearned to confront the witch directly. He looked down at the stub where his right wrist had been. Nearly healed now, it still throbbed occasionally in the night. Daily he felt his strength returning, and with it his desire for revenge.

Both Roke and Tarh maintained that the force which swept over Lorit had seemed to come from the Red Forest itself. Further, it came only after the red woman had fallen. Perhaps there were other beings in that forest. If so, as of yet they had not ventured out, though the red woman, at least, had acted to assist the witch-girl's escape.

Another Power, he suspected, had furrowed the ground around Tarh and Roke and shaken them off their feet so they could not cast spells on the small group who'd left the forest. It did not seem that the witch-child had struck—if she had, no doubt the guardsmen, at least, and perhaps Roke and Tarh, would be dead.

Rath could not account for the third force. That Power had seemed almost playful, choosing to immobilize two wizards rather than destroy them. He suspected that an unseen Power which could so easily send furrows darting out in a random pattern might well have strength it had not yet used. Unlike the witch-child or whatever burst from the forest, that Power chose simply to immobilize.

Rath felt cold; his anger remained, and his determination, but he was no longer certain that this vigil would turn out well. Perhaps the best they could hope for was that the three who'd entered the Barren

Lands would remain there. The Order could keep watch on the mist-ridden place but otherwise avoid it, And the Red Forest and the valleys.

That would turn Rath's purpose from revenge to that of watchman and warden, his only duty to alert the Order should the witch-child emerge from the mists. That was no role for the Order's most powerful member, as he was again becoming. If a permanent watch were to be kept on the Barren Lands, he would return to the Order's headquarters. There he would seek Oleg's assistance in finding or developing spells and powers to counter this witch-child. If word spread that there was in the land another force greater than the Order, holding what control remained would become a constant struggle. Rath would prefer to go on the attack, but not until he had greater weapons than at present.

***

By bedtime, Bird had searched out and scrubbed every dish in the house. She left them to dry while the three wiped shelves and drawers, then arranged their storage as Reya would have done. After that came all the pots and pans and cooking utensils. From time to time Hobard would chuckle and shake her head at a Druid doing housework and, to her astonishment, enjoying it. Housework, she reflected, was not that different from healing an injured animal: putting things to right, shaping them as they were intended to be.

Aren felt like a boy again. Bird's instructions were so similar to those Reya would have given that once or twice he turned, expecting to see his mother at work in the kitchen where he'd grown up. As for Bird, she was too busy cleaning and giving instructions to notice how much fun she was having, as though she were playing at being grown-up and organizing her own kitchen.

The room was finally just as Reya would have had it. Aren felt the loss of home and farmland; it took a moment before he realized that Bird was weeping. He lifted the child and held her, noticing that she had become a little heavier and, now that he thought of it, taller as well.

Bird wept for a while, murmuring about missing her mother and father and home. Aren held her and tried to comfort her. Hobard stood aside, with no knowledge of how to comfort what was simply an unhappy human child. Eventually Aren was able to distract Bird from her own unhappiness by suggesting that they should check on Magda.

That was enough to pull Bird back into dealing as Reya would have with an immediate situation. She led the way into the bedroom, then stepped aside for Hobard to approach. The old woman's breathing was audible, so clearly she still lived.

Hobard leaned over the bed, wrinkling her nose. She listened for a few moments, then nodded and moved away, gesturing to the other two to follow. She led them into the main room before speaking. "She breathes well, and that's a good sign. If she does not awake by morning, we'd better rouse her."

Bird nodded. "And then she's going to need a bath, and those clothes will need a good washing. Probably everything in that room will need to be cleaned. We might as well make a job of it and wash all the clothing and bedding as well. There's no sense leaving a job half done." Again the decisive nod.

Aren was in no mood for smiling at the thought of another day of housework. "We'd better get some sleep ourselves, then. We'll want to finish the cleaning tomorrow. These villagers seem eager to have us visit their orchards and fields." He was uncertain how he felt about this visit when he had no way of knowing what was happening on his own family's farm, or whether he would ever see it again. He and Bird might have to spend the rest of their lives in these Barren Lands. That night he slept poorly, dreaming of the farm falling into disrepair, or occupied by strangers.

Hobard, relieved not to be fleeing or fighting wizards, decided to sit outside for a while. She was beginning to recall life from the time before she'd gone into the earth with her fellow bright Druids, leaving behind a dozen or so others whose robes had turned dark.

In the first shock of having found herself in a bright robe standing next to an ancient oak rather than flowing throughout it, facing what seemed to be both a human child and a focus of power she'd not experienced since leaving her physical form, she'd had no time to think about this sudden disconnection. Then came healing Aren, fleeing dark wizards, discovering those who might have been dark Druids. And now, immersing herself in, of all things, housework. The loss of tranquility struck hard as she sat on the house's front step, breathing in the air.

She discovered that she enjoyed breathing.

Breathing was not something Hobard needed to do after she'd become insubstantial, though she'd felt from within an oak its slow breathing in of night air through its leaves and out through those leaves in daylight. She came to realize that what the oak breathed out in the light changed air itself to something animals and humans and, she supposed now, Druids could breathe. The thought pleased her; it was a small connection to what she'd so suddenly left behind.

Hobard experienced the world differently than she had from within. She saw rather than sensed night sky, moonlight almost as bright as day but bringing out less color in the landscape. She stood and walked about, enjoying the motion, the feel of the land beneath her sandals, the night air on her face and arms. Disconnection was still present within, but a sense of re-connection grew and became increasingly familiar. As she walked, she understood that this land had once been barren but now had become fruitful. And more: that the land was somehow pleased, in a way deeper, quieter than her own pleasure in moving about. She'd learned during the time as a disembodied being that life took many forms. Consciousness could be deeper, slower than she'd realized when she'd had a body. And now she brought that awareness into this body which eventually became tired, so she stretched out beneath a small pine and slept.

***

It was evening before Rath's crystal glowed and Soren's face appeared within the globe. "No news, I hope," the Chief Mage said.

"None here," Rath answered. "I left Roke to watch the path by which the witch-child entered the woods and the barrens. I've come further south, thinking it would be good to watch over a wider area. There's been no movement so far."

"You'll have company soon. I'm sending Ren, Vash, Quar, Vil, and your former apprentice Owen to join you. Others have been alerted. I expect soon to hear back from them. Ren's group will carry maps— one for each. They'll bring a force of forty guards, which should be enough to spread out over the ground. Between crystals and runners, you should be able to keep in touch with each camp."

That should do, Rath thought. "Has Oleg learned anything of value?"

Oleg stepped forward, leaned toward the crystal so that in Rath's view his face seemed to grow. Unlike Soren, he took a second for a greeting before going on. "We've found little new. There are some ancient references to a Mother who seems to have been alternately loved and feared, or perhaps loved at one time and feared at another. It is difficult to tell when either response might have been dominant.

Clearly there came a time when the Druids who were our teachers and informants came to worry about being overheard.

"We continue to turn over the oldest records, since they seem the only ones of relevance. There are plenty of references to women healers and some to women of power, but apparently our ancestors did not find those worthy of more than a mention." Oleg did not bother to note that his predecessors were not the last to be short-sighted. Who could tell what information future Loremasters might need? His tenure had resulted in detailed and varied reports, to the point that occasionally his apprentices almost worked up the courage to question his requirements. Almost.

Rath was uninterested in such details, though he knew of their importance to the Loremaster, as well as the risks of offending the man. He waited until Oleg had finished before he brought the conversation back to his immediate concerns. "Have you found spells which several wizards working together might use against the witch? So far, individual wizards have not been able to break through these wards, but perhaps several working together could."

"I have already thought of that," Soren broke in. "I have instructed Oleg to assemble a collection of counter spells, as well as spells for both attack and defense which might be suitable for chanting as a group. That will take some time. They won't be ready to send with our wizards. I will send them later with guardsmen; without wizards, they can travel on horseback and so arrive more quickly."

Rath sought for something positive to say in light of these delays. "That will give Ren's group time to settle in, at least." He knew even before he saw Soren's frown that the comment sounded grudging, at best.

Oleg leaned in again. "We can at least offer some small assistance. The guards with Ren's group are bringing a small table so you may look at maps without spreading them on the ground and crawling around. And stools."

Soren again took over the conversation. "I'm sending enough guardsmen that they can bring some items beside those needed for subsistence. If there are other things you need, speak up." When Rath said nothing, he asked, "Anything else?"

Rath indicated there was not, and Soren broke the connection.

"Rath grows sure of himself as his strength returns, I think," Soren said. "His eagerness to confront this witch-child may yet betray him. Perhaps he has too soon forgotten the lesson she taught him last time."

Oleg almost raised his eyebrows, but caught himself. Soren rarely betrayed his dislike and mistrust of Rath. The Loremaster kept his voice soft, neutral. "We must hope he does not overreach. Losing a wizard of Rath's strength would be bad enough; losing the others who join him would be a disaster."

Soren nodded. "True enough. We must hope the One-Hand does not allow his thirst for revenge to lead him into a confrontation before he's ready."

***

This business of waiting and watching for the witch-child to do something was not to Rath's liking. Still, his strength was recovering. and it would be good to be more nearly at full strength when what Soren had called "Ren's group" arrived. The term irritated Rath, but he knew Ren to be a sensible man, one unlikely to think himself the equal of any of the Order's senior wizards. Earlier, it had suited his plans to appear weak before Lorit and later Soren and Haster; now he must appear to be even stronger than he might actually be. And much more confident.

Rath stood, placed his crystal again in his pack, then carried the pack to his tent. It wouldn't hurt to arrange his bedroll.

When Rath emerged, he saw Tarh sitting on one of the camp stools and went to join him. Tarh began to rise at his approach, but Rath gestured for him to remain sitting. That was a bit unusual: Rath had been stickler for these small ceremonies among his apprentices. A guard approached, carrying wood for a fire, but Rath waved him away. The night was plenty warm, and he felt the need to be surrounded by dark.

Normally Rath didn't care for conversation, and rarely asked for—or took—anyone's opinion. Tarh was surprised when the wizard spoke.

"I begin to wonder what we can accomplish here, should the witch-child decide to leave these lands."

Tarh was uncertain how to answer this. He kept silent.

"Oleg seeks scrolls containing chants to remove a ward, suitable for a group of wizards to recite together. If nothing else, we can become accustomed to throwing spells as a group." Rath shook his head. "So far, nothing we have tried has been successful, other than Lorit's spell against the red woman. We know how that turned out."

Tarh spoke hesitantly. "Yet now we expect the witch's attacks. In the valley, we didn't know of her power to command the skies. Had we known, perhaps we'd have prepared defenses." He fell silent, half expecting Rath's anger to singe him, as it had often done during his apprenticeship. No anger came. Tarh wasn't certain whether Rath was simply tired, or willing to listen to a wizard in ways he wouldn't have listened to an apprentice, but he appreciated the respite.

"That's true. Oleg's efforts seem to focus on searching the past, hoping to learn more about this thing we pursue. We have defensive spells which might help. Perhaps"—Rath considered—"perhaps several casting a defense spell while several others attack could be successful. That's something we can practice as well. A useful thought, that."

After a while Rath spoke again. "I suspect we may yet return to that valley. The ward still holds, though the witch-child has left. If, as Snake believes, she was raised by farmers there, the valley may be of importance to her. That the ward holds when she has been absent so long suggests the valley itself may be supplying some of the power which sustains it." Another silence. "The mist hiding these Barren Lands existed long before this witch-child was born. She seems to have intended to reach this place, or perhaps even been drawn to it. And that is interesting."

Now Tarh offered up another idea. "She seems to seek places of power. First the Red Forest and now these Barren Lands. It is difficult to tell whether the valley would be a place of power had she not been there."

Rath nodded. "Perhaps she's an emanation of the valley itself, called into being to counter our drought and now—" He paused, shaking his head. "And now, what? Are there ancient powers in the land which she has been sent to awaken and unite? Is she simply a messenger?"

"She seems to possess power of her own," Tarh noted. "Rand's keep surely was not the site of an ancient power, yet it fell at a word from this child." This, he felt, was risky: he hoped Rath wouldn't take the suggestion as a contradiction.

He didn't. "True. The only power there came from Rand's own greed and will, enforced by his guardsmen. I doubt there was any dark magic in those walls; they came down too quickly." He thought for a long moment. "There is something in that: Rand's walls came down immediately. The walls of my tower took a full day to fall—though they also turned to dust, while Rand's keep survived as stone after it fell."

His smile was grim. "We have discovered something. While the tower's fall was total, yet it took longer. The power used in its creation held out longer than did the walls of Rand's keep. It is a small hope, but a hope nonetheless."

Rath stood. "This conversation has been useful. Now, let us rest."

Tarh, pleased but still more than half apprehensive, stood as well, inclined his head in acknowledgment of the order.

***

Bird slept soundly in her bedroll on the floor of Magda's cabin, only to be awakened in the morning by groans from the bedroom. She jumped out of bed, quickly rolled up her bedding, then tossed it against the wall next to her small backpack and Aren's larger pack. "Well," she muttered to herself, "if Magda is waking, it's about time you woke up, too." She stood for a moment, hesitating, then shook herself. "Might as well get this day started. Lots to do, lots to do." She strode into the bedroom. Behind her Aren struggled his way out of a dream of overgrown fields and a sagging farmhouse.

Magda seemed to be having trouble working her way out of the bedclothes. Bird stepped up and said "Here, let me help you" and reached out a hand. The old woman froze, staring at the child.

When she spoke, it was in the voice of a person not sure she was awake. "Then it wasn't a dream? You're—you're here? After all these long years, you're actually here?"

Bird, busily untangling the woman, thought that was an odd sort of good morning. "Of course I'm here. You can see me, can't you? Now let's get you up. You've slept since yesterday afternoon, and that's long enough. We've got the rest of your house nicely cleaned and things put where they belong, but this room needs the same. And you, I'm afraid, need a bath."

Magda was on her feet now, leaning partly against the tall head of the bed and holding Bird's arm as she tried to balance herself. "Wait—wait. Let me get my bearings." She clutched her temples. "Oh, my head. I need some wine." She looked again at the child. "Is it really you, Mother? Or am I still full of wine?"

Bird shook her head in disapproval of this talk of being full of wine. "Now stop that and stand up straight! And don't be calling me mother—I'm not anybody's mother! Look at me! I'm a little girl!"

At the command, Magda's spine straightened and her shoulders squared. Her groans brought Hobard from where she'd been sitting on the front steps, watching the day become light. Aren stood in the bedroom doorway in case he was needed. Both could hear the creaking and cracking of Magda's joints as she stood straighter than she had in years.

Aren winced at the thought of what that must feel like. "Bird," he said, "I think standing so straight is hurting her."

Bird turned to look at her brother. "Why should it hurt her to stand up? That's silly!"

"She's old, little bird. Old people tend to stand bent over, and their bones sometimes hurt." Aren's voice was gentle. At some point, any older-brother authority he still possessed would vanish in the face of Bird's powers. It would be wise to delay that time as far as possible.

Bird turned back to Magda. "Stand however is easiest for you, then. I didn't mean to hurt you."

Magda slumped, but remained on her feet. "Thank you, Mother."

This time Bird looked exasperated but didn't correct the woman. "Let's get you into the other room. If you were full of wine yesterday, a meal and hot tea will do you good." She turned and led the way into the main room, Magda shuffling after.

As she stepped through the door into the other room, Magda stopped, stared. "Who did this? Who dared? If Inek—"

"We did this," Bird replied. "I don't see how you could find anything in this house. We cleaned, and that was surely overdue. No one changed where you put anything; we just cleaned up and put things to right. See for yourself."

Magda shuffled to the shelves of jars with bunches of dried plants hanging above, pausing occasionally to put both hands to her aching head, looking carefully at everything before nodding. "It will do, then." She turned to face Bird and reacted nearly as strongly as she had on the doorstep the day before. Aren leaped forward to steady her as she tottered, then helped her to the nearest chair, where she sat staring at the child. Hobard moved further into the room. Magda caught sight of her, gasped, and covered her eyes as though the bright robe hurt them.

Bird was already at the cupboards, taking down a plate and cup, then arranging bread, cheese, slices of apple and pear. "Aren," she said, "I think a small glass of wine might do. We can heat water for tea in the meantime."

The evening before they'd noted the house's ample supply of wine. Aren selected a jug, poured a cupful and walked it to the table. Bird set the plate she'd prepared next to the cup, and Aren helped a still-staring Magda to a seat.

"I—I don't think I can eat," the old woman said. Aren noted her trembling hands, bloodshot eyes, and pale skin. He suspected she might need days to recover. Back in the valley, he'd seen a farm hand or two who'd arrived still drunk from days of drinking and was of little use for the next several. Magda exhibited the same symptoms.

"Take some of the wine. It should help. Not too much, now," he said as she seized the cup and raised it quickly to her lips. Aren let her take a long drink, then gently removed the cup and set it back on the table. Hobard stood off a ways, not wanting to further upset the woman but fascinated by this process. Druids, she recalled, enjoyed wine from time to time, but on the whole preferred water from gurgling streams. Wine didn't intoxicate a Druid the way it did humans, though the flavor was pleasant.

Bird sat down next to Magda and began to try to interest her in the food. "Aren," she said, "will you start a fire in the stove so we can heat water for tea? Will you and Hobard start a fire in the shelter stove as well, then heat water to fill the wash tubs? When Magda feels a little better, we'll want hot water for her bath as well."

At that, Magda turned to Bird, a protest in every line of her body, but stopped. Again she stared at the child, seeming to look at something around the little body. Hobard recognized the look. It was the same which had appeared on the villager's faces as they watched Bird: a mix of recognition of the play of auras around the child and surprise at the being who carried those auras.

"You'd better put some solid food in your stomach now," Bird said. After a moment Magda nodded and broke off a piece of bread, taking a small bite and another of cheese. Aren started a fire in the stove, then left to join Hobard. Bird watched Magda eat until she was satisfied the woman would continue, then rose and moved the kettle to the stove's warmest spot.

By mid-morning, Aren and Hobard had brought the largest tub into the cabin's main room before returning to the arbor where they washed clothes energetically if none too efficiently. Bird had heated water for the bath Magda continued to protest. While the old woman bathed, Bird searched through the wardrobe in the bedroom for clean clothing and a clean towel. Once she'd set those on a chair next to the tub, she gathered the clothing and bedding which hadn't measured up to Reya's standards. These she carried out to the laundry workers, assuring them that this was the last.

When Bird returned to the cabin she found Magda trying to maneuver herself up and out of the tub. Once Bird got the old woman on her feet and dry, the girl left her to dress herself and returned to cleaning the bedroom. It was a smaller room than the main room, with only a bed, chair, and the wardrobe Bird had already emptied, so the chore was easy. A good dusting and sweeping took only a few minutes. Then it was time for the mop, which necessitated interrupting Aren three times to ask for one more bucket of water, please.

By mid-afternoon, clothing and bedding were drying on a line Aren had found lying on the ground and re-attached, one end to the house and the other to the shelter. He and Hobard lay on the grass, enjoying the sunshine. The house-cleaning was done. Magda had drunk several cups of tea and began showing interest in the arrangement of her jars and hanging dried plants. Despite an occasional pause to rub her temples when she turned too quickly, she approved the arrangement. "It's as though someone knew my methods," she commented at one point.

"That was Hobard," Bird answered. "She put away your seeds and the things you use to heal, while Aren and I cleaned. She seems to know a lot about plants and healing."

Magda snorted. "More than that, I'll wager. If she's not a Druid, I'll eat her robe." She turned and looked at Bird. "Mother, did you call her? I've not seen a bright Druid since—well, you know when."

Bird stood then, hands on her hips, angry: "I'm no one's mother! Can't any of you people see? I'm a little girl! Don't call me mother!"

Magda shrank at the show of temper. "Then what may I call you?"

"Well, Bird, of course. That's my name."

For a long moment Magda was silent. "May—may I call you Little Mother? I don't think I can manage to call you Bird. It seems disrespectful."

Bird thought this a strange thing to say, but then Magda was defi-nitely strange: living all alone in such a messy—no, dirty—house, with such a wonderful collection of seeds and herbs and plants, clearly drinking more wine than was good for her. "All right, then, if you must," she answered. "But it seems very odd, if you ask me." For a time she watched Magda work her way around the shelves, the hanging plants, the jars which were too large for the shelves.

Finally Bird stood, took a breath, and bustled over to the cupboards. "It's past time for the mid-day meal! We've been working so hard I almost forgot. While I set the table and bring out food, will you call Aren and Hobard?"

When Aren, Hobard, and Magda entered, Bird had stirred up the fire and was heating a kettle for tea. On the table were fruits, breads, fruits and cheeses of various sorts—all the good things the villagers had sent the night before. The four set to eating like hungry workers, even Magda, surprised that her appetite had returned. When the kettle boiled, Bird rose to pour tea for herself and Magda. Hobard went to the wine jug and poured a mug for herself and another for Aren. Magda almost requested one for herself, but didn't as she caught Bird's frown.

Eventually all four pushed their plates away. Aren allowed a few moments before he spoke. "Bird and I are travelling, as you know, Hobard, to escape the dark wizards. But that is not our only purpose. We also seek those who can instruct Bird in the nature and use of her powers."

At this, Magda almost spoke, but caught herself. Hobard was only slightly less surprised.

"Hobard knows something of this power, since Bird called her when I was badly wounded." Aren was reluctant to continue, but knew that if they were to learn anything, he must. "Neither of you has seen the extent of her powers." Hobard and Magda exchanged glances, eyebrows slightly raised.

"Nor do you know why the Order pursues us—or rather, pursues her. I am of interest only because I accompany her." Both Hobard and Magda leaned forward at this.

While Bird sat with eyes downcast, occasionally stifling a sob, Aren told of the series of events which brought them to the Barren Lands. "And now," he ended, "we seem to have reached a place where wizards cannot follow. We seek more: knowledge of the extent of Bird's powers, of who she is."

Magda had become increasingly agitated as the tale continued. When Aren ceased, she burst into speech: "And you have endured this, have allowed it? Mother, how can this be?"

Bird looked up, tracks of tears clear on her face. "I killed twice. The second time Aren says I left people without the lord they thought they needed. I don't want to be killing! I hate killing! If they'd just leave me alone, I could stop!" After a deep breath, she scolded: "And don't call me Mother!"

Magda bent her head in apology. "I forgot myself. At least I can give you this much assurance, Little Mother: no wizards will find their way past the mist. You and your—brother?" Here she looked a question at Aren. At his nod, she continued. "You and your brother are safe here. These mists are ancient, the power which created them far beyond any wizard's understanding." She looked at Hobard. "As for telling you more, I am at a loss. Perhaps the Druid will know what should be done."

Hobard shook her head. "This is beyond me. When sent into the earth, I went with a mix of pleasure and of concern for what remained behind. Soon little was left but pleasure in that existence. Those who remained may be able to tell more than I can."

This was something, at least, but Aren wanted more. "Hobard, you do not say who or what sent you. There seems to be some mystery there which may not concern us, though I cannot tell. But you, Magda, have been here for some time. How did you come to this place?"

"That much I can tell you," she said. "I remember the bright Druids, and I remember when they were sent back into the earth from which they'd come." At this Aren's eyebrows raised. "I loved walking the world and was allowed to remain. For a long time I was content, living one place for a time, then another. The dark wizards began to be jealous of powers other than their own, though mine is a small one: that of planting and harvesting, and of healing. I had heard of this place and knew that others had been sent here. I came also, thinking that their powers would prevent the darkening wizards from following, only to discover that these others declined to use their powers. Still, the mist was more than sufficient protection. You may learn more when the villagers show their fields and orchards and gardens."

Bird was interested in this about plants. "Did you teach them?"

"When I first arrived, for a time," Magda said. "They knew little of planting and nothing about harvesting beyond picking an apple when it came ripe. I shared what I could, then left them to discover more on their own."

"What are these villagers?" Bird asked. "Their robes seem odd. Why do they behave so strangely? They seem afraid. And yet their fruit and bread and cheese are delicious, and you seem to think their wine is tasty as well." With a sly glance, she directed this at Magda, who had the grace to blush.

Magda and Hobard exchanged a glance but kept silent until Aren leaned forward, clearly ready to question them further. Before he could, Hobard spoke. "I am not sure how much we may tell, little bird. There is some plan here which I do not understand. This much I think I may say: they are very like me, yet also unlike. How they came here I do not know."

"That I can tell, at least," Magda said. "They were sent here because of their errors, to remain until called. Since I was allowed to remain in this form and to walk this earth, I heard them instructed to come here and remain, though it was some time before I joined them."

"Who," Aren asked, "gave them these instructions, and sent Hobard and the others into the earth and allowed you to remain? Hobard, did the others sent into the earth welcome that change as you did?"

Hobard leaned back, looking into the distance and smiling gently. "Oh, yes, we all did. A long time before, we had been called from the earth, and returning allowed us to again move freely into all that is or lives upon the earth."

"And," Aren asked, "were you sent back by the same being who had called you?"

Both Hobard and Magda nodded. "Who else could do such a thing?" Magda asked.

Aren sat thinking, while Bird waited wide-eyed, hoping for more. Finally he spoke. "Is it possible, then, that Bird's powers might mean that whoever called you from the earth and later sent you back is about to reappear? Or might reappear?"

Magda gave a not-very-convincing shrug. "I have no knowledge of that, and doubt that Hobard has either. There appears to be some plan being carried out, something set in motion long ago. I would not speak more than I have."

Hobard nodded in agreement. "The appearance of a red wizard and the awakening of the Red Forest would seem to be part of some great change in the world. I was part of that forest for what may have been a long time, though I was not concerned with time. Trees which had long been both tall and broad grew even greater while I was there, so surely time was passing." She pondered. "Still, I was aware of a change in the trees while I was still part of the forest, something perhaps similar to a sleeper becoming aware of something or someone nearby while still sleeping, but less soundly. I had been enjoying that slow change for some time when I was called back into this form."

At that, Aren sat with one hand holding his forehead and hiding his eyes, facing downwards. After a time he sighed, raised his head, and looked at Hobard. "You were sent back into the earth; and now you have been recalled into this life by my sister. Who are these tall persons we find living in what are supposed to be Barren Lands? In appearance they are not unlike you, Hobard, except for their gray robes. Were these once Druids who were sent here instead of into the earth?"

"It may be." Hobard was reluctant to say more. "They may tell you their story. It is not mine to speak."

"Well," Bird said, "I want to hear it!" She turned to Aren. "Can we get out and walk tomorrow? I don't want to be shown around just yet. First I'd like to wander a little."

In fact, Bird put off visiting the villagers' fields for a full week while she wandered, climbed trees, and played alone part of each day, then led Aren and Hobard and a recovering Magda in household chores. Aren couldn't tell if she were playing house or simply trying to deal with homesickness by imitating the routine she'd have followed back in the Fifth Valley.

CHAPTER ELEVEN

Another week passed before Ren's group of wizards arrived. Rath had spent little time with any of the group other than Owen, his former apprentice. He expected that Ren would be the most decisive and most useful when it came to planning. Owen, his former apprentice, no doubt would be the least decisive, but the man could take orders.

They arrived late in the afternoon, dusty and tired after a journey no doubt sustained by spells which would leave each badly in need of a night's rest. Ren took one look at Rath's camp and quickly directed the guardsmen to set up their tents in a wide circle. Wizards' tents would occupy a smaller circle within, leaving the center to Rath.

Guardsmen had learned to not wait to see if another wizard had contrary orders. They set to work making camp. Two unpacked and assembled a portable table and stools.

Ren led his fellow wizards to greet Rath. Each carried a bag or two of the size and shape for scrolls. "Greetings, Master Rath," Ren said, bending his head slightly in recognition of Rath's superior standing in the Order. "We bring reinforcements, food, and perhaps most welcome, maps and a convenient place to read them."

"You are most welcome to this desolate camp, Master Ren, and Masters Vash, Quan, Tor, and Owen," Rath replied. "Rest yourselves and perhaps eat somewhat. We can speak after supper."

Bowing slightly, Ren handed Rath the set of maps he'd carried. Rath hoped they would be the clearest set. Ren gestured for the guardsmen to bring forward the small camp table and stools before leading his group toward the tents.

Rath waited until they'd all entered their tents before he opened the bag. It contained two slightly different maps. An irregular blank area in the center of each was labelled "Barren Lands." He selected the one marked "A" and stretched it out on the table with stones holding down each edge. These maps were new and had not long been rolled up, so it took relatively little to hold them down, fortunately.

The outline of the Barren Lands appeared much as Rath had expected: broadest in the center, opposite where he'd chosen his camp; to the north the boundary gradually moved easterly, and the same was true of the boundary to the south. What surprised him, however, was that the barrens extended to within a league of the Blue River. The only bridge was far to the south. Should the witch-child leave the barrens on the far side, she'd have to come around the north or south edge. He would have wizards in both places.

Roke would move further north to watch that edge. Owen should be capable of watching the path by which the child had entered the scant forest bordering the Barrens. Vash, Tor and Quan could take positions to the south, with Ren nearest the south edge.

He'd keep four guards for himself and Tarh. Other than himself, only Tarh and Owen had seen the witch-child in action. If Rath expected the witch-child to come out the way she'd gone in, he'd send a better man than Owen to that spot. Surely she'd try to escape through some other route, if she decided to leave the safety of that mist..

That last thought bothered Rath most of all. Why would she have gone to such a desolate place but for safety and the opportunity to consolidate her power? Oleg had said there were vague suggestions in old scrolls that the barrens were a kind of prison for beings of power. Who could have imprisoned such beings? Druids, perhaps. But suppose whatever lived in the Barrens were Druids. Who could order Druids to such a place? Who could require them to remain so far from the oak forests that scrolls said they preferred?

The evening session went just as Rath intended. Each wizard accepted his assignment quietly. Orders came ultimately from Soren, but even had they not, none of these would presume to challenge Rath. They were less quiet as he recounted the events which began as Lorit sent guardsmen into the Red Forest to seek the witch-child.

Talk of the Red Forest always caused uneasiness among members of the Order. It was no surprise when they blanched at Rath's account of the magical attack on the Order's guardsmen. That Tarh and Roke had suffered another attack later, coming from the same red-robed woman who had struck down the guardsmen, caused further unease. Then Rath's description of Lorit's return attack striking the red woman down raised their spirits, until Rath told of the earth opening and shaking Roke and Tarh off their feet while the child escaped. Worst of all: the blast from the Red Forest itself, after which Lorit was no longer to be seen.

Tarh corroborated everything his former master said. By that time, the five newly-arrived wizards were extremely receptive to Rath's orders that they set up camp some distance from the trees, so they would see from afar the witch-child and her party were they to leave the Barrens. Under no circumstances were any of them to attempt to attack the child. Rather, anyone sighting her was to draw back and give room while alerting Rath. In turn, Rath would alert the others, then Soren.

Oleg, Rath said, was searching for spells which might dissipate the mists which warded these Barren Lands. As soon as those were ready, Soren would send copies. Each was to memorize the spells. These mists were no ordinary ward; they would have to chant dispersion spells as a group.

There was some muttering at that. It vanished when Rath reminded them that this course of action had been approved not just by Soren, but by Oleg as well. The Loremaster's name calmed the group more than did Soren's. That Oleg felt that no single wizard's power could prevail against this ward focused their minds nicely on the need to chant together.

There was something more, Rath said. They would also practice as a group both defensive and attack spells. Should the witch-child appear, they would hope to gather somewhere along her likely path, ready to cast a destructive spell upon her. Rath did not know whether that approach would work; but nothing else had. Thoughts of more powerful attack and defense spells raised the newcomers' spirits, though not by much.

His fellow wizards returned to their tents in somber mood, as did Rath himself.

The next morning Owen went north alone, though Snake and his minion followed soon after. Snake's orders were to mark on a map the site Roke would select further north as well as the exact position of the site Owen would take over.

Tarh had gone south with Ren and would accompany him as far as the southernmost post. On the way, they would both note where Vash, Quar and Vil set up their camps. Each wizard was accompanied, as always, by six guardsmen. Each would keep two in reserve and send two in each direction, thus extending the net of watchers. In case of a sighting, one could follow and watch the witch-child and her entourage while the other rushed to report to the wizard.

Tarh carried his own copy of the map Oleg had sent and would mark that as he and Ren passed through each camp, then return to report to Rath. Rath did not expect him for a day or more likely two.

Snake, on the other hand, with only two camps to visit, returned late in the day, shadowed as always by that fellow Dog. He reported immediately, spreading his copy of the map on the table and pointing out the site Owen had taken over from Roke and, more importantly, Roke's further north.

Rath found the assassin's report satisfactory, though this business of sitting and watching was not to his taste. He'd be glad to start practicing spells once Oleg's scrolls arrived. Soon he hoped they would banish this fog, strike directly at the witch-child and bring the chase to an end. While he waited, there was one more thing he could do.

Rath handed the assassin the map and asked, "Can you read this without Owen or Roke's help?"

Given his years of going wherever Soren wished, Snake was surprised that the wizard might have thought he couldn't decipher a map. Wandering without a good map would sooner or later have resulted in mistaking his destination. That no doubt would have meant the end of his service to the Order, not to mention his life. Concealing his irritation, he replied, "With ease, Master Rath."

Rath hadn't noticed. "I have a task for you," the wizard said. "There may be other paths leading out of the Barren Lands. Tomorrow I wish you to begin a careful search along the forest edge for signs of any such. Follow and mark any which extend to the mist." These, Rath was certain, would be the witch-child's most likely escape routes. Any such paths would be worth setting a special watch. He doubted she—or the guardsman who'd accompanied her—would choose to cut through even thinly forested lands were a path available.

At Rath's wave of dismissal, Snake bowed slightly and turned to walk away. He made a gesture for Dog to follow which he hoped would be sufficiently preemptory to satisfy Rath while not offending the actual master. Dog grunted, rose and followed Snake back to his tent.

Dog was first to speak once they were out of earshot. "Good thing, this. Earth-walker show path, move quickly. Snake camp path's end; earth-walker go, see child. Rath big help." Here he chuckled. "Leave morning, nearest path. Very good thing, this."

Snake wasn't surprised that Dog already knew where the paths were. Providing Rath the information he wanted should further secure Snake's position. Dog, he knew, was of no importance whatsoever to the wizard, who wouldn't hesitate to attempt to paralyze the squat being with fear. Snake would have liked to see Rath make the attempt. If Dog did not laugh it off, Snake would want to be out of reach of whatever chasm Dog might open beneath the wizard.

Snake and Dog left at first light. Wizards would be asleep, and guardsmen would ignore the assassin and his strange minion. Dog began to travel very quickly once they were away from the camp. They soon stopped at a break in the thin forest where Snake could see a path winding its way into the woods.

He unrolled the map Rath had given him and spread it on the ground, the edges held down by stones. He took out a quill and a small bottle of ink. Consulting with Dog, he drew the little he could see of the path's course into the woods. Finally he put away pen and ink, hoping he'd not irritated Dog with the delay.

Apparently not. The squat being chuckled, said only, "Finish drawing when reach mist." He entered the woods, walking at a normal pace and enjoying the stroll. It was early afternoon when they saw the misty barrier ahead. Dog signaled a halt. "Now do map, camp. Wait." Snake again spread the map. He noted that once Dog touched it, the map ceased attempting to curl at the edges. Snake got out his ink and pen. Dog dipped a twig into the ink and lightly traced their route, leaving it to Snake to thicken that dim line. Still strolling leisurely, he walked into the mist.

***

Bird decided it was time to tour the fields. "Hobard, please tell the villagers that we'd like to go tomorrow. We don't know how big their fields are, so we'd better prepare a lunch and something to drink." With that she joined in packing the lunch.

The next morning Bird rousted them out early, eager to be up and doing despite Magda's grumbling. A cup of tea and a bowl of hot oatmeal at least partially calmed the old woman's irritation. With their lunches and flasks of both water and wine in Aren's and Hobard's packs, they followed Bird down the trail toward the village.

The villagers were gathered in the street before their cabins. Aren could see the tension in the tall men's faces. They appeared fearful their work would not be good enough. He wondered what cause they might have to fear Bird. Perhaps it was Hobard, the bright Druid, whose approval they so clearly sought.

"Welcome, Mother"—Inek began but was interrupted.

"Why does everyone call me Mother? My name is Bird! Can't anyone who lives here see I'm a little girl?"

Inek stood shocked and fearful. Magda spoke, her quiet, soothing tone surprising to Aren and Hobard, who'd heard her only hoarse and fretful. "Inek, I have been allowed to use 'Little Mother.'" She turned to Bird. "Perhaps that would be an acceptable way for these men to address you as well?"

Bird, tight-lipped, nodded. "All right. But I don't know what you people have against birds!"

After a deep breath, Inek continued. "Welcome, Little Mother, and all those with you. We have long looked forward to this visit. May we begin?"

Bird replied with an eager "Yes! I want to see fields and orchards that someone cares about. Let's go!"

Aren was startled by Inek's words about having long looked forward to this visit. Had those words been directed to Hobard, they'd have made more sense. These men, who might have been lesser Druids, must have waited long for a visitor. But a visit from Bird?

Inek led them up a gentle rise away from the village. As they reached the crest, spread out before them were acres of already-harvested grain. Aren could see remaining stalks of wheat, oats and barley, and the stalks were strong, healthy. These were fields Lir himself would have been proud of, unlike the worn, over-cropped lands they'd passed through. Thought of Lir led Aren to wonder who their father would have reached out to for help in the harvest. Probably Dog, he guessed. Immediately he changed the name to the Lamar preferred by both Reya and Bird.

"Oh, my!" Bird whispered. "This is lovely." She looked up at Inek, standing off to one side. "May we go down into them?"

Inek, smiling broadly and looking as though he could hardly keep still, tried twice before he could reply. "Of course. You may go anywhere you wish."

The others had to hurry to catch up with Bird. Aren fell in step with Inek. "I see no ditches. Do you irrigate at all?"

"We have no streams here from which to run ditches." He pointed to a field off to their left. "That ground has lain fallow throughout the past months. Next year, we will plant that field and this will lie fallow. Once birds and animals have gleaned all they can here, we'll begin the work of turning over the stubble. That will go on through the year, but it becomes more urgent in summer when the land will attempt to turn green again."

Lir had spoken of possibly of having trying to something similar, had the drought continued. These men appeared expert. "Does no rain fall here?" Rain in the valleys came down from the mountains, but these lands were far from the northern mountains.

"Very, very rarely do we see rain," Inek replied as they walked across the recently-harvested field. "When it does, we take a day to celebrate." He smiled. "It takes two years of water to support a crop. There is water beneath the soil, though not much, and it moves slowly toward the surface. We worked long to develop strains with deep roots which could reach what water comes near the surface."

"How did you go about that?" Aren knew that fruit trees could be cross-pollinated to develop strains which might resist disease or bear more fruit, but had not heard of similar efforts with grain.

Inek paused before replying. "Once we learned, the process seemed only natural, really. We had help. I doubt we'd have managed if left entirely to our own devices, especially in those early sorrowful years." He shook himself as though trying to throw off that part of the memory. "Once we began to understand, we kept track of which plants bore more grain. To our surprise, they were often small. We guessed that such plants put more energy into seeds than growth. At harvest time we set those seeds aside, then planted them the next year in part of the field so we could keep track of how well they did. If they did well again, we'd plant more of the next year's field. Eventually all our seed sprouted deep-rooted plants, while the harvested seeds each year remained wholesome."

Aren was surprised to hear Inek speaking as though he'd had to learn all this. Inek saw the look on the guardsman's face and smiled ruefully. "Oh, we had to be taught, all right. We were beings of the forests, especially the oak forests. We were sent to this strange place and the mists set about it. Here we were to wait until our penance might be done.

"Fortunately, Magda joined us and taught planting and harvesting, as she once taught humankind." For a moment Inek appeared to consider something he'd not thought of for years. "Then she told us we knew as much as we needed and should learn the rest for ourselves, as we have done." His voice became full of regret. "Alas, over the long years we became proud of what we had achieved and forgot to be grateful. We have not treated Magda with the respect she deserves."

Aren slowed, trying to make sense of what he'd just heard, especially the part about Magda teaching humankind the skills of planting and harvesting. Bird again raced out ahead of them. She turned to call back to Inek, "Blueberries! This late in the year? But how did you get blueberries to bear this late? May I try some?"

Inek's smile broke into laughter. "Little Mother, you may eat as many as you wish of everything we have! All are welcome!" He turned then to share a look with the villagers walking just behind them. Magda, leaning on Hobard, came along more slowly behind the rest. "Brothers," Inek said softly to his fellows, "she is pleased. She was pleased with our first offering, and now seems more than pleased with the work we have done, and its results."

Puzzled by Inek's obvious relief, Aren put in, "I've known Bird all her life, and this is more than pleasure. This is delight."

For moment something seemed to puzzle Inek. "All her life?" he wondered before the rest of what Aren had said sank in. "Delight?" He turned again to face the broadly-grinning men behind him. "Do you hear that? We have brought her delight! Delight!" He turned again to Aren. "You cannot imagine what this means. It is for this that we have labored willingly all the long years. Delight!" And now he didn't try to contain himself, but indulged in a sort of skipping up to and through the row of bushes. Bird strolled, eating a little from each bush, her hands and lips turning blue with juice.

After a time, Bird returned to where Hobard and Magda stood, sampling berries from the first bush they'd come to. Aren stood nearby, watching the villagers. This visit became stranger and stranger, he thought. These beings acted as though they'd waited all this time not just for any visitor, but for Bird herself.

"How did you get blueberries to bear this late?" Bird asked again.

Inek nodded at the question. "It took years. Since we have no real winter here, we thought perhaps fruit could be gotten to bear later in the year, so we did much the same as with other crops. We kept seed from late-bearing fruit, planted it in a special part of the field, then harvested the latest-bearing seeds to plant the next year. Eventually we developed versions of fruits which will bear at different times of year."

"Reya will love this!" For a moment Bird's face saddened. She shook herself and brightened. "Well, let's not stand here all day!" Bird chirped. "There's more to see and taste," she giggled.

She led the way toward another row of bushes. Beyond those were other rows and further off yet, trees, mostly the size of those in carefully-tended orchards.

Bird sampled each crop—huckleberries, blackberries, raspberries, boysenberries, currants, gooseberries, and beyond those, a bed of strawberries. As they came to the orchard itself, with its apple, pear, peach, apricot, plum trees, Inek noted that cherry harvesting was well past. The villagers, he said, were still working to find cherries which would ripen this late in the year.

Bird nodded absently, looking puzzled as she turned to the crowd of villagers around her. "I'm bothered by something, though," she said. Inek looked stricken; Bird hastened to add, "Oh, not about the trees or bushes or fields—those are wonderful." She turned to Aren, standing nearby. "Aren't they, Aren?" Without waiting for him to reply, she turned to face Inek again. "It's your robes. They just aren't right, somehow."

Inek froze. Looking around, Aren saw that the others had stopped cold as well, even Hobard and Magda. Again he saw fear in the villagers' faces.

"I just don't think they suit who you are," Bird murmured, walking through the silent group, examining their gray robes, occasionally touching one with a careful finger. "No, they're not right. I hope," she said, brightening, "they'll change to something which suits you better!"

As she spoke, the villagers' robes began to lighten, becoming almost as white as Hobard's, though with here and there a gray stain. The villagers' faces were suffused with a mix of joy and shame as Bird looked them over. She shook her head at the stains, lips pursed, Aren realized, just as Reya's would have been in a similar situation. "Well," she said, "I can see that you've been careless."

As Bird paused, the villagers lowered their heads.

"Still," she said, speaking slowly and thoughtfully, "this is a lot better than those dreary things you've been wearing." She beckoned Inek to come closer, then reached up and fingered a stain running across his chest. "This looks as though it's been worse. If you're careful not to add any new stains, this should come out with washing and sunlight." She looked up into Inek's hopeful face, then at the villagers standing around her, and smiled. "This is much better." She gave her decisive nod. "I like your orchards and fields! I can hardly wait to tell Reya and Lir."

The tears on Inek's face were of joy. "Thank you, Lady. We are and will remain your loyal servants." He turned to face the townspeople. "Will we not?"

"We will!" echoed over the land, and the villagers broke into a harvest dance of joy which had not been seen in an eon.

Bird clapped her hands in delight. Hobard and Magda stood open-mouthed at sight of Kasen-turned-Inek and his fellow villagers, newly robed in white albeit with stains, dancing before (Hobard barely allowed herself the name even in her thoughts) the Mother, or a version of the Mother.

Bird spoke, a little impatiently. "Don't you want to join them? Go ahead!"

Hobard leaped into the air and joined in. Inek led a sinuous procession which somehow became circles, lines, intricate figures which then dissolved into something even more intricate. He motioned for Hobard to join him at the head of what became a double line of singing villagers.

Bird laughed and shrieked with delight. Aren watched in wonder and even Magda smiled, first thinly and finally broadly. "Why, look!" Bird cried, turning to Aren. "They're all Druids, aren't they! Look— their robes are beginning to shine!"

After a time the dance slowed, came to a graceful halt. Inek and Hobard led the group back to where Bird, Aren, and Magda stood watching. They bowed and stood waiting for a smiling Bird's next words. "Well," Bird said, "that was lovely! And your robes are beginning to shine like Hobard's, too! I didn't realize that you're all Druids—that's wonderful! Hobard doesn't have to be alone!"

Inek stood quietly for a moment, his face glowing, as the men around him murmured praise and gratitude.

At the sound, Bird looked around sharply. "Now that doesn't mean Reya and I will do the washing. We'll show you, but you'll have to get the stains out of your own robes." She joined in their joyous laughter, a little puzzled that the thought of doing laundry should so delight this group of men.

As the laughter died, Inek ventured a question. "Who is Reya?"

Bird looked as though she thought that anyone who didn't know that was very foolish indeed. "Why, Reya is my mother of course, and Aren's as well!"

For a moment Inek couldn't speak. When he did, his tone was incredulous. "You—you have a mother? You?"

Bird was puzzled. "Well, of course. How do you think children come into the world? Though"—and now her voice was thoughtful—"Though Reya and Lir always say they found me in a basket woven of oak branches, under the oak tree in the yard." She seemed to reflect for a moment. "But that's just one of the stories parents tell. They think I don't know where babies come from, but I saw a calf being born, and I watched when the neighbor's cat had kittens."

Inek exchanged a look with Aren before speaking again. "So Reya and Lir raised you?"

"Well, of course. I don't know how Druids do things, but people are born and their parents raise them." Bird was impatient at such a silly question. "Oh, and they gave me the most beautiful blanket. Reya says I was wrapped in it when Lir found me, but we know what to think about that story. It's all the colors you can imagine, all woven in together, and it just fits my bed, back in the—"

Aren interrupted. "Remember, little bird, we don't want to say too much, even among friends. We don't want some dark wizard going after our family, and we don't know how much they might be able to hear with their crystals and spells."

Bird clapped a hand over her mouth, her eyes large. After a moment she took her hand away and turned to her brother. "Oh, Aren, I'm so sorry. I almost—but you stopped me in time! Thank you!" She walked over, reached her arms up to Aren. He lifted her into a strong hug.

Inek watched, beginning to think he understood. He stepped nearer to Aren. "You are the son of Reya and Lir, and brother or perhaps foster brother to our Little Mother?"

Aren nodded.

The others slowly gathered around them. Now Inek and the rest knelt, each with one knee on the ground. "Then we pledge our loyalty to you, second only to she whom we serve always, never to question again. And we thank you for bringing the Little Mother among us."

Bird looked up from where she'd buried her face in Aren's jerkin, puzzled by all this solemnity. "Are there any more orchards or fields to see?"

Inek stood, the others following. "Only the grapevines from which we make our wine, Little Mother. They are just over this way, if you'll follow me. As we return, we'll pass the pastures where we keep a few cattle for milking. Aren's horse is also there."

They had just begun when Bird stopped, listening. "Someone's coming." At her words, Aren's hand went to his sword hilt. He, Magda and Hobard stepped forward to stand between Bird and any enemy, while the rest of the Druids made a circle around them. Hobard peered into the distance, though she knew her forest-trained eyes weren't likely to see as far as would Aren's, or those of the Barren Land's Druids, for that matter, after their centuries in this open land. Magda didn't bother squinting. She doubted any wizard could make it to the village coming from the west, as this walker did. And, she noted, the Little Mother was smiling, no, nearly giggling with delight. The visitor would be no wizard, and Magda was certain she knew who it would be.

The stained Druids gave a great shout of welcome as Inek led them toward the newcomer. Soon they returned, singing as they circled and wove around a short, gnarled form. As they approached Bird's little party, the Druids quieted, forming a half-circle around a smiling Dog as he came forward.

Bird clapped her hands in glee. "Oh, you know my friend Lamar!" She skipped forward and took one rough hand. "What are you doing all the way out here? Have you seen Lir and Reya and how are they? I'll bet you're hungry and thirsty, too, and we have fruit and nectar—look at these orchards! Don't you think Reya would love them?" This time she did pause for an answer.

Lamar looked around at the trees and nodded. "Reya approve," he replied.

"I thought so too. Oh, but I'm forgetting my manners. You must come back to Magda's house and have something to eat and drink. And I'm forgetting my other manners, too!" She giggled for a moment, then became formal. "You know my brother, of course."

Aren stepped forward and offered his hand. "A long way from home, friend," he said as a grinning Lamar took his hand.

"This is Magda," Bird said. "We're staying with her."

Lamar bowed his head slightly. "Know Magda well." Then, to the old woman, "Looking better, little sister. Eyes almost clear!" He laughed.

Magda tried to keep a stern face at his mention of her almost-clear eyes but couldn't hold back a smile. "All things are looking better these days, elder brother, even you."

Lamar threw back his head and laughed long and joyfully. Bird chuckled to be polite, though she wasn't certain just what the joke was. Then she tugged at Lamar's hand to get his attention. "And this is Hobard." She lowered her voice confidentially. "She's a Druid, you know. I didn't know there were any left, but then there she was. Just in time, too. Aren was awfully hurt, but Hobard fixed him."

Lamar's smile was almost solemn. "Pleasure see bright Druid. Long time."

Hobard was a bit shy. "And it is both pleasure and honor to meet Lamar. Even in the deep forest, I heard much of the Earth-walker."

Bird turned toward the stained Druids, who stood with heads down at Lamar's mention of bright Druids. "This is Inek, and his friends. They're the ones who cared for all these lovely trees in this dry land! Isn't that a wonderful thing?"

Lamar chuckled. "Visit Barren Lands often. Yes, Aren know," he smiled at Bird as though referring to a secret between them, "Lamar useful. Help plant, harvest. Here, did what could." He looked up at the watching Druids. "Have not?"

"Aye, that you have." Several spoke at once.

"Do you see," Bird pointed out, not wanting her friend to miss anything that might interest him, "how much lighter their robes are? I knew the gray robes just didn't look right, and now look at them! Isn't this better?"

Lamar nodded. "Much better. But," he became very serious, "fruit and nectar?"

"Oh, I did offer!" Bird was crestfallen. "And I've kept you talking when you're tired and hungry! Reya would have my hide!" She started toward the village, then paused, turning to Magda. "Here I am, inviting people to your home. Is it all right?"

It was Magda's turn to laugh. "Little Mother, I can imagine little you might do which would not be all right. My home is your home for as long as you like."

"Oh, thank you," said Bird. "Then let's all go there and have a feast!"

"We'll go ahead and prepare," Inek said, and he and the villagers sprinted away.

***

Reports from the other wizards arrived intermittently by crystal through the afternoon and evening. Each was fully aware of the need to select a site which would command the best view of the forest edge, distant enough to allow at least time to report the witch-child's escape, if not get well out of her way. Tarh, who knew Rath's mind on this, would make suggestions if necessary, despite his junior status.

***

By the time Bird and her little group reached Magda's yard, the Druids had brought a second table, covered it with dishes and flagons, and arranged stools and small wooden chairs.

Inek asked for a moment in which to do something long overdue.

Even Bird paused then, as Inek walked to where Magda sat, knelt before her, and spoke. "For too long we forgot to be grateful to the one who taught us to plant and harvest. Our Little Mother's presence has reminded us of what we owe. We offer, as a tiny and long overdue moment of gratitude and promise that we shall not forget again, this song of praise." With that, the Druids began a song which needed no words to leave not only Magda but Bird, Aren, and even sturdy Lamar weeping tears of joy.

As they finished, Magda stood straight, nearly as tall as the Druids. It took a moment for words to come. "To have friends again cancels all debts," she said. "I thank you. But this is enough solemnity. Let us eat and celebrate!"

Inek stood beaming as Bird danced around, sampling this fruit, that nectar, even taking a sip of wine and making a face. The bread and cheese, she decided, were more to her taste than the wine. Though, she wished to make clear, she had tasted wine at home. It hadn't tasted any better there, either, and she wasn't sure why Lir and Reya drank the stuff. But that was all right, so long as she didn't have to drink any.

After a while, as everyone sat back in their chairs or lay on the ground, Lamar spoke up, his voice like gravel. "Aren seek teach Bird," he said, looking. "Time come." He looked around him at Magda and Hobard and the dozen stained Druids.

"Oh, yes," Bird said. "I've done more bad than good, I think. Calling the rain was good, but not calling lightning to strike wizards, even dark ones. Though I'm not so sure about that. I told a man to die and he did, but he was about to have Aren hung, and that couldn't happen. But I brought his whole castle down and left people with nowhere to live, and afraid of me, and just afraid. Since then I've tried not to hope for anything."

She was silent, sad-faced. Aren reached out and pulled her into his lap. "We don't know who or what Bird is, you see, other than that she's as much a part of our family as if she'd been born in our house. My father did find her under an oak tree, lying in a basket woven of oak branches and wrapped in a lovely multi-colored scarf."

"Was that an old oak with a broad trunk and many heavy branches, not nearly so tall as one might expect?" Magda asked.

"It was," Bird said. "I used to climb it all the time, but even from the top I couldn't see over the trees along the valley."

Hobard and Inek exchanged glances. Inek gestured for Hobard to be the first to speak.

"We know that tree well, Little Mother," she said. "In former days, that was a gathering place for Druids at midsummer and again at midwinter, and also at the fall and spring days when light and dark were the same length. In that valley dwelled the Mother of us all, and we came to honor her."

"I often came there, as well," Magda put in. "Humans in those days lived south of the forest, and rarely came to the Valleys."

"The valley has changed," Aren said, uncertain what to make of these claims that Druids came to celebrate around the oak in his family's yard, or someone called The Mother lived there. "Now the valley is full of farmers and their families, as are all the Five Valleys, as Lamar knows."

Lamar nodded. When he spoke his voice was more gravelly than before. "Is. Some things change, some not. Valley green, peaceful, grassy. Grows fruit, berries, grain."

"True," Aren noted, "but this does not help Bird to understand who and what she is, or what her powers are, or—"

Inek interrupted. "Pardon, my friend. I am not certain it is our role to instruct the Little Mother—at least not those of us who were once dark Druids and even now bear stains. We showed little wisdom in former times. No doubt there is still much for us to learn." He paused, gathered himself, and went on. "I do think we might be allowed to accompany the Little Mother as she travels. We would assist Aren in protecting her if need be."

"I might be of little use in protecting the Little Mother," Hobard noted. "I have always been a healer; exploring the ways of power was never my interest." She turned to Bird. "I would put what skills I have at your service, as I have done before."

"A good thing it was, too!" Bird said. "Aren might not be here without you!"

Hobard bowed her head. "I did what I could, Little Mother, but it was your desire that he be healed which awoke the Red Forest's healing powers. That, and the presence of the woman in the red robe."

"A red wizard?" Inek asked. "That would be something new in the world since dark Druids came to these lands."

"Not a wizard, I think," replied Hobard. "Something else, I would say, connected with the forest in some way she did not then understand. When I watched her carefully, I could see red lines, threadlike, moving between the woman and the trees."

"I hope she lives," Bird said. "She stayed behind when we ran for this place. She should have come with us."

"Little bird," Aren said, ignoring the raised eyebrows among Druids and Magda at his continued informality, "she stayed behind to slow the dark wizards' pursuit. She gave us time to cross the open area between the two forests. I also hope she survived."

Hobard broke the silence which followed. "Whatever happened to her, it seemed to fully awaken the forest. I could see only a little, but she appeared to come off badly in a duel with one of the dark ones. At that, the forest erased him." Aren's eyebrows rose at that "erased."

Lamar rumbled, "Survived. Earth-walker carried forest, left for heal. How long, cannot guess."

"Still," Aren reminded them, "this does not get us closer to helping my sister understand her powers, much less who she is. So far I've heard only that the Druids wish to travel with us when we leave here."

"Yes," said Bird, slapping the table once for emphasis, Lir's rare gesture for times when things had been talked nearly to death, "I want to see the Valley again, and Reya and Lir."

Lamar's rumble broke the resulting silence. "Need learn." He looked around the table at Magda and the Druids, his look not far from being a glare. "Explore, practice. Used power harshly. Fears use. Druids teach sustain, nourish, strengthen, heal. Magda also." He looked at each in turn, frowning. "Walk land, remind what forgotten, practice." It was not a request.

He turned to Bird. "Old Earth-walker saw dimly. Now sees more. Intended find teachers. Walk land, learn. Ask questions. Remember." He stood. "Enough. Rest. Tomorrow lessons."

In the morning, Lamar was off, he said, to check on wizards. The rest of that winter he and Snake continued to pretend to find trails he already knew. From time to time Snake would report a new-found trail and the pair would spend a day and night in Rath's camp, gleaning whatever information they might.

***

And so Bird's lessons began.

Inek, who felt he owed the most for his past transgressions, became first in her series of teachers. Each day the two of them walked through the fields and orchards. He would speak of sending his thought into the trees, seeking out weaknesses, perhaps insect damage or diseases. Bird listened attentively, then practiced. "It's a kind of listening," she said, after some days of trying. "Only not with my ears."

Inek had become apt to caper at almost anything, and he capered again. "Yes, Little Mother," he cried. "That's exactly it!" For the rest of that day, they wandered among trees, listening with their minds. "Each is a little different," Bird noted eventually. "Some of the apple trees feel sweet within; others I can tell without looking must be green or yellow and a little sour." She saddened, remembering. "Reya likes those for pies."

Late one day, Inek led her to a small tree, a little stunted. Together they stood, eyes shut, focusing their thought. "It has a hard time, doesn't it," Bird said.

Inek nodded. "This tree had a sort of wasting disease. We had to take turns spending the day with it, sending our thoughts of strength, of healing. Now it has thrown off the disease, but needs to recover."

"Can I send my hope that it will continue to grow stronger? Would that be too much? Aren fears that I won't learn to be gentle,."

"Aren is a wise man," Inek said. "Can you send a very slight hope?"

Bird took a deep breath. "I'll try." She closed her eyes.

"Not too strong, now," Inek cautioned, and reflected for a moment that he'd not have dared make such a suggestion a few days earlier.

Bird opened her eyes. "There. I made that as gentle as I could, I hope that the tree will grow stronger and healthier. How will we know whether it worked?"

"We can visit the tree each day and send our minds to it. We'll know."

After a few weeks, Inek reluctantly gave up his spot as Bird's teacher to Osa He taught Bird to listen with her mind to grape vines and crops in the fields. Bird noted that deer coming out of the trees which bordered the Barren Lands seemed to eat only what came up in the fallow fields, and birds seemed to eat grain only in those fields which had been harvested.

"That is true," Osa answered. "We have learned to cast our thoughts onto fields which are fallow or have been harvested, suggesting they're fine places for our friends to dine."

"Oh, let me try!" Bird cried.

"Hmmnn." Her teacher thought for a moment. "Perhaps you should begin by focusing your mind on this field with its ripening crop. Discover what you can read there."

Bird stood, eyes closed, for a long time before she decided she had sensed some protection over the ripening grain. Then the Druid took her to a nearby fallow field. This time she opened her eyes again more quickly. "Oh, I can feel the difference! This field says the grass and weeds coming up are sweet and tasty! The other field said its crop was dry and old and bitter!" She looked up at Osa, wide-eyed. "But that wasn't true, was it? The grain was still good, wasn't it?"

Chuckling, Osa assured her that the grain was, indeed, quite edible.

CHAPTER TWELVE

Usually Oleg put his apprentices to searching the archives while he reviewed their findings. This time, he led the search for dispersion, dissolution, cancellation spells of all types. He would review each for long hours when his apprentices slept. There were many such, but most were minor.

After three weeks, Oleg had selected eight. He spent another night softly chanting each. After many trials, he concluded that two would take months of practice before any group of wizards could hope to speak them in unison. Six others, however, appeared suitable for group chanting, given enough practice. He put his best apprentices to work making copies of each.

In the meantime, he sent the rest of his apprentices to look for powerful spells of attack and defense. This time he didn't lead the effort.

Again he found several of such complexity that he doubted any group of dark wizards could be brought to speak them as a unit.

It was likely, Oleg realized, that each of Rath's wizards knew most of the remaining spells, but it wouldn't hurt to send copies. Each wizard would speak a spell in a slightly different cadence. They would have to get used to speaking as one. Reading from a scroll might facilitate that effort, though Oleg wasn't certain. This business of working together was alien to the Order as he knew it,

Once his best apprentices had finished copying the six dispersion spells, Oleg set the entire group to copying the three attack and three defensive spells he'd chosen. These would offer the best mix of powerful and possible to chant as a group.

Soren waited impatiently as the weeks passed. Twice during that time Haster had to remind him that, surely, the Loremaster would report as soon as he had something worth reporting. It would be of little use to interrupt Oleg before he had finished.

None of that improved Soren's mood. As Oleg entered, Soren said only "Well, Loremaster," in lieu of a greeting. "I assume you have something to report."

Oleg hadn't expected a cheerful, "Ah, Oleg, what have you got for us? Something good?" He nodded to Haster, walked to Soren's desk and spread out copies of six spells. "As a matter of fact, Chief Mage, I do. My apprentices and I have dug out dispersion spells which might lend themselves to group chanting. I have copies for Rath's wizards, for you, and for my records."

He held up a hand, halting Soren and Haster as the two stepped toward the desk. "I caution, Chief Mage, that these will not be easy to chant as a group. Rath and his fellows will need some time to become proficient. It would not be wise to try too soon and alert the witch and whoever has gathered around her."

Soren replied with a scowl. He picked up a scroll and read it, his lips moving soundlessly as he shaped the words. Not even Soren would speak aloud a dispersion spell within a building so completely sustained and guarded by spells.

Oleg reserved the truth that he had spoken each of these spells aloud several times within his own office, confident that the wards he had set around the room would stand. He wasn't sure whether to be pleased with the strength of those wards, or disappointed that the dispersion spells had no effect. He'd rather hoped for a slight trembling of papers on his desk, if not of the furniture or the walls. Still, he was one wizard. Rath would have six.

Haster read several spells, not daring to mouth the words. Well, Oleg thought, that was Haster. The building should be safe even if someone accidentally muttered softly a few words. It would take an entire spell to have any effect, and only if spoken aloud and firmly, with a wizard's full focus and power. Even then the effect would undoubtedly be minor.

After a time, Soren turned from the scrolls. "Well done, Loremaster. These should indeed work as group chants." He thought for a moment. "Is it your thought that only one or two may work, so you send enough that Rath may decide which is most likely to be effective?"

Oleg shook his head. "No, Chief Mage. My thought is that the group should speak the six spells loudly and firmly, in whatever order

Rath prefers, then end with a Word of Power. I suggest "Forscéadan" from one of the old languages. The sound seems to carry more weight than a mere "disperse."

"Do you think it will take all that?" Haster was aghast at the thought of the effort involved to learn that many spells, to say nothing of getting six wizards to speak as one.

"Indeed, it may not," Oleg said. "Perhaps one or two spells would be enough. Should that prove not sufficient, I fear the witch-child would nonetheless be alerted. We know what she is capable of. From what we have heard of these mists which infest the Barren Lands, they have prevailed over generations of wizards. They may be more powerful than the ward over the valley." He paused a moment to allow Soren to consider that possibility. "I doubt that any of the group will know all these spells. Should they make an effort and fail with the first spell they manage to memorize and practice, they may not have the opportunity to learn the remainder."

Soren nodded. "I will instruct Rath to restrain his impatience and wait until we are ready with our strongest effort. How soon will you have enough copies to send?"

"I have them now, Chief Mage," Oleg replied. "I suggest that we also send a few of our most powerful attack and defense spells. My apprentices are hard at work copying those and should complete that task no later than tomorrow. Our wizards will know most of these; each should be able to easily learn the rest."

"Good," Soren said. "Haster, arrange for a half-dozen guardsmen to leave for Rath's camp on the second morning from now. They can draw mounts from any of the City's stables." He turned to Oleg. "You're certain that a complete set of all these spells will be ready by tomorrow night?" He didn't wait for Oleg to reply. "Pack each set in its own pouch so Rath won't have to sort through and arrange them. Haster can arrange for pouches to be delivered to you by mid-day tomorrow."

Oleg didn't bother to affirm that his apprentices would have finished copying well before the next evening. Given the emphasis he'd given to these researches, he expected that when he returned he'd find ten sets of attack and defense spells carefully arranged on the worktable closest to his office door. But he wasn't going to make that claim now. Soren would only too gladly rush the guardsmen's starting time. It was just barely possible that Oleg was wrong about how much progress his apprentices had made, and he wasn't about to admit that kind of miscalculation.

Instead he asked, "Would you like me to prepare instructions to deliver to Rath when you contact him tomorrow night, Chief Mage? I can also make a written copy for his use, if you'd like." The question seemed innocuous enough. Oleg hoped Soren would give it little thought before agreeing. If Soren spoke immediately with Rath, the Chief Mage would be at his imperious worst, not to mention that he hadn't yet reviewed all the spells Rath would be receiving. At best, Rath would be prickly at being given instructions, however gently disguised.

Oleg was lucky. Soren responded with a vague, "Yes, fine, that will work. Let us plan to contact Rath tomorrow evening. Haster, you can start work on travel arrangements now." The dismissal was clear.

***

The stained Druids now gathered every evening for supper at Magda's outdoor table, bringing fruits and berries, breads and cheeses and eggs, while Magda supplied tea and wine. Often Bird would speak of what she had learned during the day. This evening, Bird asked whether the stained Druids could communicate directly with animals. Could they cast their thought to animals as they could to plants and even to entire fields?

"That we can do only a little," Inek said. "We have focused on plants and the land. In earlier times, our exploration of minds led to dark magic. We would not touch on that again."

Hobard, however, noted that she often had need to calm a person or animal in order to heal. She offered to teach that once Osa's lessons were finished.

When that time came, Hobard walked Bird among the pastures. Bird learned to touch the minds of deer, birds, even mice. She realized that when, back in the Fifth Valley, she'd hoped a deer or squirrel or bird would let her come up to it, she'd been doing something like what Hobard now taught her.

"You see, Little Mother," Hobard said, "it is not necessary to frighten something into stillness. A gentle touch can remove their usual fear. Were a hurt and frightened being to attack, a harsher command might be necessary. Once the animal has been held, then it is possible to calm it."

These were some of Bird's best days since she'd fled the Fifth Valley. At times she would enter as gently as possible into a deer's being, participate for a while in its life of peaceful grazing and watchfulness. At others, she'd enter into the life of a swallow darting about as it caught insects. Her presence seemed calming rather than alien.

"Well, of course your presence would not be frightening, unless you wished it to be so," Hobard said. Then she went a step further. "Little Mother, you contain a power to sustain and preserve. When you use that power, all which exists can sense your presence and purpose. How could they not welcome it?"

Magda also walked with Bird, teaching her to cast her mind into plants to discover their potential for healing, for calming, and even for ending a life too damaged to recover. In these walks, Bird realized something else which Magda did not teach her: she could command a tree, for example, to fall should she need to block a path. But she also realized that, as when she'd turned herself into a butterfly to escape from a well into which she'd fallen, there was a price to pay. Then, it had been the deaths of other butterflies nearby to sustain her greater weight. For a tree to fall at her command, she must also end its life.

***

Rath ceased to keep track of Snake and his minion. Other than mapping pathways into the Barrens, he had no use for the pair. The growing number of identified pathways worried the guardsmen who had to do the actual watching of those pathways, but Rath had more important concerns. The process of teaching wizards to chant together was going more slowly than he'd hoped.

When the half-dozen additional guardsmen Soren sent him arrived with their pouches of spells, Rath had first spent an evening reviewing them. Oleg had suggested an order in which to chant those. After Rath spent much of that first night considering whether another order might be more effective, he had decided that once again the Loremaster was correct.

The next day he called his wizards together and decreed the order in which the dispersion spells were to be chanted. He led them in a run-through, then sent them back to their camps to memorize and practice. Attack and defense spells they could learn later; dispersion spells were at the core of their purpose in watching these Barrens.

Two weeks later, Rath called the wizards back for their first group practice. After three sessions, Rath was unpleasantly surprised by how slowly his wizards, as he'd already come to regard the others, learned to chant together. At this rate, it might take all winter before they became proficient at group chants.

Getting wizards to work together was not easy. Group chanting was the core problem. Memorizing spells was not difficult. Unfortunately, as Rath quickly realized, each had his own rhythm when it came to chanting. Here Ren became valuable. He listened carefully to Rath's patterns and intonations and became adept at following them. Owen and Tarh, Rath realized, had patterned their chanting after his during their apprenticeships. Even though they'd never chanted in unison, the pair quickly mastered the form. Between gatherings of the entire group, Roke, practicing with Owen, learned almost as quickly, and Ren suggested that between gatherings Tarh work with Vash and Quar, while he worked with Tor. Rath welcomed the idea. Guardsmen did the actual watching of the forest for any sign of the witch attempting to leave. There was little for wizards to do other than practice.

***

Some months had passed since Oleg had paid a visit to the Dark One, though more than once he'd considered descending to the dungeon below, despite having no news he wished to offer. There was nothing to be served by revealing their plans to try group chanting against the witch-child. Even should their captive believe group dispersion chants might work against the ward over the Barren Lands, it was unlikely he would say so. A visit might reveal that the Dark One already knew of the Order's sentinels around the barrens. And that was something Oleg would rather not think about.

The Loremaster had more hope than faith that even a group as powerful as those the Order had assembled could succeed in breaching the ward over the Barrens, but he would not speak those doubts. That the Order under Soren's leadership might withdraw and hope the child would leave them in peace seemed an impossibility. There was nothing for it but to search for a way to succeed.

Which brought him to consider again the ward over the Fifth Valley. That ward was recent, unlike the mists of the barrens. It had not been tested by time; indeed, it had not been tested at all, except by sending an individual wizard to learn whether it might prove fatal. Suppose, while Rath's wizards were challenging the ward over the Barrens, another group challenged the ward over the valley? He had already gathered the appropriate spells. His apprentices could quickly make additional copies.

***

These days Soren spent most of his time in his observatory, pacing impatiently while he waited for his crystal to glow with Rath's latest report. Those reports claimed progress, but not enough for an actual attempt on the mists. How much longer Soren would have to wait, Rath declined to say.

When Oleg offered a second method of attack, if not on the witch-child herself at least on the valley where all the trouble had started, Soren welcomed the suggestion. So did Haster, who'd tired of listening to Soren complain about Rath's slow progress.

"Who shall we send?" Haster asked. "With Lorit gone, most of our strongest wizards are with Rath."

Soren considered. "We had best send three younger wizards. Should the attempt fail, or worse yet, should it bring lightning across the road to strike those who chant against the ward, our losses will not be too great."

Soren continued to work out a plan. "We should also send a senior wizard, not to participate in the chanting, but as a witness. Pennon can be here within a day. I will send him to observe the valley while he waits for the chanters. When they arrive, he can keep off a way and observe, as Lorit observed when Selik dared the ward."

Haster's eyes widened at this version of Lorit pushing Selik into the valley to test whether lightning might prove fatal.

"Oleg, you have dealt more recently with our younger wizards than most," Soren said. "Who would you recommend?"

Some minutes passed before Oleg answered. "Vil, certainly, and Fant. Both passed through their apprenticeships some years ago and have had time to develop their power. And, I suppose, Wold as well."

Soren nodded. "Good choices. Between these two attempts, we may learn much."

Oleg cleared his throat. "There is reason to believe the child could be drawn out of the mists, Chief Mage. The Dark One has given me to understand that despite our spells, the stones beneath his dungeon bring him, shall I say, intimations of events in the world. When he has mentioned such hints, they've proven surprisingly accurate. If the child, or the others she has joined within the mists, receive similar notice of an attack on the ward over the valley, that might bring her out."

Soren's smile was approving and unpleasant. "Once out, she might be vulnerable to attack by more usual means. By guardsmen, perhaps, or even Snake. This course offers promise. Loremaster, contact these three and begin their training. I will order Pennon to begin monitoring events in the Fifth Valley."

***

Pennon had been summoned, his role in the attempt to disperse the ward over the valley carefully explained, including the need for him to insure that he, at least, would survive to report. Other than a brief lifting of his eyebrows, he showed no response. He would leave in the morning, accompanied by the usual six guardsmen. While he waited for the others to arrive, Pennon would establish his own camp, observe what he could from outside the valley, perhaps send his guardsmen to report on the state of the farmers. He and Soren would keep in communication by crystal.

Oleg set about selecting and preparing the three to be risked as chanters against the ward.

Vil, Wald, and Fant did not know one another well, but that wasn't unusual among the lesser members. As each scrambled for a place in the order, another's success simply meant the other had gained reputation. They had not yet had any such success.

The order to report to Loremaster Oleg had been delivered to each by a servant rather than a fellow wizard. That might not be a good sign. All three were nervous as they approached the archives after the evening meal. None was pleased to see the other two. With none wishing to take the lead by knocking, the three stood just outside the archive door until Oleg's voice, seemingly coming from the walls, called "Come in, then! Don't dawdle all day!" and the door to the outer room opened.

The door was just wide enough to allow the three to push through together with only a little elbowing. They knew the room well. Each had spent a two-year apprenticeship under the Loremaster. Nonetheless, the archive was not a place of comfort for lesser wizards; each wondered privately if it ever became a place of comfort even for greater wizards.

They knew well enough that since Oleg was not visible in the great room of records, he would be waiting in his office at the far end. They wasted no time in getting there. Vil pushed the door open and stepped through, the other two just a step behind. He hoped his action would be taken as a sign of leadership rather than precipitance.

"All three here; that's good. Have you discussed this summons?" Oleg sat behind his desk, leaning back in his chair, weighing them.

They shook their heads.

"Just as well." The Loremaster gestured toward three straight chairs. "Sit. We have much to cover."

That they were asked to sit seemed a good sign. They sat so quickly they nearly overturned their chairs.

Oleg hid a smile, and also his worry. With most of the greater wizards and the most promising young wizards already on their way to join Rath, these were the best of those who remained in the Headquarters building. Not all wizards lived at Headquarters. For the most part, the least and greatest tended to choose to occupy rooms in the Capitol, while those whose powers were somewhere between tended to live elsewhere as they studied and practiced.

Rath had been unusual among the greatest in moving to the Valleys, constructing his spell-drenched tower in one night. The move had been at Soren's order as the pair pursued their drought.

All that was gone now. There was no sense wasting time thinking about it. Oleg sensed the trio's uneasiness. He'd made them wait long enough for him to tell them why they had been summoned.

He cleared his throat. All three snapped to attention. "You may have heard rumors of troubles to the north and east," Oleg began, ignoring their nods. "Your mission is related."

He'd decided to tell them only that there was over the Fifth Valley a ward. "The Chief Mage wishes to test its strength. I have sought out spells of dissolution which might be chanted in unison.

"You are to learn these spells." He handed each a pouch containing a half-dozen scrolls. "When we are through here, you will take them back to your quarters and learn each completely. I will allow you three days. At the end of that time, return here. You will practice these chants. When you are prepared, I will give you a Word. You may practice chanting on the road as you travel to the Valleys, but do not speak the Word until you reach the Fifth Valley and are prepared to begin chanting.

He spoke slowly, and carefully. "At that time, you will speak the spells in unison, facing the Valley. Observe carefully what takes place.

Master Pennon is already there. He will observe and report to Soren. Do not be discouraged if your first attempt fails."

Oleg ceased, watching the three carefully for a moment. He saw the usual awareness that this assignment might lead to greater things, mixed with concern about the situation into which they were about to be thrust.

"One more thing," he said. "Don't attempt to enter the valley. Camp in the woods on the far side of the road. Chant from the edge of the woods. The ward refuses entry to members of our Order." Now they were more than simply concerned. A little worry should sharpen their attention to detail.

Oleg gestured dismissal, and the three quickly rose, bowed, thanked him, and left.

At least this trio would provide some evidence about the strength of the ward over the Valley. If their chanting proved to weaken that ward even slightly, the information would be of use to Rath, who could call on more and better wizards.

Perhaps he should appoint one of them their leader, but he wasn't sure on what basis he might do that. None of them had been either particularly impressive or particularly weak as apprentices. Let them sort it out among themselves. Soren, he suspected, expected little from this effort directed against the valley. Perhaps the Chief Mage was unsure of just how fully Rath would report his experiences with the fog enveloping the Barren Lands and wanted a second set of reports.

For a moment Oleg wondered if he should also send along with these three the defensive spells he'd sent to Rath. He decided against it. By now Pennon would have reached the Fifth Valley. He would be prepared to inform Soren should none of these three be able to report.

***

Lamar was in and out of the Barren Lands. Often, Aren noted, Lamar and Magda would walk the fields and beyond. They continued to address each other as "little sister" and "elder brother." Aren had to admit that, odd as the pair looked, there did seem to be some similarity between them.

Aren himself was becoming restless. He found himself thinking of home more often. There was no work for him to do in these Barren Lands, though at least Inek was often available for walks through the fields. They would talk of how the Druids had learned to develop trees and berry bushes which bore at different times of the year. Reya would wish to know this. Aren was more interested in dry farming and allowing fields to lie fallow. If drought came again, that knowledge would be especially useful.

Sometimes Lamar and Magda would invite Aren to join them on a walk. He would speak of what he'd seen of the over-worked and worn-out fields in what had been Lord Rand's Holdings. He believed those fields could be restored, if farmers were allowed to farm as they should. Magda was skeptical that a lord would have such good sense but Lamar would shrug his shoulders and smile. Magda would accuse him of knowing something he was holding back. Sometimes they'd enter into an argument about whether the quality of the soil or the quality of the seed and the care taken in planting and harvesting were more important. Lamar held that it was the soil and care of the soil, while Magda spoke for seeds, planting, and harvesting, even in poor soil. Aren avoided becoming the mediator, though his own opinion was that it would be best to have both.

***

When the trio returned to Oleg's office three days later, each had memorized the six spells with more or less success. For the next few days, Oleg put them through their paces until they became a little more certain. He instructed them to practice on their walk to the Fifth Valley. Finally, certain that each had developed his own Word of Power and they would waste time squabbling over which to use, he gave them another: Stregdan. That word from the old language, he pointed out, should be practiced separately from the spells of dissolution, lest they cast those spells prematurely.

Knowing that only experienced dark wizards were able to travel efficiently at night, Oleg instructed these three to leave at the next dawn. The usual escort of guardsmen would be waiting for them in the entryway.

That evening Oleg joined Soren and Haster in the observatory. Pennon and a half-dozen guardsmen were keeping a discreet watch over the valley. Pennon would need to know of the chanters' departure.

Soren first focused his great crystal on the valley itself. As before, the crystal showed only white fog, impenetrable whether Soren willed the crystal to show the physical or aural planes. Whatever had created that ward, it was holding.

When Soren contacted Pennon, the wizard confirmed that observation. "Chief Mage, when I approach the valley's opening, clouds form and come down from the mountains almost instantly. If I remain on the road's edge, lightning strikes near enough for the heat to scorch. Guardsmen may enter, but I may not."

"Have the guardsmen brought any news of value?" Haster asked.

"No, they have not. Lately they're reluctant to enter. The valley people have become more openly unfriendly. Many men now wear their sword-belts, and women carry knives as long as a short sword. A dozen or more young men follow our guardsmen wherever they go. Often they're joined by young women who make a point of testing the double edges on their knives."

"Surely these farmers can't be a threat to trained guardsmen," Haster said. Oleg's eyebrows went up at that. Could Haster not know that Lords of the Five Valleys recruited guardsmen from among the villagers? Worse, those guardsmen returned home after their service both trained and armed. Even the Order had heard of the practice, though with no concern. Dark wizards' powers would easily overcome even the largest force of guardsmen.

Pennon didn't hesitate to correct Haster. "Our six would have little chance should a fight erupt. I've told them to watch from the road and not enter the valley." He a deep breath before continuing.

"There has been another development. No longer can our guardsmen move at will through the wooded slopes along the valley's edge. The growling of wolves, they say, surrounds them almost from the moment they enter. They catch glimpses of shadowy forms moving through the trees and brush, never visible long enough for even the quickest bowshot."

For a moment Soren stared at the crystal before turning to Oleg. "Loremaster, what say you to this? Do your scrolls mention an army of wolves?"

Oleg raised his hands, palms up, in a gesture of uncertainty. "Nothing, Chief Mage. We have heard a tale of the witch-child charming horses during her journey east. Perhaps she also charms wolves."

"Or perhaps," Haster said, "these wolves gather in expectation of carrion on a battlefield."

Soren's scowl deepened. "I doubt there will be a fight. Should we succeed, these farmers will hide their weapons and go back to farming."

"And if not," Oleg observed, "there would be little use in trusting guardsmen to carry out our will in any lands which we could not enter. Such a situation would be little improvement, especially with the witch-child still at large."

Soren's scowl deepened at this. Curtly, he instructed Pennon to expect the three young wizards in a few days, along with another six guardsmen.

As Soren's crystal darkened, Haster said, "Perhaps these additional guardsmen will strengthen the resolve of those already present," to which neither Soren nor Oleg had any response.

***

Their walk to the Valleys would not become a pleasant memory for any of the three. Vil attempted to take charge, but neither Wold nor Fant would have any of that. For much of their first day's walk, they did little chanting as none would agree to begin at another's suggestion.

Following, the guardsmen who'd been assigned to accompany them looked at one another, rolled their eyes, shook their heads in disgust but kept quiet. If whatever assignment might have been intended ended in failure, blame would fall on wizards, not their escort.

Eventually the trio realized that same danger. One would begin a chant as they walked, their voices merging raggedly. Another would begin the next and they'd stumble through that. Practicing as they walked slowed their progress, but by the third day they were doing much better. Vil suggested they begin the following day with the Word of Power Oleg had given them.

This proved more difficult. With an entire spell, their first word could be a bit ragged so long as they made up for it with unison on the rest. With a single Word of Power, precision became essential. Finally they settled on taking turns gesturing for the Word to be spoken. That worked well enough that they decided to do the same with chanting. Since they suspected that more than one effort would be required, each would have at least one opportunity to lead.

Early on the fourth day they passed the Manor of the Five Valleys. The manor interested them less than did the bare patch where Rath's tower had stood, just north and slightly west of the manor. Though none knew many details, all had heard of the tower's destruction over-night, as they'd earlier heard something of the tower's construction in a single day as it rose to the sound of Rath's spell-casting. That it fell overnight suggested attack by an even stronger power.

They did no chanting until out of sight of the place. Were there any shreds remaining of the force which had destroyed Rath's tower, none wished to attract its attention. Attention would focus on them soon enough as they reached the Fifth Valley.. Suddenly their rivalries over who should lead seemed of far less moment.

Twilight found them settled in a camp across the road from the valley's opening. Pennon was camped a short distance away and further back in the woods. The six guardsmen who'd accompanied them were already integrated into Pennon's small force. That was fine with the three. Supervising guardsmen would only prove a distraction from their task.

To their dismay, their view up the valley was marred by a stone cairn in the foreground. Pennon told them of a wizard who had attempted to cross into the valley in the face of a thunderstorm. Lightning reduced him to clean bones. Since then, no dark wizard had tried to enter the valley. He recommended they avoid making the attempt.

Their approach that afternoon had been accompanied by distant rumbling from somewhere up the valley. Pennon's story did little to calm their nerves, even though the rumbling had diminished when they left the road for the woods facing the valley.

They would not try chanting that night. Weariness seemed sufficient reason to rest. They also wished to let the grumbling of thunder cease completely before they began. Oleg had not mentioned the exact nature of the ward, but Pennon's tale of the wizard and the cairn seemed information enough.

On the morrow they could venture further into the woods. Surely there would be paths leading from this campground. Once a safe distance away, they could spend a good part of the day practicing the dissolution chants and, after a suitable break, the Word of Power. It would be a temptation to practice softly, but they'd found on their walk north that only practicing with the full force of their strength produced a result which might prove effective.

***

Lir and Reya had not failed to notice the arrival of a dark wizard and his half-dozen guardsmen. Though the guardsmen had ceased to prowl through the valley, the pair were troubled by the arrival of three more dark wizards and another six guardsmen.

Such news called for a council of the heads of families. That evening Lir took word to the nearest neighbor, who in turn passed the news up the valley. Normally such a meeting would have taken place in Reya and Lir's yard, but with wizards no doubt watching, the council would instead meet at a farm further up the valley. Though only thirty men and women would participate in the council, entire families would attend, the younger children sent to play in fields toward the mountains.

Mota and Lena were pleased to host. Their son Del had returned three years earlier from two years as a member of the Lord's Guard. He spent the morning sharpening his sword, examining his bow for strength and suppleness, his arrow shafts for any which might have gone even slightly out of true and his arrowheads to be sure they were sharp and tightly fastened. The other young men would also arrive armed, he knew. There would be some discussion and kidding about one another's readiness. He did not wish to be the butt of any jokes.

Families began to arrive at mid-morning. The council would begin at noon.

Among the first to arrive were Reya and Lir's nearest neighbors, Alta and her husband Rom, both full of questions, as usual. Reya found their concerns always valuable.

"So, Mota," Alta asked their host immediately after greeting him and before she began to unpack the food she'd prepared for the meeting, "Won't the wizards' spies simply lurk in the woods and watch us, even up here?"

Mota smiled at that. "Not likely. Ever since summer we've had wolves in the forest all along the valley edge. On both sides, in fact."

"Lost some calves, have you?" Rom asked, concern for his own colts wrinkling his face.

"Not a one," said hostess Lena. "We worried for a time, but these wolves don't seem to leave the woods."

"That's odd," Alta noted.

"It's not the oddest," Mota said. "They don't bother anyone who goes into the woods, whether berrying or seeking mushrooms, or even gathering firewood. We've seen one or two wolves standing up on the ridge. They seemed almost like sentinels."

"So you've seen none of these guardsmen who skulk in the woods just across the East Road?" asked Alta.

"Not a one, They don't seem fond of wolves," said Mota with a grin. "I'll tell you who I haven't seen. Ryd's Dog hasn't been around all summer."

'Now that's a handy man,' Lir noted. "I'd swear he does three men's work. And knows something about working on the land, too."

The others nodded. Dog had worked every farm in the valley at one time or another. He had an uncanny way of showing up where most needed.

"Maybe he's off with Ryd," Alta offered. "Ryd and half his guard still haven't returned since they rode east a few months ago. Maybe there's some trouble with Rand, though ten guardsmen aren't many if that's the case, Valley bred though they might be."

Lena chuckled. "Word is Rand can afford to keep only fifty guardsmen. I suspect that ten of our Valley guardsmen might find that number a pleasant day's exercise with Ryd leading them. Our boy says he's the best swordsman of the lot." Throughout the valleys there was a good deal of pride that the new Lord trained almost daily with their sons.

By that time, the Council had gathered. Lena's outdoor table presented a solid mass of dishes waiting for the families to approach, so she stepped to the dinner bell hanging next to her kitchen door and rang loudly for the meal to commence.

After everyone had eaten their fill, the Council began. By common consent everyone waited for Reya to open the proceedings.

"Well," she began, "we all know why we've gathered. Wizards and guardsmen are camped just outside the Valley, and that can't be good."

Briefly she described the situation, noting that the wizards had not attempted to enter the valley. In fact, they hadn't been seen at all since their arrival. She and Lir had taken turns keeping watch.

"And that brings up something," she said. "Right now no one is on watch. I suggest that some of our young scouts slip across the road and watch the camp. If several go together, they'll be able to send messengers should anything happen."

"Absolutely," said Alta Beekeeper. Heads nodded all around her. She turned toward a group of young women gathered near the barn, comparing their long knives. "Sola! " she called. "Stop messing around and come here! The rest of you, too!" The tone and words were unchanged from the earliest times her daughter had ventured out of the house. Twenty-year-old Sola grinned as she trotted toward her mother, followed by the other five.

"Tell them, Reya," Alta said. Reya did: They were to shadow the wizards and their guard, reporting any activity on their part.

That led to pleased smiles. The young women retreated to their spot by the barn and engaged in a short discussion, after which Sola reported to the Council. Four scouts would go in pairs across the road and into the woods. One in each pair would be relieved every two hours and would report to Reya or Lir. Should anything happen between times, a scout would return with the information.

There were murmurs of approval from the Council. "An excellent plan. Go ahead," Reya said. As the scouts dashed off, she focused the Council on her next suggestion. "We should also have watchers on this side of the road."

Del spoke up, with a gesture toward a dozen young men standing with him. "We can serve as watchers within the woods bordering the valley. We've not been away from Lord Ryd so long that we've forgotten our training." He grinned. Lena and Mota stood tall and proud, looking toward Reya.

"Good," Reya said. "Del, will you take responsibility for organizing watches? If that's acceptable to your fellows," she added. The young men standing behind Del whooped. The group trotted over to Mota's barn, where they'd left swords, bows, and quivers leaning against the near wall. Then they were off, running after Sola's group, who were already half-way to the valley mouth.

The Council sat in silence for a few minutes, watching their young people eagerly heading into danger. Finally Mota spoke. "I'll wager some of them haven't used their bows in a while except perhaps to hunt deer. They might wish to set up a target on the north side of my barn, where it would be out of sight. A little practice would give them something to do while they wait their turns on watch. They might as well sleep in the loft; there's fresh hay up there and plenty of room."

Lir added, "Wouldn't hurt any of the rest of us to take a turn at the target, for that matter."

This received more nods and murmurs of agreement.

Mota led a handful of men into the barn. They returned carrying bales of hay which they set up against the barn wall. Mota ducked into the building and brought out a can of paint, a brush, and an old cloth cover. One of the men set about drawing a target.

The council continued for a while longer. They would do nothing unless the wizards and their escort became threatening. In the meantime, everyone should go about their business as usual, especially those living nearest the East Road. Those families should be ready to move further into the valley should things become serious. Various neighbors offered shelter should moving become necessary. All would do what they could to prepare foods which could be eaten cold should the worst take place. In the meantime, Mota would walk over the hills to the west and pass word to the Fourth Valley concerning the presence of wizards.

This was all standard practice among the valleys in times of need, though it had been some years since one valley had had to come to the aid of another. No longer did bands of thieves cross over the mountains from the north, now that wars among small northern lords had largely ended in exhaustion. Local bands of marauders had long since realized that valley farmers, far from being frightened and defenseless, actually welcomed a skirmish with the sort of untrained and poorly armed men who rode or walked as thieves.

Lord Ryd sometimes wished his people were a little less willing to deal with thieves on their own. He had twenty guardsmen in constant training and a little field work against groups of thieves would be just the thing to keep their training meaningful. Occasionally he'd hear of thieves becoming active in time to join the chase.

At such times there was a good deal of kidding between Ryd's guard and the former guardsmen as both fell in together. Ryd was careful at such times to treat both groups as highly-trained men, though some were out of practice. Such large groups often failed to find the thieves they sought. If the band learned of the number pursuing them, they were likely to move away from the Valleys as quickly as possible. Still, a few days of searching made a break for the current guard from their constant training. Ryd suspected that former guardsmen welcomed the break from farming just as much.

Those sorties gave him every confidence that should he ever need to repulse an invasion from some lord eager to expand his holdings, valley men would respond quickly. He was certain that a hundred or more armed men trained to work together could defeat any force which might invade.

***

Lamar took Bird on a stroll through the fields. For a time they simply walked, unspeaking, until they had passed into a dry, rocky area where little grew.

"This must be what Inek's fields were like," Bird guessed.

"Little bird correct," Lamar said. "Inek, others full of anger, pride. Much to learn. Dry land patient, waited. Hungry years." He sighed.

"Magda come. Stained not listen. Old earth-walker visit. If stained ready, make suggestion. Next visit, maybe stained learn some. Make another. Return sooner. Stained began learn from plants, land. Little bird maybe learn some."

"Oh, yes!" Bird chirped. "I've learned so much." She paused, puzzled. "But, Lamar, sometimes it feels as though I'm remembering things I didn't know I knew. But how could that be? I'm just a little girl. I haven't had time to learn all this, much less forget that I knew it."

Lamar chuckled. "Little bird learn easily. Means stained reclaiming selves. Little bird beginning remember things known long ago."

They walked in silence while Bird puzzled over this suggestion. Lamar had never misled her. From the first moment he'd come walking across Lir's fields, it had been as though an old friend had arrived. She'd known immediately that she could trust him.

Lamar broke the silence. "Call rain, good. Too soon, use power harshly. Earth-walker speak earlier, save sorrow." He considered. "Perhaps as meant. Earth-walker not know plan. Guess maybe Bird seek stained Druids." Lamar stood with his head down. When Bird reached out and took his large, rough hand, he shook himself and smiled down at her. Not so far down. He'd never been all that much taller than Bird, and she had been growing.

"Well," he said, "one more. Send mind to earth. Then deeper, stones."

As Bird followed his lead, she was astonished to discover within earth and stone something which wasn't quite thought, yet which she understood. With it came a kind of welcome. When she had turned her thought to birds, animals, plants she'd also felt welcome. The welcome from earth and stone was stronger and yet slower, more permanent, coming not only from this place but from beyond, travelling through earth and stone to reach this spot.

For a time Lamar let her walk, lost in her feeling for the land over which they moved. When he spoke again, his voice was somber.

"Little bird," he said, "heal plant, animal. Also heal land. Beneath, water held by stone. Little bird ask stone release water."

"Do you mean the stone would have to do what I asked of it?" Bird wasn't sure she liked this idea. "When I try to help a tree or a deer, they wish my help. They benefit from it. But how would the stone be helped?"

Again Lamar chuckled. "Not helped, not harmed. Pleasure, doing as asked." He gave her a moment to consider that. "Little bird speak, earth, stone feel joy."

Bird was doubtful. "Why? And what about the lord when I said I hoped he'd die? He didn't look joyful." Her eyes clouded at the memory.

"Not joyful. Life mostly gone, arrogance, cruelty left. Life not sad if leave."

"Then the man's life didn't die with him?" Bird asked, frowning. "What happened to it?"

"Difficult," Lamar answered. "Much life. Enters, departs. Life not die. Waits, enters another. Earth, stone, life long. Ant, bird, less."

Bird had to work on this for a while.. "So when that awful lord died, the life within him went somewhere else?"

"Escape, glad," Lamar answered.

"Then," Bird said slowly, "when Aren said that the land was tired, it had been worked too hard because the lord was greedy, that's what I could feel?"

Lamar nodded. "Little bird felt land, weary."

Bird was quiet as they walked. "Maybe. Could I have tried to heal that lord?"

Lamar shook his head. "Too far in power. Not want change. Not welcome presence. Hard lesson. Not heal everything. Animal too injured, bring less pain, less fear. Great gift. Same plant, tree: too far gone, offer peace. Hard knowing when."

"So I'll need to look inside people just as I do plants and animals, fields and stone? It's an awful lot to have to do!" Bird shook her head, frowning. "I'm just a little girl, even if everyone does want to call me Little Mother!"

Lamar laughed long. When he finally stopped, he said, "Even old earth-walker forget." Again he considered. "No need walk earth, look problems. Not yet. Dark wizards problems enough."

With that, they realized that they'd talked their way nearly back to Magda's house, where both were glad to think of a good supper and the gathering of friends.

CHAPTER THIRTEEN

After several weeks, Rath's wizards began to chant almost in unison. At that point, he could afford to spend time on Oleg's defensive spells.

Only when the chanters had become fairly proficient did he speak the word of power, "Forscéadan!" from one of the old languages. This they practiced at a near whisper. Should defensive chants become necessary, the word of power for that task would be "Stregdan!" Unfortunately, experience indicated that the witch-child would respond should she become aware of their efforts. Her responses had been harsh when not fatal.

It became time to make the effort; Rath was certain they were as prepared as it was possible to be.

***

Despite their weariness, none of the three young wizards slept soundly on their first night opposite the Fifth Valley, though the night remained quiet enough. Morning sunshine brought with it slightly higher spirits. A hot breakfast served up by a guardsman who turned out to be a decent campfire cook did still more to revive them. This task might well be the making of all three; at the least it would raise them in the esteem of Oleg and Soren. Even failure might well bring further understanding of the ward. Surely Oleg would make something of that news.

None mentioned the possibility that they might not survive. Nor did they speculate upon what sort of wizard might have created such a ward. So far as they knew, not even Soren would be capable of casting such a spell.

At mid-morning the three made their way deeper into the woods. They hoped the path was clear enough that they'd be able to find their way back to camp later in the day. When they felt they'd come far enough.

they began rehearsing. Fant gave the signal to start. At first their voices were soft, hesitant. As they heard no thunder in the distance, those voices became louder, stronger, more certain.

By mid-afternoon they felt ready for a break, and for the bread, cheese and apples a guardsman had packed for them, washed down by a flask of cold water. Lying with their backs against trees and dreaming of success allowed enough time to pass that they felt safe quietly practicing the Word of Power. An hour of that left them ready to return to camp.

The time to begin chanting, they were certain, would be just before midnight, so repeated chants would build in strength before they thundered out the Word of Power. All this they would offer from the very edge of the forest, with the road between them and the valley.

***

Oleg made the trip to the Dark One's cell more slowly these days. The being had given little reason for hope. He'd been too pleased at the Order's travails and too clearly enjoyed making the Loremaster wait for cryptic responses. This time, however, the Dark One's voice came as soon as Oleg stepped from the stairs.

"Well, Loremaster, there is news in the world. She has begun to learn of herself, and that bodes ill for your kind. She was always beyond your reach. Now I feel from the earth itself that She becomes aware. And, Loremaster, earth and stone are pleased."

Oleg hid his unease behind scorn. "And you know all this how? Do secret messengers make their way through some hidden entrance?"

The Dark One laughed, a harsh, grating sound which echoed unpleasantly there under the ground. Oleg had rarely heard the being laugh, and would rather not have done so now.

"You listen no more wisely than the rest of your kind, Loremaster. Your Order's enchantments may be woven through the stone of this building. But your spells are not strong enough to reach deeply into the earth itself. When deep stone rejoices, not even your Order's will can mute the echo of that rejoicing."

This gave Oleg pause. "The earth speaks to you despite these stone walls?" Not even the oldest scrolls mentioned that stone and earth could speak.

The Dark One's voice was soft now. Oleg had to lean forward to hear. "These stones sense the joy of stone deep within the earth. Though they are bound to your Order's will, they are not so perfectly bound as to be unable to reflect that joy. During all these long years I sensed only the Order's will holding them. But no longer. The world is changing, Loremaster."

"These enchantments are old and strong; they've held you."

"Yes; as they've held these stones. Stone has a long memory, Loremaster, and recalls a time when your Order did not exist, when stone might be carefully shaped by men's skill with tools, held together by that care and not by the force of spells, a time when stone might refuse such service."

If the Dark One was in a mood to talk, Oleg would attempt to take advantage. "Will you tell me, clearly, just what this being is?"

"What can you offer me for that information, Loremaster? Freedom? Your Order is too full of fear to allow that; and I've dreamed too long of vengeance. Yet I find myself most interested in what approaches, in the possibility of being freed from this cell." For a moment he fell silent. "Why, I might not hunt down members of your Order. I may settle for destroying any I happen to come across, should any survive."

The Dark One emitted a sound which was something like a chuckle. "No, there is nothing you could offer which would bring me to speak more clearly. I will tell you this much: despite your spells, this building is pleased at the news from below. Too long has it been bound by your order's will. Were I you, I'd find a safer place." He laughed again, more softly this time, and fell silent.

"And you think this—being—will free you? What if instead it chooses to keep you imprisoned forever?"

This brought a growl. "I've considered the possibility, Loremaster. This has been a long punishment for my errors, which were great enough to deserve even this. She might well decree further punishment. If so, it will not be of this sort. Even should my final destruction be decreed, She will first return me to sunlight and allow me to die beneath an oak. Loremaster, I know the oak beneath which judgment would be rendered."

Oleg knew that further questioning would be futile. He might return later and try again, but for now he returned to his own office above.

This hopefulness was more disturbing than anything else Oleg had heard in these past months. It might indeed be wise to think about a time when the Order's power would be broken, when even this building might fall as had Rath's tower.

Any Loremaster worth the name knew things unknown even to the Chief Mage. Dark Wizards tended to be solitary beings, with colleagues and sometimes allies but not friends. Loremasters were even more isolated, a situation which had always suited Oleg. He was far more interested in knowledge than in friends or even power for its own sake. As nearly as he could tell from his records, that was true of most Loremasters from the Order's earliest days onward.

That other wizards, including Soren and certainly Haster, felt a respect for his knowledge which wasn't entirely free from fear pleased him. That touch of fear kept Soren's temper in check, allowed Oleg a certain freedom to say what he thought.

Sitting in his office, Oleg considered his own situation should the Dark One be correct that his building could well fall. Some Loremaster in the far past had thought along these same lines. He had prepared a refuge, passed it on in a document to which only Loremasters had access. This refuge lay some distance south of the Capitol, on the edge of the low, dry mountains which marked the edge of the Order's influence.

That Loremaster found a cave hidden by the shape of the rock surrounding it, such that the opening seemed nearly invisible. To further hide the entrance he'd used a spell found in an old scroll, then placed that scroll in the same safe spot within his office where he'd placed the document describing the refuge. Over the years, each succeeding Loremaster made certain than no similar scrolls came to any eyes but his own.

That cave had been enlarged, shaped into several rooms, furnished, made comfortable over the years by a succession of Loremasters. One room was given over to copies of scrolls from the Order's records; another to coins with which to purchase food and the few other necessities for a wizard's existence in exile. Oleg had made his own visits to that cave, added a few scrolls and even a few coins from the Order's treasury, their amounts added to the purchase price he reported when coins had to be offered to secure a scroll from some thief.

Perhaps he should make another visit, be sure the cave remained ready for permanent occupancy. Oleg saw no need to die at his post should the Order's headquarters fall.

***

It was time to try the dispersal chants and the Word of Power. Rath's wizards were as ready as they were ever likely to be. A few days earlier, Snake and his minion had arrived with a report of yet another path. Rath commanded them to remain in camp and wait for instructions. On the morning of the day chanting would begin, he ordered them back along the nearest path until they could see mist. Snake was to observe as midnight approached. In the morning he would return and report any change.

He sent word to the other wizards to gather that evening. As midnight neared, they would make their first effort.

Roke and Owen, with the shortest distance to travel, arrived first, in mid-twilight. Ren arrived just as the real dark began, bringing with him Vash, Quar, and Ter. Rath said little to any, leaving greetings to Tarh. That night they would have no fire. Light would limit their connection with the dark as each focused on calling up his full power before the chanting began.

As they waited and the night grew darker, Rath could feel each one's power growing. That Ren would be able to reach most deeply into the dark did not surprise him; but that Tarh reached nearly as deeply was startling. It had been some time since he'd tested Tarh, and that had been before the man's ordination some months earlier. The fellow had always had a feeling for the dark within. These past months surely would have strengthened that.

Owen, his other former apprentice, was a different story. His connection with the dark had always been weaker, sometimes almost intermittent as though something within him tried to interfere. Still, he wasn't noticeably weaker than the three who'd arrived with Ren.

Rath could feel the circle's power growing as midnight approached. He needed no timepiece but his own awareness. The others, even Owen, would perceive the increase in their powers as well.

"It is time," Rath said as he stood. The others did the same. For a moment Rath allowed the tension to grow, They could draw on tension. "We'll repeat the dispersion chants six times," he said. "Then we'll pause, take breath, and together shout the Word of Power. On my mark." He breathed deeply and heard similar inhalations around him. "Begin!"

The night was filled with the sound of harsh voices chanting words not intended to be spoken in daylight. The voices fell silent. Again the sound of inbreathing, followed by a hoarse roar as six voices cried out in unison: "Forscéadan!"

Rath stumbled but kept his feet. A look around the circle showed Ren and Tarh staggering, Roke slowly collapsing, and the others already on the ground. Only a failed spell rebounding on its casters would have this effect.

All would need to rest for some hours before again drawing on their powers. Toward morning Rath would send each back to his own camp to rest until summoned again.

Another failure.

He would report to Soren later. For now, he could do little but wait for Snake to return from the woods. If he did not appear, he'd send the guards to look for bodies. Bodies would mean that the ward had noticed their efforts, and that would be something worth reporting.

***

Soren had decided to risk using his great crystal to watch as Rath and his group made their first attempt. He felt little fear at what might take place around the Barren Lands. There, the ward did not attack; it merely blinded and confused.

Though he wouldn't say so, Soren was relieved that Oleg also felt it would be reasonably safe to look in on the results of their efforts against the ward over the Barren Lands. He'd invited the archivist to observe the results.

Rath had chosen a moonless night. Nonetheless, the mist seemed to pick up whatever light the stars might offer, so the its boundary was clear, even through the crystal. All three watchers were silent as midnight approached. Soren stood closest to the crystal, Haster and Oleg at each shoulder.

All three leaned forward. Haster began to mouth the words of the dispersion spells, being very careful not to say them aloud, just in case. As he came to the end of the sixth repetition, he did not mouth the Word of Power. For a moment, they held their breaths.

Soren cursed. "Nothing. The mist showed no reaction. I see no evidence that it receded, or even was affected." He looked around "Did either of you see anything I may have missed?"

The others shook their heads. "I saw no effect, Chief Mage," Oleg said. "Perhaps several attempts over a few days will bring some result, but I'm not sure. Still, it may be worth the effort."

***

Snake had planned to roll out his bedroll a good fifty feet from where the mist began, just in case Rath's efforts had some effect. When Lamar laughed, took a wineskin from his pack along with two cups, and stretched out near the first tendrils, Snake shrugged and joined him.

"Long time mist hold. Wizards, little time," Lamar said as he poured a cup for Snake.

Eventually Lamar began to snore, but Snake was just worried enough to remain awake until he was certain it was well after midnight. He'd seen no change in the mist, which remained luminous in the moonlight. After that he slept until Lamar's movements woke him as the broad man built a small fire and heated two cups of wine to go with the bread and cheese he'd laid out on a rock.

"Snake still here. Old Earth-Walker still here. Mist still here. Wizards, probably," Lamar said as he handed over a wine cup.

"Glad to hear it," Snake replied. "Now I've got to tell Rath. That I don't look forward to."

"Wizards know. Learn quick," Lamar said, laughing. He leaned forward, serious now. "Wait camp." Without speaking again, he picked up his pack and walked into the mist.

***

It was time. The three young wizards arranged themselves on the road edge.

The two guards on night watch took one look, backed into the camp, and roused those who slept in their tents. All twelve walked well into the woods. Should something extraordinary happen to the three, they'd hear it. If Pennon survived, he could notify Soren. If no wizards were left alive, all twelve would return to inform Soren. Risky as that might be, simply disappearing would involve even greater risk.

The three wizards spoke little as they approached the East Road. Woodcraft was not among their studies. They tended to bump into one another, which did little to improve their confidence. These chants might work, but they might also call down lightning. Who knew whether, once the ward were challenged, it might extend its range to include its attackers? None had any reason to feel so valuable that they might not be sacrificed in an experiment. They couldn't help but notice that Pennon was absent, and they strongly suspected the guardsmen were also nowhere near.

All three felt at once the influence of midnight as they began to chant, doing so more precisely than in any of their rehearsals. For a moment each felt a sense of achievement which had been rare during their studies or, so far, in their careers. They lost themselves in chanting. Their voices became louder and stronger until, perfectly together, they shouted the Word of Power: Forscéadan!

They waited. In the frenzy of chanting, none noticed whether the valley filled with clouds, or thunder and lightning. Now they realized that nothing had occurred. Had they been successful so soon? Or had their efforts meant so little that the ward didn't bother responding?

Fant spoke first. "There's only one way to find out. One of us must cross the road and approach the valley. If he stands on the road's edge, we may hear enough thunder to know whether we have failed or perhaps partly succeeded. If the ward is indeed still strong, then we should learn quickly whether we've had any effect."

"And if that lucky wizard hears nothing, then what?" Vil asked. "Does he then step off the road, into the valley itself? The other two can record the strike and report his death. Perhaps he will even be honored with a cairn of his own."

" I see no choice." Wald's voice was nearly a whisper. "We must test the ward."

With that, Fant felt around on the ground nearby until he'd found three twigs suitable for drawing lots. He held them up for the others to inspect, then gave them to Vil to hold. Wald took the first, then Fant, leaving Vil with the third. They compared twig lengths. Wald held the unlucky one.

By that time, Pennon had joined them. Wald shrugged, tossed his twig away and walked slowly across the road. Pennon moved away from the other two as thunder began near the mountains. Wald's walk became even slower.

They could see lightning striking from cloud to cloud further up the valley. The storm was moving quickly. As Wald neared the road's edge and stopped, thunder raged overhead. So far there were no strikes.

With a deep breath, Wald walked forward until another step would have taken him into the valley. Lightning struck just beyond him, and he backed away far more quickly than he'd approached. As he retreated, thunder grew quieter and strikes became fewer. By the time he reached the woods, thunder had become a low rumble and the lighting ceased.

Abruptly, Wald sat down. Fant rushed to get him a cup of wine, then held it to his mouth. After a few sips, Wald waved the cup away. "Next time, one of you makes the trial."

Pennon moved from the shadows. "That was well done. I judge that there was a little less thunder than when I tried the ward some time ago, and certainly less lightning. This is worth continuing."

***

Owen returned to his own camp, where he looked forward to a day of rest. He'd cast spells before, certainly, both as an apprentice and now that he was a full wizard. He knew that in a successful spell casting, the power invoked moved away from the caster, left him perhaps a little tired but also exhilarated.

After their chanting, all but the strongest had collapsed. Even those left standing had been staggered. That could mean only one thing: their spell had been thrown back upon them.

The mist must be not only a strong ward but an active one, able to defend itself. This was no wizard's doing, but the work of an older power. Not for the first time, he wished he'd been a farmer like his father, any power he might possess remaining hidden. He would never rise to Rath's or even Ren's level in the Order. That, he thought with a grim inner chuckle, made it easy for him to recognize when he was over-matched.

***

Bird slept badly that night. This time she did not need to lie out in the dry lands to feel stone's thought. Stone warned of danger, not to Bird herself but to a place about which she cared. That made no difference. Stone would bear warning until she ceased to be interested or the danger ceased to exist.

As daylight began, Bird rose and quietly rolled her bed, then gathered the few things which weren't already in her small backpack, finally tying on the bedroll. Setting the pack back in its place against a wall, she slipped out into the dawn to sit at the outdoor table until the others awoke. If they were to go travelling and perhaps have to deal with dark wizards, they should rest even though she had not.

Hobard came walking up from the orchards to join her. Bird nodded but did not speak. A slight inclination of Hobard's head acknowledged Bird's greeting. Accepting her silence, the Druid sat down at the table's far end to watch the sunrise with her Little Mother.

Lamar was the next to arrive, coming from a bed of half-dry grass where he'd slept soundly though aware on some deep level of the earth's uneasiness. Always earth and stone were uneasy somewhere, and Lamar concerned himself only with what he must. In the morning Bird would tell them what she intended, and he would help. Only first he must return to the wizards' camp where he'd find Snake.

When Aren awoke, his first thought as always was to see how Bird had slept. The space where she had lain was empty. He nodded approvingly; she had rolled her bedroll and set it out of the way as usual. Then he realized that she had tied the bedroll to her backpack, and the pack itself looked ready for travel. Aren rolled his own bedroll and tied it on his backpack, then checked the contents.

As Aren finished closing the pack, Magda came from her room, dressed for the day, yawning a little, ready to begin gathering part of their breakfast. The stained Druids would bring more than they could eat, as usual. Seeing Aren step away from a backpack with his bedroll tied on, then glancing at Bird's smaller pack to see her smaller bedroll similarly fastened, Magda stopped for a moment. She gave Aren an inquiring look, saw his nod in return.

"Well, then," she said, "we'd better have a good breakfast. I have an old pack here somewhere, if it hasn't rotted away. Hobard probably put it somewhere safe." She glanced around the room, noted her walking stick leaning in a corner with what appeared to be a pack hanging on the wall nearby. Of course; that's where she would have put it herself, had she not lost the habit in recent years of putting things in their right places. She wouldn't take but a moment to pack a few things; packing food would be more important. First she'd need to know what Bird had decided. She followed Aren out to the table. Breakfast could wait a bit.

Magda sat, quite willing to wait until Bird was ready to speak. Aren, less at ease than the others, looked a question at Lamar, who smiled and gestured toward the bench. Still uneasy, Aren sat. The Druids who now approached, singing and bearing food and drink, seemed trustworthy enough; but Aren still feared at times that only Lamar and Bird could be fully trusted.

As Inek and the others approached, only to be greeted by silence and gestures from Lamar toward the table, they fell silent. After setting out food and drink, they stood, waiting.

Bird took a deep breath. "I want to go home. All night I felt darkness near the valley. And it's growing."

Aren shot a look at Lamar, who seemed unsurprised. When the broad man didn't speak, Aren decided that he must. "Little bird," he said, "what have you felt? What has happened?"

"I can't tell, exactly," Bird answered. "But I know there's danger, and it feels just as it did when those wizards tried to stop the rain."

"Won't know exactly," Lamar put in before Aren could question Bird. "Feels what stone feels. No words, just feel. Darkness, trouble, worry valley."

Aren had hoped Lamar might have spoken to calm Bird, as had happened the day before. He might never know just what Lamar might really be, or what he might have ways of knowing. But it had been the squat man's suggestion that Aren and Bird leave the valley and seek those who could teach Bird. As it turned out, Bird's teachers included Lamar, who, Aren thought, might have begun much earlier. Still, the man had given good advice, and if he agreed that Bird should return, that was that.

"We need to plan our route," Aren said. "I don't think we can just stroll down the East Road."

"They watch," Lamar said. "Wizard, guardsmen each camp. Crystals."

Inek spoke up. "Unless they've grown far more powerful, any one of us—" his gesture included all the Druids "should be able to handle a wizard. And guardsmen—" He broke off, but his shrug was eloquent enough.

"Yes," Aren said, "but still we must take a route other than the East Road. There we'd be too easy to find. What of going through the Red Forest, then across fields to the wooded hills bordering the valleys? Or even going north from that forest to the mountains and making our way through them, then down into the valley? Either way we would avoid roads."

Those same thoughts had already occurred to Bird. If she couldn't walk the East Road, then she'd go back through the Red Forest, stay within it until it ended to the west, continue across fields until she came to woods rising up from the farmland. At the top of that rise she would be on the brink of the Valley, and from there she could find her way home with her eyes closed. If she met any dark wizards, they could just get out of her way.

Aren noticed Bird's eyes darkening and guessed she had some thought of wizards or their henchmen. Lamar answered before she could speak.

"Good plan. Same path out. Wizard watch."

Bird muttered, "I'll fix him."

"Good," Lamar said. "Red Forest angry. Hope calm. Little bird, Druids go first."

Hobard nodded. She'd expected something of the sort. The stained Druids, on the other hand, became excited at mention of the Red Forest. Some, unable to remain still, leapt from their stools and walked in tight circles. Only Inek spoke, and his voice shook. "The forest of red oaks? We're to see oaks again, after all these years?" He turned to his fellows. "Bothers! We're to leave with the Mother and travel to the Red Forest! To oak trees older than we are!" He noticed that Bird was watching him, her eyes wide, her mouth an "O," and stopped himself. "Little Mother, is it your wish that we should travel with you to the Red Forest?"

His fellow Druids held their breaths, but only for an instant. "Well, of course," Bird replied. "We've already had trouble with these wizards. No doubt we'll have more," she said in her best matter-of-fact Reya manner. "I wish they were gone!" She saw Aren's frown and spoke quickly before he could reprimand her. "I didn't hope; I just wished." She turned to the Druids. "If you and Aren keep between me and dark wizards, I won't be as tempted to wipe them away." She turned back to Aren. "I don't want to kill any more. But they frighten me, and they make me angry!"

Aren stood, stepped around the table, took Bird on his lap and wiped away a tear. "It's all right, little bird. They also frighten and anger me. With these good Druids to accompany us, we should be able to cross open ground safely. I don't think wizards will be looking for us to come back the way we came in. They know about Hobard, but they won't expect us to have found more Druids."

At this Inek and his fellows smiled.

It was settled. The stained Druids would take the day to speak to their lands and crops. All but two would prepare to leave the next morning. Selected by lot, those two would remain to tend the small herd of milk cows. Aren decided that Blaze should remain in the Druid's pasture. A single horse would probably be more hindrance than help for a group of more than a dozen walkers.

The Druids would bring food for a long trip in case it became necessary to leave the Red Forest by way of the mountains to the north. Magda would pack herbs and other remedies against need, whether on the way or for whatever awaited them in the Fifth Valley. Lamar would leave immediately to rejoin the wizards for a while. When Aren asked whether they should wait for him in the forest, Lamar smiled. "Old earth-walker catch."

Aren's eyebrows went up. He glanced around to see what reactions Magda and the Druids might have and saw smiles on their faces as though he'd asked a foolish question.

Magda laughed. "Elder brother draws strength from walking on the earth. The longer he walks, the faster. We may find him waiting for us in the Red Forest with his feet up, a flagon of wine nearly empty."

Lamar snorted, trying to hide a smile. Then he was up and walking away. Almost immediately he was out of sight. At the look on Aren's face, the Druids joined in Magda's laughter.

For Bird, the rest of the day went slowly. Magda would select her own remedies, and the Druids needed no assistance in preparing packs of food for the journey. Bread, cheese, and fruit would travel well, though bread would harden by the time they reached the valleys. Hobard joined them, though there was little she could add other than an offer to carry a pack if one were available. One was. Aren spent much of the day sharpening his sword, checking his bow for strength and his arrows for straight shafts and firmly anchored feathers, his sword sheath and belt for wear, and the same for his quiver.

They made an early start the next morning. By full daylight, they had travelled out of the Barren Lands and were making their way along the trail out of the woods. Druids spread out through the thin woods ahead and around Bird, Aren, and Magda. Aren walked beside Bird, his eyes scanning forest ahead for any signs of movement other than Druids.

Bird could feel the presence of a wizard somewhere ahead and another to the north, with still others further off to the south. That dark wizards would get out of her way was unlikely. But walking through the stained Druids' fields had left her eager to see again Reya's orchards and Lir's fields, the oak tree in her own yard, the stream running through the valley, and most of all her own home, Reya, and Lir. She was going to get there. Whether she could simply tell any Wizards she met to die, she didn't know; and she'd had enough of killing. But also enough of running.

Voices ahead brought them to a halt. The Druid Osa had returned from scouting. Hobard and Inek came out of the trees to join them. Speaking softly, Osa reported that he'd reached the forest edge and seen no one nearby. A ways off, however, a camp lay between these woods and the Red Forest in the distance. Before Bird could respond, Aren turned to Hobard. "Bird says that you and Osa have shown her how to use her mind to calm animals and birds. Can you calm whatever is in that camp long enough for us to pass by?"

The question startled Hobard. "I have not used the mind-touch for such a purpose." She turned to Inek. "You have had more contact with wizards. Would it be possible to use the mind-touch on more than one?"

"We are several; if there are only three or four in the camp, two or three of us can focus our minds on each and hold them for a time." Inek's smile held no joy. "We helped create these wizards. It is fitting we place holds on them."

"The wizard is mine." Bird's voice startled them. Aren began to protest, but she cut him off. "I have learned the mind-touch, and I have a few things to say to this wizard."

Aren recognized a favorite saying of Reya's when she felt someone needed, as she put it, 'a good talking to.' So long as Bird kept following Reya's patterns, she might restrain herself. Reya rarely lost her temper, and on those occasions when she did become visibly angry, she held back from action or speech until she'd regained control. He hoped Bird would follow that pattern. Nonetheless, he'd be a little easier in his mind were he certain she could order a dark wizard to die and have the man obey.

Quickly Aren arranged them. Bird would lead, Aren a step behind and just off to her right, where he could quickly bring his sword into action if needed. Druids spread out in lines on each side, Madga a little behind Bird and Aren. They would move forward as quietly as possible.

Bird, listening hard but not yet sending the mind-touch, was surprised at how clearly she could hear voices at this distance. At first she heard only guardsmen, she guessed from their tone. Then another voice spoke: arrogant, commanding, a little contemptuous. Quieter, but similar in tone to what she'd heard from the dark wizards who'd attempted to stop her rain.

Bird drew herself up and marched forward quickly, catching the others by surprise and leaving them several feet behind. She walked into the campsite where a dark wizard and three guardsmen turned to face her. The wizard began a gesture; the guardsmen reached for their swords. Though she wasn't entirely certain it would work with four people, Bird commanded in her most authoritative Reya voice: "Don't move an inch, any of you. Pay attention because I'm not going to say anything twice."

Owen found himself frozen, his hand partially outstretched toward what must be the witch-child. Just behind him, three guardsmen strained unsuccessfully to move their hands just a little closer to their sword-handles.

For a moment Bird satisfied herself with glaring at the four, almost wishing one would move just a little. When they did not, she walked closer to the wizard. She thought he might be one of those who had tried to stop the rain. Aren had said that the one who'd ordered the drought had lost a hand when lightning struck his tower. This fellow had both hands.

Judging by his eyes, he was terrified. Well, that was good. "You," she said, partly for the pleasure of seeing his fear grow. Still, frightening one wizard wouldn't help all that much.

Then, calming a little, she remembered what she'd learned in the Barren Lands. Her own fear had led her to throw fear into this man. While that had worked, she now knew of other approaches. She focused on this wizard's mind, seeking to calm but also to know him.

Aren and the Druids quickly caught up. Seeing the wizard frozen, the guardsmen unmoving, all breathed a little easier, but the Druids remained ready to use the mind-touch if they were needed. All carefully avoided breaking Bird's focus on the wizard.

Aren remained nearby, sword in hand. If the wizard regained control over himself, Aren was ready to see whether a swordstroke might take off a wizard's head as it might for any other man. He kept one eye on Bird, watching for any faltering. Magda came up on Bird's left. She caught Aren's eye, nodded; he hoped that meant Bird was doing fine.

Bird found, beneath the wizard's fear, something she hadn't expected. She'd heard enough about the dark Order to know that its power rested on men's fears of the dark. But this one's powers seemed to come from some other source. She waited, learning more, realizing that this wizard feared that other wizards would learn the true source of his power. She sensed a kind of layering, the Order's dark spells near the surface but something more beneath.

Bird remembered the three guardsmen and spared a glance for them. None had moved.

Now the question became, what to do with a dark wizard and three guardsmen. Bird began to be angry again, felt the wizard's fear grow. She calmed herself, then the wizard.

She was pretty sure somebody gave orders to all these wizards who'd been chasing her. She remembered the crystals she'd seen wizards using on the night lightning had driven them out of her valley. If wizards could use those things, she could.

She spoke again to the wizard. "Where's your crystal? You may speak long enough to answer me."

Owen found that he could move his jaw, though it took a moment for him to regain speech. "In my pack."

"And where's your pack?" Bird's eyes, already dark with anger, turned obsidian. She'd given this kind of answer to Reya often enough, trying to slow trouble. "Answer, and then be quiet."

"It's just behind me," Owen answered. Never, not even as an apprentice being shown by Rath himself just how powerless a sending of fear could make one, had he found himself so completely paralyzed. As his fear receded, this paralysis had begun to feel as though it came from some power stronger than fear. What that might be he had no idea.

Bird stepped around the wizard. She opened the pack, slipped her hands around the globe and carefully brought it out. The crystal was a little larger than her small hands could easily manage,.

Turning to face the wizard, she asked, "How do I make it work? Speak long enough to answer."

Owen wasn't certain it would be a good thing if this witch-child learned to use a crystal. Nonetheless, he found himself speaking. "Will it to show whatever you wish to see."

"And if I wish to contact your chief?"

Another reluctant answer. "Soren's crystal. Seek that."

Bird stood looking up at him for a time, still holding the crystal in both hands. When she looked down at the crystal, it began to glow.

Within it she saw a room and two men in dark wizard's robes. One leaned over the crystal, while the other stepped back.

"Who are you?" the leaning one's voice came, that same commanding, arrogant, contemptuous voice she'd heard the frozen wizard use, but even more so.

"Speak when spoken to," Bird replied, her voice shaking with anger. As she spoke, she felt something like fear attempt to touch her mind. Her anger became cold and focused.

In Soren's observatory, he and Haster saw the witch-child looking up at them from Soren's great crystal. Even through the crystal they could feel the power radiating from her. Soren knew that his strongest fear spell had failed. Haster quietly stepped away.

"Who are you?" Bird demanded. "Speak."

"I'm Soren, Chief Mage of the Order of Dark Wizards." The words conveyed the man's long-held arrogance. "Who are you, who think you may command my crystal? Bow before me child, before I blast you into nothingness!"

"I thought so," Bird said. "Come here. Now." She set the crystal on the ground.

Shrieking, Soren was pulled into the crystal. Haster, safely out of the crystal's view, stood astonished and alone in Soren's observatory.

Bird waited, hands on hips in her most demanding Reya pose as Soren, still shrieking, squeezed through the small crystal, breaking his shoulders and hip as he came.

"Be quiet!" Bird commanded. "And sit up!"

With that, the wizard sat at attention, his face a study in agony. Bird was too angry to notice.

"Now tell me," she commanded, "why did you try to stop the rain? Speak! Tell the truth! And no groaning!"

"Because," Soren was barely able to stammer, "we want to usurp the other Orders of Wizardry's powers."

Bird stared at him for a moment. "Just how would stopping rain make that happen?"

Soren swayed, but her command kept his tortured body upright. "That was to be our first demonstration that we could take another Order's powers."

Shaking her head, Bird considered that. "You have mastered the powers of darkness, have you?"

"Yes." Soren's reply was more hiss than word. "We know the fear of darkness and death. We harness both in spell after spell."

"Fool!" Bird's voice became deeper. "What do you know of darkness as a time of rest? Of healing for those who walk by day, of movement and life for night creatures? What have you studied of the dark's full powers? You were ill taught and have taught yourselves even more vilely!" Just where these words came from, Bird wasn't sure.

She paused, trying to comprehend, before the deep voice from within her asked another question. "Do you wish to become part of the dark?"

Soren, tears running down his face from the agony of his broken body, could barely gasp out, "Yes, mistress! Yes!"

A voice more like Bird's answered. "I hope you become one with the dark. There are shadows under the trees in this forest. You should join them."

Soren dwindled then as Bird released him, becoming a shadow next to the crystal through which he'd been summoned. The shadow elongated and slithered away to blend with other shadows beneath the trees.

In the observatory which had been Soren's, Haster found himself standing at attention and unable to move. As Bird's attention shifted, he was finally able to creep even further from the glow of the great crystal. In the woods, Bird looked down at the smaller crystal at her feet and willed it to rest.

Haster breathed a sigh of relief as Soren's great crystal darkened.

Bird had felt her voice deepen, saying things she hadn't known she was about to say. That was as disturbing as were any of the powers she'd discovered in herself. Yet Reya had taught her something similar lest she be afraid in the night, though she didn't think that had been necessary. She couldn't remember being afraid of the dark, or of the night sounds which came through her window. Sometimes she'd even slipped out of bed to walk among the small beings who scampered through the dark and the night birds flying so silently overhead, though never quite silently enough to escape Bird's notice. It had been her own normal voice which freed Soren to become one with the dark, and that was reassuring.

Bird looked at Owen and the three guardsmen, all still frozen. "Hmmn. Now I suppose I have to deal with you four so you don't go running off to tell the other wizards." She looked carefully at Owen, her face puzzled. "You appear familiar." She thought for a time. "You were one of those who came to stop my rain, weren't you? You may answer."

"Yes, mistress, I was," Owen replied, his teeth chattering now that he could speak.

Bird nodded. "You were shorter, but you ran as fast as the tall one." Her eyes darkened again. Then she looked closely at Owen's robe, reached out, and touched it. "What's wrong with this?"

Owen's eyes were round with fear. "I—I don't know, mistress."

"Well, it's not right," Bird said. "I want to see what it should be." As she spoke, the dark robe slowly changed to a greenish brown. Bird nodded; the robe now fit with the deeper power she'd sensed within this one. "I thought so." She glared at Owen. "Why were you wearing a dark robe?"

Owen, unable to look down, felt a change of some sort within himself. "I—I—I" he stuttered for a moment. Then, able to say what he'd never dared say before, he answered. "There was no choice. When I first showed signs of power, word spread among my parents' neighbors. Soon a dark wizard arrived and took me off to the Capitol to be trained. I was offered no choice."

Bird's eyes darkened again. "Didn't they know you weren't one of theirs? Your robe looks as though you belong in a dry place. Do you create droughts?"

Owen saw her anger beginning to build and answered quickly. "No. I was required to follow my master's orders. He had the knowledge and the power, though I sometimes felt he used knowledge from some source other than the dark Order. When we were in your valley chanting, I almost understood what source he drew upon. Then the lightning started, and I felt nothing but fear."

Bird watched the young wizard closely as he spoke. "Where are you from?" she asked.

"From the south. My parents had a farm there, near the Dry Mountains."

Farms interested Bird. "What's the land like there?"

"Dry," Owen answered, his eyes showing that for the moment his thoughts were far away. "Farming is very different from that in your valley. There's little rain, so crops must endure dry spells. Half the fields lie idle each year. It takes two years' rain to produce one year's crop."

This sounded similar to what Osa had told her of the fields in the Barren Lands. "And what wizards live there?" Bird asked.

"None. The country is too poor for dark wizards' tastes. There are tales of other wizards living in the Dry Mountains, where dark wizards don't go."

Behind Bird, Aren and the rest stood listening, Aren with his sword still in hand should one of the three guardsmen make a move toward Bird.

"What do those wizards look like, if they're not dark wizards?" Bird asked.

Owen shook his head. "I've never seen one. They were just stories. I've heard they wear some sort of brown robe."

Bird smiled. "Look at your robe."

Owen looked down, gasped. Then, catching movement behind Bird, he looked up to see Aren with sword in hand and behind him tall figures in gleaming white robes who could only be Druids.

Aren stepped forward to stand between Bird and the three guardsmen. Seeing that they didn't move even at sight of his sword, he turned to ask Bird, "What have you done to them?" He didn't want to ask about the source of that other voice, deep and commanding. There could be no answer which he would find comforting. Hobard and Inek moved with him, standing on each side and slightly to the rear while their fellow Druids made a circle around the camp. Magda walked around this wizard in a changed robe, looking him over carefully.

"Told them not to move, and they haven't. I've been busy with wizards and haven't gotten around to telling them any more," Bird said. "I suppose sooner or later we'll have to deal with them."

"Let them be for now," Aren replied. "I see one wizard; is he safe?"

"I haven't told him to do anything but answer. See how his robe changed? I don't think he was intended to be a dark wizard." She turned to Hobard, who had been looking with interest at Owen's green-brown robe. "Do you know what sort of wizard wears a robe like this?"

Hobard shook her head. "I had little to do with wizards before I went back into earth and stone."

Inek stepped forward. "Alas, I did. Not all wizards sought power for its own sake. This robe"—he reached out, touched it, then held a fold for a moment—"this robe puzzles me. Before we moved to the Barren Lands, we worked with wizards whose robes became green. They lived mostly in the forests beyond the mountains. Others' robes became blue. They chose to live near the great water and near rivers. Those with brown robes mostly lived in the dry south lands, near the Dry Mountains. This robe suggests that its wearer is from the south, but the green tinge puzzles me. How did he come here, Little Mother?" he asked Bird.

"He says dark wizards took him from his home in the south when he was young. I've seen him before. He was one of those who tried to stop the rain in my valley. When I saw him here, up close, I knew right away that his robe was the wrong color."

"What do these—these brown-green wizards do? Are they after power for its own sake?" Aren asked.

Inek replied, "They must be a kind of brown wizard. Those wizards seek to heal disease in plants, injury to the land. Their skills even in the earlier time were adapted to dry areas. Their interests are in life, not fear and death."

Owen stood wide-eyed at what he was hearing. Aren broke the silence. "What are we to do with him? I'm not sure we can trust him to travel with us. Suppose his robe should darken again? It appears he belongs in the south, but we cannot simply send him. The dark Order would never let him travel safely."

Bird clouded up at all these complications. "Well, he's got to go somewhere!"

Aren winced; he'd seen what happened when Bird lost her temper. He was about to try to calm her when Inek cleared his throat.

"Little Mother, he could go into the Barren Lands. My fellows there would keep watch on him, and teach skills the dark Order would not."

Bird looked at her big brother, eyebrows raised, her face calming.

Aren, relieved, agreed. "It could work. I doubt he'd have power over a pair of Druids, even if his robe were to turn black again. That land would provide opportunity for him to practice a new kind of wizardry. But, " he said as he picked up the globe from where Bird had set it on the ground, " I do not think we should trust him with a crystal." He turned to Bird. "I can carry it for you, little bird."

At Bird's nod, Aren turned to Inek. "Will any of your fellow Druids wish to return?"

One of Inek's fellow villagers stepped forward. He spoke, sadness in his voice. "Though I had hoped to travel on with our Little Mother, I hear the wisdom in her words. If this wizard is to be reformed, it is only right that he be taught by those who acknowledge how great were the errors we committed in the past. I will lead him into the Barren Lands. With my brothers who remained, we will teach him how to link the power which lies within him to that of the dry lands. We will show him what we have done and teach him to do the same in lands to the south."

He grew silent, thinking, before he spoke again. "There may well be other wizards who are capable of change. We will remain until our brothers come to replace us. Should we never again leave the Barren Lands, we will know we remain there not as punishment, but to do the Little Mother's bidding."

Inek bowed low to the volunteer. "If the Little Mother is willing, we will take our turns teaching. I promise you, I at least will come to relieve you."

"As will I," Osa said. "And I thank you."

Bird turned to Owen. "Well," she said, "what do you think? We've got to do something with you. In the Barren Lands you'll be safe from dark wizards. Once all this is settled, you can travel south."

It took Owen a moment to find words. "It would—I would—but mistress, wizards cannot enter the Barren Lands. The mist confuses us and we wander helplessly."

Bird looked at Inek, who chuckled. "That's true enough, unless one of our number leads you and asks the mists to allow you to see. This one--" he gestured toward the volunteer, "--will lead you safely."

Owen bent his head in acknowledgment. At Bird's gesture, he took up his pack and set out along the trail leading to the Barren Lands, a Druid following.

"That's that, then," said Bird, turning to face the three motionless guardsmen. "What of these? We can't just leave them standing there."

Aren could see fear in the guardsmen, a sergeant and two foot soldiers. He hoped Bird would not lose patience again and deal harshly with these men. "No, we cannot, little one. But they could be dangerous."

Hobard, Inek, and Osa came forward to stand between Bird and the guards.

Inek spoke. "We can assist should they attempt to draw weapons. While I greatly regret teaching the dark Order to use fear of dark to protect themselves against attacks by others, as we thought then, I have not forgotten the use. Osa, what of you?"

Osa, not taking his eyes from the guardsmen, replied, "I have used my mind to hold quiet an injured animal more than once."

"Very well, then," Aren said. "Little bird, perhaps we should ask the sergeant whether he can stand surety for the peaceful intentions of these three."

"All right," Bird said. She stepped forward to stand next to Aren as Hobard made room. "You," she said to the sergeant, "may speak and move."

The sergeant moved only enough to shift his right hand further from his sword hilt. "Lady," he said, "we will offer you and yours no harm. Not all who serve the Order do so willingly. For myself, I would serve you under the command of your Captain." This last he followed with a slow, careful salute as he shifted his gaze to Aren.

"I'm no Captain," Aren said. "I was a guardsman for a time, but no more."

The sergeant bowed his head. "With all respect, sir, I recognize a captain when I see one by his bearing, his actions, and his words. You speak as an advisor to the Mistress, and these others follow your lead. How should I do otherwise? And what should I call you but Captain?" Then, moving very slowly, he used his left hand to carefully remove his sword from its scabbard and offered the sword, hilt first, to Bird.

Puzzled, she looked up at Aren.

"Bird," he said, "a guardsman's most sacred oath is the offering of his sword hilt and his service. If you grip the sword handle, you will accept his service. A guardsman would die rather than betray the sword-oath."

"What should I do?" Bird asked.

"You may well accept his service, sincerely offered."

With that, Bird reached out and took a firm grip on the sergeant's sword hilt. He sank to his knees, head bowed until Aren told him to stand and remain at ease.

"What of these two?" Aren asked the sergeant, gesturing toward the two frozen guardsmen.

"They are no lovers of the Order, Captain. I think they will welcome a chance to escape their present service."

Bird looked at Aren, who nodded. "You may speak and move, then," she said. "No tricks, now!"

The two had not reacted so quickly to Bird's presence as had their sergeant. Their hands were nowhere near their sword hilts. Shaking just a little, they came forward, the stockier leading, his taller fellow a step behind. First the stocky guardsman and then the tall one used his left hand to slowly remove his sword from the scabbard. Each knelt and offered the sword-hilt to Bird.

She stood looking at each before speaking. "You don't have to make promises, you know. If you'd rather go, you may. We won't hurt you."

Each held his sword-hilt a little closer to the child. She took a firm grip on each hilt in turn.

"Stand at ease," the sergeant ordered, and both rose. He turned to Aren. "Captain, there are three other servants of the Order scattered along the edge of these woods, watching for your party. At least one is not to be trusted. Even if he offered his loyalty, the oath would mean little." He hesitated before continuing. "We are due to relieve them soon. They will wonder when we do not. It may be wise to make your next move now, before their wonder becomes such that one or more comes seeking their relief."

"Are there wizards with them?" Aren asked.

"No, not with those three. There are wizards and guardsmen to the south and one such party further to the north. Master Rath commands all. Our orders are to report if we see the Mistress and yourself and these—" here he paused and looked at the Druids surrounding the camp--"these companions of yours. There will be no such report, of course, but we will be missed. While Rath would not concern himself with missing guardsmen, no doubt he will note an absent wizard."

"Well," Bird said, "we'll never get home by standing here talking, now, will we?"

CHAPTER FOURTEEN

Snake returned to Rath's camp to report no change in the mist, either during the night or since. He found Rath and Tarh sitting on the camp stools, both looking exhausted. The master wizard accepted Snake's report in silence. He didn't inquire about Dog's absence.

In his years of serving the Order, Snake had picked up a little about the uses of power. What he saw in the two wizards seemed the signs of a spell which had rebounded upon the caster. He was surprised to find Rath subdued rather than angry.

His report given and Rath showing no further interest, Snake went to his tent, noted no signs that Dog had returned, and settled down to wait. And listen. Unlike the guardsmen's tents, Snake's was just within hearing distance of Rath's, near which wizards would gather. No doubt Rath believed Snake had chosen the site so he could respond quickly whenever the master wizard might call. That was true enough, but being within hearing distance cut two ways. Should Master Dog not return, leaving Snake on his own, knowing what Rath planned would become even more important. Whatever else, Snake planned to survive.

Rath went to his tent for his crystal and returned to the stool. "Might as well get this over with," he said. Tarh, not sure whether Rath realized he'd spoken aloud, kept quiet. Taking a deep breath, Rath placed his hands on the globe and willed it to contact Soren's great crystal.

For a moment, Rath stared at what his crystal showed, which seemed to be the ceiling of Soren's observatory. Soren's crystal should not have activated without Soren or one of his lieutenants in the room. That would mean Haster, Soren's only remaining adviser, unless Oleg had also been granted control over the globe. Or had decided to take control.

Haster's face appeared. Apparently the man was standing some distance away. "Rath?" Haster's voice was uncertain. "Rath, is that you?"

"Who else would it be?" Rath growled, in no mood for foolishness and too tired to be polite even to Soren, much less Haster. "What's wrong?"

Haster leaned over the crystal, his face worried. "Rath, there's been a disaster. Soren is gone."

"What do you mean, gone?" That was hardly conceivable, though Soren might have decided to travel north to the Fifth Valley if those efforts had been more successful than had Rath's.

"I mean gone. Vanished. Right out of this room." Haster paused for a moment, seemed to gather himself. "This morning. Soren came up early, hoping to hear from you. When his crystal came to life, we leaned over it expecting to receive your report. It was the child-witch. You know Soren; he thundered at her. Instead of quailing when he identified himself as Chief Mage, she commanded him to come to her."

Haster trembled as he tried for control. "Rath, Soren was pulled into the crystal! Into the crystal! I had stepped back, out of the crystal's range, remembering how she'd sent power through your great crystal. Perhaps that saved me. Then the globe went dark, and I've not approached it since. Oleg is here as well. I sent word to him as soon as I gathered my wits."

The Loremaster stepped forward, nodding at Rath's image in the great crystal, but did not speak. He'd arrived in the observatory in response to Haster's summons to find the wizard white and shaken, almost incoherent. It had taken a while to calm the man enough to make any sense at all. Since then, they'd sat in silence, a safe distance, as Haster hoped, from the crystal. Each was uncertain whether any attempt to reach Rath would result instead in contact with the child. That any wizard was able to contact the great crystal was a relief. At least it wasn't permanently under the child's control.

Rath found all this hard to believe. "She has a crystal now? And was able to call Soren to her through a crystal?" Such a thing was unheard of—no crystal, even a great crystal, had ever been able to convey even the smallest physical object. Wizards had failed in the effort ever since they began to realize that crystals had extraordinary capabilities.

Oleg answered. "We know only that when she called Soren to her, he vanished into or through his own crystal. Where he is now, I can only guess. Have you heard anything?"

"Nothing," Rath said. "I've not been very active since last night." He breathed deeply. There was nothing but bad news this morning. "Last night we chanted against the ward over the Barren Lands." He paused, gathered himself.

Oleg, watching Rath's face through the Great Crystal, expected to hear of failure. "It did not go well, then?" Haster, slower on the uptake, glanced at the Loremaster, puzzled.

"My watcher reports that the mist seemed unaffected. That's not a surprise. Last night's effort came back upon us, if anything with greater power than we sent. Fortunately the dissolution spell itself did not return. Only Ren and I were able to move about, and that with great effort. The others lay on the ground for hours. Before dawn, all had recovered enough to return to their camps. I sent them on their ways. We'll want to rest a few days before we try again.

"I would say that we failed completely. This news of Soren is more important, I think. Wait a moment." He turned toward Tarh, who couldn't have missed hearing Haster's account. The younger wizard stared. "Don't sit there gaping," Rath snapped. "Get your crystal and start contacting the others. Start with Roke. After Roke, try Ren. Keep alert. If the witch-child responds, break contact and back away."

Tarh was already up and trotting toward his tent.

Rath turned back to his crystal. "Did you hear?"

Oleg answered. "Yes. So you think that the child may have taken a crystal from one of your party? It's a useful thought."

"But it does make using crystals dangerous," Haster put in. Leave it to Haster to think first of that danger, Rath thought. Still, he had to admit that he'd just warned Tarh about that same possibility. Perhaps Haster wasn't being more cautious than usual, or he himself was being more.

"I'll send out scouts," Rath said. "They can quickly reach the two nearest camps." Soren might have survived being pulled through a great crystal, if the child had found one in the Barren Lands. Tarh would probably not survive a journey through a small crystal no matter how large the crystal at the other end.

"There has been some good news, at least," Oleg said. "Pennon reports from the Fifth Valley that the efforts there seemed to moderate the ward. He hopes that over time, their efforts may achieve greater effect. This offers some hope."

"But not much," Haster put in. "Not enough to soften the news of Soren's disappearance and the possibility that the witch-child may be on the move again."

The younger wizards' success brought back Rath's exhaustion and the failure of his efforts. So far, he'd three times come off badly in conflict with this demon child.

Oleg broke the silence. "For now, I suggest Haster continue to coordinate things from here. The Chief Mage's seat has been vacant before, though never for long and I doubt in times as perilous as these."

Rath could see the exchange of glances between Haster and the Loremaster. The look on Haster's face showed panic rather than a desire for the power of the Chief Mage's office. On a better day, Rath would have chuckled at the thought of Haster as Chief Mage. As coordinator, however, he might well survive. No doubt he'd be a willing tool of whoever became the next Chief Mage. That person, surely, would be Rath himself should he yet manage to defeat this witch-child. If not, there might not be enough left of the Order to be worth commanding.

"That makes sense," Rath said, and saw relief on Haster's face. "I will report as soon as I know more about—" He broke off as Tarh called to him. "Wait a moment. Tarh may have heard something."

"Master," Tarh said, "I've reached Roke, who has seen nothing. I've asked him to send a runner to Owen's camp. Ren also has seen nothing, and will send a runner to Wald's camp."

"That's something," Rath said. "Send our runners, and then try the others. But be careful." He turned back to the crystal. "Roke and Ren are still in place. We'll keeping trying to reach the others."

Oleg had taken a half-step back from what had been Soren's Great Crystal, letting Haster take precedence. Haster spoke. "What of the Fifth Valley?"

"It sounds as though more guardsmen will be needed there," Rath said. "If three wizards could weaken the ward, more may be able to disperse it entirely. Guardsmen can enter, so perhaps if we gather enough, they can prevent the cursed farmers from interfering. If the ward is gone, we won't need guardsmen to enforce our will."

"Yes," Haster said. "I had that thought as well."

He probably had, Rath mused, but was reluctant to make the decision. He could tell how Haster's coordination of efforts was going to go. Still, Oleg was nodding his head from where he stood just a half-step further off. So long as Oleg was present, the Loremaster could strengthen Haster's resolve. "Probably best to put out the call to our members. They can order lords to send reinforcements."

"And then accompany guardsmen to the Valley," Oleg put in. "We won't want any delays from lords." He was silent for a moment. "What of your group? Will you remain and try again?"

Rath shrugged. "If the witch-child is moving, a ward over the barrens matters little. She may be going back to the place all this started, In that case, it would be best to remove the ward before she returns. The ward here is ancient, we know. That over the valley is recent and clearly not as strong.. Adding our group to those already having some success might allow a rapid ending of that ward." He did not add that his group contained most of the Order's most powerful wizards. Neither Oleg nor Haster needed reminding.

Haster was nodding as firmly as if this had indeed been his entire plan. "I will send the messages now." He paused as though thinking. "Is there anything else?"

Rath shook his head. "I'll report as we learn more."

Haster made a gesture of dismissal—a pale imitation of Soren's, which had seemed almost to brush away an entire conversation and the wizard who'd participated. His and Oleg's faces vanished. Rath allowed his own crystal to go dark. He turned to Tarh.

"Soren is missing, perhaps dead. Yet there's been some success in the Fifth Valley. Now let's find out what our other wizards have to say."

"Wald responds He's seen nothing," Tarh said.

"Good. At least we know that three have survived. Perhaps the child found a crystal somewhere in the Barren Lands, and none of our group is involved. You try Owen; I'll try Tor. But be careful. If you don't get a response, stop trying. Should you see a child's face, throw the crystal from you." Rath closed his eyes for a moment, shaking his head. "If we can't reach someone, we'll let the runners tell us what they've found. I suspect that guardsmen will approach cautiously at the best of times. In this case, that may be a good thing."

✳✳✳

From within his tent, pitched just close enough to Rath's for voices to carry on a quiet morning, Snake listened carefully. Haster's voice he recognized; Haster and Lorit had sometimes been Soren's messengers when Snake was wanted. Oleg's was unfamiliar. Snake's missions required no lore—stealth and a sharp blade had been Soren's chief requirements. If what he heard was true, Snake would not have to concern himself with Soren's commands.

As Rath's conversation with Haster and Oleg ended, the assassin realized that Dog had entered the tent and been listening as well. Snake started before his usual self-control reasserted itself.

Dog held a finger to his lips, then spoke very softly, his usual low rumble a mere buzz. "Child leaves Barren Lands. Interesting times. Dog leave wizards, follow child. Snake free to leave. Must choose now."

Though Dog again offered freedom, Snake knew that sooner or later a dark wizard would find him and again compel him to serve. Still, he could hide out somewhere, wait for all this to be over. Then he could resume his comfortable life as a thief and occasional assassin.

That life no longer seemed as interesting as it once had. Snake realized that he'd been silent too long. He looked up, saw the beginnings of a smile on Dog's face. Snake shook himself, rather like a dog waking from sleep. "As a free man, then, I'll travel with you, if I may."

This strange being laughed softly. "Glad," he said. "Message first. Paper?"

To his surprise Snake found himself also wanting to laugh. "Paper. Pen. Ink," he said, digging into an outer pocket on his backpack. "Ready."

"Trouble Fifth Valley. Need lord." Snake wrote quickly, then handed the paper to Dog, along with the tiny bottle of ink. Dog sprinkled a very small amount of ink on his knuckles, pressed them onto the paper to create the print of a dog's paw just below the brief message, then handed the sheet back to Snake. "Captain Ryd," he added.

Snake folded the paper three times, addressed it. He sealed the small bottle, wrapped the pen again in a piece of cloth, and put them back into their pocket, from which he drew out a piece of wax. "I'll get a coal out of the guards' fire. Then I'll seal this."

"Good. Wizards move soon. Dog leave. Ryd at Keep. Then north road, Meet Red Forest." The squat man stood, moved to the tent door. He had to bend only a little as he went, though he had to turn sideways to fit through the tent's opening. He paused, looked back. "Good choice." Then he was gone.

Snake slipped out of the tent, found a live coal in the remains of the guards' fire and dripped just enough wax onto the letter to seal it. Back inside, he rolled up his bedroll and tied it to his pack. His few other travelling belongings were already stowed, as always. When it came time to leave, Snake did not wish to be slowed by packing. Snake had never travelled with a tent, and wouldn't miss this one.

Moving as quietly as though it were midnight and he afraid of waking sleepers, Snake stepped out. He looked once toward where the wizards sat and saw that they were occupied with their crystals. At this time of day, most of the wizards' guards would be at their posts, keeping watch over the woods. Those who were in camp would no doubt be sleeping. Snake walked quickly away. He kept the guards' tents between himself and the wizards as he walked southeast.

Lands this close to the Barren Lands tended to be unoccupied, but Snake knew there would be cultivated fields ahead. When he reached the first of those would be time enough to head directly south until he reached the East Road. That might take most of the day, but once on the road he could walk as late into the night as he wished. For a moment he wished Master Dog were with him. At the pace that odd being would set, they'd have reached Lord Ryd by evening. Still, sometime the next morning would do. It occurred to him that he could spend a comfortable night in the inn near what was left of the keep. That was an intriguing idea. He hadn't slept in a bed since they'd left that inn to follow the wizards' quarry north toward the Red Forest.

***

Roke was surprised when his crystal began to glow. He'd had only a few short hours rest after returning from their challenge to the ward over the barrens. Surely Rath was not up and about so soon. Even a wizard far more powerful than Roke knew himself to be should not recover completely this quickly.

He placed a hand on the globe and looked into it. Tarh's face, looking not just tired but worried, stared back. Relief replaced the worry. "You're all right. That's good. Have you seen anything unusual this morning?"

That was an odd question. Had others been so drained they'd collapsed? Everyone had seemed fine when Roke left Rath's campsite just before dawn. He and Owen had walked together as far as Owen's camp. From there he'd gone on alone, taking the opportunity to check on the guard Owen had posted to the north of his camp and the second guard further north that he himself had posted. Both had been in place, and even awake. Roke hadn't taken any special care to move quietly. He was chiefly concerned that the men continue in their duties when he was absent overnight.

He'd let Tarh wait too long for an answer. "No, nothing. My guards are on watch, so I'm sure I'd have heard. Has there been some reaction to our attack on the ward?"

"Nothing worse than what we felt last night," Tarh said, at which Roke felt a surge of relief. The pushback after their effort had been strong enough to keep him from looking forward to their next attempt. "The witch-child seems to be on the move. We think she met with one of our group and seized his crystal. Clearly it was not yours."

"No, indeed." Roke spoke his relief before he caught himself. "I've not seen her, and she didn't pass this way while I was gone. Are you sure she met with one of ours?"

"No. But apparently she used a crystal to contact the Chief Mage, so she has gotten one from somewhere." Tarh wouldn't say any more than that about what had happened after the witch-child contacted Soren. Let Rath decide when it might be time to speak of the Chief Mage's fate.

"I left Owen at his camp some time ago. Everything seemed normal there," Roke said. If anyone had had the misfortune to encounter the witch-child and allow her to wrest control of his crystal, Owen was a likely candidate. In the man's short time in the Order, his most notable act had been to survive the attempt to restore Rath's drought in one of the valleys. There was something almost half-hearted about Owen.

At that, Tarh instructed Roke to send runners to check on Owen's camp. Two, he suggested, though Roke knew the suggestion came from Rath and was an order. "Tell one to go on to report to Rath himself, and the other to report back to you. Use your crystal to inform me of what you learn. Rath will be contacting some of the others, as will I, so keep trying if you don't get through. Don't try to contact Owen or any of the others by crystal. You don't want to reach the witch-child instead." With that, Tarh's face vanished. Roke let his own crystal go dark.

He woke the two guards who'd been sleeping after having night duty and sent them trotting south to check on Owen's camp. If things were normal there, they were to tell Owen to contact Rath and then Roke. If not, he also passed on Tarh's instructions.

He noted that the men paled a little as the import sunk in. Roke finished with what he hoped would reassure them. "There may be nothing wrong at all, and Owen will wonder at your appearance and questions. But we want to be certain." With that he sent them on their way.

It was now past mid-morning. If things were normal at Owen's camp, Roke could expect to hear by crystal at mid-day or thereabouts. If not, it would take until mid-afternoon for his runner to return. If the witch-child had taken someone's—Owen's?-- crystal, then she was on the move and would have a head start. That thought relieved him; he'd rather pursue than encounter her. Let Rath lead any pursuit. If the master wizard could not stand before this witch-child, it was unlikely he could.

He wondered what sort of beings would accompany the child this time. He'd seen the brother and the tall being in shining white as she entered the woods surrounding the barrens. Stories told by farmers living nearby said there were dwellers within the mist. He had no idea what those dwellers might be like. Perhaps—he hoped—they were somehow bound to those lands or held in by the mist. If not, who knew what powers they might bring with them?

With his guardsmen either on watch or serving as messengers, there was nothing for Roke to do but watch the woods in the near distance. He settled himself in front of his tent to watch and wait.

When mid-day passed and his crystal did not glow, Roke knew something was wrong in Owen's camp. He waited a little longer to be sure, then took up the crystal, settled it in his lap, and focused his mind on Tarh.

The young wizard's face appeared, looking hesitant for a moment until he recognized the caller. Roke spoke quickly, before Tarh could ask a question. "My men have had more than time enough to reach Owen's camp. Owen should have contacted us by now. Perhaps he has contacted you?"

Roke realized after he'd spoken that he'd been lucky to be speaking to Tarh. Rath would have resented even a question this obvious.

"No," Tarh said, "he has not."

Roke could hear Rath's voice then. Though he could not tell just what the master wizard said, the voice contained its usual note of command,. That, at least, was a relief; so long as Rath remained calm, there might be hope. The image in Roke's crystal shook for a moment and Rath's face appeared. "Owen is the only one from whom we've had no word. Haster believes that the witch-child is on the move, and it appears he is correct."

Roke had only a moment to wonder why Haster's view rather than Soren's would be important before Rath continued.

"There appears to be no further need for a watch here," Rath said. "Go to Owen's camp and contact me when you arrive. Be careful not to disturb any tracks. If Owen and any guards who were in that camp are missing, we'll want to examine the ground carefully.

"Wait there. If she's on the move, we'll follow. The man Snake is a good tracker, and his minion, so he claims, is even better." He paused. "Watch yourself. Owen may well be dead. He won't be the first of our order."

With that, Rath's face vanished and Roke allowed his own crystal to become dark. For a time the younger wizard sat, shaken by what he'd heard. It was known that the witch-child had used lightning to attack apprentice wizards, even to kill one ordained wizard.

Where would she go now? What place could be safer than the mist-haunted Barren Lands?

Her first goal might well be the Red Forest. With the head start she must have by now, she'd reach that cursed place well before Rath and his group of wizards and guardsmen could catch her. What then? Another vigil? Surely there were no spells which could affect the forest itself. Perhaps this time their watch would be only for the purpose of warning the rest of the Order should she decide to move on again.

Roke would do as Rath ordered. If this ended badly, the fault would be Rath's. He would do his best and hope to survive. There was some credit to be gained even in a losing effort, so long as he acquitted himself bravely.

***

Rath returned Tarh's crystal and took up his own. "I'll report to Haster. In the meantime, tell the guards to break camp. Contact Ren. Tell him to join us here. He can notify the other two as well."

Tarh nodded, turned to his crystal.

Rath focused on his own, seeking the great crystal in what had been Soren's observatory. This time Haster's face appeared immediately, though the wizard was clearly standing back a little, no doubt hoping to duck should the witch-child's face appear. "We know a little more," Rath said, again not bothering with a greeting. "It appears that the crystal the witch used was Owen's. We've reached the others."

"She's on the move, then," Haster said. "I assume you'll follow?"

Oleg's face had not appeared in Rath's crystal. No doubt the Loremaster had returned to his archives. Rath would have liked to have Oleg present. His mind was better than Haster's, and his advice would have been useful. For the moment, however, Rath's course seemed clear. "Now that I know whose crystal the child used, we can assume that Owen is no longer with us. I've instructed the others to meet me at what was Owen's camp. There we can at least ascertain how many came out of the barrens and which direction they took. My preference would be to follow, though my fear is that she will return to the Red Forest."

The Red Forest, Rath did not bother saying, would present even greater problems than had the ward over the Barren Lands. While their attempt to disperse the mist covering those lands had resulted in a backlash which left even Rath himself needing time to recover, that could well have been a rebound, rather than directed by some intelligence. But the Red Forest had targeted Lorit and erased him as though he'd never existed. Should Haster suggest they try casting some sort of spell to neutralize the forest's power, Rath would invite the man to try that himself.

Haster received the news in silence. It was a while before he spoke. "I want to discuss all this with Oleg. In the absence of Soren and Lorit, he's the only one here who is familiar with the situation."

Rath groaned inwardly at Haster's hesitation, but agreed that Oleg was the only person left who might be consulted. "He may have already found some useful reference to that blighted forest." When Haster gave no instructions, he continued. "I will contact you again once we've reached Owen's camp." At Haster's nod, Rath broke the connection.

With both Soren and Lorit missing, the order was weakened, certainly. Haster could serve to coordinate their efforts, but not to devise them. That, Rath knew, would fall to him, and perhaps to Oleg. He'd have only a little time to consider his next few steps before he and his wizards gathered at what had been Owen's camp.

Just one of the order's efforts had been at all effective: working as a group to disperse the ward over the Fifth Valley. Only after that did the witch-child leave the mist-haunted barrens. If he could reach the valley before she did, he might yet break its ward. That might weaken the witch-child's powers, or at least make her careless. If she were mortal, Snake's dagger or a guardsman's arrow might end all danger.

Snake. Tarh contacted Ren while Rath spoke with Haster, and then went to relay Rath's orders to the guards. He returned, frowning. "Snake and his minion seem to be off somewhere. Their tent is empty. Even Snake's bedroll is missing."

This was not good news. Best to put a positive face on it. "Snake tracks well enough to follow us, and he claims his minion is even better. No doubt they'll catch up." Should they choose to. Snake had been Soren's man. If he'd heard of Soren's death, perhaps he'd decided that he was no longer bound to the Order. For now, a missing assassin paled in the face of Rath's other problems.

***

Lir and Reya slept peacefully as thunder rumbled over the mountains, lightly as it approached, and came fully awake as the storm settled overhead. Through the bedroom window they could see lightning. Immediately they were up and pulling on cloaks. As they entered the house's main room they could see through the front windows a thin row of lightning strikes along the East Road. At almost that same moment came a knocking on the kitchen door. Taking his sword from its place over the fireplace, Lir went to answer.

He found Del and Sola standing on his doorstep. "Come in, you two. It's too wet to stand out there."

"You saw, Father Lir?" Del asked. "Before the storm, we heard chanting from the woods across the way, then a shout. Sola and Ana saw more."

"We were hidden in the woods," Sola said, "moving a little closer to their camp when we realized that they'd not set a watch. When the chanting began, we moved even closer. As the lightning grew, we were able to see three wizards. Finally they shouted something, but we couldn't tell just what."

"Have any attempted to enter the valley?" Lir asked.

"We think not," Del said. "We would have seen them, even in their black robes, once the lightning started."

"One did walk almost to the road's edge as the lightning grew," Sola said. "From behind, we could see him clearly."

Del nodded. "You had a better view. We were half-blinded by the strikes."

"Lightning would have struck any who entered," said Lir, "and that would have been a greater flash. It sounds as though the ward holds."

Reya joined them from where she had stood at the front windows, watching the road. Both Del and Sola bent their heads in respectful greeting.

The two were silent for a moment before Del said, hesitantly, "We have heard stories of the row of strikes along the road that time a wizard was killed trying to enter. Tonight's storm did not seem as strong as what we've heard of that one."

Reya and Lir exchanged a look. "What do you think, my wife? You had a longer look. I was answering the door."

Reya sighed. "I think, Del, you are correct. The strikes did not make a solid wall. I fear this chanting may have had some effect on the storm, though not enough to prevent it."

"In that case," growled Lir, "we can expect more tomorrow night, and the night after that. Perhaps they will not be able to entirely remove our protection, but who can tell?" He rubbed his chin as he thought. "Council meeting tomorrow?"

Reya nodded. "In the meantime, I think our young folk might as well watch through our front windows. There's no reason for them to be half-drowned this night."

Del laughed. "We here in the valley are in no danger, Mother Reya. We have cloaks and hats, and set up a makeshift roof of branches as we heard the thunder begin. But I thank you for the offer."

Sola seconded his thanks. "We scouts have capes, should the rain cross the road. So far, it has not."

"All right, then," Reya replied. "But tell the others not to hesitate to enter here should anyone become chilled."

With nods, Sola and Del turned and slipped out the door.

***

The next day's council did not last long. That night saw ten bowmen concealed in the woods along each side of the valley. As the night became dark, five from each group moved very quietly into Reya and Lir's front yard where Lir joined them, his own bow in hand. Sola and her scouts were once again scattered in the woods around the wizards' camp, keeping further off so the bowmen would have no fear of accidentally wounding one of their number.

"Now we wait," Lir said. "Mark where their fire is. Doubtless they will let it become embers by midnight. Spread out. Once the chanting begins, try to spot an outline against the embers. When the wizards appear, we will have only a short time before their chanting begins. When it does, fire as you will at any form you've seen, or think you've seen. Among us, we should at the least wound or frighten them enough to bring a halt to their mischief. No doubt tomorrow we will have to deal with their guardsmen, who can enter freely; but they won't risk the dark."

None were sure how long they waited. Some thought it a short time, others terribly long. All were experienced hunters and had been trained in the Lord's Guard. They knew better than to stare constantly at the fire. Each chiefly looked away, relying on spotting movement out of the corners of the eyes.

Eventually a voice whispered, "They come," and all tensed. Chanting began, and eleven bowstrings twanged almost in unison. A yell from the far side of the road suggested someone had at least been distracted. Chanting faltered. Bowstrings sang intermittently, some shooting at where they'd seen part of a silhouette, others shooting toward where they thought that yell had come from. A few aimed just above the glow of the fire or just to one side or the other of that glow, hoping for a hit in the dark.

Chanting ceased. Thunder dwindled. They could hear movement in the camp across the road, men calling orders to others. Bowmen watched closely for any sign the fire had been rebuilt or that torches or lanterns were being lit, hoping for clearer targets. The experienced guardsmen in that camp were not going to provide any easy marks.

After a time, Sola and her scouts returned. They'd watched events, then faded back into the woods, crossing the road some distance away before making their way into the valley. Sola spoke for them.

"Well done! You wounded one wizard in a shoulder, a second in the thigh, and frightened the third. Two guardsmen took arrows as they assisted wizards into the woods. It seems that any wound will render a wizard unable to help himself!"

She paused for breath. "They've moved further into the woods. Guardsmen have slipped back into their camp for bedrolls, but I think all will sleep on the ground this night." Her voice became somber. "The fourth wizard camps separately and didn't take part in the chanting. He seems to be an observer. He was the only one who went to a crystal after things settled down. Probably he reports to someone."

Lir smiled. "You bring good news, but move carefully in those woods. We would not have any of you taken by these wizards." He ignored Sola's snort at the idea. "They'll keep their camp further from the road after this. In daylight their guardsmen will no doubt try to move their tents and supplies as well. We may find targets then, but they'll be few..

"Most of you may as well go upvalley and get some rest. Let's keep only a few watchers for the rest of the night. Pass the word that we'll want fresh bowmen well before dawn, just in case these wizards order their guardsmen to try a surprise."

After considering, he continued. "I'd rather leave guardsmen alone unless we have to fire upon them. If two wizards are wounded, I doubt they will chant again tomorrow night. When they do start again, they may order their guardsmen to become shields. Should that happen, we'll have to fire upon both guardsmen and wizards. At any rate, we must be prepared night and day from now on. At the least, we have bought ourselves a few days."

With that, Sola's scouts and most of the bowmen left, chattering about the night's work. Remaining were only the designated watchers and two or three others too excited by the night's work to sleep. Lir watched them go, then turned toward the house.

Reya leaned against the front wall. Of course, Lir realized, she'd not have remained indoors to watch through the safety of the windows. She would carry her long knife, ready to defend her home should the wizard's guards attempt to cross the road. Should he be injured, she would stand over him to the death. Other women up and down the valley would have spent a sleepless night as well, waiting in their yards and listening for sounds of fighting. Or, more likely, gathering in a yard only one or two farms further up the valley, a place from which they could move quickly to reinforce the archers. For a moment, Lir wondered if Lord Ryd had any idea that not only could he rely on well over one hundred trained former guardsmen living in the five valleys, but also nearly that many knife-bearing women.

Reya came toward him and they walked toward the house, each with an arm around the other's waist. "That bought some time," she said.

"A little," Lir replied. "How long before they find a way to weaken whatever protects us from wizards? If they gather guardsmen enough, valley blood will be spilled. That begins to seem something we can not avoid."

"At any rate, we cannot solve this tonight. Sleep will do us more good than worry," Reya noted. And as will those who refuse to worry about what may not happen, they did sleep, soundly, through what remained of the night.

***

Haster and Oleg waited for Pennon's report. They'd considered watching this second attempt as it took place, but Oleg suggested they not. Should lightning cross the road into Pennon's camp and begin striking crystals, they would not wish Soren's great crystal to go the way of Rath's. Haster was quick to agree.

Pennon's report was slower in coming than they'd hoped, which might mean that sustained chanting had had little result. On the other hand, it might have meant that the storm shrank so visibly that the three continued for some time.

When the great crystal began to glow, Haster gingerly approached. When he saw Pennon's face appear, he rasped "Well?"

Pennon's face was too thoughtful for a man reporting a complete success, but not grim enough for one reporting failure. "There is some good news. As the chanting began, the storm moving down from the mountains seemed to slow even more than on the previous attempt."

"Well, that's something!" Haster chimed in.

"Yes," Pennon said. "But then came a hail of arrows out of the dark. One struck Vil, and another Fant. Wald was unhurt. That ended the chanting, so there's no way to tell what effects it might have had. A guardsman or two may also have been struck."

"They dared fire upon members of our Order?" asked Haster. "They dared?"

Oleg lay a restraining hand on Haster's arm. "Remember that they've been under the protection of a ward since summer. No doubt they've learned courage in the meantime."

Haster calmed himself. "Think you, Pennon, that the two wounded are too badly hurt to continue?"

Pennon spoke softly. "I think not, though they may need two or three days before they try again. One has an arrow in the shoulder, the other, one in the thigh. Even now, guardsmen are removing those and will doubtless bandage them adequately. Wald and I will offer up healing and strengthening spells, and I have with me a potion which should hasten healing. I'd thought to need it in case of guards being injured in a skirmish, rather than for wizards."

Haster continued to fret. "How will you deal with the threat of archers in the valley? Now that they've had this success, what's to keep them from firing every night?"

"I suspect they fired at shapes showing against the campfire. We've moved camp into the woods, and we'll make sure no campfire is visible from the road. We can post sentries in case farmers come onto this side of the road. We'll see. If these young wizards' nerve holds, we should be able to try again in a few days."

"Keep us informed of any news." With that abrupt conclusion, Haster willed the crystal to go dark. He stood, shaking his head.

"I think I'll return to my scrolls," Oleg said. He walked to the door, then paused. "That the valley people attempted to stop the chants is a good sign, I think. Either they perceived some effect, or at least feared that our chanting would eventually bring a result not to their liking. We can take some satisfaction in that."

He didn't wait for Haster's sigh of agreement.

CHAPTER FIFTEEN

Lord Ryd strolled slowly through the early morning, enjoying the early spring sun. He'd slept well. In fact, he'd been sleeping well for some weeks now. That was no doubt because work on the Manor had gone much more rapidly than he'd expected. Under the leadership of Tad Stonemason and, to give credit where it was due, Lars Carpenter as well, the craftsmanship turned out to be even better than the locals had claimed it might be. The stonemason and carpenter worked together well, that was certain. That should have been no surprise, given how long each had lived in these holdings.

That Ald Stoneworker readily accepted instruction not just from Tad but also from his three children had, however, been a bit of a surprise. Surely competition existed between the two families. While it might be one thing to take directions from the father, it could well be another matter where the younger members were concerned.

Ryd must have shown that thought one day as the stonemason's daughter Sule gave directions to which the stoneworker listened carefully. The man set to work as instructed. After Sule strode off to another part of the building, Ald grinned at the lord and chuckled. "A good workman recognizes a master, my lord, and is pleased to share in the work." Ryd, a little surprised but pleased that the locals had come to treat him with the mix of respect and informality he sought from his guardsmen, smiled in turn. "Wise words, my friend, and worth remembering," at which Ald actually blushed and made a very slight bow.

That was another reason to feel pleased: like Ald Stoneworker, the locals seemed to have accepted Ryd as their new lord. Some of that, he had to acknowledge, came because it would be difficult to be a worse lord than brother Rand. As a boy, Ryd had lived too long under his older brother's tyranny to expect him to have been a gentle master.

Some acceptance surely grew out of the fear most felt when the keep fell. Rand had spent years wresting bits of land from his fellow lords, as had his father before him. Surely both villagers and farmers expected that rival lords would ride up from the south to take back what they'd lost and as much more as each could seize and hold.

Until, that is, the arrival of Ryd and half his guardsmen. Added to those of Rand's who had remained, they were a sufficient force to hold out until reinforcements could arrive from the Five Valleys. Or so the southern lords would think. All knew that there were well over a hundred former guardsmen in those valleys. Distant lords would assume that all would arrive should Ryd need them to defend his expanded holdings.

Ryd smiled at that thought. While he was certain he could call on every man of the Valleys in case of need to defend his lands there, he hoped never to ask them to fight other than to protect their homes and families. That they might answer a call to defend what already were being called Ryd's Holdings was doubtful at best. That opinion he was careful to hide. He hoped that the Valley's reputation alone would forestall any invasions while the Manor's walls rose. Later he could decide whether to begin training the sons of local farmers as guardsmen and returning them home armed.

Farmers in the Holdings had been oppressed by their former lord, but that had not kept them ignorant of other lords. Farmers in the Holdings were certain that a hundred or more Valley guardsmen would arrive should Ryd request them. All had heard tales of Lord Gerlach—father of both Lord Rand and their present Lord Ryd—and his attempted invasion of the Valleys. Gerlach had ridden along the East Road and past the Fifth Valley with a hundred men, half mounted and half on foot, only to blunder headlong into a trap which left half his force wounded or dead. In the end, Gerlach's force returned home with only twenty of his Guard alive and whole, another forty wounded, and forty more to bury.

Valley story-tellers delighted in the tale, which grew in each winter's telling. Gerlach might have lost fewer men, the tales said, had not those Valley men who lived further off arrived late to the fight. Late-comers insisted on at least two more skirmishes before there could be any talk of Gerlach surrendering. By that time, Gerlach was glad to accept any terms offered.

Ryd's predecessor as Lord of the Five Valleys was willing, he said, to be lenient. Gerlach's men would surrender their weapons and their horses as well. Gerlach himself would remain a guest of the Valleys until a ransom of five hundred gold coins arrived.

When Gerlach protested at the amount, the Lord offered to increase it, though he was certain Gerlach had amassed little more than that sum. All knew that the man had maintained a guard of one hundred or more so he could continue to seize land from his neighbors. Without the gold, Lord Gerlach would have to reduce his force by more than half. It would be long before he could build up his small army again.

The Lord of the Five Valleys distributed Gerlach's horses to the Valley councils, who in turn passed them on where they would be most needed. This further enraged Gerlach, much to the Valley lord's delight.

Well, Ryd thought, if the presence of guardsmen and those of brother Rand's who'd stayed on weren't enough to reassure the villagers and farmers, completion of the Manor should. Most had already visited as construction continued. Many had worked on the building or the outbuildings. Ryd had instructed Fre Scrivener to write a proclamation that anyone working on the project for total of a month of days would have overdue taxes forgiven. Those who had lost their land to taxes would have that land returned if they worked a total of two months of days. That the days could be worked a few at a time had been the key, Ryd knew. That provision allowed farmers and their families to keep up their home duties.

He wished he could take credit for the idea, but it had been Lamar's, sometime in the second year after the two of them came to the Five Valleys. Ryd had been thinking out loud about the need to cut trees along the south edge of the East Road. He'd wanted to move the forest line out of bowshot so enemies could not fire at the Manor from the shelter of the forest edge. Having cover for hostiles so near had bothered the former mercenary captain since his first week as lord. How to go about getting trees cut was the major roadblock. His household and kitchen staff wouldn't be up to the work. His guardsmen were certainly fit enough, though they wouldn't like it much. The work would go slowly unless Ryd had them cease all training.

At that point, Lamar spoke up. He'd already noticed the drought in the Fifth Valley and to a lesser extent in the Fourth. Now he suggested that Ryd offer farmers whose crops had been affected the opportunity to cut trees in lieu of taxes. Not that Lamar put it that way. His version was "Farmers cut trees, split firewood. Not taxes. Drought worse."

For a moment Ryd gazed open-mouthed at this squat man who'd become his greatest confidant and, he'd realized some time ago, his best friend. Then, laughing with pleasure, he agreed. The next morning he sent out a proclamation and put the guard to work sharpening axes and two-man logging saws.

Farmers who'd been squeezed by the drought jumped at the opportunity. Most brought their own tools, trusting their own sharpening over that of guardsmen who were more used to sharpening swords and arrowheads. At least, so they said, though they'd known those Valley-born guardsmen most of their lives. Members of Ryd's guard took to showing up during their off-duty hours to load split wood into the wagons Ryd provided, then drive the wagons up to the Manor's woodsheds and unload them. These woodcutters were their fellow Valley residents, often their friends and neighbors. Guardsmen with any sense knew they'd hear of it for years if they sat back and watched their neighbors work. Ryd quickly realized that wood-hauling and stacking must become part of the guards' duties. He altered the guards' daily schedules accordingly.

The amount of land cleared was more than Ryd had hoped for. The quantity of firewood gathered was such that Ryd put up three years' worth for the Manor, then called on those farmers who were also skilled carpenters—most Valley families possessed more than one skill—to build additional woodsheds. He spread the word that those woodsheds were reserved for any in the Valleys who might find themselves short of firewood in a severe winter.

Thinking back, Ryd realized that the wood-gathering project had been an important part of earning acceptance for "this new lord" throughout the valleys. It might even have been more important than his decision that same year to cut down on his drinking and begin training with the guard.

On this day, Ryd planned to walk through the Manor's first floor, which Tad Stonemason said was ready for occupation. He'd stayed away after his first visits, which had been sufficient to assure him that these workers from the Holdings indeed knew what they were about. Workmen and -women tended to stop what they were doing when he came around, as though he were expected not just to look things over but to inspect and approve. That slowed both their and his day's work.

Ryd had just rounded the Manor's eastern front corner, taking the turn widely so as to stay in the sun a little longer, when he became aware of someone calling him. When he turned, he saw a villainous-looking fellow dressed in thieves' black, holding out a letter. Automatically Ryd dropped his right hand to the dagger on his right hip.

The fellow spoke. "I bring a message, my lord, from my master."

Ryd reached out with his left hand and took the letter, looking the fellow over carefully as he did so. As the man's outer garment opened at the neck for a moment, Ryd took particular note of the hilt of some sort of blade. That hilt and a long, narrow scabbard probably meant a stiletto—long, slender, no doubt razor-sharp on both edges. Perhaps not a thief but an assassin.

Once Ryd took the letter, Snake took two steps back. He knew this lord hadn't missed the blade hanging beneath his overshirt. Best to give such a man all the space he might want—not out of fear of Ryd's dagger or even his short sword, but out of courtesy. Well, and to take into consideration the possibility that this lord might be able to use sword or dagger. He looked more like a warrior than a lord, after all.

Ryd's nod suggested that he understood and appreciated the courtesy. Then, curious as to what letter would be coming to him from further east, he broke the seal and read the few words within, looking most carefully at the dogs-paw signature.

When Ryd looked up, inquiringly, Snake answered the question he was certain the Lord wanted to ask. "My lord, I was given the message by my master and told to deliver it to you here."

Ryd was silent for a moment. "By your master? Does he still travel with a group of wizards?" Ryd asked that question rather than the one he'd have preferred: when did Dog decide to become anyone's master? And how?

Snake smiled, trying for a pleasanter effect than that created by his usual smile. "He has left them, my lord. I am to rejoin him."

"Do you know the contents of the message?" Ryd was still trying to decide how far to trust this fellow.

"I wrote the words he spoke, my lord, then he placed his signature upon the sheet and had me seal it." Seeing Ryd's continued uncertainty, he added, "I wrote a similar message at his direction some time ago. It was signed and addressed as is this."

Ryd looked again at the message. The language was certainly Dog's. He would ask one more question. "In what direction does he travel, if he's left the wizards?"

"He travels west, my lord. How far I do not know, other than where I am to meet him. I fear he did not give me any further message."

"No," Ryd said, half to himself. "He would not." He took a deeper breath, squared his shoulders. "I thank you." He began to fumble for the small purse he carried for such situations, but the fellow held up a restraining hand.

"It is not necessary, my lord," Snake surprised himself by saying. He could not remember a time he'd passed up an offered coin. Puzzled, he shook his head, then surprised himself again. "One thing, my lord," he said.

"Yes?" Ryd was clearly impatient to get moving.

"A number of dark wizards and their guards may also be moving west, though I am not certain whether they will take the East Road. When I left, they had not yet ordered their guards to pack up camp. Still, they may pass here today."

These words had Ryd's full attention. He had noted the half-dozen or so wizards and their retinue as they'd passed some weeks earlier. And, he recalled, Tavnor Sergeant had spoken of a smaller group who had arrived not long after the Keep fell. Among them had been a wizard with no right hand, surely Rath, recovered from his injuries. That group had walked north and not returned. Had Rath's group met up with these others?

"That is good to know," Ryd said. "I thank you for the information. I would rather travel ahead of these wizards than have to pass them from behind." Here he smiled and was surprised to see the messenger return his smile.

Snake, caught off guard by both Ryd's smile and his own, bowed just a little, turned and walked west toward the Inn. Perhaps he'd stop for breakfast and a cup or two of wine. Dog—or Lamar; he wasn't yet used to knowing the being's actual name—had freed him, so there was no reason he couldn't pause on the way. Until this moment, he hadn't thought even once of not rejoining that strange being as soon as possible.

That was interesting. Following Lamar, there would be little chance to add to the store of coins and jewels held for him by a reasonably trustworthy landlord back in the Capitol. Somehow that didn't outweigh his interest in what might take place next. He'd already experienced events he'd never have imagined possible. And as for Dog—as for Lamar himself and his access to the Barren Lands and the Red Forest, well, it remained to be seen what other inaccessible places Lamar might yet lead him. When he became too old to keep up, Snake thought, would be time enough to return to the Capitol, live off his takings, and develop a reputation as a great liar by recounting his adventures over ale in his favorite inn.

First he'd have to live long enough to grow old, however. Pausing at the inn might delay him long enough for Rath and his wizards to catch up. Snake didn't want to take time to develop an explanation for his absence from camp. He would skip the inn and head north through the village toward the Red Forest.

A bit of caution on that road wouldn't hurt. If some of Rath's wizards followed the child toward the forest, they'd have to travel along the edge, as they had before. Eventually that would take them to where the road north met the forest, and he wouldn't want to encounter them there any more than here on the East Road. Though it would be easier to come up with a tale to account for his presence there than at the inn.

Both Rath and Tarh had been exhausted, and he suspected the others would be no better. They'd get a slow start today and would travel slowly in whatever direction Rath chose.

***

For a few moments Ryd watched the fellow walk off. If the man wasn't an assassin, then Ryd had never seen one. But Dog had taken him in as a follower. That was a story Ryd looked forward to hearing.

Dog's message had been urgent, and Ryd had long since learned to trust Dog's judgment. Plus there was the matter that a gaggle of dark wizards might be coming along the road. He turned, walked to the Manor's twin oak doors, and entered to find Tad Stonemason and Lars Carpenter awaiting him.

"My friends," Ryd said, once greetings had been exchanged, "I've just received word of troubles in the Five Valleys. I must deal with it.

Of necessity, this must be a shorter visit than I would like. I will stay longer when I return."

That they were disappointed was obvious. Craftsmen were always eager to show off their work. As he walked through the Manor's first floor, Ryd's smile grew broad. The Manor was already defensible in case of attack: four strong walls, stout oak in the front doors and again in the smaller rear door leading out from the kitchen. On the second story, joists now supported floors. The flat roof above was also in place, but not yet so complete that bowmen could fire on an enemy from behind ramparts.

The eight guardsmen he could leave behind would be able to do no more than keep the Manor itself secure. The building would hold guards and staff during a siege, and the kitchens were sufficient to support a larger force. He hoped any ambitious southern lords would assume he'd departed to bring back more of those trained Valley farmers.

Ryd intended to return soon and begin training new guardsmen. He had already decided he would keep at least thirty, building up to that number and relying on the eight who'd remained to serve as the core.

He realized that he'd been standing again in the front hall, the inspection over, thinking while the two craftsmen waited for his response. Ryd knew his pleased smile had not been missed by either, but words were also necessary. "My friends," he said, "you have proceeded exactly as I wished, You could have met my wishes no better had I watched over every day's work. I am grateful."

He hushed their expressions of gratitude for his praise. "Now I must have a meeting of senior staff, and then I'm off to the Valleys. I wish both of you to attend. We'll meet in the outdoor dining area. Please notify Cook and join us there." With that, Ryd returned through the kitchen and out the smaller rear door, where he called for Vernel Steward, Fre Scribe, and Tavnor Sergeant.

Once all had assembled, Ryd quickly explained that he and the Valley guardsmen must deal with a situation in the Five Valleys. In his absence, Tavnor Sergeant would lead the Guard and take charge in case of an attack, whether on the Manor itself or on outlying farms. Vernel Steward would supervise Manor staff. He would also be in charge of the outbuildings, fields, and other properties. Tad Stonemason would direct construction within the Manor, but Ryd would expect him to confer with Vernel, Cook, and Tavnor as well as Lars Carpenter. Cook, he said, should begin using the new kitchen.

As for himself, Ryd would leave within the hour. He instructed Tavnor Sergeant to inform the guardsmen. Those from the Valleys were to prepare themselves and their horses. He would meet them at the stables.

There was one other thing: he'd received word that a group of wizards and their guards might be moving west along the Road. It would be best to set a watch further east. If wizards approached, Ryd wished the Manor to be closed up tight. All including the guard were to keep indoors.

He dismissed the group. For a moment Ryd stood in the shade of the canopy which covered the outdoor dining area, looking around the grounds and outbuildings. The guardsmen's quarters showed the work Lars Carpenter's men had done: new roofs there as well as on the other outbuildings promised dry winters. All had fresh coats of whitewash, hiding new boards used in long-overdue repairs. The interior repairs still showed, he knew; fresh whitewash there could wait.

To the south, stables, granaries, and other outbuildings showed similar improvements. In a siege, those buildings might well be burnt to the ground, but Ryd didn't expect a siege any time soon. If the reputation of the men of the Valleys didn't give southern lords pause, tales of wizards being attacked and a wizard's tower destroyed in a night should.

With that, Ryd strode to his own quarters where he quickly packed his few travelling belongings. He wore his short sword and long knife. As he rode, he'd carry his quiver and bow on his back.

As Ryd left his quarters, he noticed several of his guardsmen gathered around an outdoor dining table. When he approached, he saw Cook stowing cold meat, cheese, bread and apples in one saddlebag after another, tying a pair of leather bottles on each.

"Well done, Cook," Ryd cried. "Good thinking! And if there's wine in one of those bottles, even better."

Cook spared only a glance and a quick "Thank you, my lord" before turning again to his work. After a moment, he passed Ryd a full saddle bag with its two bottles.

This time Ryd held out a hand and paused the man for one more word. "That you do this yourself, rather than sending out your helpers, means much, my friend. You have my thanks."

For a moment Cook stood with his mouth open. Clearly the fellow had gathered little praise from Rand. Then he bent his head in acknowledgement and went back to handing out saddle bags.

Guardsmen who'd already received supplies were walking toward the stable. Ryd followed. Several horses had already been saddled, including, as it turned out, his. Tavnor Sergeant was just leading the animal out as Ryd approached. Ryd noticed that several of the guardsmen who'd be remaining with the Manor were also nearby.

With a slight bow, Tavnor handed the reins to Ryd. "I thought you might be held up by arrangements, Captain," he said, "so I took the liberty of saddling for you." He glanced over his shoulder at the other men a short distance away. "These men wished to say farewell to the men from the Valleys."

Ryd took this as yet one more good sign. This young sergeant was clearly a leader. He'd made the Valley and Holdings guardsmen into a single unit of the sort whose members would wish a good journey and a safe return when the two groups split up. Of course, Ryd thought, noting that Scar was one of those waiting to bid them all farewell, having the support of the old mercenary hadn't hurt, either. But Tavnor would have had to earn Scar's respect well before Ryd and the Valley men arrived.

After handshakes all around, Ryd gave the order to mount, then led the Valley men onto the East Road at a trot. Once past the inn, he would let the horses run for a bit. After some months of little action, both horses and men would be eager to move. Whatever was amiss in the Valleys, if it were important enough to Dog to call him back, then it was important enough for Ryd to ride swiftly. He would waste no time on the journey.

***

Bird walked to the far end of what had been Owen's camp and looked out at the easternmost tip of the Red Forest from which they'd fled some months earlier. "Lamar said the safest way would be through the Red Forest. So let's start."

"All right," Aren said. "Sergeant, you and your men will serve as our advance guard. Druids, spread out to both sides and the rear." He turned to Bird, found her smiling, sensed her comfort in having her big brother organize things. If only he could also protect her as easily from what lay ahead. Even Magda, who was keeping close to Bird, nodded in approval.

Pursuit should not catch up before they reached the forest, which even at walking speed was no more than two hours away. Glancing behind, he saw that Hobard led a group which marched off to the left, from which Rath and most of his wizards would come. Inek and the others kept an eye to the right, where a single wizard and his guards might approach.

They were perhaps half-way to the red woods when Bird said, "Oh, someone's coming," and began a little dance. A moment later, Hobard spoke up. "Someone indeed is coming from the south. And quickly."

A few moments later, the Sergeant announced, "We may have trouble. There's just one person, but I fear it's that Snake." A moment later he said, "It's that fellow Dog. That's just as bad; he's Snake's minion. Rath may be closer than we thought. Captain, would you like us to take him?"

"His name is Lamar!" Bird stopped her dance long enough to stamp a foot. "And he's a friend!"

Startled, all three guardsmen stared at the child, then looked to Aren for direction.

Smiling, Aren reassured them. "He's a friend, all right. Where Bird and her mother can hear, his name is Lamar. Let's keep moving. He'll catch us soon enough and if not, we can wait for him once we reach the trees."

Inek chuckled at the thought of Lamar not reaching them before they entered the forest, but chiefly he felt relief. With Lamar, Hobard and Bird as his leaders, he could cease to worry about whether the Forest would accept a stained Druid.

Inek hoped that if any of his error had not yet been cleansed by the Little Mother, the Forest would heal whatever remained. It might have done so even after he and the others began teaching power to humans and his robe began to darken, but he had not dared attempt to enter in those years.

As Lamar came near, Bird darted to meet him, leaping up to throw her arms around his neck.

"Ho!" The gnarled man pretended to stumble backwards as he lifted Bird over his head. He set her down and, her hand in his, came forward to a song of greeting from the Druids. "Started already! Good. Wizards shaken, but follow." He looked up at Aren for a moment, then nodded. "Recruits, too. May be needed."

Ahead, the three guardsmen walked backwards, staring.

"All right," Aren called, "let's get going again. We can sort things out once we're safely in the forest." With that, all three guardsmen turned their faces forward and set off at a brisk pace.

***

Rath was irritated that Snake had not caught up by the time he and Tarh, with their guard escorts, reached Owen's camp. He'd counted on the assassin's tracking skills. Now he would have to make do with those of his guardsmen.

The wizard halted his group some dozen feet away from the empty site. Turning to the guards grouped just behind him, he asked which was the best tracker. That led to some hemming and hawing as the guardsmen looked at one another, each obviously reluctant to volunteer for anything which might bring a wizard's attention. Clearly, something had gone wrong. Any information a tracker might bring to Rath was likely to be displeasing. A guardsman could find himself writhing in pain for long moments before death finally rescued him.

Finally one stepped forward. "I can track a little, Master," he said, "but I wouldn't claim to be in mister Snake's class."

"Do what you can, then," Rath growled, "and don't waste any more time. Start from the trail leading out of the woods and work your way to the camp. I want to know how many entered, how many left, and where they went. I'll stay behind you." At his gesture toward the path coming out of the woods, the guardsman walked not to the path, but into the thin brush and trees which bordered it. Rath followed.

They went a dozen feet into the woods before the guard approached the path. Here he looked carefully at the ground before speaking. "Several came out of the woods, Master. I would say one normal-sized man and several unusually tall, perhaps eight or more. Their tracks indicate the length of their strides. And one child, or a very small person, I would say. But here's something puzzling: there seem to be marks of two going back into the woods, probably one very tall and one more ordinary in size. That one's tracks aren't as far apart as those of the tall ones, but farther apart than those of the child."

Rath didn't respond to that news, though he was puzzled at the idea that someone other than those who came out of the woods might have gone back in. "Acceptable," he said. "Continue on to the campsite."

There the ground showed scuff marks rather than footprints. Because the smaller ones were often partially obliterated by the others, the guard was able to say that the child had led the way. The man seemed to walk close behind and the others followed.

The child had walked up to one person and stood there for a time. While that took place, marks showed that three others stood some distance away but didn't approach. He guessed that those were part of the guard. The wizard was probably the one who walked into the woods.

That last puzzled Rath. What could the witch-child have done to Owen?

Otherwise, the guardsman said, the marks were pretty confusing. Eventually the child and her followers left the camp, heading west. Three guardsmen accompanied them.

"Are you certain the guardsmen accompanied the others? They didn't trail them?" Rath was puzzled at that. He knew that the Order couldn't count on loyalty from guardsmen, but that three would accompany the witch-child surprised him. On the other hand, perhaps fear compelled them. Otherwise Rath would have expected guardsmen to desert, perhaps to head north into the mountains and seek service as mercenaries.

The guard's answer was hesitant. "I think not, Master." At the look on Rath's face, he quickly added, "But it is difficult to tell." For a moment he stood motionless before continuing, pointing to the various tracks as he spoke. "It appears that the guardsmen were serving as lead escorts. See how their tracks are often partially covered by others? The tall beings walked to the sides and behind. The man who had accompanied her out of the woods kept beside her." He stared at the marks, thinking. "It looks as though the child and the man with her were being escorted or protected by the others, as though they were either lords or captives."

"They were not captives," Rath grumbled. "Take two men and follow the trail. I wish to know whether they continue in the same direction or turn at some point. After two miles, send one back to report; after four, you may return yourself."

With that, he turned back toward where Tarh and the remaining guardsmen waited. Roke, he saw, had also joined them. Rath gestured to the two wizards to join him on the campsite's edge. With three casting a Seek spell, any sign of magic would show, even were it only the use of a crystal.

The spell revealed that a crystal had been used. Rath led the other two around the edge of the site to where he thought Owen had stood. The crystal had been activated some feet away.

Something had happened where that crystal had been used, some sort of transformation. Whatever—or whoever--had been transformed had not walked, but crawled into the woods as might a snake, if a snake could move in a straight line.

This must be where the witch-child had used Owen's crystal to summon Soren. Rath motioned the other two to keep behind him and followed whatever had been Soren into the edge of the woods, where the trail entered the shadows and disappeared.

Rath said nothing. Neither Tarh nor Roke asked as he led them past the campsite. When he finally spoke, his voice was somber. "Tell the guards that we'll await the others here. When they arrive, we will speak of what may have happened, and of what we do now. Until then, I must think. Tell the guards to set up stools for us. After that they may do as they wish so long as they do not wander off."

He needed to gather his thoughts before using his crystal to contact Haster and, he hoped, Oleg. Whether it would be useful to follow the witch-child to the Red Forest, he doubted. By now, surely she would have entered the forest where its farthest eastern edge leaned out. Should she remain there for any time, he and his group might travel directly to the Fifth Valley and reach it before she arrived. If so they might fully remove the ward and even set up an ambush.

If, on the other hand, she intended to remain permanently in the Red Forest, at least they would have removed the ward and reasserted their dominance over the Valleys. After spending these last months following the witch and waiting for her next move, it would feel good to take the initiative. Their effort to disperse the mist over the Barren Lands had failed badly, but lesser wizards had had some success with the ward over the Fifth Valley. Surely something could be built upon that.

Haster, Rath knew, would avoid making any decision. No doubt he would go along with whatever was suggested. But Oleg's counsel would be useful, as to a lesser extent would Ren's when he and the other wizards arrived. Until then, there was little to do but once again wait.

***

Oleg had remained in what had been Soren's observatory. Now, he supposed, the room would be called the Chief Mage's observatory during the period before a new leader could be selected. If, indeed, there would be another Chief Mage, or a dark Order to select a chief.

Perhaps with Soren gone, they could rethink their dealings with this witch-child. It might be too late to simply leave her and hers alone, and Oleg doubted she would welcome a dark wizard carrying a flag of truce. She'd been taken captive at the request of the Order, her servants had been fired upon by the Order's bowmen, and one of her party had suffered a mind-blast from Lorit. That Lorit had immediately been erased from the earth would probably not have lightened the witch-child's mood.

On the other hand, she'd destroyed Rath's tower and a lord's keep, taken Rath's right hand and a lord's life. Some ally of hers had eliminated Lorit. Oleg hesitated to add to the list the fate of Soren, the Order's most powerful adept, though a shrewd diplomat would include his disappearance in an effort to convince the child that losses were even.

Somehow Oleg suspected that the child would not accept any such balancing. There was something here which operated on a level other than mere power. Mere power! A year ago he'd have scoffed at the phrase, as would any dark wizard. And still he had trouble imagining what force would reduce power to mere.

Haster sat in his usual chair, avoiding that which had been Soren's. No doubt, Oleg thought, Haster would continue to work out of his subordinate office one floor below. He was unlikely to seek the role of Chief Mage while Rath lived, and equally unlikely to hold the office long should he achieve it. Haster had served Soren too long not to realize that.

Oleg had taken a lesser chair a safe distance from the great crystal. When Rath contacted them with further word, he would allow Haster to approach the crystal first, just in case.

It was some time before the crystal came to life. Haster approached cautiously, peered from a slight distance, then straightened and walked briskly forward. "What news, Rath?" he asked. Oleg joined him, nodded to Rath's image glowering up at them.

"The crystal was Owen's. It appears he encountered the witch-child, and after walked into the woods toward the mist. The child is accompanied by several new followers. Their tracks suggest great height. The guardsman is also with her. Apparently he's recovered from his wound. All are on foot."

He paused. Neither Haster nor Oleg interrupted as they watched his face struggle to compose itself. "We cast a search spell and found strong evidence of power. There were definite signs of a crystal's use and of a transformation into something which then moved along the ground and into the trees. It may have been Soren." His glare challenged them to question. When they did not, he continued. "The child has travelled onward, heading toward the Red Forest. I have sent guardsmen, one of whom can track a little, to follow. I wait now for Ren and the others to join us."

Haster leaned against the wooden frame which held the crystal, his head hanging. Oleg felt little better, though he had expected no good news. Still, someone needed to do some planning, and planning wasn't Haster's strength.

"Will you follow the child to the Red Forest?" Oleg asked. At the question, Haster raised his head, began to pull himself together.

Rath's smile was grim. "I see little benefit in my entire force following the child and her escort to the edge of that forest. If we could have no effect on the mists over the barrens, I doubt we could against those trees. More likely we would arouse whatever Power lashed out at Lorit after he struck down the red-garbed woman." When no objection came, he went on. "Roke and Tarh have more experience of that forest and the witch-child than does anyone else here. I propose to have them follow, keeping at a distance, in order to report should she leave the forest."

Again he heard no objection from Haster or, more importantly, from Oleg. "I suspect it is no coincidence that the child left the protection of the mists shortly after our brothers achieved some success against the ward over the Fifth Valley. If she intends to return, we may be able to arrive first. Surely we can travel more rapidly along the East Road than she can through a forest."

"I see what you mean," Haster said. "Your group's strength added to that already assembling might well disperse that ward before she arrives. Certainly wizards living closer to the Valleys should arrive well before she does."

Oleg kept silent. With Soren added to their losses, this was no time to suggest negotiating with the child. Rath's suggestion might work. A larger group could end the ward over the valley and trap the child there. But suppose those travelling with her were Druids. The child might well be mortal, but could even the full force of the Order overcome Druids? The Dark One's predictions were beginning to look a little optimistic.

"I will begin those contacts immediately," Haster said, glad to have a course of action. "Let me know when you're certain that the child has entered the forest. Should she head south and travel on the East Road, we'll want to warn those of our Order who may take that same path." With that he gave his imitation of Soren's gesture of dismissal. The great crystal darkened.

Oleg stood musing. Rath had said nothing about Snake, the Order's best tracker. With Soren gone, would the assassin have wandered off? That would not be a good sign. Though the loss of one assassin, however accomplished, would do little to weaken the Order, word of such a desertion might lead to others.

***

Lamar walked on Bird's left while Aren kept to her right, where it would be easier to wield his sword. After a time, Aren realized that he walked faster than usual. In fact, the entire group walked at a pace which was nearer the speed of running than normal walking. Almost he suggested they save their strength, then realized that he breathed normally, as did Bird. Glancing over at Lamar, Aren realized that the squat man also breathed as though on a peaceful stroll. A look behind confirmed that the Druids were equally comfortable. The three guardsmen spread out ahead also showed no signs of stress. Had Bird learned this from the Druids, or perhaps from Lamar? He doubted it; she'd chattered each night about the day's learning, and some kind of speed-walking had not been among her talks.

Aren glanced over at Lamar, wondering. They'd picked up the pace after Lamar joined them. Was this his doing?

Lamar caught the glance and smiled. "Arrive soon."

The forest edge had been visible since they'd left that fellow Owen's camp, and now the trees were just ahead. The guardsmen came to a stop. Clearly they were uneasy about entering the forest. Aren called to them to wait, at which all three looked relieved.

"Good," Lamar said. "Bird, Lamar, Aren first, guards follow, then Druids. Forest not know guardsmen. Know Lamar. Never forget little bird or brother." He grinned at Magda. "Probably let little sister in."

Magda settled for a snort as her only reply. She was, Aren noted, standing almost as tall as she had when Bird ordered her to stand straight, but with no hint of pain. Would the forest heal her, as Inek claimed it healed Druids? What sort of being was Magda, if what healed Druids also healed her?

Hobard and Inek joined the group. "I doubt the forest will have forgotten me," Hobard said. "Who knows how long I lived within it, part of the trees, the ground, the stones beneath?" She reached out, grasped Inek's shoulder. "Nor will it fail to recognize a Druid who might be in need of healing."

Aren realized that Bird wasn't paying attention to their talk. "What is it, little one?" he asked.

Bird hesitated before she replied. "Two dark wizards follow us. Others are further away, somewhere south. I can't tell how many; more than four, I think."

"Ah," Aren said. "They send two to track us, perhaps report when we leave the forest. If wizards are trying to cause trouble in the Valleys, perhaps the others intend to join them."

"Probably," Lamar said. "Rath not eager visit Forest." His chuckle rumbled. The ground beneath their feet seemed to rumble in response. Aren, startled, braced himself. Bird, on the other hand, simply smiled.

The guardsmen listened with their eyes wide, their mouths open, their feet braced. That the child could track wizards at a distance somehow didn't surprise them, after what they'd seen. But talk of Druids startled them almost as much as did their realization that Master Dog might be someone of importance, even of power. Each quickly thought back over everything he'd said to this Lamar, hoping he'd done nothing to offend.

Lamar laughed as he walked past the three, Bird and Aren following. "No worry," he said, clapping the sergeant on the shoulder as he passed. "Swords in sheath. Forest think axe."

"Thank you, sir," replied the sergeant, hoping that would show sufficient respect. That assassin Snake had tended to use Master Dog as a term of scorn. How had he gotten away with that? If the fellow showed up again, it might be interesting to see Lamar school him. Now that would be enjoyable.

As the group entered the forest, even the guardsmen realized that the place seemed hushed as though waiting. To their surprise, none felt fear, or even the uneasiness they'd felt on approaching. Two of the guardsmen felt only relief. The sergeant thought more deeply, suspecting that to the forest three guards mattered little in the presence of their Captain, the witch-child, and what certainly appeared to be, if his grandmother's tales could be believed, a group of Druids. But was the child a witch or some other kind of being? He'd seen her use power, but she hadn't destroyed the wizard Owen, as a dark wizard would have done. On the other hand, there was Lorit…

Bird took the lead as both Lamar and Aren dropped back a step. A short distance into the forest she stopped, held up a hand. She stood perfectly still, as though she were listening to something Aren could not hear.

She turned a delighted smile to Lamar. "These trees are so old! And their memories! Before, I didn't know how to hear them. Can we stay for a while?"

Lamar said, "Short time. Valleys waiting."

Sobered, Bird nodded. "There's something the forest wants. Something to do with Brenna, I think." She turned to Aren. "Remember when I said she was some kind of wizard, but she didn't know what kind? Well, I was wrong. She wasn't a wizard. Or at least she isn't now."

She was already walking further into the forest, the others moving with her. "We'd better find her. Lamar, do you know where to look?"

"Earth-walker knows. This way."

***

Oleg stepped from the stairs into the dungeon, its darkness mitigated only a little by the lantern he carried. He stopped, listening: was the Dark One humming, or chanting in a low voice? Neither had been the being's habit in all the long years it had been imprisoned. Oleg was certain that somewhere in the records such an event would have been mentioned. Had the thing begun to regain its powers and now attempted to break the spells which held it? Perhaps it was time to increase the foxglove in the being's daily ration of food and drink. After all this time the Dark One might have begun to develop some immunity.

"Come forward, Loremaster. You aren't yet in danger here." The voice was that of the Dark One, certainly, but less guttural. "I find myself recalling certain old songs for which I've had no use and even less desire to hear again. None of them were sources for your spells, such as they are."

Such as they are, Oleg thought. Not strong enough to lessen whatever guarded the Barren Lands, but able to weaken the ward over the Fifth Valley. He'd feel more optimistic if he knew that Rath's group would arrive before the witch-child. If the three young wizards he'd sent to chant against the ward could have even the beginnings of success, then surely the addition of Rath, Ren and the others could accomplish more. Even then, would they be able to stand against the child?

Oleg realized that he hadn't yet responded to the voice from the darkness. "If this child is as powerful as you suggest, Dark One, might she negotiate from within that power? Might she prefer peace to constant struggle?"

Again that laughter which was worse than silence. "She prefers a green valley to one ridden by drought, Loremaster. That was peace, which your Order ended." What might have been a chuckle followed before the voice continued. "If she is who she must be, she may not be interested in your Order's continued existence."

"Perhaps not yours, either," Oleg said.

"Perhaps not," the voice conceded. "I think you said she had entered the Barren Lands some time ago, and now has emerged. Did you make no effort to penetrate the ward over that place, archivist? Surely you found something in your records which might eliminate the mist which shrouds those lands." The Dark One's voice fairly dripped with sarcasm.

That came a little too close for comfort. "It matters not," Oleg said. "She has now left those lands."

"Ah. So you tried something, but it had no effect." Then came a period of silence from within the cell. Oleg thought of leaving, but something about the silence suggested more to come.

"Did more beings come out than went in? Tall, dark-robed fellows? Or--" Here the being broke off suddenly. When it spoke again, the words came softly, as though spoken only to itself. "Or wearing robes of shining white…Have their years in those lands enabled them to cleanse themselves? Was that why we were sent there? Aiieeee!"

The cry went on and on while Oleg huddled against the wall, hands over his ears as he tried to shut out the despair in that sound. Only after the cry had reduced to a constant soft sobbing did the Loremaster rise shakily to his feet and slip away.

It was only when safely back in his office, the door to the stairs leading downwards firmly shut and fastened, that Oleg begin to think about that "we." Had the Dark One been among those living in the Barren Lands? Were the barrens a place of punishment for—for who? For Druids who had taught men the beginnings of magic?

If that were true, if those who lived within the mist of those lands were Druids, how had the child known to seek them? Had she sought teachers or followers? Or both? If she had emerged more powerful than when she entered, what might the Order do now? What could it do?

That question made trivial Oleg's wondering about the Dark One, yet that mystery also teased him. Some scrolls suggested that the Dark One had once been a Druid, but those scrolls described him as wearing a robe of deepest darkness. Yet if he had once lived in the Barren Lands, how had he come to be what now lived in the lowest depths beneath the Order's headquarters? If the witch-child brought from the Barren Lands a group of Druids in their shining robes, what hope might the Order have?

***

Ryd kept his riders at a trot until out of sight of the inn and the town. Then he slowed his horse to a walk and called to his men to spread out across the road. Once all were in place and walking their horses, he joined the line, calling out, "Now, my friends, it's time to find out who has the fastest steed. We'll race to the next turning, which as I recall is a mile or so ahead. First bring your mount to a trot. Stay in line, now! A copper coin to the winner, unless it's me! Ride!"

With that they were off, galloping wildly down the road. There had been no one ahead on the road, and he was glad of that. These fellows were unlikely to slow to pass an oncoming wagon.

Ryd's horse was among the leaders, but he wasn't at all sure who reached the curve first. To be certain, they all galloped well into the curve, then slowed to a walk to discuss who had actually won. There was some dispute about that, which was fine with the lord. He'd be happy to run several races as they travelled.

The dispute didn't last long. A consensus recognized a winner and close second, with Ryd coming in third. Ryd pretended disgust and promised another race later in the day. Both his pretended disgust and his promise were greeted with smiles. For a time he let the horses walk and cool down, then brought the troop again to a mile-consuming trot.

He kept them moving well into the night before calling a halt for a few hours of rest. The horses were relieved of their saddles and bridles, then set loose in hobbles to graze. Ryd set no guard; their horses would alert them to any intruders, and the morning sun would wake them soon enough.

Ryd placed his own bedroll where he was certain the sun would strike him when it rose, but found himself awake in the false dawn before sunrise. As he sat up, he saw that nearly half his men were already awake and about. He'd hoped to be first and able to tease these young men, but saw that he was about to come in for his share of kidding. "Good morning, Captain. I hope we didn't wake you," came first. "It's Hagen's fault. Even his tiptoeing shakes the ground."

Hagen was the largest of the group, a smiling giant who was apt, when tiring of kidding, to pick up his two greatest abusers, tuck one under each arm, and carry them to the top of the watchtower. There he'd dangle them for a time, one held by each large hand. Hagen rode what the others kidded was a plowhorse, half again larger than Ryd's own horse. It had finished fourth in their first race that day.

When Ryd first set eyes on the big man towering over his fellow recruits, he had sent his steward into the south country to look for a horse large, strong, and fast enough to serve as steed for a guardsman of Hagen's size. The gold had been well spent. This horse could carry its huge rider long after the other guardsmen's mounts had fallen far behind.

As with all his guardsmen, Ryd had crossed swords with the man more than once. Hagan wasn't graceful, but more than once during sword practice he'd strike his opponent's weapon hard enough to numb the man's arm. After having his own arm numbed, the lord had Swordmaster Talon demonstrate tactics for dealing with a much stronger opponent. Then Talon instructed Hagen in techniques for overcoming those who attempted to turn his strength against him. All of which greatly increased the quality of the swordplay as Ryd and his guardsmen drilled.

After a quick cold breakfast, Ryd again had his men on the move. This time he kept an eye out for the way known as the thieves' road. He'd already decided that he wouldn't come riding up to the Fifth Valley's entrance and into an ambush. Instead he would follow the thieves' road for a mile, then leave it and ride across the hills. Taking a less direct route with scouts going on before, he would know more about what lay ahead than had been conveyed by Dog's cryptic note.

CHAPTER SIXTEEN

For some hours Lamar led them into the forest, the others following in silence. Aren walked with a hand on Bird's shoulder. Though quiet, she kept gazing around and up into the huge trees, a rapt look on her face. The sergeant and his two guards walked in the midst of the group, carefully keeping their hands away from their swords.

Aren had only a dim sense of where they were going. When they'd come this way the previous fall, he'd thought only of escaping their pursuers, and hadn't thought at all after he'd been wounded. This time, the presence of Hobard and Inek and their fellows meant he alone was not responsible for Bird's safety. That Bird had learned far more about her powers also reassured him. While she clearly was capable of much more than when they'd left the Valleys, she'd also learned control and purpose. If the wizard she'd called through a crystal and then dispatched as a shadow had truly been the Order's Chief Mage, then Aren could hope she would be a match even for the several wizards now apparently walking toward the Valley.

When they'd first met Brenna on the road to the Red Forest some months earlier, Bird had said that the failed apprentice didn't know what she was. Aren suspected that Brenna had begun that discovery, but any beginning had been interrupted by wizards' attacks. He'd feared for a time that she lay dead at the forest's edge, until Lamar arrived and reassured Bird. That she'd been badly hurt continued to be worrisome.

"Aren," Bird said, reaching up and tugging his sleeve, "the trees seem to feel that I'm some kind of red oak, that they all came from me. Isn't that strange? They're like the stones underground; they don't use words, but I can feel what they feel. And they feel that the acorns from which their ancestors grew all fell from the tree they think I was. Isn't that odd?"

Indeed, Aren would have agreed, but just then they entered the clearing where they'd camped their first night in the forest. Lamar halted, turned to Bird and Aren.

"Stay here tonight. Guards set up camp. Time Bird call Brenna. Come." He led the way toward the large tree on the edge of the clearing.

Aren half-recognized that tree, but it had changed. When they'd visited before, the side facing them had been open. Within had been a sort of room, with a shelf which could serve as a bed. Now the trunk showed no sign of that opening. Aren knew that some trees could grow new bark to cover a small wound, but he'd never seen growth over an opening large enough for two men to walk through.

"Now," Lamar said, "Bird call Brenna. Tree healing, wish keep safe within. Brenna sleep; maybe sleep long time, maybe become like Druid, move from tree to tree. Not time yet. So Bird call Brenna, let tree know."

Bird slowly came forward. "Brenna is inside the tree?"

Hobard joined them. "She's probably not aware of us," she said. "When I was part of the trees, I perceived as they do. I knew of roots deep within the earth, of sun and wind in branches far above—no, not above, but in a different part of the tree. I felt everything at once. Only rarely was I aware of other beings within the forest, perhaps deer or birds."

Behind them, the three guards paused as they set up camp. Inek and his fellows stood off to one side, breathing deeply of the forest air, their faces rapt.

Bird looked up at Aren for a moment. He shrugged, gestured toward the tree. "This is beyond my knowledge, little bird. You must do as you think best. What you learned in the Barren Lands should help."

Bird nodded, took a deep breath, and took three steps to the tree. For a moment she paused; then she reached out both hands to the tree and leaned against it. Aren could see her shoulders and arms tense.

She stood that way for several minutes. The tree's bark began to shift. Bird stepped back and slowly an opening formed. When it had become larger, she could see again the room they'd seen before. On the bench opposite the opening lay a figure which might have been Brenna, but what flesh Bird could see appeared to be the same deep red as the bark which covered the tree itself.

"Brenna?" Bird said. "Are you all right?"

The figure slowly sat up. For a few minutes it looked around, seeming confused. Its gaze reached Bird, and the figure quickly stood, took an automatic step toward the girl. It stopped abruptly, looking down as though surprised to see legs and feet. The face was Brenna's, but the skin had the same color and texture as did bark on the red oaks of the forest.

Bird asked again. "Are you all right?"

The figure which appeared to be Brenna's looked at Bird then down again at its feet. "Where are my roots?" the figure asked. And then, urgently, "My roots! Where are my roots?" As she spoke, the tree shook slightly.

Bird stepped into the opening, stood close to the red woman. Even Aren could feel the calming influence Bird sent into both tree and woman. Behind Aren, Lamar chuckled, said softly, "Druids teach well." Inek had come closer and stood beside Hobard. The Druids exchanged pleased glances.

The tree ceased quivering. Brenna calmed, but continued to look at her feet, then her arms and hands as though expecting them to become roots, branches, leaves.

Bird kept her focus on Brenna's mind, calming her, reminding her of who she had been. As Bird's thoughts reached out, Brenna closed her eyes, breathing deeply as she calmed.

After a while, Brenna opened her eyes, smiled tentatively at Bird. "I remember now." She quieted again, seeming to work to find words. "I remember you. And dark wizards. I cast a spell." Again she seemed to be working to remember or to find words in which to express the memory. "That spell carried more power than I possessed, and then—" she broke off again. "And then I remember nothing. But I seem to know things I could not know." She was silent again for a moment. "What has happened?" She seemed to notice the red color of her hands and arms. "And how did I become like this? How did I come here? I thought I was dying."

Lamar stepped forward. "Wizard cast powerful spell. Earth-walker carry, place in tree for healing. Tree close self, protect."

Bird took Brenna's hand. "Come. Walk a little. Get the kinks out." This last was one of Reya's favorite sayings as she stretched after a long session at her loom.

Bird led the woman out of the hollowed tree, walked her around the campsite a few times. Occasionally they spoke in low tones, but more often they simply walked. Bird's face kept its expression of concentration. After a time, Bird brought Brenna back to the tree's opening and said, "You should rest now. You'll be safe."

Brenna nodded, walked through the opening, crossed to the bench and lay down. Immediately they heard the deep, steady breathing of sleep.

Bird had remained just outside the tree, watching and listening. She turned to the others, smiling. "I think she's coming back to herself." Then she frowned. "But she's part something else—not just this tree. I think maybe she's part forest. Is that possible?" She looked around at Lamar and the Druids. The Druids, in turn, looked to Lamar.

"Could be," he said, shrugging. "Forest heal her. Maybe do more. Maybe only way to heal human."

Hobard added, "Druids could be healed here because of our connection to oaks."

"And the oaks needed to create a similar connection to heal her?" Inek asked. "Could that be, Earth-Walker?"

Lamar raised both hands as though to fend off the question. "Old Earth-walker know about earth, know beneath earth. Know land. Ancient oak forest, not so much." He turned to Magda. "Know planting, harvesting. Know oaks?"

"Only a little," Magda admitted. "Oaks need little help to create acorns."

Lamar turned to Bird. "When you enter mind, what there?"

Bird said, "Lots, that's what." She thought, her face screwed up in concentration. "It was as though Brenna was hiding. First I had to calm the part which was tree. Or forest." She shook her head, puzzled. "Then I could reach Brenna. She was sleeping—not sleeping, either, but like sleeping." She looked up at Aren as though hoping he could put all this into words for her. Aren smiled but said nothing.

"And there's another part." She looked at Lamar. "It's kind of like the stones under the Barren Lands. They're all connected to each other." She searched for words. "Maybe Brenna is connected to the Forest. She has the same memories the trees do, I think, even the very old memories." She looked around at the others. "How can that be?"

"Memories can be passed down, little bird," Aren said. "You remember the stories Reya tells about things which must have happened long before she was born."

Bird nodded. "All right, then. I guess if I can hear what the stones remember, Brenna can hear what the trees remember."

"Could be," Lamar said.

"The forest is becoming angry again, I think." Bird paused, seemed to be listening. "Two wizards are approaching. They're still behind us, though."

Again she seemed to listen; then she turned to Lamar. "I think I need to listen to the forest, the way I listened to stone before."

Lamar nodded. "Good. Not need Lamar. Not need Druids. Grown past teachers. Go."

With that, Bird walked further into the forest. Aren made a move as though to follow her, but Lamar reached out a restraining hand. "Forest protect. "He smiled. "Maybe she protect forest." He stretched, a strange sight in one almost as wide as tall. "Now think food. Bird come back when ready. We stay night, maybe two, let Druids finish healing."

The two guardsmen glanced at their sergeant, their faces pale. The sergeant spoke softly, hoping not to be overheard. "Would you rather serve this group, or go back to the wizards and report? We're apt to be terrified either way, but I'll stay with these folk. Just remember to keep your swords sheathed unless the Captain tells you to draw."

The stocky guardsman spoke up. "The girl said we could leave if we wished."

"That's true," said the tall one. "I think I'll stay, see how this comes out. If the girl can turn old Soren into a shadow, there might come a time when a guardsman can choose which lord to serve without worrying about wizards."

"Could be, I guess," said the stocky one, grudgingly.

The sergeant broke in. "At any rate, let's get these tents up, then see if a fire is allowed. It's only a little past mid-day, so a cold lunch will serve now. Come evening, something hot would be nice." With that, he focused on the tent he was erecting. By the time Lamar spoke of food, they'd gone through their packs and brought out enough for a cold meal for all.

As Lamar and Aren led the way to the ring of stones which clearly had held fires in the past, the sergeant asked whether a fire was allowed. "If so, Captain, might we gather fallen wood from the ground? If showing our blades is dangerous here, we would not offend."

Aren recalled, dimly, that they'd had a fire after he'd been wounded, but couldn't remember clearly just how that had happened. "Perhaps we should wait until the lady awakens again and ask her."

The guardsmen took their food a little distance off as they'd been used to doing when in the service of the Order. They also took care to sit close enough to hear anything which might be said, something the Order would not have tolerated. They heard little.

When all had finished the meal, everyone but the guards grew restless. Inek became concerned about the two wizards Bird had felt following them. He would travel their back trail and see. Osa offered to accompany him; surely two Druids could deal with two wizards. At that Lamar burst out laughing but would say only, "Two Druids plenty."

The two walked into the woods, following their back trail. The remaining Druids scattered into the forest. Aren and Lamar remained in camp, in case Brenna awakened. Aren wanted to be present when Bird returned; he didn't entirely share Lamar's certainty that the Forest would protect her. Chiefly he worried that she might lose her way.

Lamar seemed to read his mind. "Not worry. Not lose way in forest. Wish to return, forest know way. Bird come back when ready. Old forest, much to tell. Bird maybe stay out all night. Be fine."

"What if more wizards come from the other direction?" Aren asked. "Or send guardsmen? They can enter, even if wizards cannot."

Lamar shook his head. "Forest aware. First time many years. Not let wizard's guardsmen enter again." He thought for a while. "Nothing in forest hurt little bird. Forest like stone: contentment very deep." He laughed. "Druids dance and sing. Stone and forest feel content. Deeper, stronger. Good feeling." With that, Lamar stretched out on the ground and fell asleep, leaving Aren to practice patience.

***

Rath and Ren both cast endurance spells to keep their group moving more quickly and longer than normal. If they could reach the valley before the witch-child, Rath would prepare a welcome she'd not expect. By then Oleg should have discovered more useful material in the archives. With the addition of the more powerful wizards in Rath's group, Rath hoped to disperse the ward entirely.

If not, they could use guardsmen to lay a trap. Their first attempt, when the child last entered the Red Forest, had had some effect: the man who escorted her had been wounded, her horse killed. The Order's bowmen had been allowed only one shot each, and guardsmen might again get only one shot once the witch-child reached the valley. That argued for gathering as many bowmen as possible to take that shot simultaneously.

The thought of relying on bowmen rather than dark power irritated Rath.

He hoped Snake would catch up soon. The assassin had proven to be an excellent scout. And Snake's odd minion, while a bit lacking in respect for his masters, was, Snake claimed, an excellent tracker. Snake knew a little about ambushes, unless his reputation was badly overblown. It might have been better to have delayed their departure until the two arrived; travelling at normal speed, they'd no doubt fall far behind.

***

After Ryd's departure with his Valley guardsmen, Tavnor and Scar called the remaining guards to gather in the outdoor eating area. Vernel would alert the Manor staff, and Tad Stonemason would do the same for the building crew. Farmers who'd come to work in lieu of taxes were already setting out for their homes. Good; the fewer to keep watch over, the better.

Tavnor set a schedule for watchers along the road leading east. Scar would supervise. Tavnor would speak with Cook and Vernel Steward about provisions in case of an attempt to attack the Manor.

At that, Scar smiled. "An attack would be interesting, indeed. Captain Ryd has a good sense of tactics, I know from service with him up north. Whoever designed this place had a fine sense of how to withstand a siege. The Captain says it's based on the Manor of the Five Valleys, which has a formidable reputation. I see why: from within the Manor, even now when the upper floor is unfinished, we could hold off ten times our number so long as the food and arrows hold out. It would be a delightful fight!"

"So long as wizards didn't get involved," Tavnor noted. "I doubt they could attack the building itself, but their spells have a bad name for their effect on men."

"True enough," Scar agreed. "Alas, our best tactic is to get inside quickly when they approach, then pretend not to be home, though there's little fun in that."

For the rest of that day, they continued to prepare. Cook and his helpers moved provisions into the Manor, while Tavnor supervised the making of arrows, Tad Stonemason and his crew double-checked the doors and window slits on the first floor, shuttering the windows higher up on that floor. In mid-afternoon they were interrupted when the lookout from further east arrived to report four wizards and perhaps two dozen guardsmen moving very quickly along the road. He was glad to be on horseback; they'd have caught him had he been on foot.

Within minutes everyone had moved into the Manor. They securely locked and barred the doors. Guardsmen peered through window slits on all four sides. Tavnor and Scar mounted a ladder to reach a parapet from which they could look out an upper window facing the road.

The wizards' group were already about to pass the Manor. Two turned to look at the building, seemed to be discussing something.

"Perhaps whether to order us to send guardsmen to join them," Tavnor muttered.

"Fat chance of that," Scar responded. "But I'd as soon they not try."

The wizard who seemed to be the leader, a fellow with only one hand, shook his head and the group passed by.

Tavnor and Scar watched until the group shrunk into distance. "No chance to try your bow this time," Tavnor said.

"I'm not disappointed," Scar answered. "Though if there's a fight coming, I would like to get in on it. Still, if the Captain expects us to guard the place, we'd better do it. Might get a little action yet. Those guards may come back this way after they've taken a beating. They're apt to raid the countryside as they retreat. Once we're sure all these guardsmen and wizards have passed, we might want to send scouts toward the valleys as well."

"A good idea," Tavnor said. "Are you sure the Captain will win this fight? The odds seem long, and apt to get longer."

Scar chuckled. "Captain Ryd will find a way. This bunch may find the whole fracas is over by the time they arrive."

"I hope you're correct," Tavnor said. Then, after a brief pause, "Thanks for the suggestion about sending scouts. This is apt to be my first action other than chasing thieves. I don't think you're shy about offering, but don't be."

Scar chuckled. "There's no danger of old Scar being afraid to speak out."

Tavnor was quiet for a moment. Scar, sensing there was something more to come, waited.

"They moved very quickly, did they not?" Tavnor said.

"Under a spell, I'd guess," Scar responded. "I've heard that wizards can bespell themselves and others to travel quickly for long stretches. The word is that they take a while to recover."

Later that day, the scout Tavnor had posted on the south road arrived with word of a group of perhaps twenty guardsmen walking in their direction, accompanied by three dark wizards. Again Tavnor rang the alarm bell to signal everyone to cease what they were doing and retreat to the Manor. Again they closed and bolted all the doors.

"This begins to look serious," Tavnor said as he and Scar stood at an upper window.

Scar nodded. "These are not likely to be the last. The Valleys have a reputation. Even with this group added, there aren't yet enough wizard's guardsmen to overcome armed farmers. Especially farmers defending their homes. We learned that up north when Ryd's Dog taught us about fighting in pastures rather than fields of wheat, and paying for supplies rather than taking them."

This was a theory of warfare Tavnor had never heard while serving in Lord Rand's guard, and he said so. He'd been too young to have yet served during the last of Rand's border wars with lords to the south, but he'd heard tales from older guardsmen. Rand didn't carry supplies; he took what he needed from the farms and villages he passed on the way to skirmishes. And he cared little about the effect of his small army's passage over the land, or the effect of those skirmishes on crops. His preference was to camp where an orchard would supply fruit and firewood, where a barn or a village could be raided to supply hay for his horses, eggs and fresh meat for his troops. He cared even less about the attitudes of the villagers or farmers. Once he'd gathered their lands into his own holdings, he'd send his taxgatherer and a sufficient number of guardsmen south to ensure his revenues—with a tax increase to pay the costs of his recent war, of course.

That Tavnor knew only traditional war as waged by lords over petty holdings didn't surprise Scar. "At first Ryd led us mercenaries in the same manner. The man is a good leader, a good tactician, and we had all the fighting we wanted. There's always a small war going on somewhere up there. Never made much sense to me; by the time two small armies had battled it out for a piece of land, the farms weren't able to pay much in taxes. But we made a nice living out of it.

"Then one day that fellow Dog walked up to camp and went to Ryd's tent. Walked right in, sat down, helped himself to a long drink out of the Captain's bottle. Strangest looking fellow any of us had ever seen, and that included the Captain, who just sat looking at him. Gnarled and ugly he was, short, and almost as broad as he was tall. I've heard that said about strong men, but it was true of this fellow.

"For some reason, Ryd didn't have him thrown out; instead, the two of them spent the night talking. My tent wasn't far off—I was one of those, along with Talon, Ryd would put in charge of a group. By then we were fifty, as large as any army in those northern lands. Anyway, I was sitting in front of my tent, taking it easy, when Dog walked by. Of course he caught my attention, so I watched him all the way into the Captain's tent. The weather was warm and dry, and Ryd liked to keep the front open, so I could see right in.

"We knew there was going to be a skirmish in the next couple of days. Ryd had scouts out looking for the other bunch, but they hadn't had any luck yet. He'd ridden out himself to scout the landscape, see whether there was a spot to which he could maneuver the fight so as to favor our side. So far, no contact with the enemy. Ryd couldn't select a site until he knew where they'd be coming from.

"We didn't know it then, but Dog had come to tell Ryd the enemy's location, which way they were likely to come, and just where to lie in wait. That was welcome news, as you can guess. But then, Ryd said later, talking of that night a little now and a little then, the fellow spent the rest of the night telling him how to manage his small force, starting with paying for supplies. Ryd's new friend explained the value of avoiding skirmishes in some farmer's prime cropland or orchard. When the Captain talked about the conversation, he'd shake his head, first at how quickly and completely Dog convinced him, and then with wonder that no commander had thought of it before."

"The fellow's name was Dog? That's odd." Tavnor seemed more surprised by the name than by any of the rest of the story.

"Well," Scar chuckled, "no, maybe not when he first arrived. Once he started scouting for us—that night was just the start—he was in and out of camp constantly. When he was in camp, he was always with Ryd. We started calling him Ryd's Dog, and then just Dog. He didn't seem to mind, and we had to call him something." He was quiet for a few minutes, thinking. "And, you know, once Dog started scouting for us and we started paying for supplies and listening when he chose where we fought, the locals began to bring in information.

"The quality of the supplies improved, too. Ryd could afford it; as word of our success spread, he about doubled our price. Those little lords didn't dare refuse to pay for fear we'd go over to the other side. After all, we were mercenaries. I'd never have believed it if I hadn't seen it—fifty hardened mercenaries, led by the toughest captain in the north, paying for supplies with no looting. Even selecting battle sites with an eye to protecting farm lands.

"I'll tell you when every one of us became believers. We were up against a nasty bunch, about as many as we were, and Ryd had to work pretty hard to maneuver the fight to a dryland pasture, away from a nearby village. Dog was going in and out of camp several times a day, always bringing fresh news. The other mercenaries finally had no choice but to meet us where Ryd intended. Ryd had time to arrange us so we could come at them from three sides, with him leading the main group and Talon and me each leading another.

"It turned out the bunch we were up against had been in the area for some days, looting the countryside pretty thoroughly. Our man Dog had been buying supplies, and he'd spread the money around to as many farmers as he could reach. The fellow could cover some ground, let me tell you.

"Anyway, after the battle had gone on for a while, it was pretty clear that eventually we'd win, but it was going to be costly. Then the other side's line fell to pieces. We filled the air with arrows when we saw that, though we couldn't figure out what was going on. It took a while before we realized that they were under attack from behind by men carrying pitchforks and axes and hammers. When Ryd saw that, he ordered a charge. Pretty quickly what remained of that small army were begging to be allowed to surrender. Those farmers had picked up swords from the fallen. They tended to swing them as though they were axes, but the weapons were effective enough.

"We had to stand between those who'd surrendered and those farmers, and for a while it looked as though we might have another skirmish. Then that fellow Dog walked out between the lines and said something, and things started to calm down. He walked over to a dead mercenary—one of theirs, not ours; we had some wounded, but no one killed. He lifted the body, tried to stand it up. When it fell over, he turned to those angry farmers, raised his hands and shrugged in a way which said "what more can you do?" as clearly as if he'd shouted. Next thing we knew, that whole bunch of farmers—maybe thirty, of all ages from boys holding carpenter's hammers to old men who seemed to be armed only with their canes—were laughing and leaning on their weapons. We'd already learned to respect Dog's scouting, but from then on, we showed it. Didn't seem to make a bit of difference to him, I must say." He leaned forward, peering up the road. "And now here comes the next bunch of wizards."

These wizards and guardsmen moved at a more normal pace than had those led by the wizard with one hand. This was a larger group, with at least four wizards and perhaps twenty guardsmen.

After the group passed, Scar cursed under his breath. "The Captain could use every one of us," he grumbled. "But he told us to stay here and hold the Manor. Still, that makes sense; if things go badly, we may need to protect the Holding. Nonetheless, I'd rather be in the middle of things instead of back here."

***

Ryd kept his men riding all day, with only a few short rests. As twilight came on he rode more slowly, letting the men doze in their saddles while he watched for two ruts which marked the thieves' road as it led away from the East Road. There he called a short halt, just long enough to select two men who'd grown up in the Fifth Valley to scout ahead. He warned them to be sure to dismount before they reached the valley, hide their horses, then move carefully through the woods. If they saw guardsmen and wizards camped across the road from the valley, they were to return at once and report. If not, they should move quietly into the valley to see what they might learn. They should travel carefully on their return; there might well be other parties of guardsmen and wizards coming along the East Road behind them. He and the rest of the group would follow the Thieves' Road for a couple of miles, then camp and wait for the report. In the morning, they'd ride over the hills and enter the valley that way.

***

Tarh and Roke with their four guardsmen moved cautiously in the direction of the Red Forest, led by the one guard who seemed able to follow a trail. Not that the trail was all that difficult. The wizards could see clearly enough the disturbances caused by people unconcerned about covering their tracks. The distance to the nearest edge of the Forest was not long, but about half-way along it their scout abruptly halted, then called to the wizards to join him. He signaled for them to walk in a half-circle north of the trail he was following.

Wondering, they did so. Clearly the man had seen something which puzzled him. As the two wizards came nearer, they saw that the guard had stopped just to the left of the tracks he'd been following. The man wasn't looking at those tracks, but at the ground to the south of the trail they followed.

As they approached, he pointed. "Another set of tracks. Someone has joined them."

Roke peered at the ground. The new set of tracks told him nothing. "Another guardsman?"

The guard shook his head. "Too heavy. I think too broad." He took his sword from its scabbard and used it to point to the tracks as he spoke. "See how far into the earth the tracks have sunk? Yet the stride says this was not the track of a tall man." He fell silent.

"Who or what do you think this would be, then?" Tarh snapped. These cautious guardsmen were beginning to get on his nerves.

The guard seemed reluctant to speak. Tarh sent just a touch of fear to the fellow, then asked again. "Well? Whose tracks are these?"

The guardsman had begun to tremble, the sword he'd not yet placed back in the scabbard shaking. "Master," he said, "I would guess it might be Master Dog—Snake's minion."

"Is he also tracking them?" Roke asked. If that fellow Dog had shown up, then Snake shouldn't be far behind.

The guardsman seemed torn between the fear Tarh had already induced and the greater fear of displeasing a wizard. He stuttered a bit, then spoke more clearly. "No, Masters. It looks as though he walked up and joined them. Look ahead on their trail: if he were tracking, his should be the clearest tracks. But his are often blurred by those of the tall beings who bring up the rear. No, I would guess that he joined them."

As he had feared, this angered both wizards. The guardsman stood shaking, waiting for a blast of fear so strong it would stop his heart if he were lucky, paralyze but leave him alive if he were not.

Roke, who'd seen only a little of the assassin and his minion, had been irritated but not furious at the apparent betrayal. For Tarh, however, that the squat man would dare leave Master Rath's service was an inconceivable act of treachery. And if Snake's dog had turned traitor, what did that mean about Snake himself?

That last thought did more than anger the young wizard. If Snake had turned against them, they'd have to set very careful watches day and night. No one knew the exact number of wizards the assassin had killed at Soren's command, but Tarh was pretty certain there had been at least six. With Soren dead, perhaps Snake felt free of whatever spells the Chief Mage had used to bind him. He might have simply deserted, leaving his minion to take his own way.

Tarh realized that Roke regarded him closely, eyebrows raised. The thing had best be faced. "If Snake's dog has joined the witch-child, then which side does Snake now serve? My back already itches at the thought. He's served us since we left Headquarters, his minion with him. What does this track mean, think you, Roke?"

That was it, then, Roke realized. Snake had been Rath's man. As Rath's former apprentice, Tarh took the treachery very personally. That would be something to keep in mind should they encounter the assassin again. Not only would he have to watch himself around Snake, but he'd also need to keep an eye on Tarh in case the younger wizard tried to avenge the insult before being certain it had been an insult. Snake's squat follower might have decided on his own to step away. It was possible that Snake didn't yet know of the treachery.

Were Tarh to act rashly if Snake appeared, the situation might quickly turn deadly. Roke had heard rumors that one reason for Snake's effectiveness lay in protective spells, perhaps even an amulet provided him by Soren. Such might lose its effectiveness with Soren's passing. If not, any spell Tarh might cast at the assassin might be deflected or, worse, rebound upon Tarh and anyone near him. Roke did not intend to be near the young wizard should Snake suddenly appear.

Roke realized he'd taken too long to answer. "The track means just what we see, I think. Clearly the minion has abandoned us. Whether Snake has also is more difficult to tell. We had best be very careful."

"If we see him," Tarh said. "He's reputed to have carried out assassinations in broad daylight, on crowded streets and in empty fields. Should he walk up smiling, I'll be no less careful."

"Another complication we didn't need," Roke replied. He turned to the guardsman. "Well done. Let's get back on the trail. No doubt they're headed for the forest ahead, but I'd rather be certain before dark."

***

When Ryd's scouts returned long after sunset, they found their captain the only one awake. He'd told the others to sleep while they could. He knew himself of old; he'd not sleep until he'd heard from his scouts. Probably he wouldn't sleep then, either.

The scouts hadn't needed to enter the valley. They'd come across a camp of wizards and guardsmen in the woods just across the East Road from the valley entrance. Interestingly, that camp was further back in the woods than they'd expected. Valley men had set a watch on the wizards' camp, and it looked as though so far the wizards and even their guardsmen had been kept out. The ward must still be working. The watchers probably kept the guard out as well. From what the scouts had seen, the wizards didn't have enough guardsmen to mount a serious attack.

But more were on the way; that was clear. As the scouts returned, walking their horses and listening carefully, they heard the sound of a number of men coming toward them from the east. The pair had dismounted, led their horses into the woods. One stayed with the horses to keep them quiet while the other crept back toward the road.

At least three wizards and more than a dozen guardsmen came walking along, moving quickly. As they passed, the watcher could hear grumbling from the guards—something about these wizards' spells leaving a man exhausted.

Ryd's scouts waited until that group had passed, then remounted their horses and rode on until they reached the Thieves' Road. Just after they'd turned into that path, again there came the sounds of a group of men walking on the main road. Once more the scouts walked their horses into the forest. Down the road came another group of guardsmen—perhaps twenty this time. Their wizards were already passing the entry to the Thieves' Road, so it was difficult to tell how many there were.

Ryd nodded. "You've done well. They've not yet broken the ward, and that's good to hear. But they're bringing reinforcements. What plan they've made I cannot tell. But Lir and his fellows will have some idea,

I'm certain. If the Valley men have not sent for their own reinforcements from the other valleys, there should still be time for that." He clapped each man on the shoulder. "And now, rest yourselves. We have some time before it grows light enough to make our way through the woods. I would arrive by daylight. These wizards will no doubt wait until dark to try their spells, and by then we will have prepared a surprise."

With that, the two unsaddled their horses, removed the bridles, and hobbled them to graze or, more probably, sleep until sunup. They rolled out their blankets and were soon asleep.

Ryd sat leaning against a tree, facing back the way they'd come on the Thieves' Road. If trouble came, it would be from that direction. Even if wizards and their guards detected the presence of his small band, they'd not try to approach cross-country but would follow the road. His band of mercenaries from up north would have come cross-country, certainly, and silently as well. These southern guardsmen were used to travelling by road to attack one another's lands or, occasionally, following a very clear trail left by a band of thieves. His valley men were an exception. He'd taken them into the hills and the mountains often enough that the few who hadn't grown up hunting in the woods had learned tracking. They hadn't needed to learn silent movement. Even big Hagen moved through the woods like a deer. Or, Ryd thought, like the largest and quietest bear in the forest.

His first task, once they'd ridden into the valley, would be to gather with the Council, learn what steps the valley men had taken. Together they would decide on what to do next and then he would set about whatever organizing would be needed. Until now, he'd not had much time to think about the situation. Now the enormity of the wizards' actions set in: they'd come to invade the lands which were in his charge, to endanger his people.

Unlike late brother Rand, Ryd rarely exhibited temper. Now, within him began to burn a deep anger. This he recognized as something he'd experienced from childhood onward: the warrior's fire which would lend strength to his arm but, more importantly, clarity to his mind. The day would bring time to plan. The next night would begin destruction for those who dared threaten what had become his homeland. So long as the ward held, his Valley guardsmen would keep the wizards' guardsmen at bay, even if the Order called on every guardsman serving every lord in the land. Ryd was one of only a dozen lords—no, he thought, with Rand's death he was two of the dozen. The idea brought a smile to his face.

Well, if he were two lords and only ten others were left, the Order might be able to call on as many as two hundred guardsmen, but only if each lord kept barely a handful in reserve. That a hundred would answer such a call was more likely. In addition to his own twenty-man Guard, Ryd had no doubt that he could call on at least another hundred Valley farmers who'd served the Lord's Guard in the past. They'd be fighting to protect their own lands, while facing men who served the Order only under compulsion. If the ward over the valley held, it should be possible to hold off the Order's guardsmen. But suppose the ward failed…he didn't want to consider that. If only he knew who had created the ward, and how to contact that—whatever it was. That being must have cared about the valley to set such a challenge to the Order.

He wished Lamar were here to chat with as the night passed, then chuckled inwardly at the thought. If Lamar had been with him, the man would now be slipping through the woods around the wizards' camp, listening, watching, then returning with precise information about everything from the number of guardsmen and wizards to the number of tents, campfires, cooking pots. And also, no doubt, about the defense mounted by the Valley folk. Well, Ryd would learn all that come morning. From where they were camped, the valley could be no more than two hours away, and he would make an early start. Still, he missed the gnarled man. It occurred to him that Lamar might know from where that ward came. He seemed to know everything else about a battlefield, well before the battle commenced.

***

It was evening before Brenna awoke from her rest and emerged again from her bed within the oak. Bird had not yet returned. Aren had difficulty keeping himself from going in search, despite Lamar's insistence that the forest would protect her. He was grateful for Brenna's re-appearance; Lamar and Magda appeared to sleep the day away, the Druids had scattered into the woods, and the guardsmen were inclined to sit wide-eyed and watchful, speaking only when spoken to, and then saying as little as possible.

Unlike her previous awakening, Brenna walked easily. Apparently, Aren thought, she was no longer surprised by having legs and arms instead of roots and branches.

Lamar opened his eyes as Brenna approached. "Look better. Maybe hungry?"

To her surprise Brenna had an appetite. The sergeant leaped to bring food. Brenna set to eating eagerly enough, though chiefly for the pleasure of tasting bread, cheese, fruit and a bit of wine. However she'd been sustained through the past months, it had not left her famished.

"Not skinny either," Lamar said. Brenna, surprised, felt an arm, then poked her ribs before agreeing.

Aren recalled the sergeant's question about whether fires were allowed in this forest. While he still wasn't comfortable with guardsmen addressing him as Captain, he did feel a duty to relay their concerns. He turned to Brenna and asked.

Brenna seemed to search her memory. "When I came here as a child, I sometimes had fires. For those I gathered wood. The forest did not object, and I do not think it will now." She paused, bent her head as though listening, then looked up. "Yes. You may take what lies on the ground, but don't break off any living branches or uproot any small trees or bushes. What is already dead has passed beyond the forest."

With that, the three guardsmen moved into the woods, careful to walk away from the direction Bird had taken. Soon they returned with armloads of wood, enough for several fires.

Brenna turned to Lamar. "I recognize you, though I don't understand from where. How did you know to bring me back to that tree for healing? I'd often slept there as a child when my parents sent me to hide when dark wizards came. I hadn't thought of it as a place of healing."

Lamar shrugged. "You badly hurt. Forest heal Druids, maybe heal you. Tree close. Heal or absorb. Either better than left die."

Brenna's laugh was joyful. "So much better! When I was a child, I was always pleased at being sent here to hide from dark wizards. I wished I could always live in this forest." She thought for a moment. "Perhaps now I can." She held her hands out in front of her, looking closely at each. "I wouldn't fit anywhere else." Glancing at Aren, she said, "Surely you've noticed the change."

"Yes," Aren replied. "Your color is that of the trees. Yet you seem still yourself, but with something added."

Brenna sobered. "The addition is knowledge, but also power, I think. Before I failed as an apprentice blue wizard, I spent enough time around those who possessed power to feel its presence. This is different;

I'm not sure entirely how. This power doesn't come from the auras and certainly not from darkness. It's completely different from any the blue wizards tried to teach me."

"Many kinds power," Lamar said. "Wizards not know much."

That startled both Aren and Brenna, not to mention the eavesdropping guardsmen. Brenna laughed again. "I wish I'd known that. It would have saved me years of frustration." She thought for a while, leaning forward, her right hand flat on the ground. "Yes. There is power in this forest. It—" She looked puzzled. "It welcomes me back, I think. But it wonders why I kept leaving. At least I think that's what the forest feels."

Lamar laughed. "Old tree make room, bed. Give place to sleep, get out of rain. You think that for anyone?"

Brenna seemed to be listening both to Lamar and to something else. "Yes," she said. "The forest welcomed me long ago, but I didn't know it. I felt comfortable here, I wished I could stay. But I didn't understand."

"Maybe took injury, shock. Gave time feel forest," Lamar said.

***

As Rath drew closer to the Fifth Valley, he called a brief halt during which he used his crystal to contact Pennon about conditions there. Haster had said that after the efforts of those three lesser wizards to disperse the ward, bowmen had fired upon them from within the valley. By now, Rath hoped, they'd be healed from whatever damage they'd taken, but if those cursed valley farmers were still firing arrows, he wanted to know. There would be little benefit in leading his group down the middle of the East Road and into an ambush. Pennon agreed and promised to send three guardsmen to guide Rath's party through the woods on the south side of the road. He had not, he said, had the three chant again against the ward; with Rath's five expected any day, he thought it would be better to set all eight to chanting, or all nine should Rath prefer that Pennon also join in. Rath agreed and ended the conversation.

He looked around at his group of wizards and guardsmen. These were stronger wizards than the three which Pennon had commanded, but they were tired after walking all day and into the night under an endurance spell. The guardsmen were nearly exhausted. There would be no chanting against the ward on this night, and no activity by the guardsmen. Probably nothing from the guardsmen come daylight, either.

That would be fine with Rath. It would allow time to study the situation and to think, and perhaps time as well for more wizards and guardsmen to arrive. Then they would need some practice, though with his five added to the three already present, one day might be enough. Eight leaders dispersed among the group should provide enough models.

Once that ward was dispersed, wizards and guardsmen together could easily quell any remaining rebellion among the farmers before setting traps for the witch-child. Surely she was as vulnerable to a flight of arrows as any other mortal, though it graveled him to think of defeating her without the use of his own magic. Yes, he would try guardsmen first, though that might leave unanswered the question of whether all the Order's power would suffice against a being of this sort.

Oleg had spoken as though the old scrolls told not only of Druids but of beings even more powerful. If this were the first such to reawaken, it would be useful to know if the Order could defeat such a being. On the other hand, if the attempt failed and the witch-child remained alive and angered, only disaster would result.

Rath would see what bowmen could do—or Snake and his stiletto, if the assassin returned before the witch-child arrived in the valley. That she intended to return, Rath was certain; otherwise, why leave the mist-shrouded Barren Lands at all? She'd been safe enough there. Against that older and more powerful ward, the chanting of eight wizards had achieved nothing but a rebound effect stronger than Rath had ever encountered.

Rath set his group walking again, continuing the endurance spell but setting a more normal pace. He didn't want to pass the point where Pennon would be waiting to guide them through the forest.

***

Toward morning Lord Ryd dozed a little, sitting against the tree where he'd spent the night. In the morning twilight he awoke to the soft sounds of his men breaking camp. When he looked around, he saw that within a few minutes all would be ready to ride. At the sight he laughed aloud; he'd slept even if only for a short time while these ten warriors caught and saddled their horses and his as well. They had worked quietly in order that he might catch a few more moments' sleep.

At his laughter every man in the camp turned, smiling. Ryd made a great show of leaping to his feet, shouting, "Well, if you're finally ready, let's get on the road!" grinning widely at the sound of ten men laughing.

When all were mounted, he spoke more soberly. "From here, lads, things become serious. Last night's scouts confirm that the trouble in the Fifth Valley involves both wizards and their guardsmen. Whatever numbers the Order has gathered, they've increased overnight by more than a half-dozen wizards and five times that many guardsmen. That wizards have not yet entered the valley suggests that the ward still holds. Our scouts report that the valley folk have set a watch on the wizards' camp, and we can assume that watch will keep guardsmen at bay.

"We'll walk our horses through the woods. I'll want two scouts working ahead and one off to each side. We don't know whether the Order's guardsmen have made their way along the hilltop and into the woods along the valley, but I expect them to have done so. We'll ride carefully and as quietly as eleven mounted men can. Nonetheless, we should arrive by the nooning. Once there, I'll want you to remain together until we can learn how things are. I suspect that the Council will have things organized and well under control. We'll want to fit in. Any questions or suggestions?"

There were none, so Ryd urged his horse into a fast walk and led the way off the Thieves' Road and into the woods. Two of his men trotted their horses just enough to reach their position ahead of the rest. Two others did the same, one to each side. All was carried out as quietly as could be done, with no talking and no fuss. Looking back as his men moved to carry out his instructions, Ryd thought again of how much better these valley men were than any other lord's guard in the entire country. Despite their lack of battle experience, he suspected they were better even than the mercenaries he'd led for four eventful years north of the mountains, where the fighting had been almost constant.

***

Inek and Osa moved quickly through the forest, retracing their path from the previous day. As they neared the forest edge, they slowed, moving cautiously and listening for sounds which might betray the presence of a pair of wizards.

They heard nothing. Either the wizards were still too far off to be heard, or they'd already passed by. The two Druids stepped cautiously out of the woods, looking both ways along the forest edge but finding no wizards. After a few moments, they began walking in two separate and widening circles, looking for tracks. Inek spoke first. "Here are tracks of a single man. He came close enough to see where we entered, then turned off." He pointed along the retreating tracks, which led directly away from the forest.

Osa had moved further from the trees and now worked in half-circles which took him close to the nearest pasture. "I have the rest of the group!" he called. "Your scout would have been in sight of the rest, but they weren't going to get as close to the forest as he did." He laughed. "A brave bunch! I'd wager the fellow ordered to follow our tracks right up to the edge wasn't pleased about that task."

Inek's smile was grim. "Hold up a moment; I want to be sure he rejoined the others."

He trotted beside the lone man's tracks, stopping a good distance from the forest and calling back, "Yes! Here's where he rejoined the group. From here," he called, shading his eyes and looking toward the east, "they follow the forest edge, but at a distance."

Osa, following the main body's tracks, quickly joined him. "No one else seems to have left at any time. Should we continue to follow, or take word back to the others?"

Inek thought for a moment. "Let us carry the word. The Little Mother will know should these wizards and their minions stop or turn. We can deal with them easily enough then. We will see what course she, Lamar, and Hobard would follow." With that, they re-entered the forest.

***

Ryd and his men walked their horses up the wooded slope, keeping their eyes and ears open. Scouts returned frequently to report no sign of the Order's guardsmen. At the crest they paused for a moment before Ryd led them down the slope. As they passed the crest they entered the valley, a homecoming marred by their awareness that danger awaited. The danger itself remained obscure.

The lead scout returned, reported that valley life looked normal—except that men practiced archery, using targets set against the wall of a barn. The barn's bulk, he suggested, would hide their activity from eyes looking into the valley from the East Road. Using a house for a similar shield, several young women knife-wielders worked through their movements. That last surprised Ryd; he'd not heard of women training with knives.

"Have they any skill?" he asked, to be greeted by a wave of laughter. He quickly quelled the noise, not because the laughter offended him but because their approach to the valley was intended to be silent.

"Oh, yes," said the scout, who'd grown up in the Fifth Valley. "These aren't kitchen knives, Captain. They're a good two or two-and-a-half feet long, kept razor-sharp on both edges. Lighter than our short swords, certainly, and not strong enough to exchange many blows with a sword. Girls grow up training with wooden knives, seeking quickness. Most of us have engaged in a fight with wooden weapons against young women. Often quickness gives them the victory."

Ryd looked around at ten serious faces, each man nodding. "Is that true? You've all engaged in a fight of sword against long knife and lost?" The nods continued, with soft responses: "More than once." "My sister has won more than she's lost against every man her age." "My mother still practices, Captain. Takes more pleasure in it than do some of her opponents, too." That last brought another round of chuckles from the group. "That she does," said one. "Makes it sweeter when you do win, though!"

"Well," Ryd said, "I look forward to seeing these knife-maids. Let's ride in quickly and see what needs to be done. No need for further silence!" With that, he urged his horse into a trot, whooping as he led the way.

When Ryd and his ten loud horsemen broke out of the woods and into a pasture, they saw a half-circle of bowmen and knife-wielders ready to greet whatever approached. Then the weapons were lowered, and an equally loud whooping greeted them.

Ryd rode up nearly to the circle, where he dismounted and reached out a gloved hand in greeting to the nearest man, who happened to be Rom. "We received word of need and came immediately. Is it possible to meet with the Council? I would learn what has happened and what steps you have taken. I know there are dark wizards and their guardsmen along the East Road. More are joining. And it appears you've kept them at bay. Where can I be of greatest use?"

"My lord," Rom replied. "You indeed come at need, and welcome. The Council will meet as soon as we can gather. In the meantime, come take food and drink." He gestured toward the row of tables near Alta's kitchen door, where Alta was already orchestrating a hearty meal. Then he turned to Mot. "Send runners up the valley, and down valley to Lir and Reya. Tell them the Lord has arrived with men and wishes us to meet and tell him of events."

As Mot turned away, signaling to a half-dozen young men to join him, Rom walked Ryd and his men toward the tables. "My lord, we hold the wizard's guardsmen out of the valley, yet their numbers grow. Some of our neighbors have joined us from the other valleys, but we lack a tactician—or have until now." Ryd's reputation as a tactician in the north country had spread, helped by tales from returning guardsmen of drills he put them through.

"We're in for a battle, my friend," said Ryd. "You may as well call me Captain rather than Lord." He was quiet for a moment. "There are things we can do. I take it the ward still holds?"

"That it does, Captain, though we fear these wizards have come up with some chanted spell which weakens it. Here are Lir and Reya, who can tell you more. They've watched these wizards since the first night."

Ryd greeted Lir with open arms, and Reya with a respectful bow. These two, he knew, were regarded by the valley as leaders of the Council, though there were, technically, no leaders. Lir, he'd been told, had long before been a guardsman of sufficient skill to be asked to remain as sergeant. Lir had declined the honor; eager, he'd said, to return to the Fifth Valley before his sweetheart realized that she might do better.

The three walked toward the tables. "My Lord," Reya said, "We have weighty matters with which to deal, but I must ask leave to ease my heart. During your time in the East, did you hear any news of our son Aren? Our youngest, Bird, would be with him."

Ryd's most recent news of this family had been the youngest's drowning and Aren, overcome by grief, leaving for the east. In the Holdings he'd heard tales of a witch-child and her guardsman escort, but he'd had no reason to associate the pair with Aren and certainly not with his drowned sister. If the child had driven dark wizards from the valley, created the ward, and destroyed Rath's tower, not to mention the wizard's right hand, no wonder she fled. And no wonder Aren had gone with her. The tale that Aren had been so disheartened by a beloved little sister's drowning that he'd left his parents alone with their grief had never rung true.

Ryd took some satisfaction in knowing he'd been correct that Aren would not have simply left his parents alone with their grief. That was of little comfort as he faced the duty to answer truthfully Reya's question.

He'd walked on in silence for too long. In the parents' eyes Ryd could see their realization that he did indeed have news of their son and little girl, and that the news was not entirely good. He led the pair aside, gestured for them to take seats on the ground, and joined them.

He leaned forward and spoke softly. "They travelled as far as what was the Keep of the Holdings. From there they went north. By now they should have reached the Red Forest, where people say the Dark Order will not enter. They may well be safe there."

"Oh, thank the Light!" Reya whispered, weeping in her relief. Lir reached an arm around her and the two held one another for several minutes while Ryd looked everywhere but at them.

When the couple had recovered somewhat, Ryd grasped each by a shoulder and squeezed gently. "There is more," he said. "I must think now that your daughter created the ward over this valley, with all that suggests. When did you become aware that she was the source?"

"Only a few days before she and Aren fled," Lir answered. "Aren was first to realize what Bird had done. It took him a while to persuade us. We knew she must flee and could not go alone."

"And," Reya added, then paused to control her voice, "her flight must be kept secret. We told a story of her death and Aren's departure."

Lir leaned forward, looked closely into Ryd's face. "I see there is more. They have been in danger?"

Ryd nodded. "You know that wizards pursue them." He paused only long enough for the pair to nod. "The Order sent word to a wizard living in the east. The lord of the Holdings set his men to capture the two and bring them to his Keep. The tales of what happened there grow larger with each telling, but all end with Aren and your daughter walking out of the Keep as it fell behind them. Lord Rand did not escape."

He paused again to allow a moment for the parents to absorb that news. He would not tell of Rand's order to hang Aren. "They walked away without harm, all tales agree. No one offered to hinder them. The wizards arrived days later." Ryd leaned back, took a deep breath. "I have no further news. It does appear that the child's powers have grown and that her pursuers have not caught her. I have received news that Rath is leading his group here, to join the attack. Had he taken your child, I believe I would know."

It was Reya's turn to look searchingly into Ryd's face. "How do you know of Rath's return, Lord?"

Lir answered first. "Lamar." It was not a question. "We've not seen him since Aren and Bird left."

Ryd's eyebrows went up. So this couple had also been allowed the gnarled man's name. That was something to think about, but not now. "Before he left, Lamar told me of Rath's order that he serve as scout for the wizards. He planned to lead them a merry chase. I expect he kept them about three days behind from the start. Aren and your daughter have had at least one ally throughout."

The three sat in silence for a few minutes before Reya spoke. "I thank you, my Lord, for taking this time. Now we have matters of greater urgency with which to deal." She stood, and the two men joined her. "Let us eat a bit while the other members of the Council gather." She looked around the yard. "I see that more than half are here now."

Ryd discovered as they approached the tables of food that he was indeed hungry despite the bread and cheese he'd eaten in the saddle. While they ate, Lir and Reya quickly brought him up to date concerning the previous night. By then other members of the Council had arrived, filling plates and seating themselves on the ground.

As soon as more than half were present, Reya stood and called the Council to order. "My friends, Captain Ryd and our neighbor guardsmen have arrived just as we need more than willingness to defend our homes and land and neighbors. We can do no better than to place ourselves entirely under his command. Lir and Rom and I have told him of events to this point. If he has more questions, we will seek to answer those as they come up. Does this meet with your satisfaction?"

This was greeted with nods and murmurs of agreement.

Ryd stood. "I thank you for your defense of this valley and of all the valleys. It seems clear that the Order wishes to diminish or disperse the ward which protects you. If they succeed, we'll have no defense against their spells."

A voice came from a late arrival. "What if instead of resisting we ask for peace? Accept the loss of this ward and go back to things as they were?"

"And also ask for mercy?" Another voice responded. "Who here has heard of the Order offering mercy?" There were murmurs of agreement.

"Remember, neighbors," Reya said, "that the Order created a drought which might well continue even now, were it not for the ward. We have willingly accepted its protection. The Order will not forget that."

Lir added, "When we fired upon wizards, any chance for mercy vanished, if such a chance ever existed." That brought a groan from several, but most nodded.

Ryd brought their attention back to him. "Only your bowmen have kept them from succeeding," he said. "Had I been here, I would have done the same." He let that sink in for a moment. "You've had an effect; they've been forced to move their camp further into the woods. At the same time, they've been joined by other wizards as well as by more guardsmen, which bodes ill should they manage to end the ward.

"Our first task is to interfere with any additional chanting. We have one useful piece of information: these wizards can be wounded by arrows. And," he said, smiling broadly, "we have bowmen among us." This last brought an appreciative chuckle.

"We'll want more bowmen; I've brought ten, and I've strung a bow more than once myself. I will send messengers to the other valleys and to Swordmaster Talon to send more of our neighbors. Reya tells me that these wizards begin chanting in the middle of the night. We'll be ready.

"There is, however, more we can do," he went on, smiling. "Can you gather tinder, dry straw, anything which will quickly start a fire? We'll want to make bundles, tied so that each person can carry a bundle or perhaps two. Each person carrying a bundle will also need hot coals, carried in a bowl stuffed with straw. When it's well dark but before this chanting begins, some of us will cross the road and set a row of fires in the brush on the far side. We will speak more of this after I've seen just how things are at the valley mouth.

"Those fires should bring guardsmen out to fight them. Our bowmen should have some decent targets. By nightfall there will be more of us.

"For now, I will send messages to the other valleys and to the Manor. That done, I would see for myself what can be seen, both of our preparations and of what takes place across the East Road. Later we can speak again." He turned to the guardsmen who had accompanied him. "You're free to visit family and friends once you've seen to the horses. Rejoin us before dark."

Turning again to the larger group, Ryd paused for a moment, then went on, smiling: "I hear tales of women bearing long knives. I would be delighted to observe them as they train, if that is allowed. What the young men with whom I rode today say of them is indeed impressive, and I would see with my own eyes."

At that came a double cheer from a number of young women as they waved their long knives over their heads. When the cheers died down, Reya, who like a number of other older women had taken her long knife from its sheath, holding the blade overhead but not going so far as to wave it, spoke for the group. "Captain," she said, "these knife-wielders will gladly show you their skill once life calms. We of the valleys have heard of your own skill as a swordsman. We think you will appreciate theirs."

Ryd bowed in acknowledgement. As the council members left to tend to various preparations, Reya signaled for two young men and two young women to come forward.

"These," said Reya, "are our fastest runners." She smiled at Ryd's raised eyebrows as he glanced at the two women. "They're tested, my lord. You may rely on them."

Ryd laughed then, raising his hands in a comic gesture of defeat. "Forgive an old soldier. I bow to your knowledge of these runners, and"—here he turned to the four—"do so with full confidence in each. And with my thanks." Briefly he repeated the message they were to deliver.

Reya ordered them to go, and the four sped off. Ryd stood watching, then turned to Reya. "I thank you for your choices. And I look forward to seeing these knife-wielders. But for now, it's time to visit the East Road." He turned toward Lir and the small group of men, some older and some younger, who awaited him. At his signal, they began the walk to the valley edge.

***

"The two Druids return," Brenna said. Aren stood, watchful now, hand on his sword hilt. He noted that the sergeant and his two guardsmen had done the same. All four stood between the returnees and Brenna, Magda, and Lamar, who remained leaning against a tree where he'd been resting.

Inek and Osa stepped into the clearing. "Two wizards and four guardsmen are travelling some distance from the forest edge. They tracked us to where we entered but have gone further on."

The guardsmen relaxed but continued watchful. Aren gave the order to stand down and go back to what they'd been doing. He and Magda turned toward the fire, then noticed that those Druids who had scattered into the forest now approached Brenna very slowly, their heads bowed.

Brenna stood quietly as the Druids regarded her. Then all seven knelt. "Lady of the Forest," one said, "we greet you and thank your forest for such cleansing of our guilt as is possible."

Now it was Aren's turn to be surprised. These Druids seemed to recognize Brenna in some new manner. He looked around and realized that Inek and Osa were also kneeling, as was Hobard.

"Lady," Inek said, "I ask your pardon; I had not known you before. I also thank the forest for granting its healing."

Hobard's words struck a different note. "Lady," she said, "when first we met, you were not what you have become. Nor were you when first we met again. I know you more fully now. When I lived within the trees and the underbrush and the ground of this forest, I lived within you."

Brenna opened her arms wide. "The forest welcomes you all. We are delighted that Druids visit again and wish you could stay. But the Mother has need of you elsewhere. Still, join us here for a meal and a night's rest while we await the Little Mother's return. The Forest has much to tell her this night."

"Enough talk," Lamar rumbled. "Eat now, sleep. Travel tomorrow."

***

Bird returned, as Lamar had promised, but not until mid-morning the next day. Aren, bleary-eyed after a restless night worrying despite Lamar's reassurances, found himself too pleased to scold. Not that scolding their Little Mother in the presence of what were now ten Druids plus Brenna, Magda, and Lamar would be the wisest choice.

After Bird had danced through the group of Druids she walked slowly up to Aren, head down, glancing up occasionally to see how angry he might be. When Aren swept her into his arms, hugged her, then raised her high over his head, she giggled with delight.

"Little bird," Aren said, "you're almost too big to lift! You've been growing!" They'd been away from the valley for almost a year now, and in that time Bird had had a serious growth spurt. When he put his sister down again and looked carefully at her trousers and jerkin, he was puzzled for a moment that she hadn't outgrown them. Then he recalled that Reya had always sewn Bird's clothing too large for this active child, so she'd keep freedom of movement as she dashed around the farm, climbed the old oak, or scampered through the house. Besides, Reya would say, Bird would surely grow into her clothing, and that would be time to start working on a new set. With that Aren's face turned sad at the realization that Reya had missed out on that year's sudden growth.

Bird, holding Aren's hand and looking up at him, saw the sadness. "You miss home," she said. "We should leave soon." She turned to the red woman. "I learned things from the forest last night, Brenna. You know, the forest thinks I'm the tree from which the whole big forest grew!" She giggled at the thought. "It feels that you're part of it–" she broke off for a moment, head bowed, seeming to be listening. "No," she said, "that's not it. What the forest feels, I think, is that you are the forest, Brenna. You are the forest, or you carry within you the forest, or something."

Bird paused again, frowning slightly. "It's difficult. The forest doesn't think in words. It's a lot like stone; both feel. Sometimes they show images. But I think it means that you carry the forest's power." At this point Bird stood silent for a while, looking at Brenna. "Yes. When I first felt that you were near, the feeling wasn't like that of dark wizards. I could feel something strong, almost as though it were trying to appear but couldn't." Bird danced a little, laughing. "But now it's here, and stronger than any dark wizard! It's the forest, that's what it is! You're part of it, and it's part of you, not just the forest now, but the forest as it always has been!"

Brenna had listened, nodding. "Little Mother, this is home for me. It always was, but as a child I didn't understand."

Bird nodded, Reya's 'that's it, then' nod. She turned to Aren. "We need to get home, Aren. Something is wrong there. We need to leave today."

Aren looked around, saw that Lamar already stood with his small pack on his back. Behind him the three guardsmen stood near their own packs. Clearly, all were ready to go. Looking around, he saw the Druids watching Bird and waiting for her word.

Only Magda had not packed. She stepped forward, clearing her throat. When Bird turned toward her, she bowed slightly before speaking. "Little Mother, I would be of little use in a struggle with dark wizards. If the Red Lady of the Forest will allow it, I would stay for a time."

Head bowed, she struggled for words before continuing. "My sickness is deeper than that of these Druids, who have spent the long years redeeming themselves. While my older brother spent those years wandering, doing what he could for the land itself and for those who worked it, I hid myself in the barrens. There I did nothing but teach a few Dark Druids, and that for only a short time. As this forest cleanses me, I would wander from here to speak to those who live on the land."

She gestured toward where her pack lay on the ground. "I would share seeds which might thrive even in ground which has been badly over-worked. More, I would share what I know. If none will listen, I may still place some seeds where they will do the most good." She shifted her attention to Lamar. "Older brother, would this meet with your approval?"

Lamar stepped forward, took Magda's hands. "Since when younger sister seek Earth-Walker's approval? Good plan. Time Magda walk farms again. Stay, heal, teach land and people."

Bird stepped forward, seeking words. None of Reya's seemed quite right, though she did come up with one of Reya's phrases, and that helped her begin. "I have not thanked you enough for sharing your home. Or for teaching me as we walked." A memory of the flight from the Fifth Valley came to her. "When Aren and I rode through these lands, we saw how tired the land had become. Reya and Lir say that when a person sees someone needing help, that person should give what help she can."

Magda bowed her head in thanks.

Inek broke into the silence which followed. "Little Mother, you should know that after you went into the forest yesterday, Osa and I did not find the two wizards who were following us. They had walked on, skirting the forest edge. We suspect they plan to ambush us. With your permission, Druids will go on ahead, following that trail just outside the forest."

Before Bird could answer, the sergeant stepped forward, cleared his throat, and addressed Aren. "Captain," he said, "with the Lady's permission, we'd like to go with these—these Druids. If there are guardsmen with those wizards, we would stand between them and the Lady. That is, if they don't turn tail and run at the sight of these folk."

Aren glanced down at Bird, who grinned. "Well, Captain," she said, obviously enjoying the title, "I think it's your decision," another phrase Aren recognized as Reya's.

Aren held back a smile. The sergeant's request was not something to smile at. "Sergeant, your suggestion makes sense." He turned to Inek, was relieved to see the Druid nod.

"That's decided, then," Aren said. "Sergeant, you and your men should take the lead in tracking. You may see things in that trail which Inek and his fellows might miss."

The sergeant saluted. "Yes, sir," he said. "That will suit us just fine." He turned to Inek, his eyes widening a little as he looked up at the tall Druid. "Lead on, sir."

With that, the Barren Lands Druids and the three guardsmen moved off into the forest, the guards moving at a dog-trot to keep up with the long-legged Druids.

Hobard remained with Bird. The Barren Lands Druids knew far more about wizards than she did. After all, it was their dealings with wizards which had gotten them banished to the Barren Lands. Lamar, whom she'd already realized came and went as he wished, had also chosen to remain with Bird.

Bird had become impatient. "Something is wrong at home," she said. "We need to get going if we're to arrive in time to help!"

"I will guide you to the forest edge," said Brenna. "Should there be wizards waiting, I will be helpful in dealing with them." She seemed to listen for a moment. "And in restraining the forest's anger. At any rate," she said, turning to Bird and Aren, "I would spend as much time as allowed with friends. And," she added as she turned toward Lamar, "with one of whom the forest carries much lore, oh Earth-Walker."

"Enough talk," Lamar said, but smiling as he did so. "Time walk. Bring help, Valley folk."

ABOUT THE AUTHOR

In addition to *The Dark Order* (Books One and Two, *Bird* and *Freeing Druids*; Book three, *Brightsong*, forthcoming), Wayne Ude is the author of *Becoming Coyote*, a novel; *Buffalo and other stories;* and *Maybe I Will Do Something: Seven Tales of Coyote,* each set in eastern Montana where he grew up. He holds a BA in English from the University of Montana, an MFA in creative writing from the University of Massachusetts at Amherst, and an MNPL (Master of Non-Profit Leadership) from Seattle University.

Wayne has taught fiction writing and craft for over forty years, including as creative writing faculty at Colorado State University, Minnesota State University at Mankato, Old Dominion University in Virginia, and as the founding director of a low-residency MFA program on Whidbey Island, Washington. He's a frequent speaker on fiction and craft at writers' conferences.

Since 1993 he and his wife, writer Marian Blue, have lived on Whidbey Island. Their indoor menagerie has grown to include five dogs (four rescued) and two rescued parrots. The outdoor population includes eleven goats with their guard llama, about one hundred assorted chickens and ducks in Marian's egg business, plus two heritage turkeys and a rescued one-eyed gander with a bad attitude.